A WINTER HAUNTING

Other Books by Dan Simmons

Song of Kali
Phases of Gravity
Carrion Comfort
Hyperion
The Fall of Hyperion
Prayers to Broken Stones
Summer of Night
The Hollow Man
Children of the Night
Summer Sketches
Lovedeath
Fires of Eden
Endymion
The Rise of Endymion
The Crook Factory
Darwin's Blade
Hardcase

A WINTER HAUNTING

DAN SIMMONS

𝓌𝓂

WILLIAM MORROW
An Imprint of HarperCollins*Publishers*

Designed by Bernard Klein

ISBN 0-380-97886-5

This is for Karen

For he was speechless, ghastly, wan,
Like him of whom the story ran,
Who spoke the spectre hound in man.

—Sir Walter Scott, *The Lay of the Last
Minstrel*, Canto VI, v. 26

The hounds of winter,
they harry me down.

—Sting, "The Hounds of Winter"

A WINTER HAUNTING

FORTY-ONE years after I died, my friend Dale returned to the farm where I was murdered. It was a very bad winter.

I know what you're thinking. There's the old journalism anecdote of William Randolph Hearst needing someone to cover the Johnstown flood and sending a young cub reporter. It was the kid's big break. The next day the novice cabled back this lead to Hearst's paper: "GOD SAT ON A LONELY HILL ABOVE JOHNSTOWN TODAY, LOOKING DOWN IN SORROW AT NATURE'S FIERCE DESTRUCTION." Old-timers swear that Hearst did not hesitate ten seconds before cabling back this response: "FORGET FLOOD STORY. INTERVIEW GOD."

I say I died forty-one years ago and your response is, *Forget the story about Dale. Who cares? Tell us what it's like to be dead—what is the afterlife like? What is it like to be a ghost? Is there a God?*

At least, these would be my questions. Unfortunately, I am not a ghost. Nor do I know anything about any afterlife. When I was alive, I did not believe in ghosts or heaven or God or spirits surviving the body or resurrection or reincarnation, and I still do not. If I had to describe my current state of existence, I would say that I am a cyst of memory. Dale's *sense* of me is so strong, so cut off and cauterized from the rest of his consciousness by trauma, that I seem to exist as something more than memory, something less than life, almost literally a black hole of holistic recollection formed by the collapsing gravity of grief.

I know this does not explain it, but then I do not really understand it myself. I know only that I *am* and that there was a—"quickening" might be the best word—when Dale decided to return and spend the winter at the farm where I once lived and where I died.

And, no, I have no memory of my death. I know no more of that event than does Dale. Evidently one's death, like one's birth, is so important as to be beyond recall.

When I was alive I was only a boy, but I was fairly smart and totally dedicated to becoming a writer someday. I spent years preparing for that—apprenticing myself to the word—knowing that it would be many more years before I could write a real short story, much less a novel, but practicing with opening paragraphs for stories and novels nonetheless.

If I were borrowing an opening for this tale, I would steal it from Thackeray's boring 1861 novel *Lovel the Widower*:

> Who shall be the hero of this tale? Not I who write it. I am but the Chorus of the Play. I make remarks on the conduct of the characters: I narrate their simple story.

Thackeray's ominiscient "I" was lying, of course. Any Creator stating that he is a simple Chorus and impassive observer of his creatures' actions is a hypocrite and a liar. Of course, I believed that to be true of God, on the few occasions when I considered that He might exist at all. Once, when Dale and Mike and I were having a chickenhouse discussion of God, my only contribution was a paraphrased quote from Mark Twain: "When we look around at the pain and injustice of the world, we must come to the ineluctable conclusion that God is a thug." I'm not sure if I believed that then or now, but it certainly shocked Mike and Dale into silence. Especially Mike. He was an altar boy then and most devout.

But I'm digressing even before I begin the story. I always hated writers who did that. I still have no powerful opening line. I'll just begin again.

Forty-one years after I died, my friend Dale returned to the farm where I was murdered. It was a very bad winter.

Dale Stewart drove from western Montana to central Illinois, more than 1,700 miles in 29 hours, the mountains dwindling and then disappearing in his rearview mirror, endless stretches of autumn prairie blending into a tan and russet blur, following I-90 east to I-29 southeast to I-80 east to I-74 south and then east again, traveling through the better part of two time zones, returning to the checkerboard geometries of the Midwest, and forcing himself down through more than forty years of memories like a diver going deep, fighting the pain and pressure that such depths bring. Dale stopped only for food, fuel, and a few catnaps at interstate rest areas. He had not slept well for months, even before his suicide attempt. Now he carried drugs for sleeping, but he did not choose to stop and use them on this trip. He wanted to get there as soon as possible. He did not really understand why he was going there.

Dale had planned to arrive at Elm Haven in midmorning, tour his old hometown, and then drive on to Duane's farmhouse in the daylight, but it was after eleven o'clock at night when he saw the ELM HAVEN exit sign on I-74.

He had planned to move into Duane's old house in early or mid-September, allowing plenty of time to enjoy the fall colors and the crisp, sunny autumn days. He arrived on the last day of October, at night, in the last hours of the first Halloween of the new century, hard on the cold cusp of winter.

I screwed up, thought Dale as he took the overpass above I-74 and followed the night-empty road the two miles north toward Elm Haven. *Screwed up again. Everything I haven't lost, I've screwed up. And everything I lost, I lost because I screwed it up.*

He shook his head at this, angry at the bumper-sticker-stupid self-pity of the sentiment, feeling the fog of too many nights with too little sleep, and punched a button to lower the driver's-side window. The air was cold, the wind blowing hard from the northwest, and the chill helped to wake Dale a bit as he came out onto the Hard Road just a mile southeast of Elm Haven.

The Hard Road. Dale smiled despite himself. He had not thought of the phrase for decades, but it immediately came to mind as he turned back northwest onto State Highway 150A and drove slowly into the sleeping town.

He passed an asphalt road to his right and realized that they had paved County Road 6 between Jubilee College Road and the Hard Road sometime in the last few decades—it had been muddy ruts between walls of corn when he had lived here—so now he could drive straight north to Duane's farmhouse if he wished. He continued on into Elm Haven out of curiosity.

Morbid curiosity, it turned out. The town itself seemed sad and shrunken in the dark. Wrong. Smaller. Dead. Desiccated. A corpse.

The two business blocks of Main Street along the Hard Road had lost several buildings, disorienting Dale the way a familiar smile with missing teeth would. He remembered the tall facade of Jensen's Hardware; it was now an empty lot. The A & P, where Mike's mother had worked, was gone. He remembered the glowing windows of the Parkside Cafe: it was now a private residence. Lucky's Grill on the other side of the street appeared to be some kind of flea market with stuffed animals staring out at the Hard Road through dusty black eyes. The Corner Pantry market was boarded up. The barbershop next door was gone. Bandstand Park was worse than gone—the tiny yard-sized space was now cluttered with a tiny VFW hall and various tin sheds, the bandstand torn down, the trees uprooted and their stumps cut out, and the war memorial hidden by weeds.

Dale made a U-turn and drove back east, turning north onto Broad Avenue. The clouds were low and the wind was cold. Leaves blew across the wide street ahead of his Toyota Land Cruiser, their dry scraping sounding like the scuttle of rats. For an instant, fatigue convinced Dale that these *were* rats, hundreds of them, rushing through the cones of his headlights.

There were no streetlights on Broad Avenue. The great elms that used to arch over the wide street had fallen victim to Dutch elm disease decades ago, and the trees planted since seemed smaller, stunted, irregular, and ignoble in comparison. Some of the fine old homes along Broad still stood back behind their wide lawns, the houses dark and silent against the night wind, but like an old war veteran at a reunion, Dale was more aware of the missing houses than of the few survivors.

He turned right onto Depot Street and drove the few blocks to his childhood home across the street from where Old Central School had stood.

His home of seven years was recognizable, but just barely. The huge old elm that had stood outside his and Lawrence's bedroom was gone, of course, and the new owners had long ago paved the short driveway and added a modern garage that did not go well with the American-square design of the house. The front porch was missing its railings and swing. The old white clapboard had been replaced with vinyl siding. Jack-o'-lanterns and a bulging straw man in bib overalls had been set out on the porch in celebration of the holiday, but the candles had burned out hours earlier, leaving the jack-o'-lanterns' triangular eyes as black and empty as skull sockets; the rising breeze had scattered the straw man's guts to the wind.

Old Central, of course, was gone. Dale had few clear memories of the summer of 1960, but he vividly remembered the building burning, embers flying orange against a stormy sky. Now the once-grand square city block was filled with a few ratty-looking ranch houses—dark and incongruous amidst the older, taller homes on each side of the square—and all signs of the former school building and its huge playground had long since been eradicated.

The tall sentinel elms around the school block were gone, of course, and no trees had been planted in their place. The tiny houses on the square—all built after 1960—looked exposed and vulnerable under the black sky.

There were more gaps in the rows of homes facing the former schoolyard. The Somerset place next to Dale's old home was just gone, not even its foundation remaining. Across the street from the Somersets', Mrs. Moon's tidy white home had been bulldozed into a gravel lot. His friend Kevin's family home—a ranch house that had seemed modern and out of place in 1960—was still there on its slight rise of ground, but even in the dark Dale could see that it was unpainted and in need of repair. Both of the grand Victorian homes north of Kevin's house were gone, replaced by a short dead-end street with a few new homes—very cheap—crowded where the woods had once started.

Dale continued slowly east past Second Avenue, stopping where Depot Street ended at First. Mike O'Rourke's home still stood. The tiny gray-shingled house looked just as it had in 1960, except for the rear addition that obviously had taken the place of the outhouse. The old chickenhouse where the Bike Patrol had met was gone, but the large vegetable garden remained. Out front, staring sadly across First Avenue at the harvested fields, the Virgin Mary still held out her hands, palms outward, watching from the half-buried bathtub shrine in the front yard.

Dale had seen no trick-or-treaters. All of the homes he had passed had been dark except for the occasional porch light. Elm Haven had few streetlights in 1960 and now seemed to have none at all. He had noticed two small bonfires burning in yards along Broad, and now he saw the remains of another fire—untended, burned down to orange embers, sparks flying in the strong wind—in the O'Rourke side yard.

He did not recall bonfires being lighted for Halloween when he was a boy here.

Dale turned left past the small high school and left Elm Haven behind, turning west on Jubilee College Road at the water tower and accelerating north on County 6, hurrying the last three miles separating him from Duane McBride's farmhouse.

TWO

I NEVER left Illinois during my eleven years of life, but from what I've seen of Montana through Dale's eyes, it is an incredible place. The mountains and rivers are unlike anything in the Midwest—my uncle Art and I used to enjoy fishing in the Spoon River not far from Elm Haven, but it hardly qualifies as "river" compared to the wide, fast, rippling rivers like the Bitterroot and the Flathead and the Missouri and the Yellowstone. And our lazy sitting on a bank and watching bobbers while we chatted hardly qualifies as "fishing" compared to the energetic fly-fishing mystique in Montana. I've never tried fly-fishing, of course, but I suspect that I would prefer our quiet, sit-in-the-shade, conversational creekside approach to catching fish. I'm always suspicious of sports or recreational activities that begin to sound like religion when you hear their adherents preaching about them. Besides, I doubt if there are any catfish in those Montana rivers.

Dale's corner office on the campus of the University of Montana, his former family home in the old section of Missoula, and his ranch near Flathead Lake are all alien to me but fascinating. Missoula—for a city of only about 50,000 people—seems cordial to the things I probably would have loved had I lived to be an adult: bookstores, bakeries, good restaurants, lots of live music, a very decent university, movie and live drama theaters, a vibrant downtown section.

Dale's psychiatrist, a man named Charles Hall, had his office over one of these older used bookstores. Dale had been seeing Dr. Hall for the last ten months before his trip back here. Dale had first visited the psychiatrist two days after he had set the muzzle of the loaded Savage over-and-under shotgun against his temple and pulled the trigger.

Dr. Hall's office was small but comfortable—books, artwork on the wall, a window looking out onto leaves, a desk off to one side, and two worn leather chairs facing each other with a small glass table between. The table held only a pitcher of ice water, two clean glasses, and a box of Kleenex. Dale had needed the Kleenex only on his third visit, when he'd had a spring cold.

During their last session in mid-October, the leaves had been red outside the windows and Dr. Hall had been concerned about Dale's decision to spend the winter in Illinois. Eventually, however, the subject changed from emergency phone numbers and the necessity of Dale's getting in contact with another doctor to provide the necessary antidepressants and sleeping pills.

"You understand that I strongly advise against your plan to spend the winter alone in Illinois," said Dr. Hall.

"Noted," said Dale.

"Does my advice make any difference?"

"I'm spending a hundred and twenty-five dollars an hour for it," said Dale.

"You're spending a hundred and twenty-five dollars an hour for therapy," said Hall. "To talk. Or in your case, Dale, not so much to talk, but to get the prescriptions you need. But you're still going to spend the next ten months or so alone in Illinois."

"Yes," said Dale. "But only nine months. The usual gestation period."

"You realize that this is a classic pattern."

Dale waited and listened.

"A spouse dies and the survivor moves away—especially men, Dale—and tries to 'start a new life,' not realizing that what's needed at such a time is continuity, contact with friends, a support system . . ."

"My spouse didn't die," said Dale. "Anne is alive and well. I just betrayed her and lost her. Her and the girls."

"But the effect is the same . . ."

"Not really," said Dale. "There's no continuity here. My home here in Missoula is off-limits except for supervised visits and divorced-daddy Sunday pickups. I hate that. And you agree that spending another winter at the ranch is a bad idea . . ."

"Yes, of course," said Dr. Hall.

"So I'm headed back to the Midwest to spend part of my sabbatical. Back to The Jolly Corner."

"You never explained why your friend Duane called his home The Jolly Corner," said Dr. Hall. "Did he see it as a happy place? You said that the boy lived with just his father and that his father was an alcoholic. Was he being ironic? Is it possible that an eleven-year-old would use such irony, or have you supplied that irony in the decades since then?"

Dale hesitated, not sure how to respond. He was embarrassed that Hall did not recognize the allusion to "The Jolly Corner." If his psychiatrist didn't know Henry James, how smart could he be? Should he tell Hall that Duane hadn't told him about "The Jolly Corner" when he was eleven—Duane had died at age eleven—but had used that name for his farm when Dale had first moved to Elm Haven in 1956, when both boys were eight? An eight-year-old hick farm kid had known the Henry James story, and now Dale's $125-an-hour shrink had never heard of it.

"I think Duane McBride is the only real genius I've ever met," Dale said at last.

Dr. Hall sat back in his chair. Dale thought that for a psychiatrist, Hall did not have a very good poker face. He could see the skepticism in the doctor's slight rise of eyebrows and forced neutral expression.

"I know," continued Dale, "genius is a powerful word. I don't use it often . . . hell, I *never* use it. And I've met a lot of powerfully intelligent people in my lifetime—writers, academics, researchers. Duane is the only *genius* I've known."

Dr. Hall nodded. "But you knew him only as a child."

"Duane didn't live long enough to get out of childhood," said Dale. "But he sure was a strange kid."

"How so?" Dr. Hall put his yellow notepad on his lap and clicked his ballpoint pen open—a habit that Dale found distracting and vaguely annoying.

Dale sighed. How could he explain? "You would had to have met Duane, I think, to understand. On the outside, he was a big slob of a farm kid—fat, sloppy, lousy haircut. He wore the same flannel shirt and corduroy pants all the time, summer and winter. And remember, this was back in 1960—kids actually dressed up for school in those days, even in little hick towns like Elm Haven, Illinois. Nothing fancy, but we had school clothes and play clothes and knew the difference, not like the slobs in school today . . ."

Dr. Hall's supposedly neutral expression had shifted to the very slight frown that signaled that Dale had wandered from the subject.

"Anyway," said Dale, "I met Duane shortly after my family moved to Elm Haven when I was in fourth grade, and right away I knew that Duane was different—almost scary, he was so smart."

"Scary?" said Dr. Hall, making a note. "How so?"

"Not really scary," said Dale, "but beyond our understanding." He took a breath. "All right, summer after fifth grade. The bunch of us boys used to hang around together in a sort of club we called the Bike Patrol, like a junior Justice League of America . . ."

Dale could tell that Hall had no idea what he was talking about. Perhaps male psychiatrists had never been boys. That would explain a lot.

"Anyway, our clubhouse was in Mike O'Rourke's old chicken coop in town," continued Dale. "We had a sprung sofa in there, an old easy chair from the dump, the shell of a console radio . . . that kind of crap. I remember one night in the summer after fifth grade when we were bored and Duane started telling us the story of Beowulf . . . word for word. Night after night, reciting Beowulf from memory. Years later, when I read the epic in college, I recognized it . . . word for word . . . from Duane's storytelling on those summer evenings."

Hall nodded. "That's unusual for someone that age, to even know of Beowulf."

Dale had to smile. "The unusual part was that Duane told it to us in Old English."

The psychiatrist blinked. "Then how did you understand . . ."

"He'd rattle on in Old English for a while and then translate," said Dale. "That autumn, he gave us a bunch of Chaucer. We thought Duane was weird, but we loved it."

Dr. Hall made a note.

"Once we were hanging around and Duane was reading a new book . . . I think it was something by Truman Capote, obviously a writer I'd never heard of at the time . . . and one of the guys, I think it was Kevin, asked him how the book was, and Duane said that it was okay but that the author hadn't gotten his characters out of immigration yet."

Dr. Hall hesitated and then made another note. *Maybe you don't understand that,* thought Dale, *but I'm a writer—sometimes I'm a writer—and I've never had a goddamned editor make a remark that insightful.*

"Any other manifestations of this . . . genius?" asked the psychiatrist.

Dale rubbed his eyes. "That summer Duane died, 1960, a bunch of us were lying in a hammock out at Uncle Henry and Aunt Lena's farm, just down the road from The Jolly Corner, it was night, we were looking at the stars, and Mike O'Rourke—he was an altar boy—said that he thought that the world all existed in the mind of God and he wondered what it would be like to meet God, to shake hands with Him. Without hesitating a second, Duane said that he'd worry about that because he suspected that God spent too much time picking His mental nose with His mental fingers . . ."

Dr. Hall made no note, but he did look at Dale almost reproach-fully. "Your friend Duane was an atheist, I take it?"

Dale shrugged. "More or less. No, wait . . . I remember Duane telling me one of the first times we hung out together . . . we were building a three-stage rocket in fourth grade . . . he told me that he'd decided that all the churches and temples to the currently fashionable gods . . . that what he called them, 'the currently fashionable gods' . . . were too crowded, so he'd chosen some minor Egyptian deity as his god. Learned the old prayers, studied the rituals, the whole nine yards. I remember him telling me that he'd considered worshiping Termi-nus, the Roman god of lawn boundaries, but had decided on this Egyptian god instead. He thought the Egyptian god had been ignored for many centuries and might be lonely."

"That is unusual," allowed Dr. Hall, making a final brief note.

Now Dale did have to grin. "If I remember correctly, Duane taught himself how to read Egyptian hieroglyphics just for that purpose—to pray to his forgotten little god. Of course, Duane spoke eight or nine languages by the time he died at age eleven and probably read a dozen more."

Dr. Hall set aside his yellow legal pad, a sure sign that he was becoming bored with the topic being discussed. "Have you had any more dreams?" he asked.

Dale agreed that it was time to change the subject. "I had that dream about the hands again last night."

"Tell me about it."

"It was no different than the previous ones."

"Yes, Dale, that's more or less the definition of 'recurring dreams,' but it's interesting how one can find slight but important differences when the dreams are actually discussed."

"We haven't discussed dreams much."

"That's true. I'm a psychiatrist but not—as you know—a psychoana-lyst. But tell me about the hands dream anyway."

"It was the same as always. I'm a kid again—"

"How old?"

"Ten, eleven, I don't know. But I'm in our old house in Elm Haven. Sleeping in the upstairs room with my little brother, Lawrence . . ."

"Go on."

"Well, Lawrence and I are talking, there's a night light on, and Lawrence drops a comic book. He reaches down and . . . well, this hand comes out from under the bed and grabs him by the wrist. Pulls him down."

"A pale hand, you said last time."

"Yes. No. Not just pale, white . . . grub white . . . dead white."

"What else about the hand . . . or is it hands, plural?"

"Just one hand at first. It grabs Lawrence by the wrist and pulls him off the bed before either one of us can react. The hand—the white hand—is weird, long fingers . . . I mean, *way* too long . . . eight or nine inches long. Spiderlike. Then I grab Lawrence by the legs . . ."

"He has already been pulled under the bed at this point?"

"Just his head and shoulders. He's still screaming. That's when I see both of the spidery white hands, pulling and cramming him under the bed."

"And sleeves? Cuffs? Bare arms?"

"No. Just the white hands and blackness, but blackness darker than the dark under Lawrence's bed. Like the sleeves of a black velvet robe, perhaps."

"And you don't succeed in saving your brother?"

"No, the hands pull him under and then he's gone."

"Gone?"

"Gone. As if a hole has opened up in the wooden floor and the hands had pulled him in."

"But your brother—in real life—is still alive and well."

"Yes. Sure. He runs an insurance investigation agency in California."

"Have you discussed this dream with him?"

"No. We don't see each other that much. We talk occasionally on the phone."

"But you've never mentioned the dream?"

"No. Lawrence . . . well, he's a big, gruff guy sometimes, but he's also sensitive . . . he doesn't like talking about that summer. Or about his childhood, actually. He had a rough time as a teenager in Chicago and had sort of a nervous breakdown after he dropped out of college."

"Do you think that he also has memory gaps about that summer of . . . when was it?"

"1960."

"Do you think that he has the same gaps?"

"No. I don't know. I doubt it. He just doesn't like talking about it."

"All right. Back to the dream itself. How do you feel when you lose this . . . tug of war . . . and your younger brother disappears?"

"Scared. Angry. And . . ."

"Go on."

"Relieved, I guess. That the hands had grabbed Lawrence instead of me, I think. Dr. Hall, what the hell does this mean?"

"We discussed the fact that dreams don't have to *mean* anything, Dale. But there almost certainly is a reason for having them. It sounds like a straightforward anxiety dream to me. Do you feel anxiety about the months ahead?"

"Sure I do. But why this dream?"

"Why do *you* think anxiety shows itself through this dream?"

"I have no idea. It couldn't be a repressed memory?"

"You think that you have an actual memory of white hands dragging your little brother under the bed?"

"Well . . . or something like that."

"We discussed repressed memories. Despite all the movies and TV talk about them, they are actually very, very rare. And a repressed memory would deal with a *real* event, such as physical or sexual abuse, not a fantasy nightmare. What is it? I can tell by your face that you're disturbed."

"Well, it wasn't the recurring nightmare that woke me up last night."

"What was it?"

"A sound. A scrabbling noise. Under my bed. Is our time up?"

"Just about. I do have one final question."

"Shoot," said Dale.

"Why go all the way to your childhood friend's house in Illinois to write this book? Why leave everything you know, everything you have in life, and go back to this empty house in a state you haven't lived in for forty years?"

Dale was silent for a full minute. Finally he said, "I have to go back. Something's waiting for me there."

"What, Dale?"

"I have no idea."

To get to Duane McBride's farmhouse when he was a kid, Dale had pedaled his bike about a mile and a half west on the gravel of Jubilee College Road, turned north on County 6, an even narrower gravel road, passed the Black Tree Tavern on his left, swooped down and up two steep hills, past the Calvary Cemetery where Elm Haven's Catholics were buried, and then straight on another half-mile of flat road to the farm.

Jubilee College Road had been paved and widened. The Black Tree Tavern was gone, as far as Dale could tell in the dark—the building torn down, a cheap mobile home tucked in under the trees where yellow bulbs on wires had once hung—and County 6 here had also been asphalted and widened. These two hills had been death traps when Dale had lived here: wide enough for only one car, slick with gravel, dark even on sunny days with the overarching trees and the weeds coming right to the edge of the road, no shoulders for escape. It was exciting to pedal down and then coast up them on a bike, trying to keep on the hardened ruts of the road, and even the adults tended to play an elaborate game of chicken on the hills, accelerating their cars and pickup trucks down them in a cloud of dust and gravel and roaring to the top of the next hill with only the hope that no car was doing the same coming the other way. Frequently the drivers were drunken farmers headed home from the Black Tree. Uncle Henry and Aunt Lena—who had lived in the neat little farmhouse just beyond the hills—had always joked that Calvary Cemetery had been put where it was—on the top of the middle hill—just to save everyone the bother of dragging the victims of the car wrecks back to town.

Now the asphalted road was easily wide enough for two cars to pass, and the woods and weeds had been cut back on either side.

Dale pulled the Land Cruiser onto the grassy berm outside the Calvary Cemetery, stopped the engine, left the headlights on, and stepped out into the night.

The wind had come up more strongly now, and the low clouds seemed to be rushing by just yards overhead. There were no stars. The cemetery's tall black iron gate and the long spiked iron fence were visible in the headlights and looked just as he remembered them, except for the fact that they appeared to have grown black bat wings or witches' robes—long, flapping streamers of what seemed to be black crêpe paper. It was no illusion. Dale could hear the frenzied flapping of the streamers and see different lengths of tattered black material waving and blowing eastward along the full length of the fence and all around the arched gate.

Corn husks, thought Dale. *"Shucks," we used to call them.* He had seen this post-harvest phenomenon when he was a kid here, and he often thought of it on windy days in Montana when tumbleweeds lined the fences of the highways. To the east of the cemetery, across County 6, had been Old Man Johnson's farm when Dale was a boy, and whoever now owned the land still raised corn. Hundreds of these dried shucks and husks had blown from the field and tangled themselves on the black iron gate after the harvest.

Harvested by a combine with rolling-chain corn pickers, just like the machine that killed Duane. Had Duane's torn clothes and flesh flown through the night wind like this, catching and flapping on some barbed-wire fence along this road?

Dale shook his head. He was very tired.

Dale had no family in the cemetery—his folks had not been

Catholic—but he knew that the O'Rourkes and many of his other Elm Haven friends and acquaintances had people buried there. *Some of those old friends of mine are probably buried there now as well,* he thought. He would come back in the daylight and check. He would have plenty of time in the coming weeks. He climbed back into the Land Cruiser, started the engine, and headed down the next hill, leaving the flapping, waving, crackling apparitions behind.

It was another mile to Duane McBride's farm. Dale passed his great-aunt Lena and uncle Henry's farm to the right—the house was dark—and wondered who lived there now. Uncle Henry had died in 1970, but someone had told Dale that Aunt Lena was still alive in a home in Peoria—suffering from Alzheimer's, beyond communication for the last two decades or so, but still living. If the report was true, then the old woman had lived through parts of three centuries. Dale shook his head at the thought. What would it be like to outlive one's spouse by more than thirty years? He felt a lurch in his belly at the thought. He no longer had a spouse, and the idea still seemed strange to him.

He almost missed the driveway to the McBride farm. The place had always been marked by two things—Mr. McBride's refusal, because of his late wife's request, to grow corn that would conceal the farmhouse from the world, and vice versa, in summer, and a quarter-mile of flowering crabapple trees that had lined the lane.

Now the fields were stubbled with still-standing stalks of harvested corn and most of the crabapple trees were gone. Dale knew just enough about farming to know that the remaining stalks meant that whoever was farming this land was using the "plain-tilling" method.

Dale drove slowly down the lane. When his headlights illuminated the dark farmhouse, his first thought was, *Jesus, it's smaller than I remember.*

The place was dark, of course, without even the usual farmer's pole light illuminating the area between the house and the sheds and barn. There was a front door, but Duane and his father had never used it, so Dale pulled around the side of the house and looked at the side door. Sandy Whittaker, the real estate agent, had said that no one could find a key but that it would not be locked and that the power would be turned on by the time Dale arrived.

He left the engine running to keep the headlights on the doorway as he trotted over. Both the screen and the inner doors were unlocked. Dale stepped into the kitchen.

He raised his hand to his face and almost jumped back outside. The place smelled terrible—rotten, musty, decayed, worse. Something had died in there.

He flicked the light switch. Nothing. The place was as dark as an unlighted cave, with only the slightest hint of light through the one kitchen window.

Dale went back out to the truck, grabbed his halogen flashlight, and went back in.

The kitchen looked as if it had been abandoned in mid-meal. There were plates on the counter and more in the sink. The stench grew stronger with each step he took, and Dale covered his mouth and nose with one hand as he crossed into the dining room.

Jesus, the place is full of children's coffins. Dale froze in place, flicking the light in all directions. Instead of one dining room table, there were six or eight rough benches set on sawhorses, and on each bench was a long, dull-metal box the size and shape of a small coffin. Then he saw the slots for punch cards, rudimentary keyboards, and small windows on the metal boxes.

Learning machines, Dale remembered. Duane's Old Man—always his friend's affectionate term for his father—had been an inventor. These were the pre-electronic "learning machines" that the Old Man had always been tinkering with, never completing to his satisfaction, and rarely selling.

Amazing, thought Dale. Duane's aunt—the Old Man's sister from Chicago—had lived in this place from 1961 right through to the eve of the millennium and had never moved all this junk. Forty years of living with these things in the dining room.

The smell was stronger in here. Dale panned his flashlight around, found the light switch, and flipped it on. Nothing.

Something had died in here; that was certain. Probably a mouse or rat. Possibly a larger animal. Dale had no intention of moving his stuff in or sleeping in here until he found the corpse, got rid of it, and aired the place out.

He sighed, went back out to his Land Cruiser, shut it off, reclined the passenger seat as far as it would go, cracked all of the windows a bit, pulled an old blanket from the back seat, and tried to go to sleep. Dale was exhausted to the point that when he closed his eyes he saw interstate highway center lines moving in headlights, overpasses flashing above him, exit signs flitting by. He was just dozing off when some fragment of dream or thought startled him awake. Dale reached over and pushed the button that locked all of the doors.

THREE

I T was snowing when Dale awoke to dull morning light.

Where the hell am I? It was an honest question. He was stiff, sore, still exhausted from the long drive, disoriented, cold, and achy. His head hurt. His eyes hurt. His back hurt. He felt as he usually did after the first hard day of a backpacking or horse-packing camping trip with its inevitable restless first night of fitful half-sleeping on the cold ground.

Where am I? The snow was falling in discrete pellets, pounding and bouncing on the hood of the Land Cruiser—not quite hail, not quite snow. *Groppel* was the word they used in the West. The windshield was iced up. The fields of harvested corn were glazed over. *Duane's house. Illinois.* That made no sense. *Snow?* It was the first day of November. Dale Stewart was used to snow in early autumn in Missoula, even more so at the ranch near Flathead Lake because of the elevation there, but in Illinois? He had lived in Elm Haven for seven years of his childhood and could not remember snow before Thanksgiving in any of those years.

Shit, he thought, rooting through his closest duffel bag for a jacket.

Blame it on el niño *or* la niña. *We've blamed everything else on them for the past five or six years.*

Dale stepped out of the Land Cruiser, tugged on his jacket, shivered, and looked at the house looming over him.

As a writer, Dale had been forced to learn a little bit about basic house types and architecture—writers have to learn a little bit about almost everything, was his opinion—and he recognized the McBride farmhouse as a "National Pyramidal Family Folk Home." It sounded complicated, but all the term really meant was that it was one of about a million plain, equilaterally hipped-roofed houses in the Midwest, built around the time of the First World War. The McBride place was a two-story pyramidal—tall, with no side gables or interesting windows or details. Flat all around, except for a tiny porch roof over the side door that Dale remembered the McBrides using almost exclusively. Most pyramidal family farmhouses had large front porches, but this front door boasted only a stoop and a bit of skimpy lawn. The side door opened onto the muddy turnaround area between the house and the outbuildings—two tool sheds, a couple of small-garage-size general utility sheds, a chicken coop, and a huge barn where Mr. McBride had kept his farm equipment.

Dale just hoped that the plumbing worked. He had to piss as bad as the proverbial racehorse. *Plumbing?* he thought. *I don't need no steenking plumbing.* He was at an abandoned farmhouse three miles from a dying little Illinois village. Dale glanced once down the long, dreary driveway toward the road and then went around to the east side of the Land Cruiser to pee. The light snow was trying to turn to rain, but his urine melted a small circle on the frosted mud of the McBride's turnaround.

A car horn bleated not far behind him.

Dale zipped up quickly, guiltily, rubbed his hands against his slacks, and came around the Land Cruiser. A large, dark Buick had pulled up while he was peeing. The woman who got out was probably around Dale's age, but fifty pounds heavier, matronly, with frizzy hair dyed a totally false blond. She was wearing a long beige-quilted-goose-down coat of the kind that had gone out of fashion about fifteen years earlier.

"Mr. Stewart?" said the woman. "Dale?"

For a second, he was totally at a loss. Then the slow tumblers clicked into place. "Ms. Whittaker?"

The heavy woman began walking carefully over the snow-covered ruts. "Oh, for heaven's sake," she cried, coming too close to him, "call me Sandy."

Dale had found the McBride house for rent on the Internet. When he had contacted the local real estate company handling the house rental—a place out of Oak Hill—he had spoken to the woman for ten minutes about the details of renting the vacant house before the two realized that they knew each other. She had said her name was Mrs. Sandra Blair, but only after he told her on the phone that he had lived in Elm Haven for a few years as a child did she say that actually she was divorced—she still kept the Blair name for business purposes because her ex-husband had been an important personage in Oak Hill and Peoria—but that her friends called her by her maiden name, Sandy Whittaker.

Dale dimly remembered Sandy Whittaker as a thin, blond, quiet girl who hung out with Donna Lou Perry, the best pitcher in their informal but daily summer baseball league. Now, as he stood looking at this heavy, hippy, jowled, top-heavy woman, all the time hoping that she had not seen him taking a leak as she drove up, he could make no connection at all with the eleven-year-old girl from his past. Perhaps she had the same problem: he hadn't put on as much weight as she had, but his salt-and-pepper beard and glasses certainly hadn't been part of his image as a kid.

"Good heavens, Dale, we didn't expect you until tonight or tomorrow. The place has been cleaned up a bit and the electricity was to be turned on today, but when you called from Montana we thought you said November first or second."

"I did, actually," said Dale. "I just kept on driving. Shall we get out of the snow?"

"Yes, of course." She was wearing high-heeled shoes. Dale could not remember the last time he had seen a pair of stiletto heels like these, especially on a woman so formidable. He held out his hand to help her across the frozen ruts and through the snowy patches. "Very strange weather for so early in autumn," said Sandy Whittaker.

"That's what I thought," said Dale as they came up onto the tiny side porch. "But then I thought maybe I'd forgotten what November was like here in Illinois."

"Oh, no, no. Usually very nice. It must be that terrible *el niño* thing. Have you been in the house?"

"Only briefly last night," said Dale. "The power was out and . . . I should warn you . . . something died in there. A mouse or rat, perhaps. It smelled pretty bad."

She paused at the doorway and arched one painted eyebrow. She was wearing so much makeup that it seemed to Dale that she was wearing a flesh-colored Kabuki mask. "Smell?" she said. "I was here yesterday with a cleaning lady and the propane people. There was no smell then. Do you think it's a gas leak?"

"No," said Dale, brushing the snow from his hair. "You'll see." He opened the door for her.

Sandy Whittaker batted at the kitchen light switch, and the bare bulb came on. The dishes on the table and counter, Dale could now see, had been freshly washed and stacked. There was no smell whatsoever.

"That's strange," he said. He stepped into the dining room where the cold daylight illuminated the gray boxes of the learning machines. There was no smell there, either. "I was sure that something large had died in here."

Sandy Whittaker giggled nervously. "Oh, no, Mrs. Brubaker—that was Mr. McBride's sister—died in the hospital over at Oak Hill, where I live. Oak Hill, I mean, not in the hospital. That was almost a year ago. And Mr. McBride died in Chicago . . . oh, when was it?"

"1961," said Dale.

"Yes, of course, the winter after . . . well, after that terrible accident to little Duane out here."

Dale had to smile despite himself. His childhood friend had weighed over 200 pounds at age eleven. No one had ever called him "little Duane."

"And he died in a farm machinery accident some distance from here, didn't he?" continued the Realtor.

Dale realized that she was worried that he would think the house was haunted. "I just meant that last night it smelled as if a mouse or something died here," he said. "Whatever it is, it's gone."

"Yes," said Sandy Whittaker, all business now. "Would you like to look at the house? I know that the snapshots I sent you via e-mail weren't all that clear. I don't have one of those newfangled digital cameras . . . I just scan in the snaps from my little Instamatic."

"No, they were very helpful," said Dale. He glanced at his watch. "Aren't you working a little early . . . oh, wait, I forgot that I lost an hour driving to the Central Time Zone. My watch says seven forty-five." He started to reset it.

"No," said Sandy Whittaker, with a small frown, consulting her own watch, "your watch is right. It's just seven forty-five."

Dale paused. He was sure that he hadn't reset it during his drive. Then he realized the obvious: Daylight Standard Time had begun while he was traveling. *Fall back*, thought Dale. Indeed, he seemed to have fallen all the way back into his childhood hometown, his childhood friend's house, and this conversation with his elementary-school classmate without gaining or losing a minute of his life.

Just forty-one years, thought Dale with a slight tinge of vertigo bordering on nausea.

Sandy led the tour, starting with the ample kitchen. "I'm afraid only one burner works on the old stove. It's gas, of course. Everything runs off the propane tank out by the tool shed. I'm sure you can get some place in Oak Hill or Peoria to come fix it. The stove, I mean."

"I probably won't need more than one burner," said Dale. "Actually, it's a microwave I'll miss. I've been subsisting on Hungry-Man frozen dinners. I guess now I'll just have to suck on them frozen."

Sandy Whittaker actually stopped and stared at him in something like shock. He could see that she was revising her estimate of him down several notches. "I'm sure that there's an inexpensive microwave available in . . ."

Dale held up his palms. "I was just kidding. An old Woody Allen line, I think."

The Realtor frowned and nodded. "The refrigerator is small, but it still works. Plates and glasses and everything you'll need are in the cupboards here. Mrs. Brubaker was a very tidy person, but I had Alma— that's our cleaning person—wash everything again anyway. And the dining room here . . ." The floorboards creaked under Ms. Whittaker's weight. She paused to fiddle with a wall thermostat, and Dale heard an old furnace kick on seconds before the house filled with that not-unpleasant dusty smell of the first-time heat of autumn.

"Well," she said, stepping further into the dining room, "we just didn't know what to do with these . . . machines. They were too heavy for Alma and me to carry all the way out to the old chicken coop or the barn, and of course the propane men were too busy to be bothered. I have no idea what these contraptions were, but obviously Mr. McBride had been working on them years and years ago—you may have noticed that Mrs. Brubaker kept everything as she found it, although cleaner, of course."

"Why did she do that?" said Dale.

"Do what?"

"Keep everything as she found it?"

Sandy Whittaker shrugged. "You remember how . . . eccentric . . . little Duane and his father were. Well, Mr. McBride's sister was the same way, I guess. She kept to herself. I don't think anyone ever visited except the Meals on Wheels people during her last year here. And Sarah from Meals on Wheels said that the house never changed. Mrs. Brubaker had kept it up like a museum."

"What did she die of?" asked Dale.

"Cancer," said the Realtor. The floorboards creaked again as she crossed the dining room, passed through a small arch with missing pocket doors, and stopped in the small, dark living room. "The living room," she said. "I don't believe the McBrides ever spent much time in here . . . or Mr. McBride's sister, for that matter."

Two ancient chairs, a side table with a circa-1940s lamp, a sprung sofa, and a rug with huge white flowers grown gray over the decades. No radio. No television. No phone. The two tall windows here were so heavily draped that almost none of the weak morning light found its way in.

Dale started to tug the drapes apart, found them pinned, undid the pin and struggled to open them. Another layer of draperies was pinned inside the first.

"You should have seen the dust before Alma and her daughter vacuumed," said Sandy.

"I believe it," said Dale. This inner layer of dark drapes had actually been sewn together. "Mrs. Brubaker must have been a vampire." He pulled a folding knife from his pocket, flicked open the gravity blade, and cut through the stitching. The drapes did not want to slide along the heavy rod, but eventually he wrestled them back. A once-white curtain turned the sunlight a dim, watery yellow. He tugged the curtains down. "I'm going to need more light in here to work," he explained, dropping the brittle curtains on the old couch and squinting up at the high draperies.

"I don't think so," said Sandy Whittaker.

Dale folded his knife away and looked at her.

"A vampire," she said. "I don't think that Mrs. Brubaker was a vampire."

The tour of the rest of the first floor took only a few minutes. A "National Pyramidal Family Folk Home" was pretty much like Dale's former American-square home in Missoula before the additions had been added—square, four rooms, a narrow hallway, and a bathroom. Going counterclockwise: the tiled kitchen (one window and a door), the large dining room (two windows with drapes and curtains), the small front living room (two heavily draped windows), the front entrance hall that ran back to the kitchen (its front door had leaded glass—the only decorative item Dale noticed on the first floor), the front "study" across the hall from the living room—a small room, but surprisingly cozy, with an old rolltop desk, built-in bookcases along the north wall, a single window looking down the front drive, and a long daybed with sleighbed headboard and footboard.

"This is where Mrs. Brubaker slept and—I believe—Mr. McBride before that."

"They didn't sleep upstairs?" said Dale.

Sandy Whittaker smiled. He was standing close enough to smell her talcum powder and perfume. "No. I believe I mentioned the reason in my first e-mail to you."

They paused by the first-floor bathroom: a pedestal sink, a wonderful clawfoot tub, but no shower. The black and white floor tile was chipped. The toilet actually had the flush box on the wall behind it, making Dale think of the scene in the first *Godfather* where Michael Corleone goes in the rest room of the Italian restaurant to find a pistol with which to kill Tattaglia and the police captain, played by Sterling Hayden.

"No shower?" he said.

"There's one downstairs and one upstairs, I believe. But they never used the upstairs shower."

"Why not?" said Dale.

"I'll show you," said Sandy.

As it turned out, she did not accompany him upstairs. It was a narrow stairway, winding, enclosed in the wall between the bathroom and the front door. It had no light switch and was very dark. Dale was gallant—thinking of the steep, narrow stairway and Ms. Whittaker's size—and suggested that he go up alone, clumping up the steep winding staircase in the dark. There was a dim light at the top.

A thick spiderweb covered the door to the second-floor hallway.

Something distorted and huge—a spidery shape as tall as Dale—moved in the layers of web, its limbs shifting and twitching, reaching for him.

Dale simply froze. Later, he was glad that he did not scream. Certainly *that* story would have soon gotten around Oak Hill and Elm Haven: Dale Stewart, learned professor, rugged Westerner and author of the *Jim Bridger: Mountain Man* series, scared by his own shadow.

There were multiple layers of thick, clear construction plastic nailed across the doorway. The plastic had warped and yellowed with age—Dale remembered now that Duane McBride had said that his Old Man had "shut off the second floor for heating reasons" after Dale's mother had died. That must have been around 1952.

Dale reached out and gingerly touched the first layer of plastic. Thick. Brittle. There must have been four or five layers nailed into place, each with its own latticework of folds and cracks. Dim light from a second-story window barely made it through the discolored layers. No wonder he had thought it was a web. The giant spider, of course, had been his own distorted reflection. He leaned closer but still could see no detail of the hallway or rooms beyond.

Dale clicked open his knife, set the blade to the plastic, and then thought better of it. He went carefully down the steep stairway.

"Is it still all sealed off?" asked Sandy Whittaker.

"That's an understatement," said Dale. "I was going to cut through the plastic, but I figured I'd better ask you if there was some reason for the second floor being off-limits. Ebola virus or something."

"Pardon me?" said Sandy Whittaker.

"Just kidding. I'm just curious as to why all the plastic sheeting."

"Don't you remember in the e-mail I sent you?" said Sandy. "I mentioned that Mrs. Brubaker had never heated the second floor—that it was shut off."

"I thought you meant the heating vents," said Dale with a soft smile. They had walked back into the kitchen where there was more light. "I didn't know you meant that Mr. McBride had hermetically sealed the whole second floor."

"Alma wouldn't go up there," said Sandy.

"Why?" said Dale. "Is it haunted? Is Mr. McBride's crazy second wife sealed in up there or something?"

Ms. Whittaker could only stare. Her lipsticked mouth hung slightly open.

"Just kidding again," Dale said hastily, making a mental note not to joke with Sandy Whittaker again. Had she been this literal as a kid? He could not remember. He had not hung around the girls much. "Now I remember when I lived here as a kid," said Dale, "Duane saying something about their second story being shut off because of the heating bills."

Sandy Whittaker finally managed a nod. "I assure you, Dale . . . Mr. Stewart . . ."

"Dale," said Dale.

"I assure you, Dale, that as far as I know, that's absolutely the only reason for the second floor to be sealed off. The old coal furnace was converted to propane in the 1950s and was never as efficient afterward. Mrs. Brubaker slept in the study—I think Mr. McBride had slept there as well after his wife died—and, well, no one needed the second floor."

"I just made the joke because you said Alma—the housekeeper, right?—Alma wouldn't go up there," Dale said lamely.

"Alma is seventy-four years old," said Sandy. "With a bad hip. It's the staircase she's afraid of. Now . . . you've rented the entire house, Mr. . . . . Dale. If you would like the upstairs to be opened up, I'll get my nephew over here to take the plastic down and then Alma—or Alma's daughter—will help me clean and air out the rooms. I imagine that the air up there could be a little stale if it's been shut off for almost fifty years . . ."

Dale held his palms up. He had almost made a joke about unsealing Tutankhamen's tomb, but stopped himself in time. "I don't need the second floor," he said. "If I do, I'll tell you. And for a hundred and seventy-five dollars a month, the first floor and that nice study should work for me."

"If you think the rent is too high . . ." began Sandy.

Dale had to sigh and shake his head. "Even in Missoula, you couldn't rent a decent room for that amount, Sandy. Everything's fine. Did you say that there's a shower in the basement?"

FOUR

THERE was more than a shower in the basement. Dale had forgotten that Duane had more or less lived in the basement of this farmhouse.

When Dale had been a boy in Elm Haven, he had been terrified of his own basement. It had been a labyrinth of small rooms with the coal bin far in the back of the maze, and he'd been frightened every night when he had to go down and shovel coal into the hopper.

The McBride basement could not have been more different. Essentially it was one large room—the huge furnace taking up much of the south end—but clean, tidied up, with workbenches along one wall, an old washing machine with wooden rollers, coils of clothesline, a huge jerry-rigged shower tapping into the plumbing under the first-floor bathroom, an old-fashioned but complete darkroom setup near the water pipes, and Duane's corner.

Dale remembered that he had been in Duane's home only once—breaking in through one of the six narrow windows set high up on the cement walls here—after Duane had died. He had come for Duane's private notebooks, and he still had them—wrapped and secure out in the Land Cruiser. Thirteen thick, spiral notebooks filled with Duane's small, almost illegible shorthand script.

Duane's "room" was still there: a corner of the basement partitioned off by a quilt hanging on a clothesline—the quilt smelled freshly laundered to Dale as he stood next to it—and by various crates piled high and filled with paperbacks. Dale slid back the quilt.

Duane McBride had assembled an old brass bed down here, and the thick mattress looked more comfortable than the smaller daybed in the parlor upstairs. All around the bed were more bookcase-crates, filled with paperbacks and old hardcover books, and on top of most of the crates were radios: clunky 1960 transistor radios, complicated receivers obviously made from kits, simple crystal sets, several Bakelite 1950s models, and even a huge Philco floor radio against the wall near the foot of the bed. At a small desk between the bed and the Philco sat a real shortwave radio—able to send as well as receive—with antenna wires running up and out the narrow window.

"I forgot that Duane had been a ham radio operator," Dale said softly, almost whispering.

"We don't know if it still works," whispered Sandy Whittaker. "But Mrs. Brubaker kept everything clean down here as well."

"I'll say she did," said Dale. "This basement is cleaner than my ranch in Montana."

Sandy Whittaker did not know what to say to that, so she pursed her lips and nodded.

"Seriously," said Dale, gesturing around the large basement, "there's more light here than upstairs." Besides the six uncovered basement windows—working almost like clerestory windows set high on the wall—there were four hanging lightbulbs illuminating the open space and two small lamps that still worked next to Duane's old bed. The place was actually cozy.

Sandy Whittaker glanced at her watch. "Well, I just wanted to make sure that everything was ready for you. I'd better get back to the office."

They paused in the kitchen. The snow had stopped, but it was still cloudy and cold outside. "I wish I had something to offer you," said Dale. "Maybe a glass of water?"

Sandy Whittaker frowned at the tap. "We think the water is all right—it's well water, not city water—but you might consider bringing in bottled water to be safe."

Dale nodded, smiling again. He had not heard the phrase "city water" for more than four decades. All of the implications came back to him now: Elm Haven's tap water had been sulfurous, gritty, nasty, undrinkable. Even people in town had used backyard wells.

The Realtor was handing him several pieces of paper: a receipt for the checks he had mailed her for damage deposit and first and last months' rent—he planned to stay nine months; a list of emergency phone numbers, most of them in Oak Hill, he noticed; her number; the addresses of a medical clinic in Oak Hill, a dentist, and various stores.

"I need to do some grocery shopping before nightfall," said Dale. "I noticed that the A & P and Corner Pantry were gone. Where do people in Elm Haven shop these days?"

Sandy made a gesture and Dale noticed how dainty her wrists and hands were, even with such plump arms. "Oh, most people drive to the old Oak Hill grocery store a block from the park or into the west side Peoria Safeway. Or, if they're in a hurry, out to the KWIK'N'EZ." She spelled it for him. "It's that travel convenience store built onto the Shell station out at the I-74 interchange," she explained. "Bread, milk, that sort of thing. Prices are ridiculous, but it's easy to get to."

"KWIK'N'EZ," repeated Dale. He hated chain stores and convenience stores only slightly less than he hated TV evangelists and World War II–era Nazi war criminals.

Dale accompanied Sandy Whittaker out to her huge black Buick. The woman paused by the car. "Do you hear from any of your old friends from the old days, Dale?"

"Elm Haven pals, you mean?" said Dale. "No. I wrote letters for a while after we moved back to Chicago in 1961, but I haven't heard from any of the old gang for years. Any of them still live here?"

The Realtor thought for a second. "Not that group you were with— Mike O'Rourke, Kevin Grumbacher, those boys, right?"

"And Jim Harlen," said Dale with a smile.

"Oh, well, maybe you know that Jim Harlen became a U.S. senator from Illinois."

Dale nodded. Harlen had been in the Senate twenty years before a sex scandal had ruined his chances for reelection in 2000.

"The O'Rourkes—the parents—still live in the same house," said Sandy.

"My God," said Dale, "they must be a hundred years old."

"In their eighties," said Sandy. "I haven't spoken to them for years. I understand that Michael was hurt real bad in Vietnam and then became a priest."

"That's what I heard as well," said Dale. "But I can't find any trace of him on the Internet."

"And Kevin Grumbacher . . ." continued Sandy, not listening to him. "His parents died, you know. The last I heard he was working for NASA or some such."

"Morton Thiokol," said Dale. He noticed the lack of comprehension in her eyes. "That's the company that builds the solid rocket boosters for the space shuttle. I found some old articles—evidently Kevin was working for them during the *Challenger* disaster in 1986 and blew the whistle on them . . . testified about the fact that the company knew about the faulty O-rings."

Sandy Whittaker still stared blankly at him.

Dale shrugged. "Anyway, he resigned in protest in '86 and I couldn't find any other articles or listings about him. I think he lives in Texas." He felt uncomfortable talking about his old friends with this woman, even though he was curious about what she knew. To change the subject, he said, "What about your old school friends from Elm Haven? Still in touch with Donna Lou Perry?"

"She's dead," said Sandy. "Murdered."

Dale could only blink.

"A long time ago," she said. "Donna Lou married Paulie Fussner in . . . I think it was 1970 . . . and she tried to get a divorce in '74, I think it was. He tracked her down and beat her up. She went back home to live with her folks in Elm Haven, but he waited for her one morning and shot her."

"That's terrible," said Dale. Donna Lou was the one female from his childhood here whom he'd hoped to run across, to apologize for something that had happened on the baseball diamond forty-two years earlier. Now he never could. "Jesus," he said.

Sandy nodded. "It's been a long time. The new century makes me feel like we're all ancient, talking about people and things from the middle of the last century and all. Who else was in that group of yours?"

"Cordie Cooke," said Dale, still thinking about the murdered Donna Lou.

"Don't know what happened to her."

Dale did—he had found out through the Net that the moon-faced little white-trash Cordie Cooke had become a millionaire a hundred times over, had sold the largest waste management company in America a few years ago, and was currently running an expensive rehabilitation center for cancer victims on the Big Island of Hawaii. He didn't take time to share all this with the Realtor.

"There was some other boy in your bunch," said Sandy.

Dale thought for a moment. "My kid brother Lawrence?"

"No, someone else . . ."

"Duane McBride?" he said.

Sandy Whittaker actually blushed. "Yes, I guess that's who I was thinking of." She got in the car and started the engine.

Dale stepped back, preparing to wave good-bye, but Sandy rolled the window down. "Oh, I meant to tell you, Dale. My cousin's boy— Derek—when he heard you were renting the place, he said he knew all about you."

Oh, Christ, thought Dale, a *Jim Bridger: Mountain Man* fan.

"Derek's sort of a . . . well, a problem child, I guess you could say, though he's nineteen now, so not really a child. Anyway, my cousin Ardith says that Derek knew your name from his Internet friends. That they'd sent your photograph and articles out to all the others."

"Articles?" said Dale. "Do you mean novels?"

"No, the articles that were in some Montana newspaper."

"Oh, Christ," Dale said aloud. "Do you mean the editorials on the Montana Militia?" At the height—or depths, to be more accurate—of his clinical depression a year earlier, he had written a series of editorials about the right-wing militias. "I thought those were only being routed around to other neo-Nazi groups and skinheads."

Sandy bit on her lower lip. "I don't think Derek is a whatchamacallit Nazi, but he does hang around with skinheads. Heck, he is a skinhead. Anyway, I wanted to tell you. You don't want to get on the wrong side of Derek and his friends."

"Sounds like I already have," said Dale. He folded his arms. *Great beginning to my sabbatical.* It was starting to rain again.

"Call me if you need anything," said Sandy Whittaker. She rolled up the window, ponderously turned the huge Buick around in the muddy lot, and drove down the long driveway in the rain. In the dim daylight, the dead crabapple trees looked even sadder and more skeletal.

Dale shook his head, went over to the Land Cruiser, and started hauling his boxes of junk—his life—into the McBride farmhouse.

FIVE

THE last time Dale had seen his young lover, Clare, more than a year earlier in the clean, bright, achingly blue-sky Montana mid-September, they had saddled up at the ranch—she on the spirited roan he had bought for his oldest daughter and that his daughter had ridden only twice but that Clare had ridden a score of times, he on the docile, older gelding that had come with the ranch—and then they had led two pack mules up into the high country for a three-day camping trip. The weather stayed perfect during the entire long weekend. The great clone groves of aspen covering the subalpine hillsides had gone golden earlier that week and because it had been a wet, warm summer, the leaves were a perfect yellow-gold, shimmering against the blue-vaulted sky and filling the hillsides and valleys below them with a constantly dancing light. Clare reminded him that aspen leaves glittered that way because they were attached to the branch at a slight angle so that both sides of each leaf could photosynthesize during the short growing season. Dale reminded her that he had taught her that a year earlier.

The first night they camped below treeline, and they allowed themselves the luxury of a small campfire, sitting around it and talking over coffee for hours as the stars burned almost without twinkling above them. Before Dale lit the fire, Clare gave him a small box wrapped in perfect gold paper. He looked at her quizzically.

"A small present," she said.

"What's the occasion?" asked Dale.

"Open it," said Clare.

Inside the box was a beautiful gold Dunhill cigarette lighter. "It's beautiful," said Dale. "But I know that you know that I don't smoke."

"You don't light campfires all that well, either," said Clare. "I remember Ghost Ridge. Your matches are always wet or missing or something. That thing might save your life someday."

Dale had laughed and lighted their stack of kindling and wood with two flicks of the lighter.

There had been several nights of frost, so there were no mosquitoes. The breeze from the high ridges was cold, but the fire was warm and they were comfortable in leather riding coats over fleece vests and flannel shirts. Clare told him about the first days of her graduate program at Princeton. He told her about the new book he had begun—a "serious" novel about Custer at the Little Bighorn, from the Native American perspective. Clare winced, as she always did, at the term "Native American," but she made no issue of it this time. Neither of them mentioned the reason for her long flight back and extended weekend with him at such an important time in her life: namely, their plans to get together this year—Dale's hopes of spending Thanksgiving break with her—their earlier plans to travel to Barbados during her Christmas break—their ultimate plans of Dale moving near Princeton to be with her starting the following summer, taking at least a year of sabbatical from his university and perhaps quitting to write full-time. All of their plans. All of their futures.

They made love for hours by the dying campfire that first night, spreading Dale's sleeping bag out on the soft grass and using Clare's as a blanket over them when the cold winds blew over their sweaty bodies. Eventually the campfire embers dimmed and they slept a while, making love in the middle of the night and again just after sunrise. Dale noticed that Clare's lovemaking was more intense than ever—as if she were trying to lose herself in the intimacy, thus putting distance between them—and he knew then that when they did talk, the news would be bad.

The second night, camped high on the ridge above treeline, they used only the white-gas backpacking stove for cooking and adjourned early to the tent as a freezing wind from outer space seemed to blow in. There was even less atmosphere up there to make the stars twinkle, but they seemed to shake more, as if also blasted by the arctic winds that made Clare and Dale huddle in their goose-down bags as they stroked each other and made love repeatedly, finding their orgasms separately and then together, knowing and respecting each other's bodies and needs in the way only lovers long experienced with each other can appreciate true lovemaking. It was not enough. Dale again felt the distance and lay awake after Clare's slow breathing began—the soft sighing of sleep lost in the wind-against-rainfly-nylon noise, but stirring warm and tactile against his bare shoulder. He knew for certain now that something was wrong. The day's dialogues had been enthusiastic but abstract, intimate but impersonal, occasionally touching on their past experiences but never turning toward a shared future. This was profoundly different, and as Dale lay awake feeling his young beloved breathe on his shoulder, he thought of Anne and the girls, lost to him now by choice and action, and of the house in Missoula and of his job and the long academic year ahead—an unbelievably empty year if he was not pursuing his sabbatical as he and Clare had planned—and now he felt the cold and vacuum of the dark sky enter into him until he was shaking even in the warmth of the enveloping sleeping bags with Clare's warm, bare breasts and thigh against him. He shivered and waited for dawn.

She told him the next day, as they led the pack mules down the couloir toward the high pastures above the ranch.

"It's not going to work, Dale."

He did not have to ask her what was not going to work—it was the Great Unspoken Topic of the long weekend, of their life—and he played no games just to make himself feel better by seeing her feel worse. "All right," he said. "Why not?"

She had hesitated then. It was a warm day and she was wearing his oldest, most comfortable flannel shirt—the blue one that she had worn that first weekend more than four years earlier and that she wore each time they spent time together—wore it open today, sleeves rolled up, a white T-shirt showing the strain of the full breasts he had kissed at sunrise just hours ago.

"It's . . . the way you predicted," she said at last.

"I'm too old," said Dale. They had come to a steep pitch and he instinctively leaned back in the saddle and put more weight on the stirrups to help the gelding keep its footing. Clare was doing the same with the roan.

"I'm too young," she said. For four years she had insisted—sometimes violently—that their age difference had made no difference. He had always disagreed with her. He wished she would disagree with herself now.

"There's no room for me in your life at Princeton," he said. "You're with people your own age and it's a relief."

"No," she said. And then, "Yes."

"You're with someone else," he said, hearing the hopeless flatness in his voice despite himself. They rode into an aspen grove alive with shimmer and the dry-autumn rasping of heart-shaped leaves.

"No," she said again. "Not completely *with*. Not in love. I don't think I'll be in love again for a long, long time. But there is someone I'm attracted to. Someone I've been spending time with."

"During the summer pre-program seminars?" Dale hated asking questions right then but could not have stopped himself if his life depended upon it. Perhaps his life did depend upon it. His voice sounded alien and dead even to him. The aspen leaves rattled and the wind stirred the dry, high grass as they rode out into the upper pasture. Clare's nipples were hard against the thin cotton of her T-shirt. Her cheeks were flushed. She looked beautiful. At that moment, he almost hated her for that.

"Sure," she said. "I met him then."

"Have you . . ." He stopped himself just in time and looked away, west down the long canyon. The ranch was not quite in sight. He knew that it would not look the same to him when it did appear through the pines.

"Slept with him?" finished Clare. "Yes. We've had sex. It's part of my new life there. Exciting."

"Exciting," repeated Dale. One of their generational differences over the past four years of surprise encounter, attraction, involvement, had been her use of the phrase "having sex" and his old-fogey insistence on his version of "making love." Eventually she had spoken of their lovemaking only as lovemaking. Dale had seen it as a great step forward in their relationship. He chuckled at that now, feeling no mirth whatsoever. The gelding tried to look around at him as if he had given it a confusing command through his legs or the reins. He kicked it in the ribs to keep up with Clare's roan, who had to be held back from a canter this close to the ranch.

"Exciting," said Clare. "But you know me. You must know how little it means."

Dale now laughed with some sincerity. "I don't know you, Clare. That's all that I *do* know right now."

"Don't make it difficult, Dale."

"Heaven forbid."

"You predicted this a thousand times. No matter how often I said that it wouldn't play out this way, you insisted it would. Every time I wanted to settle things between us . . . about Anne and the children . . . this was one of your reasons for waiting. What I didn't understand was that . . ."

"All right," said Dale, interrupting her with a harsher note than he had meant to use. "You're right. I understood then. I understand now. You just denied that it could happen so many times that I got stupid. I sold myself on the fantasy."

"I don't want to hurt you any more than . . ."

"What do you say we shut up for now and just talk later, during the drive back to the airport? Let's just enjoy the last half-hour or so of the trip."

They did not, of course. Enjoy the end of the camping trip. Or talk during the ride back to Missoula.

It was the last time he had seen Clare. It was two months before he loaded the Savage over-and-under, set the barrel against his brow, clicked off the safety, and pulled the trigger. It was ten months before he decided to spend his sabbatical year writing in Illinois. It was one year, six weeks, and three days before he arrived at his dead friend Duane's house in this godforsaken exile in Illinois. But who was counting?

It took Dale a while to unload the Land Cruiser and to find someplace for his stuff. The boxes of books and winter clothes could wait, of course, but he wanted to set up his ThinkPad computer somewhere comfortable and to dig out the clean sheets, pillowcases, towels, and other items he had brought from the ranch. Everything personal, he realized, was going into the parlor/study where Mr. McBride had slept long ago and where Mr. McBride's aging sister had lived—without changing anything—for most of the past forty years.

The ThinkPad went on the old desk comfortably enough—the wall outlet had no polarizer holes, but Dale had anticipated that and brought a two-prong adapter for the surge protector. Sandy Whittaker had warned him that there had been no phone lines to the house since 1960, but Dale had brought his cell phone. The phone was equipped for e-mail, of course, but he was old-fashioned and he made the infrared connections to the Thinkpad and dialed up the Peoria AOL access number. His phone informed him that there was NO SERVICE. None at all. He could not even make a telephone call.

"Shit," said Dale. He had deliberately checked with Illinois Bell to make sure that there *was* service to this part of the county.

Well, this had to be some sort of local glitch . . . a cell shadow or perhaps even a problem with the cell phone itself. He could always drive a few miles to get back into clear reception to make his calls and launch his e-mails. The thought gave him a *frisson* that was not totally unpleasant. It had been years since he had been so isolated. Even at the ranch he'd had the C-band antenna pulling in a score of satellites for TV—some of them broadcasting in high-definition now—and two regular phone lines, one dedicated for fax, as well as his mobile phone. Now he was . . . quiet. *Hell,* he thought, *I wanted time for serious reading . . . research. This will help.* He wanted to believe it.

Dale unpacked more stuff through the dim afternoon. He knew that he should drive to Oak Hill and do some grocery shopping—he'd be damned if he'd go to something called the KWIK'N'EZ—but he had packed a cooler for the trip with some sandwiches, three bottles of beer, some orange juice, a few apples and oranges, other stuff, and it seemed still good. He set these few things in the refrigerator, decided he was hungry, and had one of the ham sandwiches and a beer for lunch.

For years, every time he had packed a lunch to eat in his office at the university or for a trip, Anne had done something she first started while packing picnics during their honeymoon twenty-seven years earlier: when Dale unwrapped his sandwich, there would always be a single bite taken out of it. A salutation. Beatrice saying "*salve*" to young Dante. A reminder.

There were no bites taken out of this sandwich. Nor would there be any in the future.

Dale shook his head. He was still tired and the beer had not helped that, but this was no time for more self-pity.

He carried the last couple of boxes in from the truck. The sheets and clean blankets and pillowcases and towels were in the last box, of course, and he took his time unpacking them. The sheets were too big for the small bed in the study, but he folded them over until they fit without too much wrinkling. The thick towels looked out of place in the severe bathroom.

It was getting dark. Dale went into the parlor and wandered through the dining room and back into the kitchen. No TV had magically appeared. It would have been nice to watch the network news and then the local news from Peoria . . . even nicer to catch *CNN Headline News* or call up some news sites on the Net. He went back to pull the last of the extra towels and sheets from the boxes.

His Savage over-and-under shotgun/.22 rifle was packed beneath the bottom layer of towels, wrapped in plastic, broken into its two component parts, but clearly oiled and ready.

Dale actually took a step back from the box in shock. He not only clearly remembered *not* packing the weapon, he remembered where he had put it—in the basement at the ranch, wrapped in its soft gun case, far back on the highest and hardest-to-reach storage shelf.

Dale's hands were shaking as he lifted the old weapon out of the box and carefully unwrapped it. At least there was no ammunition—neither .22 shells nor shotgun shells for the .410. He looked in the lower breech.

A shotgun shell was nestled there. Dale had to try three times before his fingers could extricate it.

It was *the* shell. The one from 4:00 A.M. on November fourth, almost a year earlier. Dale could clearly see the indentation where the firing pin had struck the center of the shell.

Fire in the hole, he thought. A shell on which the firing pin had dropped could, theoretically, go off at any time.

Even more clear than his recollection of wrapping and storing the Savage in the basement of the ranch was his memory of throwing the shell far out from the porch, deep into the Douglas fir and lodgepole pines there.

I am nuts. I've gone fucking crazy again. He reached for the phone and actually speed-dialed Dr. Hall's office number before the NO SERVICE sign on the LCD reminded him that such a quick sanity fix was no longer an option.

"Jesus Christ," Dale said aloud. He set the phone back, weighed the death shell in his palm, went to the back door, walked out into the muddy lot in the freezing rain, and threw the shell as far out into the stubbled cornfield as he could. Then he went back into Duane's farmhouse and went through every other box he had brought in, dumping scores of books on the floor of the dining room and study, throwing clothes on the sagging furniture, leaving his stuff on every surface until he was confident that he had not packed any other ammunition.

Finally he carried the rewrapped Savage over-and-under down to the basement—Duane's basement, filled with lamps and warm from the furnace—finally setting one piece of the weapon behind a workbench and the other piece in a small niche filled with bell jars in which small, bloody human organs seemed to be floating. Tomatoes, he thought.

Then he went upstairs, read for an hour or two—starting with Dante's *Inferno* but soon switching to a Donald Westlake Dortmunder comedy mystery—and turned off the light by 8:00 P.M., but not before he went into the bathroom and took two flurazepam and three doxepin. He would sleep this night.

Sometime around 3:30 A.M.—he could not quite read the dial of his watch because his mind and eyes were so fuzzy from the medication—Dale woke to the sound of the dog growling in the kitchen. He realized that he was not at the ranch, that he must have fallen asleep again on the leather couch in his study in the Missoula house, and he wished that Anne or one of the girls would let the dog, Hasso, out. The growling grew louder and then faded. Dale started to fade as well, but then the girls began stomping and thumping upstairs . . . no, the footfalls were much too heavy to be the girls. They must have some boys visiting. *So late?* Dale thought fuzzily. *And isn't Mab in college?*

While he tried to sort this out and simultaneously figure out why his leather couch was so hard and lumpy, the upstairs thumping stopped but another dog began howling just outside. Probably the Beckers' dog outside again. He knew he should get up and let Hasso out, then go upstairs to bed—Anne would chide him in the morning about falling asleep downstairs again—but he was just too damned tired.

He went back down into a drugged sleep to the sound of Hasso's nails scraping on the tile of the kitchen just down the hall.

SIX

I SAID that I did not know the details of my own death—and that is true—but I know very well, better than Dale himself, the details of Dale's attempted suicide.

He had been alone at the ranch for almost five months when Clare visited for the last time in September a year ago. He had confronted Anne in the spring, moved out of his Missoula home in April, saw the girls only sporadically over the summer—and never at the ranch, since Mab refused to visit there and Katie followed her lead—and then was truly and totally and irreversibly alone come the middle of September when Clare said good-bye and flew back to Princeton.

Dale had not been sleeping well during the spring and summer, and by the time the cottonwood and aspen leaves had fallen in the hills and valleys around the ranch, he was not really sleeping at all. Night was a vortex of thought, a firestorm of frenzied and useless mental activity. He would wander the dark rooms of the ranch, ending up in his study there, the wind rattling the wall of windows, sitting in the blue-lighted dark writing letter after letter—usually to Clare, but sometimes to

Anne, frequently to Mab or Katie, occasionally to friends he had not seen for years—and then, come dawn, he would destroy the letters and try for an hour or two of dream-plagued dozing. His teaching at the university—already on autopilot—went to hell. The head of the department—no friend—called him in to warn him. The dean, an old friend, finally followed suit, explaining that she knew about Dale's divorce, knew that he had been drinking, and suggested ways that she and his other colleagues could help. Dale ignored the suggestions.

Dale had not been drinking. Alcohol interested him no more than did food. He lost almost thirty pounds between the middle of September and November 4 of that year. His short-term memory had all but ceased to exist, and he had reached the point where he was getting essentially zero REM sleep. One of his English department colleagues suggested that Dale's eyes looked like two cigarette holes burned through a white sheet. Dale had never heard that cliché before—he had been spared it until then, he told the colleague—but now that he had heard it, he thought of it every time he looked into a mirror.

Dale rode the gelding through the valleys and orchards near the ranch, sometimes staying out for days at a time, eating nothing but the occasional hardtack, brewing thick coffee over campfires, and sleeping under thin blankets. He was sure that the gelding thought he was crazy. He was not sure that the gelding was wrong.

In the third week of October that year, after having written and deleted more than a score of letters, after having picked up the telephone a hundred times only to put it down after dialing the number in Princeton but before he heard a ring, Dale threw some clean underwear, extra jeans, his old blue flannel shirt, and a water bottle into his canvas pack, jumped into the Land Cruiser at 10:30 one night, and drove toward Princeton, following I-90 through Wyoming, South Dakota, Minnesota, Wisconsin, Chicago, northern Indiana, northern Ohio, the corner of Pennsylvania, and western New York until he finally pulled over to sleep on the New York Thruway sixty-three hours after he had left, awoke, realizing that this was the wrong thing to do,

and drove slowly back to Montana, swinging north from Minneapolis
to I-94 and then across a suddenly wintery North Dakota.

In the last few days of October, he had written a sixty-four-page
poem—a combination epic odyssey of his drive and a letter of love and
understanding to Clare. Personally, I think the thing is a masterpiece
of madness—a logical explication of total freewheeling insanity—and
perhaps the most interesting thing Dale Stewart had written to that
point.

Unfortunately, while he would never have lifted such a pathetic
thing set down on paper, placed it in an envelope, found a stamp for it,
and driven it to a mailbox, he had written it as an e-mail attachment.
Weighing on him so heavily, it had no real weight. He e-mailed it at
3:26 A.M. on November 1, using Clare's new university e-mail address,
which he had looked up on Bigfoot. Dale slept for six hours that day—
the longest uninterrupted rest he had enjoyed in more than a month.
The one-line note and sixty-four-page attachment returned later that
day, forwarded back to him without comment, almost certainly
unread. Dale was not surprised. He deleted all copies of the poem.

The next seventy-two hours are essentially lost to Dale—his sleep
deprivation had reached the point of brain cell death—but I am aware
of every hour and minute of his wandering through the ranch, his muttering in the middle of the night, his repeated walks to the barn as if to
saddle up his gelding—which was already stabled for the winter down
in Missoula—and his hundred false starts at e-mailing or calling
Clare . . . or Anne . . . or someone.

At a little before four o'clock on the morning of November 4, Dale
got out of bed after six hours of lying there awake, wrote a brief note on
a Post-it pad—the note read "Don't come inside. Call the county sheriff" and gave the sheriff office's phone number, which he had to look
up in his county directory—stuck the note on the inside of the back-
door windowpane, pulled his Savage over-and-under out of the closet
and out of its old canvas case, went into his office, unlocked a drawer,
fumbled a .410 shell out, loaded the shotgun, paused a moment to
consider which room would be most appropriate, and then went into

the master bathroom, knelt on the tiles, set the muzzle of the shotgun against his forehead, selected the correct firing chamber with a click, and—with no hesitation or final thoughts—pulled the trigger.

The hammer fell. The firing pin clicked. The shell did not fire.

Dale knelt there for several minutes, waiting. It was as if time had stretched out in his final instant of life—rather like the mathematics of a person falling into a black hole where seconds become eternities just before time itself disappears into the singularity forever—but the shotgun blast never came. Eventually Dale lowered the barrel, broke the breech, and looked at the shell, wondering if some cowardly part of his subconscious had selected the .22 barrel rather than the loaded shotgun.

No, the firing pin had fallen on the shell. Dale could see the dent in the center of the brass circle.

Dale's father had given him the Savage over-and-under when Dale was eight years old. He had fired it hundreds of times, cleaned and oiled it well, stored it carefully, and never abused it. It had never misfired before. Not once.

After a while, Dale's knees became sore from kneeling on the bathroom tiles. He got up, removed the shell, propped the shotgun against the bedroom wall, set the misfired shell on the bookcase, took the note down from the back door, and slept for three hours. When he awoke, he called his doctor. Within forty-eight hours he had an appointment with a Missoula psychiatrist, Dr. Charles Hall. The talk therapy was useless. The Prozac began to help about two months later.

What I find interesting about this is not that Dale tried to kill himself—it was the fatigue and depression that led to that, not any self-pity he was generating, and I can say with more confidence than he could what his motivations were during this entire pathetic, disoriented time—but the fact that he chose suicide at all. Dale Stewart had always despised the idea of suicide and felt anger toward those who tried it and a real fury toward those who succeeded at it. These included a close friend in college, an even closer and much older friend in Missoula, and one of his students whom he had thought the world of.

Even before Dale's own descent into functional insanity, he had understood that suicides were not usually responsible for their deci- sions—his older friend, a French woman writer named Brigitte, had spent years battling depression before she locked herself in her bed- room and took two vials of horded sleeping pills—but Dale had always hated the narcissism of self-destruction, the ineluctable selfishness of the act. Brigitte had left four school-aged children behind. His former student, David, had left a pregnant young wife to deal with the trauma of finding his body hanging in the garage. It was, to Dale, inexcusable to leave such messes behind. Dale hated messes as much as he despised self-pity.

Dale had once taught a semester-long seminar on Ernest Heming- way, and he had fallen into flat-out argument with a few of his smarter students on the writer's culpability in ending his life the way he had.

"The selfish bastard pulled the trigger on his Boss shotgun right at the foot of the stairs," he had half yelled, "so that Miss Mary would have no choice but to walk through the puddles of blood and brains and shards of skull on her way to the phone."

"His dear Miss Mary had been the one to leave the keys to his gun case in plain view on the kitchen windowsill," said his sharpest stu- dent, not retreating a bit. "Perhaps he was just acknowledging her choice and making her pay for it a bit."

Dale had actually glared at Clare across the seminar table. "Don't you think that he was making her pay too high a price for agreeing with him that access to a man's property was his right?"

"After he'd received shock treatment for depression?" said Clare. "After he'd tried to walk into a spinning propeller during the flight to the clinic? After Miss Mary had needed to call a friend over to the Idaho house to wrestle a shotgun away from Hemingway the week before? No, I don't think he made her pay too high a price. Besides, she received—and exploited to the teeth—all of his copyrights, includ- ing those miserable posthumous books that he never would have chosen to see in print. I think Hemingway knew exactly what he was doing when he sat on the steps to blow his brains out, knowing full well what Miss Mary would have to step through to get downstairs to the phone. They each got what they wanted."

Dale had blinked at Clare's toughness on this. He had had no idea.

Dale Stewart!"

Dale almost dropped the last sack of groceries he was putting in the rear of the Land Cruiser. The last thing he expected to hear in the parking lot of the Oak Hill City Market was someone calling his name.

Two women walked quickly toward him across the wet tarmac. The one who had called his name was vaguely familiar but still a stranger to him: indeterminate middle age, red hair that had been cropped short, once-fair skin that had been tanned to the consistency of leather, evidence of plastic surgery in the sharp face and neck and breasts—breasts too large and round and firmly packed even glimpsed through a sweater—hardly an Oak Hill or Elm Haven sort of person. The other woman was short, scowling, stocky, and sporting a Phys Ed woman teacher's butch haircut. Dale, who was usually naive about such things, knew at once that the redhead and the short brunette were a couple. Dale, who had practiced safe political correctness for more than twenty professional academic years, indulged himself in the thought, *Dykes.*

"You don't remember me, do you?" said the redhead.

"I'm sorry," said Dale. "I'm not sure . . ."

"Michelle Staffney," said the woman. "Now I go by Mica Stouffer."

Dale could only stare. Michelle Staffney had been the little sex grenade of his fourth-, fifth-, and sixth-grade classes at Old Central School. Every boy in Elm Haven during the period 1957–1960 had probably celebrated his first erotic fantasies with Michelle Staffney in a starring role (unless they opted for Annette Funicello). And now, this worn and sharp-boned middle-aged woman with breast implants and a whiskey-cigarette voice.

"Mica Stouffer?" Dale said stupidly.

"I was out in L.A. for a lot of years," said Michelle as if that explained everything. "What the hell are you doing back here in Illinois?"

"I'm . . ." began Dale and then stopped. "How on earth did you recognize me, Michelle . . . Mica?"

She smiled. The smile, at least, reminded him of the delectable, soft-voiced little girl he had known. "One of the producers I was living with had a copy of your book that some lamedick screenwriter was trying to push . . . a second *Jeremiah Johnson* or something. They wanted Bob Redford for the leading role, but Redford wouldn't even read the treatment. But the book was always lying around in the bathroom or somewhere. I read the bio under your photo one day and decided that you were the same Dale Stewart I knew in Elm Haven about two hundred years ago."

"My book," repeated Dale. "Do you remember which one?"

"Does it matter?" said Michelle, the little-girl smile flickering into something much older and tougher. "I didn't read the thing—didn't read it personally, as they say out there—but the screenwriter told my producer friend that all of your books were essentially the same one, big tough mountain man shit. He said that if we optioned one, we'd really own all of them. Oh, this is Diane Villanova."

Dale shook hands with the brunette and had to flex his fingers afterward.

"So what are you doing back here, Dale Stewart?" said Michelle/Mica.

For a mad instant, Dale considered telling her the whole sad story of the last few years of his life, right down to his last view of Clare and all about Anne's contemptuous farewell. Instead, he said, "Writing a book . . . I think."

"I thought you were a teacher or something as well."

"Professor of English," said Dale, wondering if that were still true. "University of Montana at Missoula. On sabbatical." He could hear the staccato telegraph-style of his speech and wondered where it was coming from.

"And you're staying in *Oak Hill?*" There was incredulity in her voice.

"Near Elm Haven, actually," he said. "Renting Duane McBride's farmhouse for a few months."

Michelle Staffney blinked at this. "Duane McBride? The kid who was killed in that awful farm accident when we were ten or something?"

"Eleven or twelve," said Dale. "Summer of 1960. Yeah."

Michelle looked at her friend and then back at Dale. "That's weird. But no weirder than our situation, I guess."

Dale waited.

"Diane and I are spending a few months at my folks' home in Elm Haven."

"On Broad Street," said Dale. "The big house with the big barn behind it."

"Yep. The same. Only when I lived there as a kid, it was a great house . . . hell, even a great barn. Now it's all a ramshackle fucking mess. Di and I are trying to get it fixed up a bit so we can sell it. Hoping that there's some rich, snot-nosed young couple out of Peoria who wants a big Victorian house and who won't check the wiring or the furnace or anything."

"Are your parents . . ." began Dale. He always felt strange asking someone his own age about their parents. His own folks had died young in the 1960s.

"Dad died in . . . Jesus, 1975," said Michelle. "But Mom just hung in there—senile as a loon, warehoused away in Alzheimer Manor here in Oak Hill for a few decades—until she died a couple of months ago."

"I'm sorry," said Dale.

"Don't be. It would have been a blessing for everyone if she'd shoved off years and years ago. Anyway, the house was empty and needed work, so it gave Di and me an excuse to get out of L.A. and away from the Industry for a while."

Dale heard the capital "I" in Industry. *Just like everyone else in L.A.* he thought.

"You were involved with movies?" he said politely. "Producing?"

"No," said Michelle, the Mica smile returning and then fading. "I was mostly fucking producers. Even married two of them. I was an actress."

"Of course," said Dale, making a conscious effort not to drop his gaze to the obviously unfettered and obviously unnatural breasts under her sweater. "Have you been in anything I might have seen?" He hated questions like that. *Why did I ask it?* When people asked him, "Have you written anything I might have read?" his impulse was always to say, "I don't know. Do you read anything decent, or just the occasional John Grisham crap?"

"Did you see *Titanic*?" asked Michelle.

"Wow," said Dale. "You were in that?"

"Nope. But I was in *It's Alive IV* that went straight to video the same month *Titanic* came out. And I was one of the alien dancers in the spaceship scene in *The Fifth Element* with Bruce Willis. The one with the bare blue tits. That was the last time anyone hired me . . . more than four years ago."

Dale nodded sympathetically. *Bare blue tits*, he thought, keeping his gaze level with hers through an act of will.

Diane touched Michelle's arm as if reminding her that it was cold and wet out here in the parking lot.

"Yeah," said Michelle. "Well, hell, we really should get together sometime and swap lies about the good old days. Di and I will probably be here through Christmas . . . maybe longer, given the mess we have to deal with. You got a card with your phone number?" She took out a pen and scribbled her number on her grocery receipt and gave it to him.

Dale dug out a business card, using her pen to scratch out his ranch, university, and home phone numbers, and circling the mobile phone number. "The only problem," he said, "is that cell phones don't seem to work around Elm Haven."

Michelle raised an eyebrow. "That's what I'm using there as my only phone. It works fine in town."

Dale shrugged. "Well, I guess there's a dead area out near the McBride farm."

Michelle looked as if she was going to say something, stopped herself, tapped him on the arm, and said, "I'm serious about gabbing. Come on over and we'll cook you a good dinner and drink a shitload of tequila."

The two women walked back to their Toyota pickup and drove off.

"Michelle Staffney," said Dale, still standing in the rain. "Jesus Christ."

SEVEN

D ALE had driven only a few miles south out of Oak Hill toward Elm Haven when the two pickup trucks cut him off.

At first he thought it was Michelle and her friend in the white pickup approaching quickly in the rearview mirror, but then he saw that it was not a new Toyota truck, but a beat-up old Chevy, with another old pickup—this one a scabrous green Ford—roaring along just behind it.

Dale slowed down, waiting for the idiots to pass, but the first pickup pulled up alongside and stayed there, slowing when he did, accelerating when he did. Dale glanced over, saw the black leather jackets and the shaved heads, and thought, *Oh, shit.*

The white Chevy pickup passed him and then slowed. The green Ford pickup pulled closer to his rear bumper. Suddenly the white pickup in front of him hit the brakes.

Dale braked hard, lurching forward against the Land Cruiser's shoulder harness, but still had to swerve right to avoid the Chevy. Luckily there was a gravel turnout by the side of the road—some sort of small picnic area rest stop. The Land Cruiser slid to a stop in the gravel there, and the green and white trucks blocked his way out.

Three young men spilled out of the white Chevy pickup. Two more jumped out of the cab of the green Ford. All five of them had extremely short hair or shaved heads. All five wore black leather coats and combat boots. The tallest of the five had a swastika tattooed on the back of his right hand. The tallest was also the oldest—perhaps in his middle twenties—and the youngest looked to be about sixteen. At least three of the five were taller and heavier than Dale.

Dale had perhaps ten seconds to decide what to do. It wouldn't have been a problem for Dale's father; he had always carried a lug wrench tucked under the driver's seat of the family station wagon. Dale had always noticed that fact but had never asked his dad why he carried the heavy lug wrench there. Now he knew. But Dale Stewart—even while living and traveling in the wilds of Montana—had never thought that he needed a weapon handy.

He wished like hell that he had one now.

Heart pounding, Dale briefly considered locking the truck's doors and waiting in the Land Cruiser. He even considered throwing the truck into four-wheel drive, going up and over the curb, driving through the grassy picnic area and the adjoining cornfield if necessary, and making a run for it down the county road. His pride kept him from doing either.

Dale stepped out and down just as the five skinheads made a semi-circle around him. *Well*, he thought, *there's still an outside chance that they* are Jim Bridger: Mountain Man *fans*.

"You the Jewboy Zionist motherfucker?" snarled the tallest of the skinheads.

There goes the fan theory, thought Dale. He was amazed to realize that his pulse rate had fallen back to near-normal and that he was no longer frightened. Perhaps the situation was just too absurd for him to take seriously. It seemed like a bad postmillennial remake of *Gentleman's Agreement* by way of *Deliverance*.

Dale took his cell phone out of his jacket pocket and held it up with his thumb over the speed dial button. None of the programmed speed-dial numbers would do him a damn bit of good—even if the phone condescended to work out here in the boonies—but maybe the skinheads didn't know. Standing there, phone poised, Dale felt a bit like Captain Kirk preparing to have Scotty beam him up. *Yeah, I wish*, he thought.

"One of you named Derek?" said Dale, his voice strong and steady, all the while shooting an *I'm-an-adult-and-you're-going-to-be-in-deep-shit-in-a-minute* look at each of the punks.

The skinheads blinked. The next-to-youngest, an overweight mouth-breather who looked to be the least sharp knife in this particular drawer, actually blushed through his acne and took a step back. Dale fixed his heavy glare on Derek for a minute and then moved it to the leader's face.

"You didn't answer *our* question, asshole," said the leader, a gaunt-faced, hollow-eyed fascist if there ever was one. "You that nigger-loving Jewboy that wrote those magazine things?"

"Articles," said Dale. "Magazine and newspaper *articles*. That's your vocabulary word for the day. No charge."

Four of the five stared blankly at him. Obviously they had not imagined the dialogue going quite this way in their fetid little power fantasies, and the discrepancy threw them off stride. The leader reached into his jacket pocket with a menacing glower.

Will it be a knife or pistol? wondered Dale as he raised his own weapon—the useless cell phone. He heard himself say, "I know Derek, of course," looking straight at Derek, "but I'll need to know all of your names when I punch the state police number here. But I guess they'll already know who Derek hangs around with."

Four of the skinheads looked at their leader. The older man's hand came out of his pocket.

Ah, thought the strangely detached part of Dale's mind. *Knife it is.* He had always hated edged weapons.

The other four clicked out their own knives: not switchblades, but ridiculously long survival knives that came from scabbards under their jackets.

Dale punched Clare's speed dial number at the same time, surreptitiously touching CANCEL as he heard the dial tone and the first rings, and raised the phone.

"Get the fuck out of here and stay out," said the oldest skinhead. He nodded to his pals.

The younger boys slashed the closest two of Dale's tires. Dale made no move to stop them.

The lead skinhead gave Dale the finger—an oddly childish gesture under the circumstances, Dale thought—and then all five were scrambling back into their pickups and roaring away, throwing gravel against the Land Cruiser and Dale.

Dale waited a minute to make sure they were really gone and then checked the damage.

He had a can of flat sealant in his emergency kit in the back, but these tires were well and truly slashed. And he had only one spare.

Dale dialed 911. Amazingly, someone answered. "Creve Coeur County Emergency Services. Please state the nature of your emergency."

Feeling sheepish, Dale explained his situation and asked for the number of a towing service in Oak Hill. The 911 lady did not chastise him for using the emergency number for frivolous purposes, but gave him the number of a repair garage with towing service, offered to connect him, told him to call back if the belligerent youths—her phrase—returned, and then told him to sit tight, that someone would be there in fifteen minutes or less.

"I don't need . . ." began Dale but the 911 lady had signed off.

Dale had not called the sheriff, but the sheriff arrived before the tow truck. Dale took one look at the fat man getting out of the green county sheriff's car and felt his heart pounding with fear.

C. J. Congden looked nothing like he had in 1960—the thin, lanky bully had gone to fat—but the mean eyes and yellow teeth and stupid expression were somehow the same. *It can't be him*, thought Dale, but the fat man wheezed closer and Dale saw the name tag over the badge—"C. J." Dale tried to remember the last time he had seen C. J. Congden: an image came back of the sixteen-year-old, mean-eyed bully hanging Dale over the edge of the Spoon River Bridge while Dale's eleven-year-old friend, Jim Harlen, aimed a snub-nosed .38 revolver at Congden's hot rod and threatened to pull the trigger if the bully dropped Dale into the river.

What the hell was that all about? wondered Dale. If it was a real memory, it was one that he had forgotten for more than forty years.

Sheriff Congden stepped closer, looked at the Land Cruiser's deflated tires, and said, "What the hell happened here?" It was the same bully's voice, thickened by decades of cigarettes and power, but the same voice.

Dale had to clear his throat before speaking. He told Congden about the skinheads, all the while praying that Congden wouldn't recognize him. *Do bullies remember their prey?*

"Yeah, I know 'em," said the sheriff, squinting at Dale through sunglasses. He was talking about the skinheads. "But do I know *you*?" said Congden.

Dale shook his head, afraid to speak, afraid that C. J. would remember his voice.

The sheriff walked around the rear of the Land Cruiser and squinted at the license plates. "Montana. You just passin' through, Mr. . . . ?"

"Miller," said Dale and immediately realized that if and when Congden asked to see his license, he'd be in trouble—certainly more trouble than the local skinhead punks. "Tom Miller," said Dale. "Yeah, I'm just driving through on my way to Cincinnati."

Congden squinted at him and rested his thumbs in his gun belt. Leather creaked. The sheriff's gray shirt was dirty and straining at the belly.

If he asks me for my license and registration, I'll say that I forgot them, thought Dale in a panic and realized at once that this would not work. He'd just end up in the county jail while they traced the registration. He shook his head. *What the hell am I panicked about? I haven't done anything wrong. I'm the* victim *here.* That was the reasonable point of view, but Dale remembered those mean pig eyes of C. J. Congden's behind a shotgun aimed at Dale's head when he was a boy. There was no statute of limitations on bullies and their victims.

The fat sheriff opened his mouth to speak, but right then the radio in his cruiser squawked and hissed. Congden leaned into the open door, listened a minute, said something into his radio, and hung it up.

Congden straightened up, rested his hands on his gun belt again, and turned back to Dale. "You want to ride back to Oak Hill with me? We gotta get some paperwork done if you're going to swear out a complaint."

I'd rather have a colonoscopy with a Roto-Rooter, thought Dale. He shrugged as if it didn't matter to him. "I'll ride back in the tow truck. I need to get some junk out of the Land Cruiser."

Congden squinted at him again as if trying to remember where they'd met. Finally he shrugged. "Suit yourself. Just make sure that you stop by the sheriff's office."

Dale nodded and watched the former bully wheeze his way back to his sheriff's car, get in, and drive off.

The tow truck arrived less than a minute after Congden's sheriff's car disappeared. The two mechanics, Billy and Tuck, were efficient in getting the Cruiser slung into its towing cradle. "We could change the one tire here for you," said Billy, the older of the two brothers. "Wouldn't do no good, though. I don't think anybody in Oak Hill's got any of these tires in stock. Probably have to bring one in from Peoria or Galesburg. Tomorrow afternoon maybe."

Dale nodded. "Is there a place to rent a car in Oak Hill?"

The brothers shook their heads. Then Turk said, "Wait a minute. Mr. Jurgen over at the Happy Lanes rents out his dead wife's car sometimes."

"That'll do," said Dale.

*   *   *

Dale did not get out of Oak Hill until after 7:00 P.M. The tires would be delivered the next day and he could pick up the Cruiser the next afternoon. He ate dinner at the counter of a five-and-dime on the city square—not a Woolworth's, they had all disappeared from America years before—and Mr. Jurgen brought his late wife's blue Buick by from the bowling alley. The Buick was older than most people Dale knew, it reaked of cigarette smoke, and it cost Dale more to rent than it would have to rent a luxury car from Hertz and he had to leave $300 for a damage deposit, but he was glad to pay and get out of Oak Hill before C. J. Congden thought to come looking for him.

It started to snow again during his drive back to Duane's farmhouse. Dale was sleepy as he turned down the long lane and drove past the dead trees, snow dancing in his headlights, but he woke up quickly and slammed on the brakes a hundred yards from the farmhouse.

Dale had not left any lights on when he had driven off to buy groceries earlier in the day. The downstairs was dark.

But there was a light burning on the second floor.

EIGHT

DALE sat in the reeking Buick, looked at the light glowing in the second-floor upper left window, listened to pellets of sleet bouncing off the windshield, and thought, *Fuck this.*

He backed the rattling old car down the long lane, pulled out onto County 6, and headed back south. Dale had seen enough scary movies in his life. He knew that his role now was to go into the dark farmhouse by himself, call, "Is somebody there?," go fearfully up the stairs, and then get cut down by the waiting ax murderer. Either that or Realtor Sandy Whittaker had let herself in with her key, cut through the layers of plastic at the top of the stairs, and even at that moment was waiting for him, naked, on one of the beds up there.

Fuck that, too.

Dale drove up the second hill and paused at the stop sign at Jubilee College Road. He wasn't sure where to head next.

Montana, came his answer.

He shook his head. Besides a natural reluctance to abandon his $50,000 Land Cruiser in swap for this cigarette-stinking old Buick, he had nowhere to go in Montana. The ranch was rented out. Missoula was hostile territory for him these days. He had no job this year at the university there.

Oak Hill?

That made sense, since his truck was there and would be ready the next afternoon. But Dale could not remember if Oak Hill even had a motel—and if it did, it was a primitive one.

He crossed Jubilee College Road, took the narrow cutoff road through frozen fields to 150A, kept going straight, and turned east onto an empty I-74. Twenty-five minutes later he was in Peoria. Exiting onto War Memorial Drive, he found a Comfort Suites, paid with his American Express, asked the counter guy for a toothbrush, and went up to his room. It smelled of carpet cleaner and other chemicals. The king-size bed was almost obscene in its immensity. A card on top of the TV offered him recent-release movies, including softcore dirty movies.

Dale sighed, went back out to the rented Buick, and grabbed the sack of groceries that held fruit drinks and some snacks. He rooted around in another bag, found the new tube of toothpaste, and tossed it into the bag. That left only another $230 worth of groceries in sacks covering the back seat, the rear floor, and the front seat of the car. He carried the bag back up to his room, kicked off his boots and sweater, and munched Fig Newtons and sipped orange juice while watching CNN. After a while, he turned off the TV, went in the bathroom and brushed his teeth.

Eventually he went to sleep.

Dale awoke with the kind of absolute, heart-pounding, bottom-dropping-out-of-everything sense of desperation that comes most solidly between 3:00 and 4:00 A.M. He looked at the motel alarm clock. 3:26 A.M.

He sat up in bed, turned on the light, and ran his hands over his face. His hands were shaking.

He didn't think that it had been a nightmare that had brought him swimming up out of a troubled sleep. It was simply a sense that the world was ending. No, he realized, that wasn't quite right. It was simply the conviction that the world had *already* ended.

The clickover of the century and millennium had been problematic for Dale. Of course, his life had turned to shit about that time and he'd tried to kill himself, but even more troubling than that had been his deep and silent conviction that everything of value to him had been left behind in the old century. Tonight that conviction was totally pervasive and endlessly empty.

Christ, thought Dale, *I left my Prozac, flurazepam, and doxepin at Duane's farmhouse.* He had to smile at the thought. An old short circuit brings a light on in the second floor of a farmhouse and Professor Dale Stewart blows his brains out for lack of meds. *Difficult*, he thought. *I left the Savage over-and-under at the farmhouse, too.*

Dale glanced at the phone. He could call Dr. Hall. It was earlier in Montana—only about 2:30 A.M. Psychiatrists must be used to that crap.

What would I tell him? Well, the black dog was back. That had been Dale's term of choice for deep depression, borrowed from Winston Churchill, who had been plagued by his own Black Dog for decades. Churchill had saved his life by taking up oil painting.

Why is the black dog back? Dale went into the bathroom, ran some tap water into one of the little plastic glasses—sanitarily wrapped for his protection—and came back and sat on the small couch and thought about it.

I don't like running away from here. From Duane's place. Why not? Duane's farm and Elm Haven and Oak Hill and C. J. Congden and even Michelle Staffney were depressing enough in their own right. Wouldn't it be a good idea to leave now?

No. Missoula and the ranch were out of bounds for him now. He knew that. If he returned, it was probable that he would finish what he started on November 4 a year earlier.

But why Duane's drafty old place? Why Elm Haven? Because he had old connections there. Because the place had changed—for the worse—but so had he, and perhaps it was necessary for him to find that connection to his childhood, to something good about himself, to Duane, to the reason he become a writer and a teacher.

And there's the book. This is the only place I can write it. For the first time, he consciously acknowledged that he was going to spend his sabbatical year writing a novel about Duane, about Elm Haven, about 1960, about the summer he had so much trouble remembering, and, ultimately, about himself.

Vanity, vanity, vanity. He knew better. It would take great humility to write this novel: humility, not the professorial, historical, commercial, and auctorial cleverness that went into his Jim Bridger mountain man books. This novel would be just for him. And he would need both Duane's notebooks and a connection with Duane's life to write it.

The heater hummed on. A big truck roared up through its endless gears out on War Memorial Drive. Dale turned the light out and went back to sleep, even without his Prozac and flurazepam and doxepin.

Stewart! Dale . . . Stewart!"

Dale paused just outside the garage where the mechanics were finishing mounting the Land Cruiser's wheels with his two new tires. He looked over his shoulder, but he had recognized the voice.

Sheriff C. J. Congden was strolling across the oily concrete driveway toward him. Congden had one hand on the revolver in his holster. He was wheezing slightly as he came. Dale waited.

"Miller, huh?" said Congden. "*Tom* Miller. Yeah, cute. Well, I knew I'd seen your ugly-ass face before."

"Do you want something, Sheriff?" Unlike the day before, Dale's pulse did not race. He felt completely calm.

"Why'd you lie to me, Stewart?" snapped Congden. "I ought to fucking arrest you."

"For not telling you my real name?" said Dale and smiled.

"For misrepresenting yourself to a peace officer," wheezed Congden. His fat fingers continued tapping at the grip of his revolver. Leather creaked.

Dale shrugged and waited.

Congden squinted at him. "I remember you, Stewart. You and that fucking bunch of weasel friends of yours."

"Watch your language, Sheriff," said Dale. "You're a public servant now, not the town bully. Get nasty with me and I'll swear out a complaint."

"*Fuck* your complaint," growled Congden, but he looked around the garage to see who was listening. The *brrrpp-brrrpppp* of the air wrench putting on the Land Cruiser's lug nuts sufficiently covered the conversation. "And *fuck* you, Stewart."

"You have a nice day, too, Sheriff," said Dale and turned back to watch them lower his truck on the lift.

Congden walked toward the open garage door and then paused. "I know where you're staying."

Dale was sure that he did. It was a small county.

Congden walked away and Dale called after him, "Hey, Sheriff—any luck finding those punks who just cost me more than three hundred dollars?"

C. J. Congden did not look back.

The beautiful morning had shamed Dale. The snow had turned into sleet during the night, the sleet into rain, but the morning dawned sunny and warmer and sweet-smelling. Dale went out to breakfast at a pancake house across the parking lot from the Comfort Suites. The food was good, the coffee was good, and the waitress was friendly. Dale read the morning *Peoria Journal Star* and felt better than he had in weeks.

War Memorial Drive became Highway 150 outside of Peoria, and Dale drove the Buick the back way to Elm Haven, leaving the window open to air the cigarette smell out of the car. He was surprised to note that half of the trees still had their leaves and that those leaves still held deep fall colors. It was a beautiful day.

Just at the edge of Peoria's western limits—about ten miles beyond the city he'd known as a boy in Elm Haven—there was a plaza with a hardware and a sports store. Dale visited both and came out with a thirty-six-inch crowbar and a Louisville Slugger baseball bat. He tossed both in the trunk of the Buick and drove on to Duane's farmhouse.

The fields on either side of the approach lane were wet and sweet-smelling. Dale stopped the Buick in front of the house, but there was no way he could tell if the upstairs light was on in all that blazing day-light. He pulled to the side, parked the Buick, retrieved the baseball bat from the trunk, and walked up to the side door.

It was locked, just as he'd left it. Dale let himself in and stood in the kitchen a moment.

"Hello?" He heard the slightest echo of his own voice and had to smile. He'd be damned if he'd yell "Is anyone there?" just before the supernatural killer in the hockey mask jumped out to cut him down.

He searched the first floor. Everything seemed to be as he'd left it. He went down into the basement. No hockey-mask killers there. He remembered that he'd stored his Savage over-and-under down here in two pieces, but after checking that the pieces were where he'd put them, he decided not to add it to his Louisville Slugger arsenal. Besides, he'd thrown away the only shotgun shell.

Dale went up the stairs.

The layers of yellowing plastic were intact. Dale checked the nails and staples around the wood frame, but they had not been pulled out or replaced. The frame itself had been nailed into the door frame at the head of the stairs—decades ago. Dale pushed against the plastic, but it yielded only slightly, crackling a bit. If someone had visited the upstairs, they'd not come this way.

Not if they're human.

Dale had deliberately phrased that thought to amuse himself, but in the darkness of the stairway, it didn't seem that funny. He leaned closer to peer through the heavy plastic. The vague outlines of a hallway and a table. Sunlight through thick curtains. Nothing moved.

Dale pulled out his multi-use knife and set the longest blade against the plastic. He hesitated a second and then folded the blade back and set the knife back in his pocket. He laid the baseball bat against the yellowed plastic and tapped it lightly. *Let sleeping dogs lie.*

As if on cue, there came the scrabble of claws against the linoleum downstairs.

Dale whirled, bat raised, just in time to see a very small black dog run from the parlor hall into the kitchen.

"Jesus Christ!" said Dale, his heart pounding.

He clattered down the stairs and ran into the kitchen just in time to see the outer screen bang shut. He'd left the inner door open and the little dog had been able to push the screen door out.

Dale ran outside and stood on the stoop, bat ready. He half expected the small black dog to be out of sight—a delusion—but there it went, running hellbent-for-leather toward the outbuildings behind the farm, its little black ass wiggling as it ran.

Dale almost laughed. He'd been ready for the undead killer in the hockey mask and instead he'd found a lap dog. Whatever the little thing was, it was definitely a dog and definitely a shrimp—terrier-sized, but short-haired. All black except for a glimpse of pale or pink on its muzzle. Short ears.

"Hey, dog!" yelled Dale and whistled.

The little black dog did not slow down. It disappeared through a hole in the first outbuilding—the one Dale remembered Duane calling the chicken coop.

If the dog was in the house, why didn't I find it when I searched? Dale shook his head but walked out to the chicken coop.

The shed was a mess. The door had been wired shut—Dale had to unwrap a yard of rusted wire—but one side of the structure had rotted away between the wood and the foundation until the hole was large enough for that dog to slip through. *But it was a runt of a dog.*

Dale propped the door open and looked in the coop. "Jesus Christ," he said again, softly this time. He took the gold Dunhill lighter out of his pocket and flicked it on, holding the lighter high. There was just enough light to see by, but not enough to show detail. He walked back to the farmhouse and returned with a flashlight.

The interior of the coop had a fossilized layer of chicken manure mixed with embedded white feathers. The roosts were empty and the straw was ancient. The boards, walls, and floor were covered with dried blood, aged to a deep brown patina. There was no sign of the dog.

"What the hell happened in here?" Dale said aloud, but he knew the answer. *Fox. Fox in the henhouse.* Or a dog. He had to smile again. Not this dog. It was too small. Hell, a chicken could have beaten up this little black dog.

Dale looked in all of the roosts and niches, but no black dog. On the west wall, however, there were more slats missing. The pooch had probably run right through the chicken coop.

Dale went out into the bright sunlight and wonderful autumn air and checked in the mud at the west end of the coop. Sure enough, tiny dog tracks crossed the lot toward another of the handful of small sheds and outbuildings.

Well, I guess it isn't a ghost dog. It left tracks.

He tried whistling and calling again, but no dog appeared. Knowing that he should be hauling his groceries in, Dale checked out the other sheds.

The dog's prints had disappeared here where grass grew, but the second shed had an open door. Dale's flashlight flicked across hanging harnesses, hanging blades, hanging saws, hanging butchering equipment. All of it was rusted.

The next shed boasted a padlock, but the hinges had given way and Dale merely lifted the door to one side. Inside was a circa-1940s electrical generator, a mass of black cables, and half a dozen gas canisters. Only one of the jerry cans held gasoline. Dale checked over the generator, but even a cursory inspection with the flashlight showed insulated wires that had been chewed through by mice, rusted and corroded points, missing leads, and an empty fuel tank. Behind the generator shed was a huge oval fuel tank set low in girders—obviously a fueling station for the farm equipment. Unlike the other sheds and equipment, this gas tank looked as if it was still in use; the rubber hoses and nozzles had been maintained or replaced, which made sense if Mr.

Johnson next door stored his tractor and combine in the barn and still tilled this land. Dale rapped on the two hundred–gallon tank. It sounded full. He had to remember that if his Land Cruiser ever ran out of gas.

There were three more tiny outbuildings, but they had all but collapsed. The black dog might be hiding in any one of them, but Dale had no intention of crawling in after him.

That left the barn.

Dale had planned to visit the barn at some point. It might as well be now. Holding the flashlight in one hand and the Louisville Slugger in the other, he approached the huge structure.

Dale had vague memories of being in Duane's barn as a kid. Of all of Illinois's glories, the giant barns might have been the most interesting to a kid. Some of the farms boasted barns big enough to play baseball in, the lofts thirty feet high and filled with sweet-smelling hay. Perfect places to play as a boy.

This barn had a main door on the east side, but it was chained and padlocked. The huge barn doors on the south side did not budge— locked from the inside or frozen on their metal tracks. Dale hesitated. He didn't know if his rental agreement allowed him to wander around the barn and other outbuildings. He imagined that these were used for storage by Mr. Johnson.

Dale walked back to the Buick, ignored the waiting groceries, and traded the Louisville Slugger for the crowbar. He walked the sixty yards or so to the huge, looming barn, stuck the flashlight in his jeans pocket, forced the curve of the crowbar into the gap in the large doors, and struggled and cursed until something snapped—in the door, luckily, not in his back—and the doors squealed back on their rusted tracks.

Dale stepped into the darkness and then took a fast step back out into the light.

The huge harvesting combine all but filled the central space. Long, rust-mottled gatherer points thrust toward Dale from the thirty-foot-wide attached corn head. The glass-enclosed cab, seeming infinitely high above, was dark. Dale breathed through his open mouth, felt his heart pound, and was amazed that he remembered terms and details about the combine: corn head, snapper rolls, lugged chains, shields.

It can't be the same machine.

His friend Duane had been chewed up and swallowed by a combine here, under circumstances no one had understood then or now. At night. When Duane was alone at the farm. Duane's Old Man— Duane's invariable term for his father—had a solid alibi (drunk, in Peoria, with half a dozen cronies), and no one had suspected the Old Man.

It can't be the same machine. This combine was old enough to have been there then, but it was green. The machine, old even in 1960, that had killed Duane had been red. *How did I remember that?* thought Dale in something like wonder. But he did remember it.

And the metal shields over the gatherer points and snapping rolls had been off when they found the machine in the field and Duane's remains in the works. Mr. McBride had removed them weeks or months earlier, meaning to repair the rolls. Now this huge green combine had its shields in place.

Dale shook his head and walked around the combine, running the flashlight beam over the empty glass cab and the maze of metal ladders and catwalks on the giant machine. As large as it was, the combine took up only a third of the floor space in the huge barn. Doors and gates led to side rooms off the central space, and wooden ladders ran up to not one but half a dozen lofts. Dale flicked the flashlight beam up toward the eaves fifty feet above, but he saw only darkness. But he heard the frenzied flutter of wings.

Bats, he thought, but another part of his mind said, *No, sparrows.* He remembered now. That was the first time he had been in Duane's barn. A summer night when he and his brother, Lawrence, and their friend Mike O'Rourke had walked the gravel road from Uncle Henry and Aunt Lena's farm and shot sparrows in Duane's barn. First they froze the sparrows in the beams of their flashlights, and then they shot them with their BB guns. Not all of the sparrows had died. The BB guns were not that powerful. Duane had opened the barn doors for them, but he had not taken part. Dale remembered Duane's ancient collie—Wittgenstein—hanging back with Duane in the dark doorway, the dog excited by the boys' bloodlust and the wild fluttering of the sparrows but not leaving his friend's side.

"To hell with this," said Dale. He went out of the barn, pulled the screeching doors as shut as he could get them, and went back to unload his groceries.

On the way, he walked around the farmhouse, checking to see if there was another way anyone could have gotten to the second floor. The tall old farmhouse had no easy way to the six windows more than fifteen feet up there. The windows were all shut, most covered on the inside by drapes or curtains, or both. Someone with a tall ladder might have done it, but the dirt around the farmhouse was all mud after the night's rain, and there were no footprints or marks from a ladder.

I guess whoever turned on the light lives up there, thought Dale. It was hard to scare himself in the bright daylight under the blue sky.

He set the crowbar and the baseball bat just inside the kitchen door and went out to ferry in his small-fortune's worth of groceries, trying not to track in too much mud as he did so.

NINE

Driving to pick up his truck that afternoon, Dale took the Catton Road shortcut to Oak Hill Road. A few miles away from Duane's farm—the dead zone, as he thought of it—his cell phone came alive again. The asphalt road was empty. The day was still warm. Dale drove with one hand on the wheel and punched in Sandy Whittaker's real estate number.

"Heartland Realty." It was Sandy answering. Dale identified himself, and there was the expected salvo of niceties. They both agreed that it was a beautiful fall day and very welcome after the cold and snow.

"Is everything all right, Mr. Stewart . . . Dale?" said Sandy.

Dale hesitated. He was tempted to ask about the upstairs light, but what could he say? *"Say, Sandy, any reports of phantom lights on in the McBride farmhouse?"* Instead, he said, "Yeah, I was just wondering if you knew anything about a dog hanging around the farm I'm renting."

"A dog? What kind of dog?"

"A little one," said Dale. "A black one."

There was a pause on the other end of the line. Dale drove by clean white farms and large barns. The road stayed empty.

"Never mind," said Dale. "Silly question."

"No, no," said Sandy Whittaker. "Have you seen a dog on the property?"

"In the house, actually."

"In the *house*?" said Sandy.

"I left the inside door open this afternoon. I guess the screen was open just enough to let a dog in . . . a little thing. It ran off and I just wondered who it might belong to. Duane's aunt didn't own a dog, did she?"

"Mrs. Brubaker?" said Sandy. "No . . . no, I'm sure she didn't. No one saw her much, but everyone knew that Mrs. Brubaker was crazy about keeping things clean and tidy. I'm sure she didn't own a dog."

"Maybe it was a neighbor's dog," said Dale, already sorry that he'd called the woman. "Coming over to check me out."

"Not if it was a small black dog," said Sandy. "Mr. Johnson to your south owns two hounds for hunting, but they're big and brown. The Bachmanns—the young family who moved into your aunt Lena and uncle Henry's place over toward the cemetery—they had an Irish setter, but it was killed by the milk truck last summer."

Christ, thought Dale, *talk about small towns.*

"What kind of dog was it?" Sandy asked again.

Dale sighed. Some cows in a muddy field looked up as he drove past, and he wondered if his expression was as vague as theirs. "I don't really know dogs," he said.

"I do," said Sandy Whittaker. "I own five and subscribe to the AKC journal and watch the Westminster Dog Show on satellite every year. Describe the dog and I'll tell you what kind it is."

Dale rubbed his head. It was beginning to ache. "A little thing," he said. "About ten, twelve inches tall, I guess. Not much longer. Black. I thought that maybe it was a terrier."

"Did it have longer hair?" said Sandy.

"No, it didn't really have hair."

"*No hair?*" said Sandy. She sounded shocked, as if he'd said something obscene.

"I mean really short hair," said Dale. "Very short. Black."

"Well, American staffordshire terriers and toy terriers and pit bull terriers and Boston terriers and their type all have very short hair," Sandy said dubiously, "but none of them are all black. And no one in the county owns any of those breeds. Did you see the dog's head?"

"Sort of," said Dale.

"Was the snout long, thin? Or sort of pushed in?"

"Sort of pushed in, I think," said Dale. He had to grin. He felt like a crime witness being grilled by a relentless cop. "Sort of like a bulldog's."

"Hmmm," said Sandy Whittaker, sounding judicious. "American bulldogs and Old English bulldogs are larger than you described, unless you saw a puppy . . ."

"I don't think it was a puppy," said Dale, no longer sure what he'd seen.

"Then it could have been a pug or a French bulldog. Was it slim and sleek, or did it have a sort of barrel chest?"

Dale was tempted to close his eyes to remember. A pickup passed the other way. Dale kept his eyes open. "It did sort of have a barrel chest—powerful—and little tiny legs, but solid—not like one of those ratty little Chihuahuas."

There were several seconds of silence. "Two of my five dogs are Chihuahuas, Dale."

Dale rolled his eyes. "Well, gosh, thanks for your help, Sandy . . ."

"What kind of tail did this black dog have?" she asked, all business now.

"Tail?" He called back the memory of the little dog's black ass retreating toward the chicken coop. "I didn't see a tail. I don't think it had a tail."

"Pugs have curled tails that sort of sit up on their backs," said Sandy Whittaker. "What about this dog's ears? Were they flat or raised?"

"Raised," said Dale, not really caring any longer. "Triangular. They stuck up."

"Then it's not a pug," Sandy Whittaker said. "Their ears curl down. Do you remember anything else about the black dog?"

"It had sort of a pink splotch on its face, muzzle, whatever," said Dale. He was almost to the outskirts of Oak Hill. He could just stop by Sandy Whittaker's office if he wanted. He had no intention of doing so.

"Yesss," said the woman, "it sounds like a French bulldog. They grow about twelve inches tall, weigh about twenty-five pounds. They have a puglike face, barrel chest, and pointy ears. And they have a broad, short, snubby nose with slanting nostrils and a pink flush to their muzzle."

"Well, thanks, Sandy. You've been a big help and . . ."

"The only problem," interrupted Sandy Whittaker, "is that French bulldogs come in fawn coloring, pied—that's black and white—red brindle and black brindle—that's sort of reddish and black. Never pure black. Are you sure that the dog you saw wasn't pied?"

Absolutely, positively coal black thought Dale with absolute, positive certainty. "It could have been pied, I guess," he said. "Well, thanks again, Sandy, you've really . . ."

"The other problem with a French bulldog," said Sandy Whittaker, "is that there aren't any around here. Not in Elm Haven. Not in Oak Hill. Not anywhere around here. Not even on any of the farms in your part of the county. I would have noticed."

After confronting C. J. Congden in the garage and paying for the new tires, Dale drove back to the farm. He had always hated confrontations, especially confrontations with any sort of authority, but rather than being rattled by the encounter, he found himself slightly amused by it. And the previous night's sense of being displaced far from the center of things—even from himself—had receded. He had his truck back, the farmhouse was full of food and drink, and if he wanted, he could drive west—or east—anytime he wanted. Things looked better.

But the weather did not. Dark clouds were moving in from the west. The warm autumn day slid slowly but exorably into a winterish chill.

He was almost back to Elm Haven when he noticed how low he was on gas. There was nothing for it, he thought. He had to deal with the KWIK'N'EZ.

It was raining when he got to the gas station/convenience store. Trucks hissed past on I-74 just down the slope. Dale pumped the gas and cleaned his windows. There was no pay-at-the-pump option, so he took out his American Express card and walked into the store to pay.

Derek, the skinhead nephew, looked up from behind the counter. He was wearing a brown and orange KWIK'N'EZ shirt and a cap with the company logo on it. His face froze when he saw Dale.

Dale laughed out loud.

"What's so fucking funny?" said the boy.

Dale shook his head and set cash down instead of his credit card. "Derek," he said, "the day just keeps getting better and better."

The day got worse and worse. The clouds lowered, the breeze turned into a windstorm, and the temperature dropped forty degrees by nightfall. That evening Dale retreated early to the relative warmth of the basement to read in Duane's old bed and listen to the old-time radio station being picked up by the big console radio. Outside, the wind howled.

Inside, the wind howled. Dale lowered his book and listened to the sound—first a whistling, then dropping suddenly to a bass growl. He walked from one of the high windows to the next, checking for cracks or broken panes, but the sound was not coming from any of the windows. It was coming from the darkened coal bin behind the furnace.

Dale took out the Dunhill lighter that Clare had given him, flicked it on, and peered into the lightless hole. There had been a hanging light there once, but the bulb had long since been removed. The noise was very loud in the small space. Dale stepped up into the coal bin and moved the lighter flame in a circle, looking at the floor and walls.

Traces of coal dust remained on the concrete floor all these decades later. The gap where the coal hopper had been before Mr. McBride had switched to gas had been bricked up, as had the opening to the coal chute itself. There were no windows in the cramped space. There *was* a huge, square board, probably four feet by four feet, screwed into the bricks on the west wall. The howling was coming from there.

Dale bent low to cross to the west wall. He set his hand against the thick square of plywood. The wood pulsed as if something on the other side was pushing back. Cold air gusted through chinks along the top of the rotted wood and the howl returned, then rose to a whistle.

It took Dale only a minute to use his fingers to pry the old screws out of the decaying mortar between the bricks. Parts of the wood splintered when he pulled the barricade back and away.

Cold air blew freely now, carrying with it the dank stench of cold earth—the smell of the grave. Dale held his flickering lighter forward, throwing pale light down what had to be a tunnel—perhaps three feet wide, almost four feet tall. Corrugated red earth and stone were visible for twenty-five feet or more, to a dirt wall where the tunnel either ended or doglegged to the right.

It can't end there. The wind's coming from somewhere.

Dale considered exploring the tunnel for a full two milliseconds. No way was he going crawling into that wet, half-caved-in hole in the ground. Bringing a screwdriver, hammer, and nails from the workbench in the basement, Dale set the barricade back in place, reset the long screws in the crumbling mortar as best he could, and then drove in ten of the longest nails he could find. The wind continued to push and pulse against the wood, whistling through the splintered gap at the top.

Replacing the tools and washing his hands in the basement utility sink, Dale thought, *What the hell is that? Where does it go?*

He was almost asleep an hour later, the wind having dropped and been replaced by a heavy, sleety rain, when he remembered the Bootleggers' Cave.

Every summer during his four years in Elm Haven, Dale and his brother Lawrence had joined Mike and Kevin and Harlen and Bob McKown and some of the other town kids in searching Uncle Henry and Aunt Lena's property north of the cemetery for the legendary Bootleggers' Cave—a combination of underground speakeasy and liquor depot rumored to have been operated up County 6 during Prohibition. None of the kids knew what Prohibition had been, exactly, but that did not keep them from digging holes all over Uncle Henry and Aunt Lena's hillsides in search of the legendary cave. Many of the old-timers swore that the bootleggers had operated out of their cave somewhere up County 6, always on the lookout for revenuers—none of the boys had a clue what "revenuers" were, but it sounded scary to them as well. By the time the Bike Patrol kids started digging up Uncle Henry and Aunt Lena's property for the first time in the summer of 1959, the legend of the Bootleggers' Cave had become gospel and had grown to include a complete speakeasy buried somewhere under those hills, complete with several Prohibition-era cars entombed there, hundreds of barrels of whiskey, and possibly a dead gangster or two. Dale and his friends had moved several tons of soil in the fruitless search.

But Duane almost never joined them on those outings. Dale had always thought that it was because the fat boy did not want to work at the digging, but Duane worked harder on his farm than any of the city kids, so one summer day Dale had asked him why he didn't want to find the Bootleggers' Cave with them.

"You're looking in the wrong place," Duane had said.

Dale had ridden his bike out to Duane's farm alone—Lawrence was in bed with the flu—and Duane's Old Man had sent Dale up to one of the high, hot lofts in the barn, where his genius friend was busy writing what looked like hieroglyphics on the barn wall. It turned out that they *were* hieroglyphics—Duane had decided to become religious and worship some Egyptian god or goddess—but Dale hadn't been interested in that right then, even though Duane had accumulated quite a treasure trove of animal and bird skulls at his makeshift altar in the loft. Dale wanted to know about the Bootleggers' Cave.

"What do you mean, we're looking in the wrong place?"

"And for the wrong thing," continued Duane, dabbing white paint on his row of bird-and-eyeball-and-wavy-line hieroglyphics.

"What do you mean?"

"The bootleggers didn't have a cave, just one of these farmhouses with an escape tunnel they dug. The tunnel's not even that long."

"How do you know?"

"They used our house," said Duane.

"You've seen this tunnel?"

"I haven't been in it."

"Where would we dig for it?"

"You don't have to dig. It runs right out of the basement of The Jolly Corner."

"And are there cars and stuff in it? Like dead guys?"

Dale had laughed and rubbed his nose with the paintbrush. "I don't think so. More like rats and sewage. I doubt if the gangsters dug a very good tunnel. It must go right by where the old outhouse used to be."

Dale had wrinkled his nose. "That isn't the Bootleggers' Cave. The real cave is huge—with cars in it and stuff—and lots of whiskey. We're pretty sure it's down by the creek on Uncle Henry and Aunt Lena's farm."

Duane had shrugged, and that had been the end of it. Dale had never asked him about it again.

Now, more than forty years later, Dale went to sleep smiling at the memory. He did not hear the scratching that had replaced the howl of the wind—a scratching coming from the darkness behind the furnace where the opening to the coal bin was.

TEN

URING the next few weeks at the farm—the first three weeks of November—Dale began to enjoy himself. It was a brief respite before the nightmare.

It turned out that almost all of the disadvantages of the place and situation worked to his advantage in one way or another. The lousy weather—the warm fall days lasted only a day or two more before the snow and gray skies returned—kept him inside and drove him deeper into himself in that indefinable way so important to writers. And writing was what this so-called sabbatical was all about. Dale was using my old notebooks to retrieve the sense of being eleven years old in the Elm Haven of the summer of 1960. He had never clearly expressed to himself his goal of writing a book about that summer—or even of finally recapturing clear memories of that time—but this is what he proceeded to do in the weeks after his arrival at The Jolly Corner.

At first, the lack of connection there—no telephone, no Internet, no television—almost gave him a sense of vertigo. Despite his previous discipline as a writer and academic, he was still used to being con-

nected. But as the days turned into weeks, the silence, especially the
mental silence that comes from not being hammered by e-mail and
phone calls, turned first into a pleasant advantage and then into a
necessity. He thought of making the occasional call when in Oak Hill
or Elm Haven— to his agent, to his daughters—but he did not *need* to
make the phone calls and soon found reason to forget them.

He found a newspaper kiosk in Elm Haven and occasionally
bought the *Peoria Journal Star*, ostensibly for national news,
although it was the provincial Peoria and rural news that really
caught his attention. More frequently, often after writing for hours,
he would come down into the basement where I used to sleep and
listen to one of the radios there—relaxing on my bed and listening to
distant St. Louis's one good jazz station much in the way that I used
to spend hot summer nights listening to Cardinals and Cubs games,
the voices rising and falling across the static of the breathing earth's
ionosphere, the sense of distance and space implicit in the ambigui-
ties of the reception.

Most of the time, however, Dale Stewart celebrated his isolation.
The weirdness of the house, the phantom light on the sealed-off second floor, and the encounters with skinheads and a former bully
bemused him more than concerned him. It gave a flavor of strangeness
without the harshness of real threat. It kept him inward-turned and
progress-aimed.

He began to take walks. After decades living in the American West
where the view is everything, where the scope and scale of nature is all
but overwhelming, Dale found great satisfaction in finding a modest
view from the small hill a quarter of a mile behind the barn—the flat
area where I had buried my dog, Wittgenstein, more than forty years
earlier, although Dale did not know that—and then following the
frozen creek south another three-quarters of a mile to the Johnsons'
small woods. The gray skies and flat vistas seemed to make the scale of
nature smaller here, more accessible, more observable, and Dale soon
began to walk an hour or two each day, despite the harsh weather.
Sometimes, heading back up the creek toward the farm or cutting

across the frozen fields, Dale could not even see the farmhouse until the last few hundred yards, the barn appearing first, looming out of the snow and gloom, then the rusted oval of the fueling station gas tank hanging in its iron girders, then the washed-out, pale box of the house solidifying in the flat light.

He would make himself lunch—usually soup and French bread and some cheese—and then return to my Old Man's study with its rolltop desk, bookcases, sleigh bed, and decent light. There he'd work, typing on his ThinkPad for several more hours, often printing out the day's work on the compact HP Laserjet printer he'd brought along so that he could edit and revise the hard copy in the evening or the next morning. Then dinner—usually something more substantial than soup and bread—and another hour or two of writing before spending the evening reading or going to the basement to listen to jazz through the console radio's scratchy but wonderful speaker.

Dale was writing easily, but not well. Both his academic background and commercial writing experience had trained him to start from the outside in: that is, to structure the tale, research the characters and settings, and then write inward, the way a whittler carves a shape from a stick. I was just a kid when I died, but I had already discovered one important truth about writing—to do it well, one has to work *from the inside out*. That is, there has to be a quiet but unshakable center to the tale, whether in the core of the characters or the story or, preferably, in both, and everything must spiral outward from that point. Dale was still whittling away, trying not to cut across the grain and hoping to find honest shapes in the wood.

His sense of place in the unformed novel was very strong. What, after all, is more real to us than the geography of our childhoods? Occasionally he would get in the Land Cruiser and drive slowly through the streets of Elm Haven to refresh himself on some item of geography, but in truth he wasn't writing about the sad and battered Elm Haven of this shoddy new century. Dale was living in the summer of 1960 now, and when he drove the streets of the little town he was looking at structures and people who were no longer there, who would never be there again.

Dale had no guilt at borrowing my own journals of jottings and vignettes and character scribbles to capture the kids of the summer of 1960—including himself. After my death, Dale had promised himself that he would become the writer that his friend Duane had wanted to be, so it seemed natural that he would build on my old notes and observations to write this particular book.

But they were *my* notes and observations, not Dale's. He still had not discovered his own key to the door opening on that largely forgotten summer. So when he began the early-chapter descriptions of our eleven-year-old friends—Mike O'Rourke, Kevin Grumbacher, Jim Harlen, Donna Lou Perry, Cordie Cooke, and the others—they were *my* perceptions and misperceptions, not Dale's. Not even the images of young Dale himself and of his little brother, Lawrence, came completely from Dale. Perhaps he was afraid to go back to those memories all by himself.

The black dog returned nineteen days after he arrived.

It was late afternoon and Dale was taking his favorite walk, heading west to the flat rise, following the creek south to the woods on Mr. Johnson's farm, then cutting northeast along a gully, coming out at Calvary Cemetery on County Road 6. Then it was less than a mile along the gravel road to the driveway back to the farmhouse.

This afternoon, he had just reached the woods and was preparing to cross the creek before hiking east when he saw the dog twenty yards or so behind him, on the same side of the creek cut. When Dale stopped, the dog stopped.

For a moment he was sure that he had solved the tiny mystery; if the dog was here in the Johnsons' woods, then the dog must belong to Mr. Johnson. But then Dale realized that the hound had followed him from Duane's farm.

Dale took a few steps toward the dog. The small black dog retreated a few steps, then turned and waited. Dale stood looking at it, wishing that he'd brought his binoculars.

The black dog appeared a bit larger than he remembered it, but the rest of his description to Sandy Whittaker still applied: a relatively small dog, all black except for a patch of pink on its flattened muzzle, floppy ears, no tail visible, and barrel-chested. He tried to remember the breed that Sandy had mentioned—a French bulldog?

The dog waited for Dale to begin walking again before it followed. Dale slid down the steep creek bank and jumped the narrow, half-frozen stream. The dog picked its way across twenty yards to the north and scrambled up the steep slope.

Dale followed his usual route back to County 6, following old cow paths along the rim of a narrow ridge that ran between two gullies. The stream in the south gully had been named Corpse Creek by Dale and his buddies forty-five years earlier. There had been a three-foot-deep pool on the east side of the gravel road where the creek ran through a tall culvert—a favorite hiding place for the boys—and frequently, dead animals hit by speeding cars on County 6 had ended up in the pool. Thus, Corpse Creek.

The black dog stayed twenty yards back, picking its way across frozen grass in that tenderfooted way that some dogs have outdoors. At one point, Dale stopped and threw a rock in the dog's general direction—not trying to hit it, merely trying to get it to go away. The black dog sat on its haunches and stared at him.

Then the dog licked its muzzle and showed its teeth—not, Dale thought, in any sort of snarl, merely in a doggy grin.

Dale felt a chill of unease flow through him. He knew it must be a trick of the overcast day and distance, but for an instance it looked as if the black dog's teeth were wrong.

It looked as if the dog had human teeth.

Dale shook his head, angry at himself for generating the image, and when he looked back, the dog was no longer showing any teeth. He climbed over Johnson's wire fence at a sturdy fence post and walked out onto the asphalt of County 6 in front of the hilltop cemetery. It was a cold day, and windy. Usually the cemetery was empty of visitors during Dale's weekday afternoon walks, but he realized with a start that this day someone was standing thirty or forty yards into the graveyard. The lone figure was male and oddly dressed—wearing what appeared to be high leather boots, khaki wool as in old military uniforms, and a Boy Scout–type broad-brimmed hat. *An old veteran?* thought Dale. It was impossible to tell the age of the man at this distance, but the slimness and suppleness of his silhouette suggested someone younger.

There was no car in the grass parking berm along the black iron fence.

The man in the cemetery looked up from the headstone he was contemplating and stared in Dale's direction. Dale waved. He wondered if it was someone local—perhaps the male half of the young couple who had bought Uncle Henry and Aunt Lena's farm—or someone else who lived within walking distance of the cemetery. It would be nice to meet someone normal around Elm Haven.

The man stared but did not wave back.

Dale mentally shrugged and began his walk north down the steep incline, making sure, as always, that no car or pickup was roaring down behind him on the narrow asphalt road. When he thought to check, there was no sign of the black dog.

It was an hour later, after he'd finished some tomato soup and returned to his computer in the study, that he realized that someone had been in the house.

The IBM ThinkPad had been left on. The last sentence Dale had typed was still on the screen—

The summer lies ahead like a great banquet and the days are filled with rich, slow time in which to enjoy each course.

Dale had thought about that sentence during his walk and decided that the simile might be too flowery, but it was not the possible excess in the writing that concerned him now. Below his sentence had been typed—

gabbleretchetsyethwishthounds
hehaefdehundeshaefod&hisloccaswaeronofer
gemetside&hiseaganscinonswaleohteswamorgensteorra
&histethwaeronswascearpeswaeoforestexas

He didn't pay any attention to the gibberish yet. He was more interested in who had written it. Dale reached under the sleigh bed in the study and pulled out the new baseball bat he'd put there. The crowbar was heavier, but it was in the kitchen cupboard.

Hefting the bat, walking as lightly as he could, Dale went down the hall to the kitchen, through the kitchen and out onto the side stoop. It had begun to rain again, but it was light enough for him to see the muddy turnaround area. It had been wet and muddy before he left. The only car tracks led to his parked Land Cruiser. The only footprints were the ones he had left coming and going.

Not satisfied, Dale went back into the house. He traded the bat for the crowbar, locked the door, and went from room to room, switching on lights as he went. He checked behind furniture and drapes and under the bed. He opened closets. He went down the basement stairs and checked behind the furnace and under Duane's old brass bed. He checked the empty coal bin.

Upstairs again, he rechecked all of the ground-floor rooms. Then he went up the stairs to the second floor.

The heavy plastic remained stapled firmly in place. The second-floor hallway was dim behind the yellowed sheets of construction plastic.

Dale checked everything again. Nothing. No one. The house was so empty and silent that the sound of the furnace kicking on made him jump and hold the crowbar at port arms.

He retrieved the baseball bat and went back to the study, hoping that the words would be gone from his screen. They were still there.

Dale sighed, sat in the old swivel chair, and printed out the page.

As he saw it, there were only two possibilities—either someone had been in the house while he was walking, or he had typed these lines without being conscious of it. Either possibility made him slightly ill.

He looked at the first line—**gabbleretchetsyethwishthounds.** The word "hounds" leaped out of the line. Whoever had typed this mess had not taken time to hit the space bar.

Dale went through the manuscript with his blue pen, setting diagonal slashes where he thought the breaks should be. The message became—

gabble retchets yeth wisht hounds
he haefde hundes haefod & his loccas waeron
ofer gemet side & his eagan scinon swa leohte
swa morgensteorra & his teth waeron swa scearpe
swa eofores texas

Unfortunately, most of it made sense to the English professor.

Dale Stewart's expertise was in twentieth-century literature, but he had taught his share of Chaucer and enjoyed his seminars on Beowulf. This Old English was closer to Beowulf's. "Gabble retchets" rang vague bells, but did not immediately translate. He didn't believe that was Old English—Welsh, perhaps. "Yeth" meant "heath," so the end of the first line meant something like "heath or wisht hounds." He would have to check references for the "wisht."

The rest of the message was straight old English. *"He haefde hundes haefod"*—"he had the head of a hound."

Dale lowered the paper and rubbed his cheek, hearing the stubble there scrape. His hand was shaking ever so slightly.

"& his loccas waeron ofer gemet side"—"and his locks were extremely long."

Dale smiled. When he had first seen the typing, he'd been afraid that Derek and the other skinheads, or even Sheriff C. J. Congden, had sneaked into the place to spook him. He felt he could safely rule them out. He doubted if any of the locals he'd met so far were literate in Old English. *Careful, Dale old boy*, he warned himself, *intellectual pride goeth before a fall.*

"*& his eagan scinon swa leohte swa morgensteorra*"—"and his eyes shone as bright as the morning star." Someone with the head of a hound, long locks, and blazing eyes. Lovely.

"*& his teth waeron swa scearpe swa eofores texas.*" Texas. Dale wished it was a note about Texas. This line translated as ". . . and his teeth were as sharp as a boar's tusks." *Texas.*

Dale deleted the lines of Old English and tried to get back to his novel, but somehow he could not transport himself back to the rich summer vacation of 1960. After a while he gave up, pulled a cold beer from the fridge, grabbed his dogeared copy of *Norton's Anthology*, found the *Beowulf* section, and went down to the basement where it was brighter and warmer.

He turned on the console radio and listened to the scratchy jazz coming from St. Louis. As he skimmed over *Beowulf*, the last of the day's light faded and died through the windows high on the cement wall. The furnace came on with its wheeze and roar, but Dale was too lost in the *Beowulf* tale to notice.

The monster Grendel and his mother—not to mention the wolves circling close around the beleaguered mead hall—were described several times by the word *wearg* or its variant, *wearh*. A marginal note in Dale's own hand read, "German form *warg*—wolf, but also denotes *outlaw*—someone who has committed a crime that is unforgivable or unredeemable." Then, next to his note, in Clare's slanting script, "Those cast out from their communities and doomed to wander and die alone. *Warg* = corpse-worrier (from Indo-European *wergh*, to strangle = 'one who deserves strangulation'). The outcast human *warg* could be killed on sight with impunity."

Dale's hands were shaking again as he lowered the heavy anthology.

He'd forgotten that he'd loaned Clare his text when she'd audited his Beowulf graduate class four years ago.

Dimly, slowly, Dale became aware of the blues song being played on the old radio. It was as if someone had turned up the volume. He dropped the book and reversed positions on the bed, leaning closer to the glowing dial.

It was a powerful and classic piece of blues. Legend said that the composer/player, Robert Johnson, had sold his soul to the devil to be able to write and play such music. Johnson had never denied the rumors.

Dale closed his eyes and listened to the ancient recording of Johnson wailing to the tune of "Hellhound on My Trail."

ELEVEN

Two weeks after Clare Hart joined Dale's 20th-Century American Authors class and a week before they became lovers, Dale—Dr. Stewart—had her stay a few minutes after the seminar ended. It was a beautiful early autumn day that felt like summer, and the windows to the old classroom were open, looking out onto green leaves and blue sky.

"You're Clare Two Hearts," said Dale. "Mona Two Hearts's daughter."

Clare frowned at him. "How did you find out?"

"Some supplementary transcripts arrived from the university in Florence and your real name was on them . . . unlike the earlier transcripts. Your mother's name was also on one of the documents."

Clare stood silent, looking at him. He was soon to learn just how still and silent this young woman could be. After a moment, Dale cleared his throat and went on, "I apologize . . . I mean, I really wasn't snooping. But I was just curious why . . ."

"Why I hid my identity?"

Dale nodded.

Clare had smiled without warmth. "Dr. Stewart . . . it isn't easy being a famous diva's daughter. Not even in Italy. And that part of my identity had no role in my graduate work here."

Dale nodded. "I knew that your mother had grown up on the Blackfeet reservation up north . . ."

"Actually, she didn't," said Clare in that no-nonsense tone that he'd already grown to enjoy in class. "All of Mama's press kits say that she grew up poor on the reservation—not far from St. Mary—but in reality she was born there but grew up in Cut Bank, Great Falls, Billings, and half a dozen other little towns before she went to Juilliard and then on to Europe." Clare looked him straight in the eye. "Mama's mother had married a white man who was ashamed of the rez. I'm part halfbreed."

Dale shook his head at that. "Miss Hart . . . I really didn't mean to put you on the spot. I just noticed the difference in names, recognized your mother's name. I thought that I should tell you about the supplementary transcripts."

"Does anyone else know?" asked Clare.

"I don't think so. I just happened to see the file on the day that the transcripts came in because we were trying to allocate credits for the nondegree graduate students." He pulled the file out of his drawer, removed the telltale transcripts, and handed them to her. "I'll refile the rest," he said. "The supplements weren't necessary."

Clare slid the papers into her backpack without looking at them and turned to go. She stopped at the door and looked back at him. He expected to hear a "thank you," but what she said was "I've been in Missoula for almost a month, but I haven't had the nerve to drive up to the reservation."

Dale had amazed himself by saying, "I go up to Glacier and the reservation every fall. I could show you around there if you want."

Clare had looked at him with that neutral, intense stare of hers, and then turned and left without another word. Later, after he came to know her as well as he could—perhaps as well as anyone could—he realized that she had probably decided to have an affair with him at that moment.

Dale awakens to a loud banging.

He looks around. He is in the study—he'd fallen asleep in the chair—and with the exception of the single desk lamp, the farmhouse is dark. He does not remember dozing off or what he was working on here when he fell asleep. The ThinkPad is turned off.

The banging is coming from upstairs.

To hell with this. Dale is suddenly very angry. He looks around for the baseball bat, but he's left it in another room or it has rolled under the bed.

The banging intensifies.

Dale leaves the lighted study and walks down the darkened hallway, up the narrow steps. A pale light glows through the yellowed plastic.

He pulls out his pocket knife, selects the sharpest blade, and makes rough incisions through the plastic, diagonally, X marks the spot. He tears at the layers of brittle plastic with his hands until he rips a hole, widens it, tears plastic from the frame.

The air wafts out from behind the plastic and it carries the scent of lilacs and decay. *Tutankhamen's tomb.* Dale steps through the torn plastic, feeling the strands of the brittle stuff trying to hold him back, and then he is standing on the faded runner in the upstairs hallway, the stale air still rushing past him and downstairs as though he had opened an airlock.

There is one open door on his right, two on the left. The light is coming from the rear room on the left.

The banging has stopped.

Still holding his small utility knife, Dale strides down the hall, pausing to glance in the first room on his left and the open door to his right. A small bedroom to his left, an even smaller bathroom to his right. Both rooms are dark. The light from the rear bedroom flickers like candlelight.

Pausing in the doorway, Dale peers around the door frame.

A tall bed, a massive chest of drawers, a low dressing table with an opaque mirror, a flickering kerosene lamp on the dressing table, and a hand-built closet—painted a faded yellow—that seems strangely familiar to Dale. The windows are so heavily curtained and draped that no hint of moonlight or sunlight could find its way in. Holding the pathetic little knife ahead of him, Dale crosses to the bed.

There is a dark outline there on the age-tarnished quilt. At first Dale thinks it is a figure, then he sees it is merely an indentation in the quilt, but as he steps up to the high bed he sees that it is more than an indentation.

The center of the bed has sagged into a deep hole shaped in the form of a man. Or of a corpse laid out there. Even the pillow is dented down a foot or more into the mattress, the hole shaped like the oval of a human head. Dale hears the slightest noise from the deep indentation and leans over the bed, trying to ignore the stench—the same death-smell he had encountered on his first moments in the house—and wishing that he had brought a flashlight.

The bottom of the human-shaped pit in the mattress is crawling and oozing with life. *Maggots. Worms.*

Dale backs away, holding his free hand to his mouth, glancing behind him at the dark hallway.

The old oil lamp flickers as if to a strong breeze, the light almost going out but then steadying at the lowest glimmer.

The banging resumes—louder, wilder, more insistent. It is coming from the hand-built closet in the corner.

Dale looks at the closet and realizes that it is a huge coffin, crudely painted yellow and set on end. The door splinters and begins to open as he watches.

* * *

Dale awoke to a loud banging.

He sat up. He was not in the study, but in the basement, the heavy Norton anthology lying next to him on Duane's old bed. The console radio was still whispering static and music. It was not night. Midmorning light shone through the narrow windows at the top of the basement wall.

The banging resumed.

Dale looked around for the crowbar or baseball bat and remembered that he had left both of them upstairs last evening. He shook his head, ran his fingers through his tousled hair, and went up the steps and through the kitchen toward the banging.

Michelle Staffney was knocking at the side door.

Dale rubbed his face and opened the inner door.

"Dale, I hope you don't mind that I dropped by." She looked him up and down.

Dale shook his head and stepped back, welcoming her into the kitchen. "Uh-uh," he said. "Sorry for the way I look, but I must've fallen asleep last night. I was downstairs on . . . I mean, I didn't really go to bed last night. I fell asleep reading and listening to music. What time is it . . . ah, Mica?"

"Michelle will do," said the redhead with a slight smile. "And it's about nine-thirty. I guess you were tired."

"Yeah," said Dale. He crossed to the refrigerator. "Like some orange juice?"

"Sure."

"Take your jacket off. Just set it on the chair there. Do you want some breakfast?"

"No thanks, Dale. I already ate. I just wanted to give you an invitation. I would have called, but . . ."

Dale handed her a jelly glass half-filled with orange juice. "Yeah," he said. "It's sort of hard to get in touch with me by phone." The taste of the orange juice helped reduce the buzzing in his head. He felt hung over but didn't remember drinking more than one lousy beer the previous evening. "Invitation?" he said.

"For Thanksgiving," said Michelle Staffney.

Dale motioned to the kitchen table, and the two sat across from one another. The morning light was weak through the windows. Another gray day.

"Thanksgiving?" said Dale.

"Next Thursday," said Michelle. "I hadn't planned to be here this long, but it looks as if I will. I don't know anyone else around here and I thought that we could . . . well, hell, I don't know, cook a turkey together. Drink some wine. I don't know."

"So are you and your friend throwing a party . . . I'm sorry, I forget her name," said Dale.

"Diane Villanova," said Michelle, and looked down at the table. "No, Diane headed back to California yesterday. I just thought it would be nice if you and I . . . I mean, that we not spend Thanksgiving alone . . . but I bet you're headed somewhere or expecting someone . . . sorry, bad idea, Dale . . ."

"No, no," Dale said hurriedly. "I didn't even know that Thanksgiving was coming up. I've sort of been ignoring the calendar. Are you sure it's next Thursday?"

"Pretty sure," said Michelle.

"I'd love to have turkey together," said Dale. *Well, not really,* he thought. It would just remind him of Anne and the girls—the girls would be home from college—and of holidays past and holidays lost.

Something must have showed in his expression. Michelle said, "It's probably a dumb idea. In fact, my kitchen's all torn up and I'm not even sure I can get it in working order by Thursday. Diane and I had planned . . . well, this was a dumb idea."

Dale didn't know what kind of falling-out the two women had suffered, or why Michelle had remained here in Illinois, but he did know that he'd been a boor. He stood up, showing energy and enthusiasm he didn't feel at the moment, and walked over to pat the huge old stove. "Let's cook it here," he said brightly. "Otherwise I'll never use anything but the burners on this damned thing. I'm tired of soup. I'd *love* to share a turkey with you on Thursday."

Michelle nodded, but in a distracted way. "Are you all right, Dale?"

"Sure. Don't I look all right?"

"Well, I don't know you, of course. But you seem . . . tired."

He shrugged. "Haven't been sleeping too well and then last night . . . zonko."

"I have some sleeping pills," said Michelle, obviously making an offer. "Prescription. Plenty of them."

Dale held up his hand. "I have a prescription, too. It knocks me out eventually, but gives me shitty dreams . . ." He paused. *The yellow coffin-closet.* He remembered now where he'd seen it before. Their old house in Elm Haven had had such a closet in the room where he and Lawrence had slept.

"Dale?" Michelle stood and walked over next to him.

"Sorry. I just remembered the nightmare I was having before I woke up." He found himself telling her about it, keeping his voice light.

"My God," said Michelle, not at all amused. "Is the upstairs here really sealed off like that?"

"Come on," said Dale. "I'll show you."

Before they got to the stairway, he was suddenly and absolutely certain that the plastic would be torn and ripped where he had opened it, that a dim light would be burning at the end of the hall, that the air blowing out through the ripped plastic would smell of a tomb, and that there would be a dark figure standing at the head of the stairs.

The plastic was solid and secure in its frame. Only pale sunlight showed through the yellowed membrane.

"This is really spooky," said Michelle. She backed down the steps, one hand on the railing, as if not wanting to turn her back on the sealed doorway.

Back in the kitchen, she said, "What do you think's up there?"

Dale shrugged. "What do you say we work up our courage after dinner on Thursday—a lot of glasses of wine, maybe—and we end the evening by going up there and cutting that wall of plastic away and exploring the second floor?"

Michelle smiled, and Dale suddenly remembered the days and years of his longing for her in fourth through eighth grade. "It'll take more than wine to give me that much courage."

"We can arrange that," said Dale, smiling. He thought, *What the hell am I saying? The last thing I want right now is to be flirting with some woman.*

Michelle walked to the door, tugging on her jacket as she went. "I'll talk to you before I buy the turkey . . . oh, I forgot. I can't call."

"I'll call you," said Dale. "My cell phone works when I get out of this part of the county. Here, give me your number again." He handed her a pencil and yellow pad from the counter.

She scribbled the number, nodded, and went back out to her pickup truck. She started the engine but then rolled down the window. Dale leaned out from the stoop to hear her. It had started to rain.

"I forgot to tell you," she said. "I almost ran over your black dog on the way in. It just stood in the driveway, looking at the house, not even turning around when I honked the horn. I had to drive around it on the grass."

Dale shook his head. "Not my black dog. It's just been hanging around here. A black pooch with pink on its muzzle, right? Real small—maybe ten, twelve inches tall?"

"Black with pink on its snout," agreed Michelle. "But not that small. It must have been a couple of feet tall. Big chest."

"Too big to be the black dog that I've seen," said Dale. "Must be its big brother."

Michelle nodded. "Well, see you on Thanksgiving." She sounded a bit uncertain now that it had been planned.

Dale smiled. "Talk to you on the phone before then."

She waved and drove down the lane in the rain. There was no sign of the black dog. Dale went back in to turn up the heat and make some breakfast. He decided to splurge and have some bacon and was draining the grease from the pan, setting out a paper towel to blot the bacon itself, when a loud voice came from his study.

"You've got mail!"

TWELVE

>**Welcome back, Dale.**

Dale stood in the study staring at the screen of his IBM ThinkPad. There was nothing unsettling about receiving an e-mail except for the fact that (a) the modem was not currently connected to a cell phone or to any phone line, (b) the message had not come through his AOL account, and (c) the computer was not even running in Windows. Somehow the computer had exited to DOS and the message had been typed directly after the C prompt.

Then where the hell did the "You've got mail" *voice come from?* It had been the AOL voice. There was no mistake about that.

Dale came closer to the desk and studied the computer. Had he turned it on—or off—the previous evening before going down to the basement and falling asleep while listening to the radio? He couldn't remember.

The message burned white against the black screen. Without touching the keyboard, Dale checked the serial ports, the PCMCIA slots, and the other connections. He knew that more and more computers and PDAs were operating wirelessly these days, but as far as he knew, his older ThinkPad didn't have that capability. And even if it did, it would require Windows and his AOL account for him to receive or send mail. He subscribed to no other ISPs and had long ago deleted the other Internet alternatives that had been bundled with his laptop.

Which means that someone typed this directly onto the screen. Dale sat, keeping his fingers away from the keyboard, looking over his shoulder. *Did Michelle come in here during her visit?* They had gone up the stairs together to look at the plastic sheeting, but Dale could not remember her being out of his sight at any time.

Someone could have come in the house during the night. The door was unlocked this morning. That seemed more probable, but why this silly welcome note? Why not just steal the computer and be done with it? And where the hell *did* the AOL "you've got mail" voice come from? Dale was not terribly techno-savvy, but he'd been writing with and grading on and Internet researching with computers long enough to know that the AOL sounds were stored in wavefile form on the computer itself, so if someone wanted to activate it, all they would have to do would be . . .

But why? What kind of joke is this?

Dale sat staring for several more minutes, waiting for another line of letters to appear. None did.

Sighing, he tapped *Enter* and typed on the next line, **>Thanks.** Then he went back to the kitchen to reheat the bacon and make some toast. He had just carried the plate of toast and bacon to the table and was sipping his coffee when he heard, "You've got mail!"

This time he walked through the other ground-floor rooms with crowbar in hand before entering the study. Even from six feet away he could read the screen—

>You're welcome, Dale.

Dale realized that he was breathing shallowly and that his heart was pounding. He took some deep breaths before sitting and typing—

>**Who are you?**

He sat there another ten minutes, watching the screen and waiting, but no new words appeared. A *watched pot*, he thought and lifted the crowbar and went back into the kitchen, locking the outside door. His coffee and food were cold, but he ate and drank anyway, listening all the while.

After five minutes or so he peeked into the study. No new words were on the screen.

He had just carried his plate over to the sink and was rinsing it when he heard, "You've got mail!"

Dale ran into the study, forgetting the crowbar.

>**barguest**

Dale laughed out loud. What kind of self-respecting ghost would identify itself as a bar guest? This was the kind of stupid screen name that hackers and technogeeks loved to go by. He typed, >**Where are you e-mailing from, Barguest?**

This time he waited a stubborn fifteen minutes, wanting to see words appear on the screen, but nothing happened. Finally he lifted the baseball bat out from under the bed and went downstairs to check the basement. He'd just finished looking in all of the dark corners and hidden spaces when he heard the familiar AOL voice upstairs announcing e-mail.

Familiarity may not always breed contempt, but it does lessen fear of the unusual. Dale was more curious than anxious when he walked into the study to see what the uninvited hacker had to say.

>**thaere theode thaer men habbath hunda haefod & of thaere eorthan on thaere aeton men hi selfe**

Dale felt the flesh above his spine go cold. "Barguest" sounded like some young hacker's screen name, all right, but how many teenage hackers knew Old English? Dale stared at the words, forcing himself to slip into his English professor mode.

"From the nation where men have the head of a dog and from the country where men devour each other." Nice. Dale didn't know where the quote was from—it sounded like a quote to him—but he knew that it wasn't from *Beowulf* or any of the other epics he'd taught. ". . . the country where men devour each other."

Thinking of *Beowulf*, he looked back at the word "barguest." It wasn't in any form of Old English that he recognized, but it had that Germanic feel to it. "*Geist*" meant spirit or ghost, and "*bar*" could stand for "bier"—as in "funeral bier." He flexed his fingers over the keyboard and took a few more deep breaths before typing, >**Well, you're clever, but rude, Barguest. Speaking from ambush isn't polite. I'll chat with you if and when you tell me how you've hacked into my computer and who you are. Do you prefer modern English or Old English?**

This time he did not wait around. He had not quite made it to the kitchen when the voice announced new mail.

>**Welcome back, Dale. But be careful. We must find what we have lost.** *Cerberus der arge/und alle sine warge/die an hem heingem.*

Dale exhaled slowly. If he was not mistaken, the last part of the message was Middle High German. Dale didn't speak or read all that fluently in modern German, much less Middle High German, but he'd been required to do some doctoral research in the language, and at least one of his colleagues had been urging him for years to study and teach certain Middle High German epics as a prelude to *Beowulf*. He tried to print the page, but his printer would not go online unless he was in Windows 98 and he was sure he'd lose the DOS page if he opened Windows, so Dale grabbed a legal pad and pen and copied down everything on the screen. Beneath those notes, he translated the poem.

Cerberus the *arg* ("arag"? Old Norse "argr"?)
and all the *wargs* (wolves? outlaws? corpse-worriers?)
who follow him.

It was strange that he had seen that Old English word "warg,"
derived from the German, only last night—in both his handwriting
and Clare's—in the margins of his *Norton's Anthology's Beowulf*. His
hands were shaking slightly as he turned back to the keyboard:

>**Enough. Who the hell are you? How do you know me? And
what, exactly, have we lost?**

He walked back to the kitchen and waited, but no AOL voice summoned him back. Several times he returned to the study, saw the lines
on the screen but nothing new, and then walked out of the room, pac-
ing through the dining room with its coffinlike learning machines,
standing in the living room looking out at the gray rain, even going
down into the basement awhile. No voice. No new message.

Finally Dale went back to the study and loaded Windows 98. He
clicked on the AOL icon and tapped in his access code. The modem
in the ThinkPad clicked, but the message came up, **"No dial tone."**
Angry now, Dale went out to the Land Cruiser and dragged in his cell
phone. He hooked the phone to the modem and tried again. Now the
modem found a dial tone, but the legend came up, "Unable to connect to AOL number." On the phone itself, the display continued to
read NO SERVICE. He exited Windows to DOS. The screen was empty
after the C prompt. He loaded Windows and AOL again, but could
not get on-line.

After twenty minutes of messing with it all, Dale ripped the phone
out, exited AOL, and shut off the goddamned computer. He looked at
the notes on his legal pad again. "Cerberus the *arg* and all the *wargs*
who follow him." He knew Cerberus, of course—the three-headed
dog who guarded the entrance to the underworld, the infernal regions,
the land of the dead—but he had no clue as to what the quote meant.

Whoever this asshole hacker was, he was clever and literate, but he was still an asshole.

Too agitated to try to write, Dale grabbed his parka—returning to the study for the baseball bat—and went outside for a walk. The rain had stopped and the air had actually become warmer, but a fog had rolled in. Dale guessed that he could see less than fifty feet. The black, contorted silhouette of the first dead crabapple tree along the driveway was visible, but the barn and outbuildings had disappeared. His white Land Cruiser, beaded with moisture, looked only semisolid in the weak light and creeping fog. The eaves dripped.

From somewhere in the direction of the invisible chicken coop, a dog howled. It howled again.

Dale actually grinned. After hefting the baseball bat and slapping it against his palm a couple of times, he tugged the hood of his parka up and went hunting for the hound.

The fog changed the straightforward little Illinois farm into a foreign country. The dog had ceased howling the instant that Dale had stepped off the side porch, and he could not be certain of directions, since the shifting walls of fog both muffled and distorted sounds. He walked toward the chicken coop. The house and his truck disappeared in rolling gray behind him.

We must find what we have lost. Aloud, speaking in a Jay Silverheels voice, Dale said into the fog, "Who's this 'we,' white man?"

His voice sounded strange and lost in the gray blankness.

We must find what we have lost.

"Here, doggy, doggy, doggy," called Dale, swinging the bat in one hand. He had no intention of hitting the pooch—he'd never hurt an animal, or a human being, for that matter—but he was tired of being spooked by the thing. Anne had done a lot of research on dogs before they bought Hasso, their little terrier, and she had explained how they were still pack animals—obeying a pack hierarchy, demonstrating either dominance or submission. For instance, they had never cured

Hasso of licking—a classic submissive behavior most people confuse with affection. A submissive dog in the wild licks the pack leader or those hounds above it in pack hierarchy in order to receive food in return. This black dog probably hadn't worked out its dominance/submission issues with Dale yet. He decided that he'd help it along.

We must find what we have lost. Setting aside the royal "we" for a moment, Dale pondered that phrase. He had come here to Duane's old farm because he felt that he had lost everything—Anne and the girls, Clare, his job, the respect of his peers, his self-respect, and his ability to write—but down deep, Dale knew that this attitude was all self-pity and mummery. He still had some money in the bank; the ranch could be his again in ten months after the renters' lease was up; he might not truly be on sabbatical, but odds favored him returning to teach at the University of Montana again next year if he so chose. He had a $50,000 sport utility vehicle parked in the farmhouse's muddy turnaround, and it was fully paid for. He was sixty-some pages into a new novel and he had a publisher who hadn't given up on him yet. No, he hadn't lost everything—far from it.

We must find what we have lost. Perhaps it was a case of "what we have lost." Not just him, but everyone in this new century. His generation, at least. Writing about the eleven-year-old kids in the summer of 1960 made Dale's chest ache every time he sat down at the computer—not just because of the nostalgia of that half-lost summer of so long ago, but because of some indefinable sense of loss that made him want to weep.

"Yoo-hoo, dog," called Dale, opening the door to the chicken coop. He wished that he had brought a flashlight. He stepped into the darkness and then froze as a powerful smell struck him.

Not the smell of decay, thought Dale. *Stronger. Coppery. Fresh.* He blinked in the dim light, raising the baseball bat like a club.

The smell of blood.

He almost left then, but he had to see. In a minute or two his eyes adapted well enough for him to make out the long, low room of empty roosts and matted straw and splattered walls.

The walls and floor had been splattered with ancient, dried blood the first time he had looked in here. They were splattered with blood now, but even in the dim light he could see that it was fresh blood—wet, dripping, some of it actually running down the rough boards as he watched.

Time to go, thought Dale. He backed out of the chicken coop, setting his back to the wall and raising the bat again. The fog had closed in tighter. The light had failed even more. Dale felt his heart pounding and his ears straining to make out any sound—the soft squelch of mud under boots, the movement of four-legged things. Water dripped from the eaves of the coop. From somewhere to the north there came a loud, strangely familiar rasp of wood on metal. *The big barn doors being slid open?*

Time to go. Not just back to the farmhouse, but out of here—away from Illinois and its penny-dreadful little mysteries. Back to Montana, or farther east to New Hampshire or Maine. Somewhere else.

No. Here is where we can find what we have lost. The thought made him stop, not just because it had come unbidden and out of context, but because it seemed to have been stated in a mental voice other than his own.

Dale was striding quickly now, trying to keep his boots from being swallowed in the mud, listening hard for something moving behind or ahead of him.

He was almost back to the farmhouse when he saw two huge red eyes glowing at him through the fog.

A second later a car engine started up. *Not eyes, taillights.*

Dale ran, bat in hand, sure that someone was stealing his truck. The taillights glowed crimson a moment and then shut off as the vehicle drove quickly away through the fog.

Dale slid to a stop on the muddy turnaround area. His Land Cruiser was still where he'd parked it. He beeped the security system. It had been locked. But it seemed to have sunk into the mud . . .

"God*damn*it," growled Dale as he stepped closer. All four of the tires were flat. Dale assumed that they had been slashed again.

Dale walked out in front of the house, bat raised to his shoulder and ready to swing. He could hear a truck driving away on County 6, moving much too quickly for the foggy conditions.

There were tracks in the gravel and mud driveway—one pickup truck from the looks of the wheel tracks.

"Not funny, Derek," yelled Dale into the fog. "Not one bit fucking funny. You assholes are going to jail this time."

Tracking mud, Dale went into the farmhouse and looked around.

I've been here—what—three weeks, and how many dozen times have I had to search this fucking house? He searched it again.

No muddy bootprints except his own. No sign of anything missing or disturbed.

Except the fucking laptop. The ThinkPad was on again, the screen black except for three lines of white letters burning after the C prompt. This time Dale was sure that he had shut the computer off before leaving.

Disgusted, he walked over to flick the power off, not wanting to read another irritatingly cryptic message. But the stanza form of the message made him read, and the content made him pause. This was no High Middle German or Old English—Dale Stewart, Ph.D., even recognized the source. It was from Sir Walter Scott's *The Lay of the Last Minstrel*, Canto VI, if he remembered correctly. Clare could tell him. She had been auditing the graduate-level Eighteenth-Century Literature seminar the last time he'd taught this poem. Clare remembered everything. But Clare was not around to remind him, and odds were overwhelming that she never would be again.

>**For he was speechless, ghastly, wan,**
Like him of whom the story ran,
Who spoke the spectre hound in man.

Still disgusted, knowing that he would have to walk a couple of miles in the fog just to get his cell phone to work in order to call the Oak Hill garage to get his truck fixed, furious that he would have to deal with C. J. Congden again, knowing in his heart that these punks were never going to be caught or punished, feeling that the mystery of the blood in the chicken coop had been solved in the all-too-mundane fact of the tire slashings, tired of this hacker bullshit, Dale pushed the OFF button and watched the computer screen wink to a point of light and then die to black.

THIRTEEN

BOY, I hate movies like that."

"Movies like what?" said Dale. It was late on Thanksgiving Day. Duane's farmhouse smelled of turkey and stuffing and a dozen other cooking smells. Dale had ended up doing the shopping for the turkey and the wine, but Michelle Staffney had done most of the cooking that day. By early evening, Dale and Michelle had eaten a good portion of the twelve-pound turkey, had drunk a couple of beers before dinner, and were on their second bottle of white wine. They had washed the dishes and returned to the dining room. Dale had lugged all of the ancient learning machines out to a shed, but there had been no dining room table, only the benches on which the machines had sat. Dale had done his best, dragging the benches to the basement, moving the kitchen table into the dining room for the big day, and covering it with an ancient linen tablecloth he had found in the hall closet. Now the sunlight had faded away, but only a couple of lights were on in the house. Music from the console radio wafted up the stairway from the basement.

"You know," said Michelle, holding her wine glass in both hands. "I hate those formula scary movies. Horror movies. Slasher movies. Whatever."

Dale frowned. He had been telling her about the events of the past week—the blood in the chicken coop, finding his truck with flattened tires, the other truck driving off in the fog—something he probably wouldn't have talked about unless he'd had too much wine. "You comparing my life to a slasher movie?" he asked, pretending to be indignant—and actually feeling a bit indignant beneath the friendly buzz of the wine and beer.

Michelle smiled. "No, no. But you know—I always hate that part in the movies where the people know that something scary's going on but they stay anyway. And then the monster comes out and gets them. You know, like in the old *Poltergeist* or that mess of a remake of *The Haunting* or those slasher movies with the guy in the hockey mask or whatever."

Dale shook his head. "I intended to leave. But I thought that those idiots had slashed my tires again."

"But they hadn't."

"No," said Dale. "After I hiked all the way to Elm Haven in the fog, called the Oak Hill garage, and waited more than two hours for the guys in the tow truck to show up and drive me back to the farm, we discovered that someone had just let the air out of all the tires."

"But you thought they'd been slashed again."

"Yeah." Dale smiled ruefully and drank some wine. "I was stupid. The garage guys helped me get the tires inflated. At least I didn't have to deal with Sheriff Congden again."

Michelle poured more wine for both of them. Now she was also shaking her head. "C. J. Congden a sheriff. I remember him from high school here. What an asshole." The redhead held up one manicured finger. "But you stayed. They fixed your truck . . . but you stayed here."

Dale shrugged. "Well . . . it seemed silly to leave after all that anger at slashed tires that weren't really slashed . . . just a stupid practical joke. And I was still working on the novel and this seemed like the right place to write it." *The only place to write it*, Dale thought. He looked at her. "And besides, we had this date for Thanksgiving."

Michelle smiled. Her smile in sixth grade had been dazzling. Now, forty years and thousands of dollars of Beverly Hills dentist bills later, it was flawless. "So did they catch them? The skinheads? I assume that they were the ones who let the air out of your tires."

"Nope," said Dale. "It turns out that the one kid I knew by name—Derek—had an alibi. He was in Peoria with his aunt, Sandy Whittaker."

"Sandy Whittaker!" said Michelle. "My God. Do people just stay within five miles of home here until they die? Sandy Whittaker. I bet she got fat and married a Realtor."

Dale slowly shook his head. "Not quite. She got fat and *became* a Realtor. Anyway, the sheriff's deputy I talked to on the cell phone the next day wasn't too interested in trying to track down some kids who just let the air out of some stranger's tires. So I dropped the whole thing."

"And what about the blood?" said Michelle. When she leaned forward as she was doing now, Dale could see her full breasts press together down the low neck of her green silk blouse. Her California tan had begun to fade, and the freckles on her chest blended into the softest-looking white skin imaginable.

"What?" said Dale.

"You said that there was all this blood in your chicken coop. Do you think that the skinheads who let the air out of your tires threw this blood around your chicken coop?"

Dale held his empty hands out. "Who knows? The deputy I talked to said that it just wasn't in the Sheriff's Department's charter to be chasing down foxes and stray dogs who kill chickens."

"Do you think it was foxes and stray dogs?"

"No," said Dale. "And it wasn't chicken blood, either. There haven't been any chickens in that coop for forty years or so."

"It would have been cool if someone had done a DNA test on that blood," said Michelle. "You know, find out if it was animal blood or . . . whatever."

There was a silence after this comment.

Finally Dale said, "So you don't like the logic holes in these movies. Slasher movies. Horror movies. Whatever."

Michelle studied her glass of wine while thinking about this. The lamp behind her made her short-cropped red hair glow like a soft flame. "I don't like it when the writers and directors have the characters act like idiots just so they can get killed."

"Do you think I acted like an idiot by staying here?"

"No," said Michelle. "I'm glad you stayed here. I'm glad we got to cook a turkey together. It was a nice surprise not to spend Thanksgiving alone." She leaned forward again, and for a moment Dale was sure that she was going to put her hand over his where it lay on the white tablecloth. Instead, she pointed upward. "Speaking of surprises . . . weren't we going to go upstairs, take down the plastic, and see what's up there?"

Dale swallowed the last of his wine and looked toward the ceiling. "You mean you don't mind the parts in those dumb slasher movies where the characters go somewhere they've been warned to stay away from?"

"Actually," said Michelle Staffney, "I love those parts. That's the point in the movie where I quit rooting for the humans and start cheering for the monster or psychopath or whatever. But I think we have to find out what's up there."

"Why?" said Dale. "It's been closed off for decades. Why do we have to find out now?"

She showed that wonderful smile again. Dale found himself wondering why she hadn't succeeded as an actress. "We haven't been here for decades," she said lightly. "I, for one, can't leave Elm Haven without knowing what's up there behind that plastic."

"Oh," Dale said casually, "I already know what's up there."

* * *

Clare Two Hearts's first words when Dale picked her up for their long weekend of traveling to Glacier National Park and the Blackfeet Reservation were, "Does your wife know we're going away together?"

Dale had prepared himself for the content of that question but not the clarity of it. He actually blushed before saying, "Anne's used to my off-season camping trips up there. I often take students if students want to go. She doesn't mind. We have a pretty solid marriage." This last part was true, but the overall statement was a lie. He had never gone north with just one student, and usually it was a couple of male graduate students who loved to climb and camp who hitched a ride to the park with him. Anne, distracted by a swarm of life's demands, simply hadn't asked who he was going with this autumn.

Clare had looked at Dale as if reading all of this information from his blush and expression. Then she had thrown her gear in the back of the Land Cruiser and climbed into the leather passenger seat.

They both had a Friday free of classes—not too surprising, since, for reasons unknown to the instructor, Ms. Clare Hart seemed to be taking just the graduate courses that Dr. Stewart taught—so they had decided to leave on Thursday afternoon and camp near Flathead Lake that night before continuing on through the national park and then east to the reservation. It was early October, and while Dale had learned to mistrust the weather in Glacier and points north any time of the year, this autumn—and the winter to come—would be amazingly warm, with few blizzards. The cottonwoods and aspen were at the height of their color.

Dale drove west from Missoula on I-90 for a few miles and then exited to follow Highway 93 north about sixty miles to Polson and the south end of Flathead Lake. Past the little town of Ravalli, they jogged east a bit and then turned due north. Dale mentioned the National Bison Range that ran west of the highway, but Clare only nodded and said nothing. They passed through St. Ignatius, a sad little town on the

Flathead Reservation, and Dale glanced at his passenger, but Clare only watched the passing examples of depressed reservation living without comment.

The ride to and past Flathead Lake was always beautiful—the sharp-toothed Mission Mountains spiking skyward to the east—and it was all especially striking in the afternoon autumnal light, the aspen stirring gold in the breeze, but Clare Two Hearts rode in silence and Dale would be damned if he'd be the first to mention the astounding beauty all around them.

It was almost dinner time when they came close to Polson, but Dale knew of a nice place to eat in the old timber town of Somers twenty-some miles further on and he had planned to drive straight through Polson, following 93 around the west shore of Flathead Lake. But about two miles south of Polson, Clare suddenly said, "Wait! Could we stop there?"

"There" was the Miracle of America Museum, billing itself on faded signs as "Western Montana's Largest Museum." Dale had stopped there years ago with Anne and the girls, but had not paid attention to it since. He pulled into the lot.

"This is a dusty old place," he told Clare. "Tanks, tractors, collections of tractor seats . . . it's more a hodgepodge of an attic than a museum."

"Perfect," said Clare.

They spent more than an hour in the ramshackle museum, almost half of that time listening to recorded music in the place's "Fiddler's Hall of Fame." Clare smiled at everything—the tractor seat collection, the armored tanks from three wars, the motorized toboggan, the yellowed old newspapers behind glass, the old toys with flaking paint. Dale had to admit that it *was* sort of interesting, in a nondiscriminating, kitschy way.

It was almost dark when they got going again, passing through Polson and heading north along the lake. Here the view east toward the high peaks was especially beautiful—Dale's ranch was across the lake here, near the U. of M. biological research station—but he was determined to mention it only if Clare said something about the view or the hills. She didn't, so neither did he.

They had dinner in Tiebecker's Pub in Somers, on the north end of the lake. Clare ate only salad and paid for her own meal, despite Dale's offers. After dinner, they drove a few miles east to a good campground that Dale knew right on the water at Wayfarer State Park. They were almost two hours behind the schedule he'd planned, so they set up their camp in the dark, using flashlights and the Cruiser's headlights. Clare did not seem to mind.

Outdoors people can tell a lot about other outdoors people by the gear they use. Dale was wearing quality old boots, but he had brought an expensive North Face backpacking tent in his Gregory expedition backpack, a top-of-the-line L. L. Bean goose-down sleeping bag, and a high-tech gas backpacking stove for cooking, with lots of freeze-dried packets of food. Clare had brought only an old Swiss canvas military rucksack. Her camping gear consisted of only a tarp—which she pitched in little more than a minute, using a hiking stick for a center pole and rocks bunched in the nylon for grommets—and an old military-spec down bag that literally looked as if it had been left behind in Italy after World War II by the 10th Mountain Division. Her food supplies consisted of a water bottle, some fruit, and crackers.

Dale suggested that they build a campfire—the evening wind had turned cold—but Clare said that she was tired and disappeared under her tarp. Dale had stayed outside to watch the stars for a while, but soon he crawled into his seven-hundred-dollar tent and tried to get some sleep.

The next morning—cold and clear—they made coffee at the campsite, had a real breakfast at a cafe near the summer playhouse in Bigfork, and drove north to West Glacier.

Their plan had been to cut through Glacier Park to the Blackfeet Reservation and then head south along the Bob and the Front Range to the little reservation town of Heart Butte where Clare's mother had been born. On Saturday they planned to head straight back to Missoula on Highway 2, turning south again along Flathead Lake. Dale had argued for the side trip through Glacier—it was part of his annual late-autumn outing—but mostly he wanted to show off Montana to this young visitor.

The fifty-two-mile-long Going-to-the-Sun Road was famous, but one had to see the incredible scenery to understand how spectacular it really was. Heading east, they drove along the narrow but very deep Lake McDonald for eight miles or so, then started curving and climbing toward Logan Pass. Dale kept glancing at Clare. The young woman was attentive but did not appear to be enraptured by the incredible view.

About four miles beyond the lake, Dale pulled into the Avalanche Campground turnoff. "Want to walk for a few minutes?" he asked. "I know a nice little loop trail up the road here."

"Sure."

The Trail of Cedars was a tourist walk—partially built on a boardwalk to protect the delicate undergrowth of ferns and moss—and it wound through a forest of 200-foot-high hemlock and red cedar. There were no other visitors on this beautiful October morning. A soft wind stirred the branches high above them, creating a regular sighing that Dale found as calming as the susurration of ocean surf. Patches of light filtering down through greenery above filled the air with the scent of sun-warmed pine needles and decaying humus. Where the boardwalk crossed Avalanche Creek, water tumbled over moss-covered rocks into the steep and narrow gorge.

"Don't you wish we'd brought a camera?" said Dale.

"No," said Clare Hart.

"No?"

She shook her head. "I never travel with a camera. Occasionally a sketch book, but never a camera. It always makes me sad to see tourists snapping away with their cameras and staring through video viewfinders—waiting to get home to see what they didn't really see when they were *there*."

Dale nodded, pretending to understand. "But you have to admit that this is some of the most beautiful country in the world."

Clare shrugged. "It's spectacular."

Dale smiled. "Isn't that the same as beautiful?"

"Not really," said Clare. "Spectacle is just more accessible to the dulled sensibility. At least that's the way I think of it. This kind of country is hard to ignore. Rather like a Wagnerian aria."

Dale frowned at that. "So you don't find Glacier Park beautiful?"

"I don't find it subtle."

"Is subtlety that important?"

"Sometimes," said Clare, "it's necessary for something to be subtle to be truly beautiful."

"Name a subtly beautiful place," challenged Dale.

"Tuscany," said Clare without hesitation.

Dale had never been to Tuscany, so he had no response. After a moment, moving onto the trail beyond the boardwalk, he said, "Your people considered these mountains to be sacred."

Clare smiled at the "your people" but said nothing. As they came back toward the campground, she said, "Can you think of any mountains anywhere in the world that some primitive people did *not* consider sacred?"

Dale was silent, thinking.

"Mountains have all the attributes of the gods, of the Jehovah God, don't they?" continued Clare. "Distant, unapproachable, dangerous . . . the place whence cometh the cold winds and violent storms of rebuke . . . always present and visible, looming over everything, but never really friendly. Tribal peoples worship them but have the sense to stay away from them. Western types climb them and die of hypothermia and asphyxia."

"Whoa," said Dale, rolling his eyes a bit. "Theology. Social commentary."

"Sorry," said Clare.

They continued the drive across the incredible Logan Pass. Dale told Clare that the pass was usually closed even this early in the autumn, but that the snows were coming late this year. She had nod-ded, her eyes on a mountain goat hundreds of yards above them on the rock.

Going west to east, Dale had saved the most spectacular scenery for last— St. Mary Lake with the high peaks to the west, little Wild Goose Island in the foreground. He realized, looking at the scene, that if he had a dime for every photograph taken from precisely this spot, he'd never have to teach or write again. Clare said nothing as the view receded behind them. They reached the east portal to the park before lunchtime.

Passing out of the park and through the little reservation town of St. Mary, they headed south into the flatter, sadder belly of the reserva-tion, driving toward Heart Butte. Dale found himself irritated at his passenger—at her arrogance, at her refusal to be amazed by the amaz-ing scenery, at her dismissal of her own heritage. He was sorry that they had another night of camping and day of driving ahead of them before he could get back to Anne and the girls and his work. He was sorry that he'd invited this spoiled little diva's daughter on a trip that usually made him calm and happy to be living in Montana. He was sorry that he'd ever spoken to Clare Two Hearts about her real name.

He was only hours away from becoming Clare Hart's lover and, much worse, from falling in love with her.

Dale?"

He looked over the top of his wine glass at Michelle Staffney.

"You still here, Dale?"

"Sure," he said. "Just gathering wool."

"You were going to tell me what's upstairs behind the plastic and how you know."

He nodded and set his wine glass down on the wine-stained table-cloth. "The Jolly Corner," he said.

Michelle's expression showed no recognition.

"When we were kids, I remember Duane calling this house 'The

Jolly Corner,' " continued Dale. "It's a story by Henry James. A sort of ghost story."

"Like *The Turn of the Screw?*" asked Michelle. She had lit a cigarette and now exhaled smoke from her narrow nostrils. When she'd asked earlier if she could smoke after dinner, he'd said "No problem," but he was surprised that she still smoked. Now he was surprised that she knew about *The Turn of the Screw*. *Quit making assumptions about people*, he warned himself. He heard Anne's voice saying that, since she had suggested that to him hundreds of times during their marriage.

"Not quite like *The Turn of the Screw*," he said, "but subtle in the same way." *Subtle*. *"Sometimes it's necessary for something to be subtle to be truly beautiful."*

Michelle batted ashes into the small bowl she'd brought out to use as an ashtray. She waited.

"In 'The Jolly Corner,' " continued Dale, "James has one of his typically Jamesian protagonists—a fifty-six-year-old guy named Spencer Brydon—return to New York and the States after decades spent in Europe. Brydon's coming back to check on some property of his, including a tall old home in Manhattan where he grew up . . ."

"A place his family called The Jolly Corner," guessed Michelle.

"Right. Anyway, the house is empty—no furniture—but in the story, Brydon becomes obsessed with it, returning night after night to climb the stairways and wander through the empty rooms in the dark, carrying only a small lantern or a candle . . . searching for something . . . for someone . . ."

"A ghost," said Michelle.

"A Jamesian ghost," agreed Dale. "Actually, Spencer Brydon is convinced that The Jolly Corner is haunted by the ghost of his alternate self."

"Alternate self?" Michelle's eyes were very green in the dying candlelight.

Dale shrugged. The cigarette smoke made him want a cigarette, although he had not smoked in more than twenty-five years. "The person he could and would have been if he had stayed in the United States," he said. "If he had pursued money rather than the finer things of life he found in Europe."

"Whoo," Michelle said sarcastically. "Sounds scary. Real Stephen King territory."

"Actually, it *is* sort of scary," said Dale, trying to remember whether Clare had been in any of his graduate classes where he discussed "The Jolly Corner." He thought not. "When he finally confronts the ghost of his alternate self," he went on, "the apparition is pretty awful—brutal, missing fingers, a sort of Mr. Hyde to Spencer Brydon's sophisticated Dr. Jekyll." Dale closed his eyes for a second, trying to remember James's phrasing. " 'Rigid and conscious, spectral yet human, a man of his own substance and stature waited there to measure himself with his power to dismay.' "

"Cool," said Michelle. "You have a good memory."

Dale shook his head. "I just emphasize the same phrase over the years of teaching the story . . . over the decades of teaching the story." He frowned. "Anyway—not much more to the tale. Spencer Brydon confronts the ghost of himself in the middle of the night and . . ."

"Dies?"

"Faints," said Dale. He smiled. "This *is* a Jamesian hero, after all."

"That's how the story ends?" said Michelle, stubbing out her cigarette and looking dubious, a producer who had not especially liked a screenwriter's pitch. "He faints? That's it?"

Dale rubbed his chin. "Not quite. You get the idea that Spencer Brydon might have died—he's unconscious for hours—except for the fact that his older lady friend, Alice Staverton, I think her name is, had come to the house with premonitions of danger for him. She gets the housekeeper—Mrs. Maloney or Mrs. Muldoon or some such—to let her in, and Brydon comes to with his head on Alice's lap. His head pillowed, I think James puts it, 'in extraordinary softness and faintly refreshing fragrance.' "

"Sexy," said Michelle.

Dale actually blushed. "I don't think he . . . I mean, not deliberately . . . anyway, you get the idea in the end that he's been saved from his alternate self by the love of a good woman . . ."

Michelle snorted politely. "The love of a good woman," she said softly. "That's a phrase I haven't heard for a while."

Dale nodded, still blushing like an idiot. "So it ends with Alice Staverton saying to Brydon, 'And he isn't—no he isn't—you,' or something like that, and hugging Brydon to her breast." Dale quit, feeling sorry that he had brought the whole thing up.

Michelle smiled again and looked toward the ceiling. "So that's what we're going to find up there? Our alternate selves? Who we would have been if we'd both stayed in Elm Haven?"

"Scary thought, isn't it?" said Dale, returning her smile.

"Terrifying," agreed Michelle. She stood, reached into the purse she'd hung from the back of her chair, and removed a box opener. She thumbed a catch that slid a razor blade out of the end of the thing. "I came prepared."

"Is that to fight off the ghosts?" said Dale, rising with her.

"No, stupid. It's to cut through the plastic."

FOURTEEN

I COULDN'T have told Dale what was waiting for him upstairs. I didn't know. The Old Man had sealed off the second floor when I was three years old—not long after my mother died—and I had no memory of ever being up there. It may seem weird to have spent eight years in a house with the second floor sealed off behind plastic, but it didn't seem that strange at the time. The Old Man was a fanatic for saving money, and I knew that it cost too much to heat the whole house for just the two of us. Also, on the second floor was their bedroom—the Old Man's and my mother's—and I understood early on that he hadn't wanted to sleep up there after she died. Not that she died in the room. She died in the hospital at Oak Hill. At any rate, sleeping space was no problem as I got older—as old as I got—since the Old Man slept in his study and I began sleeping in the basement even before I went off to kindergarten.

As for calling the farm The Jolly Corner, well, that was just a conceit of mine after I'd read the James story when I was about seven. Essentially, I just liked the sound of the name. It's true that the farm was anything but jolly with the Old Man on his regular drunken binges—he got angry when he drank—and both of us living our mostly silent and separate lives there. If there were any "alternative selves" haunting the house then, they belonged to the Old Man. My father had been intelligent enough, but he lacked that human gene that allows people to finish things. He'd dropped out of Harvard before World War II for no reason that he ever explained to me, and even with the GI Bill, he'd never gotten around to returning to school. His brother, my uncle Art, had not only graduated from college but had taught on the university level for a while. In a real sense, my uncle Art was the Jolly Corner-ish alternate-self ghost that the Old Man had to confront—Uncle Art had avoided the booze, written books, taught, traveled, married frequently, and basically just enjoyed himself through his life. Perhaps the Old Man lacked this enjoyment gene as well.

This Jolly Corner-ish idea of who he had become and what he had lost along the way had been buzzing through Dale Stewart's brain for months. In writing his novel about the kids of Elm Haven in the summer of 1960, Dale had been staring unblinkingly at an innocence and breadth of potential that might have remained better off forgotten.

Potential, Dale had decided, was precisely the sort of curse that the *Peanuts* character Linus had once said it was. It was a burden before it was realized, and a constant specter after it had been failed to be realized. And every day, every hour, every small decision made, eliminated the remaining set of potential until—in what post-fifty Dale considered his last home stretch of life—that potential was fast dwindling toward zero.

Clare had once described the topography of life in those terms—an inverted cone dwindling to zero potential. Now Dale agreed with that figure.

The reality of opening up the second floor of the house had sobered Dale a bit. He had Michelle wait while he went into his study and returned with the baseball bat.

"Is that going to protect us from the ghosts?" she asked.

Dale shrugged. He'd also brought a flashlight, and he held it on the barricade of yellowed plastic as Michelle pulled out her box opener. "Do you want to do the honors?" she asked.

Dale's hands were full with the bat and flashlight, so he just nodded to her. "You go ahead."

Michelle did not hesitate. She cut through the first sheet of plastic with a lateral incision that ran four or five feet from the upper right to the lower left. Then she made a diagonal cut in the opposite direction. The brittle plastic peeled back as she tugged the first layer open. A second and third layer remained.

"Still time to change our minds," said Michelle. Her eyes were bright.

Dale shook his head, and Michelle cut through the remaining plastic, pulling it free from the frame as if she were eagerly opening a Christmas present.

Dale didn't know what he had expected—a sigh of sour air, perhaps, or a rushing in or rushing out of sealed-in atmosphere. But the plastic folded back, and if the air on the other side was anything but colder than the downstairs air, he could not detect it. He *could* detect the cold, however. It flowed out through the torn plastic like a frigid river. Michelle clicked shut the box opener and hugged herself. The cold made her nipples press against her blouse.

"Dark in there," she said softly, almost whispering. "Cold."

Dale nodded, stepped into the upstairs hallway, and jerked the flashlight beam to and fro. It was not much like his dream. There were no rooms to the right of the bare hallway, and only two closed doors on the left. He could see the same narrow table against the wall that he'd glimpsed the first time he peered through the plastic. There was a Victorian-style lamp on it. Heavy drapes covered the windows. The hardwood floor—no rug here—seemed strangely absent of dust. Could this space really have been sealed off for almost five decades without accumulating dust?

Propping the baseball bat against the table for a moment, Dale turned the old-fashioned switch on the lamp. Nothing. Either the bulb was burned out or Mr. McBride had cut off power to the second floor. *Well, duh,* he thought. *It was fifty years ago.*

Michelle took his arm. "Why didn't we do this in the daylight?" she whispered.

"Too stupid," said Dale. His voice sounded loud in the hardwood hallway. "Plus we had some drinking to do." He lifted the bat again and took a few steps into the hall, with Michelle following closely. "You'd better stay over there by the stairs," he said, all gallantry.

"Uh-huh, yeah, sure," answered the redhead. "Like in the movies— *Let's split up.* No offense, Dale Stewart, but fuck you."

Dale grinned at this. They paused by the door to the front bedroom. The room held only an old-fashioned bed—stripped of sheets and pillows, the mattress pad yellowed with age but otherwise looking oddly clean—and a single dresser with no mirror. There was a built-in closet, but the door was open and it was empty. Without entering the front bedroom, Dale moved on to the second room, trying to remember the details of his dream.

Whatever the scary details had been, the second bedroom did not live up to them. The room was empty except for a small child's rocking chair set precisely in the center of the square space, but directly above the rocking chair hung a massive and ornate chandelier. A huge, sepia-colored water stain covered much of the ceiling, looking like a faded fresco or a Rorschach test for giants.

"That's weird," whispered Michelle. "Why would they put a big chandelier up here? And that child's rocker . . ."

"If it starts rocking," said Dale, "I'm going to . . ."

"*Shut up!*" whispered Michelle with an urgency that may not have been pure acting.

They went into the room. Dale flicked a light switch. Nothing. He played the flashlight over the walls, the heavily draped windows, behind the door. Nothing of interest. Even the wallpaper designs had faded to indecipherability.

"Just think," Michelle said softly, "the last time the air up here was breathed, Dwight Eisenhower was president."

"That's just because whatever walks up here doesn't breathe," said Dale, using his best Rod Serling voice.

Michelle made a fist and hit him in the upper arm. It hurt.

"Let's take a look at that front bedroom." He paused out in the hall and played the flashlight beam over the north wall of the hallway. "Odd," he said, "the landing comes around here as if there should be a room on that side. There's certainly room for it—it'd be over the kitchen." The flashlight beam flicked back and forth, but there was only the ancient, faded wallpaper, with no sign of a doorway having been sealed off.

"The lost room," whispered Michelle.

" 'The Cask of Amontillado,' " said Dale.

"Pardon?"

Dale shook his head and led the way to the front bedroom. The cold up here really was brutal. He began wondering about re-fixing the plastic to seal off this floor again.

He stepped into the room without any sense of drama, but the sensation hit him so hard that he stopped in his tracks, almost stepping back into the hall. "Jesus Christ," he said without meaning to.

"What?" demanded Michelle, squeezing his arm tightly.

"Don't you feel that?"

"Feel what?" She looked at him in the reflected light from the flashlight beam. "Don't kid anymore, Dale."

Dale was not kidding. Not being well versed in the supernatural, he did not know what to expect in a so-called haunted room—the usual, probably: a deathly cold spot, the kind of smell of rotting meat that had greeted him during his first moments in the house, perhaps a sense of something cold and dead brushing past him like a blind breeze.

This was none of that.

The instant Dale had entered the room, he had been all but overcome by a wave of absolute physical desire. No, not desire. That was too weak a word. *Lust.* His erection had been immediate and powerful, and the only thing that kept Michelle from noticing it now was the darkness and the fact that he had worn a long cardigan sweater for the semiformal Thanksgiving dinner.

But even more powerful than the erection was the frenzy of lust that surged through his system. He turned to Michelle, not knowing what to say, and he immediately noticed the nipples still visibly straining against her blouse, the exposed cleavage there, the curve of her hips, her red hair—her pubic hair would still be red, the skin on her soft abdomen almost certainly a soft white, the lips of her sex a pale pink— and he had the urge, no, almost the absolute need, to drop the stupid baseball bat, set the flashlight down, pull her onto the bed, press her down, tear her clothes off, and . . .

"Jesus Christ," Dale said again and stepped back out into the hallway.

The waves of lust abated the instant he stepped across the threshold. The erection remained, but it no longer controlled him.

"What?" demanded Michelle. She had followed him out into the hall but was looking back into the room with real alarm. His flashlight beam wavered on the hallway wall, and the bedroom was black with darkness. "What?"

Dale shook his head. He had the wild urge to laugh senselessly. Whoever heard of a haunted room that gave you hard-ons? Not a haunting, but a boning.

"What is it?" asked Michelle, dropping her grip on his arm but stepping in front of him.

Dale took a step back, half afraid that his erection would brush against her, afraid that even the softest touch of her large breasts against him would set him off again. He held the flashlight to one side, allowing the darkness to conceal him.

"Did you feel anything?" he asked at last.

"No. Did you?"

"Yeah," said Dale. That syllable was an understatement. He had come very close to raping this visitor, this near-stranger, this fifty-one-year-old woman. Dale shook his head again, feeling the last tidal surges of lust disappearing. He had not felt such an erotic moment since his late adolescence, and possibly not even then. *This*, he thought, *must be the kind of wild loss of sexual control that the brain-dead fundamentalists are afraid of when they try to ban pornography— to ban anything erotic. Sex with no humanity at all. Pure sexual energy, absolute desire. A fucking frenzy.* He looked back at the darkened doorway. The Scientific Method demanded that he step back through there and see what happened.

Not today, Charlie, thought Dale.

"What was it?" said Michelle, no humor in her voice now. She grabbed Dale by the upper arms and shook him slightly. "Did you see something? Smell something?"

Dale raised the flashlight between them, causing her to release his arms, and tried to smile. "Just an . . . emotion," he said huskily. "Hard to describe."

"Sadness?" said Michelle.

"Not quite."

"What, then?"

He looked at her pale face in the reddish light. "You didn't feel anything in there? Nothing at all?"

She squinted slightly. "Right now I'm feeling pissed off. If this is your idea of a joke, it's not really funny."

Dale nodded in agreement and tried to smile again. "Sorry. I think it's just the effect of the wine and beer. I don't drink that often and . . . well, I'm taking some medicines that may interact with it." *True*, he thought, *but both the Prozac and the sleeping pills make me impotent, not horny.* "Maybe we'd better go back downstairs," he said aloud. Part of his hindbrain was still commanding him to drag Michelle Staffney into that darkness and fuck her brains out.

"Yes," said Michelle, looking intently at him, "maybe we'd better go back downstairs. It's getting late. I'd better be going."

FIFTEEN

Driving into the Blackfeet Reservation that lovely autumn day four years earlier, Dale tried to make conversation with Clare Hart—aka Clare Two Hearts. This area was known to Montana residents as "the Rocky Mountain Front"—or more simply, "the Front"—and the aptness of the phrase was everywhere visible, with the snowcapped peaks rising up high to their right as they headed south on Highway 89 and the rolling, empty plains sprawling off to infinity on their left. Dale glanced at his passenger several times, awaiting some comment, but Clare had nothing more to say about the view than she had in Glacier Park.

"Do you want to stop at the Museum of the Plains Indian?" asked Dale as they entered the reservation town of Browning.

"No," said Clare. She watched the shabby town fall behind with its tourist traps and shops—many closed now after the end of the tourist season—selling their "authentic Indian artifacts."

"Does all this make you angry?" asked Dale.

She turned to look at him with those piercingly clear eyes of hers. "No. Why should it, Professor Stewart?"

Dale lifted a palm. The homes on either side were rusted-out trailers with junked pickup trucks lying about in the gravel and scrub brush. "The injustice of the history to . . . to your people. Your mother's people. The poverty."

Clare smiled slightly. "Professor *Stewart*. Do you get all worked up about historical injustices to your Scottish ancestors?"

"That's different," said Dale.

"Oh? Why?"

Again he gestured with his open hand. "I've never even been to Scotland."

"This is the first time I've been to Blackfeet country."

"You know what I mean," said Dale. "This economic injustice against the Blackfeet—the alcoholism, the illiteracy, the unemployment on the reservation—it's all still going on."

"And Scotland still isn't independent," Clare said softly. She sighed. "I know what you're talking about, Professor Stewart, but it just isn't in me to have much interest in all of the historical grudges in the world. My mother and I lived in Florence, but my stepfather's ancestral house is in Mantua. In that part of the world, every city has tales of oppression by every other city. Every old family remembers a thousand years of injustice and oppression at the hands of almost every other family. Sometimes I think that remembering too much history is like alcohol or heroin—an addiction that seems to give meaning to your life but just wears you down and destroys you in the end."

Why the hell are we here on this godforsaken reservation, then? Dale wanted to ask. He kept silent.

The followed Highway 89 down into the river bottom around Two Medicine River, then up, then down again across Badger Creek.

"Turn here, please," said Clare, looking up from a road map and pointing to a paved road that ran west. A small sign read HEART BUTTE ROAD. They drove west along Badger Creek toward the mountains and then south again, paralleling the foothills. Heart Butte, when they reached it, was a sad scattering of falling-down houses, trailers, a few double-wide mobile homes, and a concrete-block "recreation building" that looked as if it had been abandoned shortly after its completion. It was hard to tell the discarded pickups from those still in use. Everything had a psychic stench of poverty and despair hanging over it.

"Your mother was born here?" said Dale. That was what Clare had told him, but he wanted some conversation to leaven the sad scenery they were passing.

Clare nodded.

"Are you hunting for the house she lived in?" asked Dale. A few Blackfeet children watched them drive past. The children's expressions were dead and incurious.

Clare shook her head. "It burned down a long time ago. I . . . there, please stop." She pointed to a small trailer no different than most they had passed.

Dale pulled into the dusty drive behind an old pickup and waited. "Do you know these people?"

Clare shook her head again. They sat in the Land Cruiser and waited. After a while, a middle-aged woman came to the screen door of the trailer and looked at them with no more curiosity than the children had shown. She disappeared from the door for several minutes and then returned and stepped out onto the cinderblock stoop.

"Please stay here," whispered Clare and got out of the truck. She walked over toward the woman, stopped about five feet away, and began speaking softly. The woman responded brusquely and squinted in Dale's direction. Clare spoke again. Dale heard only snippets of the conversation but was surprised to hear that they were speaking in Pikuni, the language of the Blackfeet.

Finally the Blackfeet woman nodded, spoke a few syllables, and went back into her trailer. She reappeared a moment later and climbed into the ancient pickup truck.

Clare walked back to the Land Cruiser on the driver's side. "Do you mind if I drive for a few miles?"

Mystified, Dale only shook his head, clambered out, and went around to the passenger side. The Blackfeet woman backed past them in a cloud of dust.

Clare adjusted the driver's seat and backed out, hurrying a bit to keep the woman's pickup in sight without driving into the dust cloud the vehicle kicked up on the gravel road.

They followed the other truck away from Heart Butte, down several crude BIA roads, along Jeep tracks, then west along another BIA road that headed off toward the foothills. They stopped several times for the older woman to get out of her truck and open stock gates. Each time, after they drove through, Clare would clamber out and close the gate behind them.

Once a man on a roan horse stopped the pickup, spoke briefly with the driver, and then rode back to stare at Clare and Dale for a moment. The man was dressed in basic cowboy work clothes, sweat-stained hat and all, and the only hint that he was Blackfeet was the dark, wide face with deep-black eyes.

He brusquely addressed Clare in a Pikuni dialect—Dale had heard the language used on campus by some of the Native American students and one professor, although these words sounded different some-how—and Clare answered his questions in the same language. The man finally fell silent, stared at Clare a long moment, nodded ever so slightly, wheeled his horse around, and rode away to the east.

The pickup started up again, and the Land Cruiser followed slowly.

Two miles further the BIA road ended. The Blackfeet woman turned her truck around and climbed down. Clare got out. Dale hesitated, wanting to speak to the other woman but not wanting to intrude on the silent scene. He stayed where he was.

The older woman said something that sounded angry but then quickly hugged Clare, got back in her pickup, and drove away in a cloud of dust.

Clare came back to the Land Cruiser. "We have to walk from here," she said.

"Where?" said Dale. He looked around. No ranch houses or trailers were in sight. Nothing man-made was visible except for a distant fence.

Ridges rose higher as they ran west to the Front. The land here was high desert and grasslands blending into the forested foothills. The only road visible was the one they had come in on.

"A mile or two," said Clare. She squinted at the afternoon sun lowering itself toward the high peaks. "We'll have time. Let's use some of that backpacking equipment you have."

"Will you tell me what our destination is?"

"Sure," said Clare. She was already pulling their packs and hiking boots out of the back of the Land Cruiser. "I'd like to spend the night at a place called Ghost Ridge."

It began snowing in earnest the day after Thanksgiving. Dale walked for hours that day, hands deep in the pockets of his wool peacoat. He had not remembered autumns in the Midwest being so wintry.

Duane's farmhouse was colder after the removal of the plastic barrier at the head of the stairs. It was as if a cold wind was blowing down from the second floor—or as if the heat of formerly inhabited parts of the house was bleeding away into outer space through some hole upstairs. Dale had shivered in the study until almost 3:00 A.M. after Michelle Staffney left and then had given up and gone down to the basement to sleep. It was warm near the furnace and the glow from the furnace and the old console radio, volume set low so that the music was not much more than a whisper, lulled Dale to sleep.

The next morning he had cleaned up the last of the clutter from their Thanksgiving dinner and then had gone upstairs. It was bitter cold there. Hesitating a second, Dale finally worked up courage to step across the threshold of the front bedroom.

Erotic excitement hit him like a tsunami. He forced himself to stand there, just inside the doorway, letting the tide of lust flow over him.

Dale had always thought of himself as a physical, if not overly sensual, person, but this wave of desire was pure lust—physical excitement completely removed from thoughts of romance or love or the reality of another person. Dale was bombarded with half-images of penises, breasts, vaginas, pubic hair, sweat, nipples, erections, and semen spurting; he heard the moans of passion and the whispered filthy nonsense that only the drunkenness of desire could free one to whisper. Blood flowed into his own straining erection, and his pulse pounded in his ears.

Dale staggered out into the upper hallway, caught his breath, and went down to the relative warmth and sanity of the kitchen to recover. It took ten minutes for his body to release the coiled spring of desire.

What the hell is going on? Dale had never heard of a psychic phenomenon consisting of a place haunted with . . . with what? Sexual stimulation. "Fucking weird," he said aloud and had to smile at the appropriateness of that phrase.

He went into the study to work on his novel. The screen was black except for a message on the black DOS screen.

>The lords of right and truth are Thoth and Astes, the Lord Amentet. The Tchatcha round about Osiris are Kesta, Hapi, Tuamutef, and Qebhsenuf, and they are also round about the Constellation of the Thigh in the northern sky. Those who do away utterly sins and offenses, and who are in the following of the goddess Hetepsekhus, are the god Sebek and his associates who dwell in the water.

Dale stared at the message for a moment. Finally he typed—

>You're getting long-winded. What's with this Egyptian shit? I thought you just communicated in Old English. Who the hell is this? What do you want?

He waited, but there was no answer. Dale walked out to the kitchen, poured a glass of orange juice, and returned to the study. Only the previous lines of text glowed on the screen.

>**Fuck you and the Nile barge you rode in on,** typed Dale. He turned off his computer, went back to the kitchen, pulled on his pea-coat, and went out into the snow for a walk.

The black dog was following him. Dale was about half a mile north and west of the farmhouse, walking along the line of trees toward the creek, when he looked back and saw the dog moving slowly along his trail. The heavily falling snow made it hard to see details, but it was obvious that this hound—although black with a pink patch on its muzzle—was four times the size of the little dog that he had first seen. Even more disturbing was the fact that four other black dogs—all large, but not as large as the hound in the lead—were also following his tracks in the snow.

Dale stopped, heart pounding, and looked around for a weapon—a fallen fence post, a heavy stick, anything. Nothing came to hand.

The hounds had stopped about forty yards away. Their coats were impossibly black against the snowy fields and falling snow.

Dale began moving more quickly—not running for fear that he would cause the hounds to give chase, but walking in a half-jog—trying to get to the little patch of woods, where he could find a tree big enough to climb. The saplings along the fence here were far too small.

The black dogs shuffled along behind him, keeping their distance but following relentlessly.

Dale was panting when he reached the trees. He climbed the fence and moved quickly into the woods, looking for a tree with stout branches.

What am I afraid of? Am I really going to let some stray dogs tree me way out here? He looked back through the snow and the tree trunks, saw the black dogs pausing at the point where he had entered the thin screen of trees—saw how huge the lead hound really was, larger than any rottweiler or Doberman Dale had ever seen—and realized instantly that the answer to his question was *You're damned right I am.*

Dale found a tree with branches that would hold his weight, grabbed a branch in readiness to climb, and looked back, half expecting the black hounds to be bounding into the darkness of the woods, tongues lolling, teeth bared, eyes burning red . . .

The dogs were gone.

Dale stood there breathing hard, swiveling, certain that the pack of wild dogs had moved to flank him somehow.

The only sounds in the little woods were his ragged breathing and the soft fall of snow.

He waited ten minutes—until his hands and feet were freezing and the drying sweat on his face and body had started to chill him—and then he ripped one of the stouter lower branches off and walked back the way he had come.

The dogs were gone. But dog prints were everywhere. *Ghosts and demon dogs don't leave paw prints,* he thought, and tried to smile at his own silliness. Tried and failed.

The prints headed back toward the farm, disappearing into the falling snow.

Dale headed east, following the ridgeline back to County 6 where it came out at Calvary Cemetery. Clambering over Mr. Johnson's fence across the road from the cemetery, Dale saw a man moving at the far end of the graveyard.

Give me a break, thought Dale. *More ghosties.* In truth, however, Dale was relieved to see someone. Perhaps the man had a car or pickup back there, obscured by the heavily falling snow.

No tire tracks leading into the cemetery, he thought. The snow was four or five inches deep already and falling more heavily than ever.

"Hey!" shouted Dale, waving across the black iron fence at the distant figure. "Hey there!"

The form paused. A blank face turned Dale's way. Even from fifty yards away, through the heavy snow, Dale could see the khaki-colored army uniform and the old-style campaign hat with its broad brim. He saw no eyes, nor any features. The distant face was a pink blob.

The man started moving his way, but not walking—there was no gait and rise and fall of walking—but, rather, gliding—seeming to slide over and through the gray tombstones and low bushes.

Okay, thought Dale. *Fuck this.* He ran and slid down the steep hill, panted up the steep rise past Uncle Henry and Aunt Lena's old place, and did not stop running until he was a quarter of a mile beyond the cemetery, glancing over his shoulder the whole way. The khaki-clad figure had not pursued him.

Dale half expected to see the black dogs waiting for him in Duane's long driveway, but there was only snow, piling up deeper by the moment. But there were tire tracks being buried in that heavily falling snow. Dale put his hands in his peacoat pockets, tucked his chin down, and walked into the westerly wind, blinking snow out of his eyes.

A sheriff's car was parked in the turnaround. Sheriff C. J. Congden levered himself out of the driver's seat and stepped out as Dale came up to the driveway. The fat man had one hand on his gunbelt and the other hand on the butt of his pistol.

SIXTEEN

IT was almost dark by the time Clare and Dale set down their packs. Ghost Ridge looked like any of the other nearby ridges. A cool evening wind from the west stirred the tall grass around them.

"Are we camping here?" asked Dale, trying to catch his breath. Even though Clare had insisted on taking the backpacking tent in her rucksack, she had set a fast pace.

"No," said Clare. The wind stirred her short dark hair. "This place is sacred to the Blackfeet." She pointed to a long, narrow lake running east below the ridge. "We can camp down there as long as we move around to the other side of the lake."

"Why is this place sacred?" Even as he asked the question, Dale remembered her earlier comment of how almost every natural site was sacred to someone.

"About six hundred Blackfeet died near here during the bad winter of 1883–84," said Clare. "The tribe buried the bodies here." She looked around, reached into her rucksack, and took out a battery-powered backpacker's headlamp. "I can lead the way down to the lake."

"Wait a minute. How did you know about this place?"

"My mother told me. She used to ride her horse here from Heart Butte when she was little."

"And did your mother teach you Pikuni?" asked Dale.

Clare nodded. Dale realized that he could see her more by starlight now than by the fading twilight. She had not yet switched on the small headlamp. "My mother and I used to speak the Blackfeet language when we wanted privacy," she said softly, her voice almost lost under the sighing of the high grass in the night breeze. "That was the older, traditional dialect that I used with Tina."

"Tina?"

"The lady who led us here. Her Blackfeet name is *Apik-stis-tsi-maki*—Crystal Creek Woman. She used to run the *I-am-skin-ni-taki* before she moved to Heart Butte."

"*I-am-skin-ni-taki*," repeated Dale. "That sounds as if it has to do with skinwalkers and tribal medicine. Was she a . . . a shaman? A holy woman?"

"*I-am-skin-ni-taki* translates as 'Cut Hair Salon,' " said Clare. "It's a hairstyling place in Browning that offers skin therapy, massages, and saunas as well as cuts."

"How'd you know that she could speak traditional Pikuni?" asked Dale.

"There were indications outside her house."

"What kind of indications?"

"Subtle ones," said Clare. She gestured toward the lake. "If we don't get hiking, we're going to be setting up the tent in absolute darkness."

"Okay," said Dale, but he hesitated. "Do you want to do anything here on the ridge first?"

"Like what?" said Clare. "Take a leak?"

"I was thinking of a prayer or something," said Dale. "Some sort of Blackfeet ceremony."

He could see Clare's teeth flash in the starlight. She set the headlamp straps on her head and clicked on the light. "I don't know any

Blackfeet prayers," she said, "and I'm not big on ceremony." She began hiking down the hill.

Dale paused in the farmhouse driveway. C. J. Congden was between him and the side door. The snow was turning into a cold rain.

"What do you want, Congden?"

"It's *Sheriff* Congden to you, Stewart," rasped the fat man.

"Fine," said Dale. "Then it's *Mr.* Stewart to you, Sheriff. What do you want?"

"I want you to get the fuck out of here."

Dale blinked at this. "What?"

"You heard me. You don't belong here, *Mr.* Stewart."

"What the hell does that mean?" said Dale, trying to be amused by this *Deliverance*-style dialogue.

"Something bad's gonna happen if you stay here."

"Is that a threat, Sheriff?"

"I don't make threats," said Congden in a flat, almost lifeless voice. "That's just the way it is."

"I'm not bothering anyone here," said Dale, trying to keep his voice from showing the real anger he felt at this redneck talk. "Why don't you earn your salary and find the people who let the air out of my truck tires rather than threatening law-abiding citizens?" He could hear how stilted his words sounded even as he spoke them.

Congden stared at him through the sleeting drizzle. The brim of his Western-style hat dripped. The sheriff's eyes were thin black slits in his fat face. "You heard me, *Mr.* Stewart. Get the fuck out of here before something happens."

"I think that the next thing to happen is me calling my lawyer about this harassment," said Dale. It was pure bluster. Except for a divorce lawyer he'd consulted once a year ago, Dale knew no lawyers.

Congden turned away, lowered himself ponderously into his sheriff's car, and drove away in the snow.

What next? thought Dale. He went into the house, took off his soaked peacoat, boots, and socks in the kitchen, stood over the heating vent for a moment, and then went into the study to get dry clothes.

The computer screen was still on DOS, but there was a new line of text under his "Fuck you and the Nile barge you rode in on" line.

>**He's right, Dale. If you don't get out of here, you'll end up as dead as Congden.**

Dale stood staring at the two sentences. It was the first time the unknown hacker had written anything that didn't amount to abstract drivel. Whoever was writing this shit knew who he was and where he was and that he'd just spoken to Congden.

How? And what the hell does it mean—". . . as dead as Congden"? Is something going to get both of us? Perhaps it was his wet feet and jeans, or perhaps it was the chill breeze sliding down the stairway from the frigid second floor, but something caused Dale to start shivering, his teeth literally chattering.

So, do you believe in ghosts?" asked Dale about half an hour after he and Clare had crawled into their sleeping bags. They had made a quick dinner of soup, Dale had spent ten frustrating minutes trying to get the campfire lighted with old matches blowing out in the wind before Clare removed a cigarette lighter from her pocket and lighted it with one try, and—even though they'd pitched the tent in case of rain—they'd set their bags out under the stars. Wind-driven waves lapped at the shore of the small lake fifteen yards away.

"My mother does," said Clare. "She saw several right here at Ghost Ridge."

Dale looked up at the hill looming above them. The rustling grasses sounded like urgent whispers. "But do you?" he asked.

"I don't believe in ghosts," Clare said softly, "but I saw one once."

Dale waited, lying on his stomach in the comfortable confines of the sleeping bag and cupping his chin in his palm.

"I mentioned that my stepfather has a place in Mantua," continued Clare at last. "My father was an artist in Florence, but after he was killed in an auto wreck, Mother married this older man from Mantua—his family has earned uncounted millions selling salami. The Salami King. A perfect title for the husband of one of Europe's foremost divas.

"Anyway, I was about ten when Mother married this guy—his family made me nervous because the Salami King had a son six years older than me who's always on the make—and we went to stay at his house in Mantua. We still spend several weeks every spring and autumn there—the summers and winters are miserable. Do you really want to hear this story, Professor Stewart?"

"Yes," said Dale.

"The Mantua house is truly incredible," said Clare. "The Salami King commissioned an architect back in the seventies to combine three old homes dating back to the sixteenth century and a courtyard into one huge home with interior design straight out of the twenty-third century. The stairway up to the library, for instance, doesn't even have railings—just a single spiraling ribbon of steel for support and raw wood steps with skinny steel cables hanging on either side. It looks like some sort of dinosaur vertebrae rising up between these ancient terra cotta walls covered with the remnants of frescoes from the seventeen hundreds.

"Anyway, my room is just off the library, near the service elevator, and I have windows that look both outward onto the piazza and inward down onto the ancient courtyard that the architect had enclosed with clear Plexiglas doors and roofed in with steel. One night that first autumn we visited, I awoke some time after three A.M. to the sound of a woman weeping. At first I was afraid it was Mother—this was less than a year after Father's death and I knew she sometimes cried in private—but this crying was louder, coarser than anything I'd ever heard from Mother. I ran to the open interior window, since the crying was coming from inside the house.

"It was a woman dressed in black, just like so many of the old Italian women in Mantua and Florence today. But this was not an old woman. She wore a scarf, but I could see long, lustrous black hair escaping from it, and I could tell by her carriage and figure that she was a younger woman—in her twenties, perhaps. And she was carrying a baby. A dead baby."

"How could you tell it was dead?" whispered Dale.

"I could tell," said Clare. "The baby's eyes were sunken and glazed over and staring. Its flesh was bloated and white beyond white. Its little hands were frozen into claws by rigor mortis. I could almost *smell* it."

"Your window onto the courtyard was that close?" said Dale, trying not to sound skeptical.

"It was that close," said Clare. "And then the woman looked up at me. Not at me, not through me, but *into* me. And then she just . . . disappeared. One instant she and the baby were there, the next instant they weren't."

"You said you were ten," suggested Dale.

Clare had been lying on her back, looking at the stars as she recited all this, but now she rolled over to look at him. The little backpack stove sat between them, separating their bedrolls like a modern-day sword of honor.

"I was ten, but I saw what I saw," she said softly.

"And, of course, there's a legend in the town about a woman whose baby died in that house," said Dale.

"Of course," said Clare. "Actually, the baby had drowned in the well that used to be in that particular courtyard. The mother—who was only twenty, it turned out—refused to allow the child to be buried. She carried it around for weeks until the Mantuans restrained her and buried the child. Then the mother threw herself down the same well. That all happened late in the sixteen hundreds."

"Good legend," said Dale.

"I thought so."

"Any chance that you heard the legend *before* you saw the ghost?" he asked.

"No," said Clare Two Hearts. "No chance at all. My stepfather and his family wouldn't talk about what I saw. I finally coaxed the story out of an eighty-six-year-old cook whose family had served the household for five generations."

Dale had rubbed his chin, feeling the stubbled whiskers there. "So you do believe in ghosts," he said.

"No," said Clare Two Hearts. There was a silence, and then the two of them laughed at the same time.

"What *do* you believe, Clare?" asked Dale.

She looked at him for a long moment. Then she unzipped her old sleeping bag and folded back the top, in spite of the cold air. She had slipped out of her jeans and sweatshirt before crawling into the bag and now her bra and underpants glowed very white in the starlight.

"I believe," she said, "that if you come over here, Professor Stewart, our lives are going to be changed in some way that neither one of us can imagine."

Dale had hesitated, but only for the space of ten or fifteen wild heartbeats.

The five black dogs circled the farmhouse for days. When Dale came outside, they retreated to the fields or disappeared behind the out-buildings and barn. When he went back inside, they moved in close, circling, sitting, watching. Their tracks were everywhere in the melting snow and mud. At night he could hear them howl.

Finally he got tired of them, went out to his Land Cruiser, and drove to Oak Hill. There was a hardware store there that sold firearms and ammunition. Dale bought two boxes of .410-long shells. Driving out of Oak Hill, he saw the tall cornices of the Carnegie Library and pulled into the tiny parking lot. He had come here a few times as a kid—the Elm Haven library had been tiny, its books musty with age—but Dale knew that Duane had used this library regularly, sometimes walking all the way from his farm on the railroad tracks to do research here.

A weight seemed to lift off Dale's shoulders as he settled into a study carrel and began to read from the heap of books he had collected in the stacks. This was more his métier—the books, the quiet hum of purposeful reading, the lamps on the tables—a clean, well-lighted place.

Dale took a crumpled page of yellow legal-pad paper out of his pocket. He had been carrying around the handwritten list of DOS messages for days. Now he looked at the last quote.

>**The lords of right and truth are Thoth and Astes, the Lord Amentet. The Tchatcha round about Osiris are Kesta, Hapi, Tuamutef, and Qebhsenuf, and they are also round about the Constellation of the Thigh in the northern sky. Those who do away utterly sins and offenses, and who are in the following of the goddess Hetepsekhus, are the god Sebek and his asso-ciates who dwell in the water.**

Dale had never researched or taught Egyptian mythology, but as an undergraduate decades earlier he had gone through an avid Howard Carter phase, so he remembered some of this context and knew the source. These words were from the papyrus of Ani, also known as *The Egyptian Book of the Dead*. Amazingly, the Oak Hill Library had a copy of this book, and now Dale used the index to look up the various names.

Anubis, although not mentioned directly had to be involved and was the easiest god to track down: also known as Anpu, Anubis was the jackal-headed son of Nephthys and Osiris and the deity given the greatest duties in guiding souls to the afterlife and protecting them once they were there. Anubis was the god of embalming and the god of the dead, although it became obvious in *The Egyptian Book of the Dead* that this role was usurped by Osiris as the centuries rolled past. It was thought that Anubis wore the head of a jackal, or a dog, because of the jackals and wild dogs that lurked around the Egptian tombs, graves, and cities of the dead, always waiting for a rotting morsel.

Dale followed the research trail to Plutarch. The ancient historian had written:

> By Anubis they understand the horizontal circle, which divides the invisible, to which they give the name of Isis; and this circle equally touches upon the confines of both light and darkness, it may be looked upon as common to them both—and from this circumstance arose that resemblance, which they imagine between Anubis and the Dog, it being observed of this animal, that he is equally watchful as well by day as night. . . . This much, however, is certain, that in ancient times the Egyptians paid the greatest reverence and honor to the Dog, though by reasons of its devouring the Apis after Cambyses had slain him and thrown him out, when no animal would taste or so much as come near him, he then lost the first rank among the sacred animals which he had hitherto possessed.

Dale read on, following the maze of connections through the available books and then onto the Internet, using one of the library's surprisingly new computers. In all the sources, Anubis emerged as a psychopomp—the creature charged with ushering the souls of the dying from this world to the next. It was Anubis who mummified and prepared the corpse of Osiris. It was also the jackal god who assisted Maat in judging these souls for truth and was considered the primary messenger from the underworld. Anubis was the Opener of the Way, presiding over the oval gateway to the realm of the dead—that gateway known to the ancient Egyptians as the Dat, or Duat, or Tuat. Dale blinked at this, realizing that the Egyptian gateway to the dead was in the form of a vagina—that portal both to and from this life.

"Twat," he said aloud, appreciating the etymological geneology, and then realized that an elderly woman at the next computer was scowling fiercely at him. Dale smiled wanly and went back to his study carrel.

He realized that it would take days to track down the provenance of all the other spirits and gods mentioned in his short e-mail message, but he stayed at the books long enough to confirm that the "Constellation of the Thigh" was now known as the Great Bear and that the "Tchatcha," or spirits, of "Kesta, Hapi, Tuamutef, and Qebhsenuf" were the chosen from the Seven Spirits whom Anubis had appointed as guardians and protectors of the dead body of Osiris. The goddess Hetepsekhus, he discovered after two more hours of reading, was "the eye of Ra." He had no idea what that really meant, although it sounded like a sunbeam to him. He was getting tired.

Dale returned the Egyptian books to their shelves and looked at his crumpled paper. He looked at the first line of the first message he had copied:

gabble retchets yeth wisht hounds

Dale checked a library clock. It was after 6:00 P.M. The library closed at nine. He was starving. Sighing, unwilling to give up the hunt just yet, he went back to the stacks.

A moldering old book with a surrendering spine, a book that had, according to the still-used checkout stamps glued in the front, last been checked out on June 27, 1960—exactly the kind of book, Dale knew, that would have long since been thrown away by any "modern" library—provided him with the jackpot. The book was titled *English and Cornish Regional Myths and Folktales*. The "Yeth or Wisht Hounds" were, as he thought, Heath Hounds—demonic dogs given to wandering the moors. Hounds of the Baskervilles. Always black dogs. It turned out that demonic black dogs, phantom dogs, spectral dogs, had quite a history in Lancashire, West Yorkshire, Cornwall, and the Quantock Hills of Somerset.

At Brook House, Snitterfield, in an ancient home formerly called the Bell Brook Inn, during World War II, guests and locals observed a big black dog haunting the grounds. The dog had red eyes, and it left no footprints in the freshly tilled garden.

In 1190 A.D., near the Welsh Marches, a chronicler named Walter

Map wrote of spectral black hounds, huge and loathsome, haunting the fields. These spectral hounds invariably presaged violent death in the area.

On Sunday, August 4, 1577, the parishioners of the church in Bungay, Suffolk, huddled against a memorably violent thunderstorm. In several written accounts it was told of a terrifying black dog that suddenly appeared inside the church, slavering and howling, roaming the aisles while the faithful cried out for divine help. Three people touched the hound: two of them died instantly and the third shriveled up "like a drawne purse." In separate accounts but on the same August day in 1577, the same or similar hounds appeared in the church in Blythburgh, seven miles away, killing another three people there and "blasting" others.

Dale skipped ahead to 1613 A.D. when "a blacke dogge as bigg as a bull" suddenly appeared during services at Great Chart in Kent, killing more than a dozen people before demolishing a wall and disappearing.

Dale pulled down more old books, tracking the Black Dog legends all the way to *Beowulf*—learning that Grendel was primarily lupine, "him of eagum stod ligge gelicost leoht unfaeger"—"from his eyes shone a fire-like, baleful light," before watching the legend disappear into the mists of prehistory via the Frankish *Lex Salica*, the *Lex Ripuaria*, the legends of Odin's wolves in *Grímnismál*, and the Eddic poem *Helreith Brynhildar*, which spoke of the *hrot-garmr*, the "howling dog" that ate corpses and breathed fire. All of the black dogs in all of these legends seemed to be associated primarily with corpses, the dead, funeral grounds, funeral pyres, and the underworld. Dale was reminded that the *warg* was "a worrier of corpses."

Dale realized that he could make a doctoral dissertation out of this crap, given the proper primary sources and a few years. It looked as if the connection between spectral black dogs and the "realm of the dead" ran through Indo-European mythologies into prehistory, through Vedic, Greek, and Celtic myth, offered hellhounds in such epic Scandinavian poems as *Baldrs draumar* (Balder's Dreams), left paw prints through American Indian legend, and offered death-bound devil dogs romping through Altaic shamanic ritual and pre-Classical Greek thought and the Hindu *Mahabharata,* while all of it pointed straight back to old Anubis and his Egyptian underworld pals.

It gave Dale a headache.

He shelved the last of the books, realized that he was the only person in the building other than the librarian, saw with a shock that it was three minutes before 9:00 P.M., and went out into the cold night to his truck.

Dale was halfway between Oak Hill and Elm Haven when his cell phone rang. The sudden noise startled him enough that he almost drove off the dark county road. He grabbed the instrument from the passenger seat, where it had been lying for days.

"Hello?"

Silence on the line, but a sense of presence. In a wash of emotion that made him pull the truck to the side of the empty highway, Dale knew that it was his lover Clare on the line—Clare calling him after more than a year—Clare telling him that his life and reality could resume once again.

"Daddy?"

For an instant Dale felt only vertigo. The voice, the two syllables— all lacked context.

"Daddy? Are you there?" It was his older daughter, Margaret Beth, Mab, away at Clermont College in California.

"Mab? What is it, baby? What's wrong?"

An exhalation through the receiver. "We've been going crazy trying to get in touch with you, Daddy. Where have you been?"

Dale shook his head in confusion. A pickup truck drove past him in the night, an old man's face checking the Land Cruiser to see if Dale needed help.

"I've been right here in Illinois, kiddo. Right where I told everybody I'd be. Is everything all right?"

"Everything's all right here, Daddy. But you don't have a phone number there and you never answer your cell phone number. Katie and I have been trying to call you or write you. Did you get the letters we sent?"

Dale blinked. He had told his daughters as well as his colleagues and business associates that he would pick up his mail care of General Delivery in Elm Haven. He had never thought to do so.

"Sorry, kiddo," said Dale. "I've been . . . busy." He heard how silly that phrase sounded. "What's up, Mab? Are you calling from Clermont?"

"No, Daddy. I'm home for Christmas vacation. We needed to know if you were coming . . . back this way." Dale heard the unheard word—*home*.

"Christmas vacation?" he said, confused again. "It's weeks until your Christmas vacation, Mab. Why are you home early?"

There was a silence broken only by the idling of the Land Cruiser and the hiss of static and distance over the frozen fields. Then Mab said, "Dad . . . it's not early. Today's December twenty-second."

Dale laughed. "No it's not, kiddo. Thanksgiving was just a few days ago . . ." He paused, not wanting to tell his daughter that he had spent the holiday with a woman they had never heard about. "Seriously, why are you home early?"

"*Daddy,*" real frustration audible now. "It is *December twenty-second*. Tomorrow is the day before Christmas Eve. Now stop it. You're scaring me."

"Sorry, kiddo." It was all that Dale could think of to say. He looked at his watch, switching on the overhead light in the truck to check the date. The watch had stopped at 4:15. The date said the 8th, although he had no idea what month.

Another voice spoke. His younger daughter, Katie, her voice still cooler but deeper than Mab's. "Dad?" Katie had never called him Daddy.

"Hey, Butch," said Dale, using his old joke name for her. He tried to keep his voice light. "How's everything?"

"Where *are* you?" asked Katie.

Dale looked around at the dark fields, but he could see only his own reflection in the windows and windshield. "I'm here where I said I'd be. I'm sorry I haven't called or checked the mail. I just . . . got busy. I'm writing a novel. An important novel. I sort of . . . lost track of everything, I guess."

The cell phone's low battery indicator blinked once. Dale cursed softly to himself. He did not want to lose the call now.

"Daddy," said Mab, "are you coming home for Christmas?"

Dale felt as if someone had cut through his ribs and squeezed his heart once, very tightly. He took a breath. "I hadn't thought about it, kiddo. The ranch . . ." He stopped. The girls didn't want to hear about the ranch or its renters. He tried again. "Your mother . . ." he began and stopped.

"Mom didn't know if you'd be back in Missoula for Christmas," said Katie. It seemed to be a question.

"I don't think that she'd think that it was a good idea," Dale said at last.

The low battery indicator glowed steadily.

"Daddy," said Mab at last, "Mom's just run out to the drugstore for something, but she should be home in a minute or two. If she called you . . . if she called your cell phone number in just a couple of minutes . . . would you talk to her about you coming home while we're all here for Christmas?"

Dale could not speak. His mind seemed as wind-blown and empty as the fields beyond the reflections on the glass.

"Good," said Mab as if he had agreed. "Stay where you are. Mom'll call back in the next two minutes."

The line went dead. Dale clicked off the phone, left its power on, and set it on the console between the two front seats. It was beginning to snow, flakes visible in the twin cones of the headlights. No other vehicles had passed him.

Dale sat there for ten minutes—his watch was still stopped, but the green letters of the dashboard clock read 9:52. He stared at his cell phone. The Low Battery glowed, but the power was still on.

The phone rang. Dale jumped as if a rattlesnake had made a noise inches from his hand. He grabbed the phone.

"Hello?" His heart was pounding, and he heard the shakiness in his voice.

"Dale? Dale, it's Michelle."

"Who?" Dale said stupidly.

"*Michelle*. Michelle Staffney. Dale, I've got a problem." Her voice was also trembling.

For a minute, Dale could not shift mental gears. It was as if Michelle Staffney had been only a dream and now he was beginning to doze again. She had never called him on his cell phone before. He could not remember giving her his cell phone number.

"Michelle?" he said thickly.

"I'm at the school grounds, Dale. In Elm Haven. On the playground where Old Central School used to be . . ."

Dale waited, wondering if he should hang up. The low battery indicator was very bright.

". . . and the dogs are here, Dale. They're all around me."

"What?" said Dale.

"The black dogs. The ones from Duane's farm. They're here . . . in town. They're all around me."

The phone went dead.

SEVENTEEN

AT this point I begin to worry about Dale. The missed phone call from his wife, Anne—if, indeed, Anne had called back at all—seems the kind of turning point that too often converts light farce to tragedy.

Obviously I know nothing about women. I grew up with just the Old Man and Uncle Art around and paid almost zero attention to the girls at Old Central School. I remember Michelle Staffney as the fifth- and sixth-grade redheaded sex grenade, but since "sex" didn't really mean much to kids back in that prehistoric era circa 1960, none of the boys in the Bike Patrol really paid much attention to her other than to act like idiots whenever she was around.

Through Dale, I have memories of sexual intercourse—with girls he knew in high school and college, with Anne, even with the self-appointed Beatrice of his idolatry, this aptly named Clare Two Hearts—but memory of lust, much like memory of pain, is a surprisingly unspecific, clouded thing, and I can't say I feel that I missed too much of that particular aspect of not having lived to adulthood. I confess that I regret more never having seen *King Lear* performed than never having had a sexual encounter.

But I don't think that Dale rushed into Elm Haven this December night on some lustful errand; he had found some respite from solitude in talking with Mica Stouffer née Michelle Staffney, but at this point he certainly did not desire her other than in the most passing way. His affair—his romantic interlude—with the person called Clare had driven him quite far from desire's dark shores. Of course, so had the clinical depression that had rendered him impotent for months and the heavy dosage of Prozac and other drugs that followed. One might say that Dale Stewart's libido had taken a direct hit from a pharmaceutical heat-seeking missile.

If I had lived and become a writer, I might have tried to explain the role that *eros* plays in the lives and misfortunes of men, but I suspect that it would have been in a classical and twice-removed fashion. When I lived outside of Elm Haven, reading away my less-than-dozen winters and summers and equinox months, my ideal of the perfect woman was the Wife of Bath. I suspect that if I had grown up, moved on, sought, and found such a woman—identifiable, I always assumed, by that delightful, sensual gap between her front teeth—I would have, in the end, fled from the vitalism of such a sexual life force. More to the point, what would she have wanted with me—the sedentary lump, the solipsistic, overweight, clumsy, and poorly dressed geek?

But then again, Arthur Miller ended up with Marilyn Monroe, however briefly.

Of more interest to me now than Dale's imperfect memories of past lovemaking were the images and recollections of his two daughters. Perhaps it is only with one's mother and girl children that a male human being can really hold any hope of knowing and understanding women.

Margaret Beth—Mab—his oldest girl, was always the apple of his eye. Remembering her through his remembering, I cannot help but think of literary equivalents I had encounted—Aaron Burr with his beloved daughter, Sir Thomas Moore with his. These intellectual equals were the real women in these famous men's lives, and there was some of that with Mab and Dale . . . at least until this Clare appeared on the scene.

Katherine Sarah—Katie—rises less frequently in Dale's thoughts, but I see a wonderful person there, at least equal in her compassionate way to Mab's fierce intelligence. Katie was a feminine definition of empathy and connection, a gestalt humanist, the likes of which I never encountered in Elm Haven, either in the girl-children there or in their mothers. Where Mab delighted her father with precocity in language and precision in logic, Katie was quiet as a child—observing, feeling, preparing to give of herself. Dale did not ignore this trait in his youngest daughter—he loved both of his children and admired Katie's empathy beyond words—but where Mab's strengths might reflect (and thus confirm) his own, Katie's human beauties were most like her mother's. It might be this sharp fact that made him think more of Mab in his exile than—more painfully—of Katie. I won't speculate further here. I understood very little of being a son and nothing at all about being a father of girls.

Before we return to Dale's chivalric rush to save Ms. Staffney from the black dogs, we should discuss the book he is writing—the Elm-Haven-in-summer book—and the issue of his writing in general.

Dale was not a good writer. Trust me on this. I was a better writer at age nine than my friend is in his fifty-second year. The reason is, at least partially, I suspect, that he was not born to the craft, not driven to the task by the non-negotiable flames of internal fires, but, rather, made a conscious decision to become a writer at the end of that summer of 1960, the summer in which I died. Added to that is the simple fact that in training to be an academic, Dale was crippled by the need to write in academese. It is not a language formed by any human tongue, and few, if any, academics survive the degradation of it to move on to actual prose. Finally, there is the choice of Dale's fiction—"mountain man" stories. This was a conscious choice on his part—an attempt to retain his professorial status by not slumming in such genres as mystery or science fiction or, god forbid, horror—but, again, a cool one, a cerebral one, and not one forged by desire. Patterning his style on the work of the limited genre's masters—Vardis Fisher, for one—Dale wrote about the few white men in the West of the 1830s and the Native American tribes (his professor self made it almost impossible to be politically incorrect enough to think "Indians"—even though his mountain man characters did so frequently enough—much less frame some obscenity like "savages").

Hemingway once wrote that a true writer had to "work from the inside out, not from the outside in." The difference, he explained, between art and photography, between Cézanne and mere documentation. All of Dale Stewart's so-called Jim Bridger books, as I have said before, were written from the outside in.

Clare had confronted him with this fact more than once and Dale had demurred rather than defend himself, but he was hurt. He thought of his books as a contribution to literature, sort of. She would not allow him that illusion, just as, in the end, she allowed him none of the illusions one needs for survival.

This Elm Haven book that Dale is so enthused about—the book that makes him willing to stay at The Jolly Corner despite its discomforts and psychic uneasiness—is, at least, different from the mountain man books. But it is also, in its own exuberant way, a lie. It is all sunlight and summer days, swimming holes and dirt-clod fights, bicycle freedoms and idealized friendships. Dale had sworn, in his own mental preparation to write this book, to be "true to the secrets and silences of childhood," but in his actual writing of it, the secrets have become smug and the silences far too loud.

Dale Stewart's work lacked irony without even the protective camouflage of the postmodernist abandonment of irony. Dale the man might have been ironic at times—this time seeking protective camouflage—about the whole idea of writing mountain man tales, but the tales themselves were almost never leavened by irony or self-judgment. A work completely devoid of irony has no more hope of becoming literature than does the most sincere piece of Christian apologetics or Marxist polemic. As Oscar Wilde once said, "All bad poetry is sincere."

Dale's writing, in both the mountain man entertainments and his Elm-Haven-summer-of-1960 manuscript, was overwhelmingly sincere.

Of course, this is just my opinion. And I hope that I would not have become a literary critic (or its idiot sibling, a reviewer of books) had I lived. Certainly my pedantic and opinionated side would have gravitated to that vocation, but all good things beyond sleep come precisely because we defy gravity while we live. Besides, somewhere in the basement of The Jolly Corner to this day, mildewing amidst the pages of an equally mildewed paperback, is a 3-×-5 card on which I had scribbled this quote from Flaubert:

> Books aren't made the way babies are: they are made like pyramids. There's some long-pondered plan, and then great blocks of stone are placed one on top of the other, and it's back-breaking, sweaty, time-consuming work. And all to no purpose! It just stands there on the desert! But it towers over it prodigiously. Jackals piss at the base of it, and the bourgeois clamber to the top of it, etc. Continue this comparison.

I was eight when I jotted down that quote, but even then, the part I enjoyed the most was the delightful "Continue this comparison." And even then, I understood at once that the pissing jackals were critics.

It was only a little after 10:00 P.M. when Dale drove into Elm Haven, but from the darkened and abandoned feel of the little town, it might as well have been 3:00 A.M. on Walpurgis Nacht.

The fastest way from Oak Hill to Elm Haven was the old way—Oak Hill Road, which ran north and south, crossing 150A just east of the Elm Haven city limits. Dale drove quickly down Main, noting but ignoring the dark storefronts, the empty lots, and the lack of streetlights, then turned north up Second Avenue to the school yard.

He saw Michelle Staffney and the dogs almost at once. The schoolyard, once the near-majestic tableaux of the huge Old Central School on its low hill, surrounded by ancient playgrounds and sentinel elms, was now just this flat and treeless patch of weeds poking through dirty snow, the field littered with some sad plastic playground equipment, an empty parking lot, and some town storage sheds.

Michelle was at the top of the slide. The five dogs—the lead dog looking impossibly large in the headlights, as if it could easily leap to the top of the slide without exertion—stood around the slide like points on a five-sided star.

Dale stoppped the car sideways in the asphalt street, headlights cutting white cones from the old schoolyard's darkness, and hesitated. The dogs did not turn toward the light or acknowledge the Land Cruiser's presence. Michelle Staffney's face was white and her eyes wide as she raised one hand more in appeal than greeting.

Dale drove off the pavement, across the low ditch that had been much deeper when he had crossed it every day on his walk across Depot Street to the school, and accelerated across the snowy field toward the slide.

The five black dogs did not move. Their gaze stayed locked on the middle-aged woman at the top of the ladder.

Dale felt panic and tasted bile. For an instant he was sure that the five dogs were going to attack Michelle before he closed the last ten yards, then drag her down and off into the deeper snow and higher weeds behind the steel storage shed.

The dogs did not move. In a surge of absolute, senseless hatred, Dale gunned the throttle and slewed to run down the largest dog, the one he thought of as the original black dog, even though it was four times too large to have been so.

The dog whirled and ran an instant before Dale had to decide whether to brake wildly or actually run down a defenseless animal, probably someone's pet. The other four dogs also turned and loped into the darkness, each of them running in a different direction and all five blending into the night in seconds.

Dale slid the Land Cruiser to a stop, throwing up snow and dirt as he did so. Leaving the headlights on, he stepped onto the running board. "Michelle? You all right?"

The white face nodded. She was wearing a light parka and a scarf and mittens. In the harsh glare of the halogen headlights, Michelle looked simultaneously much older than she had the last time he had seen her and somehow much younger, childlike. Dale thought that perhaps it was the mittens.

He walked over to the slide and held his hand up as she descended. She ignored the hand but touched his arm when she reached solid ground.

"What happened?" said Dale.

Michelle shook her head again. "I don't know. I was out for a walk . . ."

"This late?" said Dale and realized how silly that sounded. At 10:00 P.M. in Beverly Hills she would probably still be at dinner before the late screening of a new film.

"They just . . . appeared," said Michelle and began shaking.

Dale reached a hand out to reassure her just as an extra pair of headlights swept across the schoolyard and pinned them. A car was driving across the snow toward them.

The car stopped next to Dale's truck, but the headlights blinded them. The silhouette of a heavyset man emerged from the driver's side.

"Trouble here?" came C. J. Congden's phlegmy voice.

Michelle suddenly leaned against Dale. She was shaking very hard now. She turned away from the sheriff's headlights, almost burying her face in Dale's coat.

"No trouble," said Dale.

"You drove up on city land here, Mr. Stewart," said Congden. Dale could see the headlight glare reflecting off the underside of the sheriff's Smokey hat, but the big man's face was still in shadow. "City property. You been drinking, *Professor?*"

Dale waited for Michelle to say something, but she kept her face against his chest.

"Ms. . . . Stouffer here was taking a walk," called Dale, his voice sounding very loud to himself in the cold night. "Some huge dogs appeared and started to attack her. I saw her and drove out here so the truck's lights would drive them away." He was irritated at himself for providing such a detailed explanation to this fat slob of an ex-bully.

"Dogs," said Congden, his tone dismissive and amused. To Michelle, he said, "You'd better come with me, Missy. I'll drive you home."

Michelle gripped Dale tightly now, her arms hugging him fiercely through her parka and his jacket. "*No,*" she whispered to Dale.

"I'm taking her home," said Dale. He put his arm around her and led her to the passenger side of the Land Cruiser.

The sheriff's car was at enough of an angle that the vehicle and its driver remained just dark silhouettes against the night. The cheap plastic slide and swingless swing set looked unreal—too bright, too orange and red, too fake—in the twin sets of headlights.

"She should ride with me," said C. J. Congden from the other side of the police cruiser. His voice was flat, emotionless, but somehow both amused and threatening.

Dale ignored the sheriff, helped Michelle up into the truck, shut the door carefully, and went around to the driver's side. For an instant he wondered what he would do if Congden came around his own car and tried to stop Dale from driving off. *Why would he do that?*

Because you questioned his authority, stupid, was Dale's answer to himself.

Congden did not come around.

Dale backed the Land Cruiser up, turned it around on the snowy field, and drove back to the asphalt line of Second Avenue. Checking in his rearview mirror, Dale could see only the headlights of the sheriff's car. Congden did not follow.

Dale drove up to the junction of Depot Street, where his old house—dark now—was illuminated in the headlight beams, started to turn left, but paused.

"Do you want to go home or come out to . . . the farm?" he asked.

Michelle was still shaking violently. She hadn't seemed so frightened of the dogs out at The Jolly Corner. Dale wondered if it was from the cold.

"Home," she said softly.

Dale dutifully turned left on Depot Street and drove toward Broad and the old Staffney house there.

"I mean home in California," said Michelle.

Dale laughed. He turned to look at her, to smile reassuringly, but he could see only the pale white oval of her face in the darkness. He had an irrelevant memory of the faceless man in uniform he'd glimpsed twice on his walks past the cemetery.

The Staffney house was absolutely dark. Her own truck was not in the driveway, nor were there tire tracks.

"It's in the shop in Oak Hill," said Michelle, her voice more steady now. "It's some black box screwing up the ignition system. They say it'll be a few days before they get the part in."

"You all right for groceries . . . and everything?" said Dale.

Michelle nodded and touched his arm again. "Thanks for saving me."

He tried to sound light as he said, "I don't think the dogs meant to hurt you."

The white oval of her face bobbed up and down, although he could not tell if she was agreeing or signifying that the dogs *had* meant her harm.

"I'd never get in a car with him," she said softly and it took Dale a few seconds to realize that she was speaking of Sheriff C. J. Congden.

"I don't blame you," he said. "Shall I come in with you until you get the lights on?"

"No need," said Michelle. She handed him a square box, and it took him a minute to realize that it was the box of .410 shells he'd bought in Oak Hill earlier that evening. "This was on the passenger seat and I didn't want to sit on it," she said.

Dale set the box of shells in the backseat. *I could have thrown them at the dogs*, he thought.

The overhead lights came on as she opened the passenger door, but her face was turned away so Dale could not see her expression, see if she had thought his invitation to see her inside had been a come-on. Walking around the truck to stand outside his open driver's-side window, the snow crunching under her feet, she said, "Just watch until I get down the drive, would you? Make sure the hounds don't get me?" Her voice sounded normal. "The power's off right now, so I'm using candles and flashlights until it's fixed. Don't worry if you don't see any lights."

"If the power's off, do you have heat? No need to stay here in a cold, dark house." Dale tried to think of where he'd sleep—Duane's bed in the basement, giving her the daybed in the study, or upstairs while she took the more comfortable bed?

"The furnace works," said Michelle. He could see starlight reflected in her eyes now. "It's on a separate circuit. Diane and I blew some fuses when we were messing around with the old wiring. I've got a guy coming from Peoria to fix it tomorrow. Good night, Dale. Thanks again for rescuing me." She reached out and squeezed his bare hand with her mittened one.

"Anytime," said Dale. He watched as she walked carefully down the snowy lane and disappeared around the back of the house. As advertised, the house stayed dark, but he thought he detected the slight glow of a flashlight through a dark side window.

He backed the Land Cruiser out and headed back down Depot Street toward First Avenue and the road to The Jolly Corner. There was no sign of Congden or his car.

The interior of Duane's farmhouse, except for the cold draft sliding down from the second floor, seemed warm after the cold night air. Dale went from room to room, turning on lights as he went.

He carried the shotgun shells down into the basement and retrieved the two parts of his Savage over-and-under from where he'd stored them. It was time, he thought, to have a real, loaded weapon on the premises.

Dale was attaching the over-and-under barrel when he saw that there was a shell in the shotgun breech. He removed the red shell carefully, shocked that he would ever store a loaded weapon, even one that was broken down this way. He'd learned better than that at his father's knee when he was six years old.

The shell had an indentation, the mark of a fallen firing pin, near the center of its brass circle. This was *the* shell—the one that had misfired a year ago November when he had tried to take his own life.

Dale stepped backward and sat on the edge of Duane's old brass bed. The springs creaked. He took out his treasured Dunhill lighter, flicked it on, and turned the shell around and around in his hand, looking at the gleam of light from the lighter flame glint on the brass. There was no doubt. This was the suicide attempt shell.

I threw it away. Here at the farm. Before I stored the weapon. Threw the shell far out into the field.

Had he? Dale had a distinct memory of walking out across the frozen mud, past the burned-out pole light, to the opening in the fence where the rows of frozen corn began, and tossing a shell far out into the night.

Maybe it was a different shell.

That made no sense. He had found only the one shotgun shell when he had discovered that he had somehow packed the shotgun with his books and plates and other possessions.

And I'd never have stored the shotgun with a shell in place.

Dale shook his head. He was very tired. The heavy reading at the Oak Hill library and the strange scene with Michelle and the dogs had filled his head with blurred images.

He propped the assembled over-and-under against the wall, making sure that it was open and unloaded, and went upstairs to lock the kitchen door and shut off the lights there.

The ThinkPad had been turned off when he left. Now words glowed on the black screen after the C prompt.

>Which way I fly is hell; my self am hell;
And in the lowest deep a lower deep
Still threatening to devour me opens wide,
To which the hell I suffer seems a heaven.

Dale stood a long minute staring at the stanza and scratching his chin. It was Milton. Definitely Milton, but not from *Paradise Lost*. Perhaps from one of the surviving drafts for Milton's *Adam Unparadised*.

Unlike in *Paradise Lost*, where Satan is the most human and compelling character but the reader never sees Satan in his unfallen state as the beautiful Lucifer, the "morning star" of heaven, most favored and beloved of all of God's angels, this was hell-bent Lucifer's lament. It was derivative, Dale guessed, of Marlowe's Mephistopheles—"Why this is hell, nor am I out of it."

Dale was too tired to play literary trivia games. He typed—

>Tell me who you are or I'll shut this fucking computer down forever.

Then he shut off the light and went downstairs to sleep in Duane's bed.

EIGHTEEN

ABOUT three months after Dale began his affair with Clare Hart (aka Clare Two Hearts), he traveled to Paris as a guest of his French publisher and the Ministry of Culture for a conference on "Liberation Fiction of Indigenous Peoples." It was January break at his university after a depressing Christmas that he spent at home but not really at home, and Anne had not even considered accompanying him to the conference. Dale himself had originally decided to skip the conference despite the rare treat of a free trip to Paris—he knew that the invitation was based on a French misreading of his third Jim Bridger book, *Massacre Moon*, in which several of his mountain man characters, including several impossibly benevolent French beaver trappers, sided with the Blackfeet to help the tribe avoid a massacre by encroaching federal troops. It was the most politically correct of all his novels and the most historically inaccurate. The French had loved it. In the end, Dale had decided to accept the invitation at the last minute, both to bolster his sagging credit with his dean and department and to get away, even if just for the seven days of the conference, from the double life in Missoula that had been driving him crazy.

Montana had been uncommonly warm and relatively snowless that winter, but Paris was wet and freezing. The conference writers were all being put up at the swanky Hotel Lutetia on the Boulevard Raspail, but of the ten American writers there, only Dale seemed to know that this hotel had been the headquarters for the Gestapo all during the Occupation. A faded bronze plaque near the entrance announced the historical importance of the hotel only in terms of it having been the headquaters of the Red Cross after the war and the locus for attempts to reunite refugee families.

Dale's editor from Editions Robert Laffont had been busy squiring around his *real* writers—Dale was the only non–Native American author invited from the States—so he was met at Roissy–Charles de Gaulle airport by a woman representing the Ministry of Culture's Agence Pour l'Organisation de l'Accueil des Personalitiés Étrangères from the Ministère des Affaires Étrangères, which Dale immediately translated through his jet lag as the Poor Organization to Acquire Strange Personalities, a part of the Ministry for Strange Affairs. Since the woman's job was to deal with foreign artistic types, specifically Americans, she spoke zero English and was obviously shocked that Dale spoke no French. She quickly led him through the Death Star concrete bowels of the airport to a Renault in the oppressive parking garage and drove him into Paris in a silence broken only by her exhalations of cigarette smoke.

His work at the conference began that evening. The meetings were being held in the ornate Hôtel de Ville—the city hall—and the first evening was given over to a series of greetings by the mayor, by various ministry officials, by the organizers, and by others—possibly including the president—although Dale would never be certain who was who because all of the proceedings were in French and there was no one to translate for him. He was just happy that he had worn his best black suit that evening and that he was able to stay awake through the jet lag and that he never heard his name called so that he did not have to speak. Actually, none of the thirty or so writers present, mostly African other than the exhausted-looking Native American writers and himself, were asked questions that evening, not even by the French media who crowded the anterooms and wide hallways outside the conference room and shouted questions only at the French politicians and ministry officials.

This sense of being lost in a jet-lagged nightmare in which human speech dominated everything yet in which almost nothing could be understood continued through the next two days, although by that time his editor had spared him some time and he had been assigned an interpreter—a pale young woman who chain-smoked Galoise's and who interpreted only the parts of the conference that directly required Professor Stewart's attention, which was almost none of it.

Dale's editor was in his early thirties—twenty years younger than Dale—and was very pale, a condition emphasized by the unrelentingly black turtlenecks, suits, and sport coats the young man wore. The editor specialized in Native American fiction and boasted that during his six visits to the United States, comprising more than three months in the country, he had never set foot anywhere other than Native American reservations, with the exceptions of several Indian war battlefield memorials and, of course, the rides to and from airports. His paleness was also emphasized by a small mouth that looked unnaturally red—although Dale was never sure that his editor wore lipstick—painted eyes and eyebrows, and severely cropped black hair with a small, sprayed, upturned crest in front. His name was Jean-Pierre, but Dale immediately thought of him as Pee-wee Herman and was never able to rid himself of that image.

On the second day, his publisher had arranged a small press conference for Dale at the Hôtel de Ville, and Jean-Pierre, whose English was atrocious, took over the interpreting duty from the bored, chain-smoking woman whose name Dale never quite caught.

The first question from the press was translated as "When the armed revolution from the oppressed indigenous peoples of America becomes reality, on which side will the bourgeois pseudo-intellegentsia such as yourself proclaim?"

To which Dale could only reply, "What?"

On the third day, just as Dale was leaving for the late-morning beginning of the conference, Clare arrived.

Dale stopped in the lobby and stared at her in pure shock and surprise. The night before he had phoned Anne and they had actually talked—the first real conversation they had enjoyed for many weeks. Dale knew that it was only his sense of feeling homesick and out of place that had prompted the call and tone of the conversation, but it felt natural nonetheless. Now this. Now Clare.

He had no idea how she had found him. She had gone home for Christmas break—home being Italy—and Dale had not expected to see her again for another two weeks. He had never told her that he had decided to go to Paris for this conference, and there was no one at the school to give her the hotel address. How had she tracked him down?

"Don't be silly," said Clare, taking his arm as they returned to the elevator and went back up to his room to make love, the first hour of the conference day be damned. "I'm part Blackfeet. That's what they do—track people. Don't you read your own books?"

After this, the week changed magically. Clare had her own plans for Paris, but she found time to accompany him to what she called the Liberal Fiction of Indigenous Pimples, to dismiss the chain-smoking non-interpreter, and to whisper translations to him during the stultifying proceedings. Her French, Dale soon realized, was perfect, unaccented except for its Parisian sophistication. The conference proceedings amounted to even more bullshit shoveling than Dale had imagined, but Clare livened it up with commentary so that sometimes the presiding academician or politician had to look over at their end of the table like a schoolmarm frowning at giggling children.

In the late evening, after the de rigueur three-hour conference or publishing-related dinners, which Clare attended without asking permission of Dale or anyone else, invariably identifying herself only as

"Clare" to the obviously curious French hosts and indigenous-peoples'-writer guests, at the midnight hour when Dale had just begun dragging himself back to the Lutetia and bed for the first two nights, now he and Clare would go out and see Paris.

Clare took him to a wonderful all-night jazz club with the ironic name of Montana. They had memorable chocolate mousse at 1:30 A.M. at a place near the Pont Neuf called Au Chien Qui Fume, went to Montmartre to watch topless dancers at the Lili la Tigresse, stopped at a fantastic little bar off the Boulevard Raspail that Clare insisted had been a favoring watering spot of Hemingway that no tourists knew about—they were all over at the overpriced Harry's Bar—and which offered more than fifty varieties of single-malt scotch, popped over to the Right Bank for more music with a young crowd at the Le Baiser Sale, took a cab to the Alsace brasserie on the Champs-Élysées to eat seafood as the street-sweeping machines swished down the avenue in the pre-dawn, and walked along the Seine as the sky lightened to the east.

In midmorning, after hours of lovemaking, Clare insisted that they take the corny Bateux-Mouches tour on the Seine even though the day was freezing, and they sat huddled together for warmth on the upper deck. Afterward, they walked slowly through the Jardin du Luxembourg and then sought out Baudelaire's tomb in the Cimetière de Montparnasse. When Dale suggested that this common Parisian activity of visiting tombs was a bit macabre, Clare said, "Macabre? You want macabre? I'll show you macabre."

Clare took him down the Boulevard Raspail past the avant-garde building housing the Foundation Cartier center for modern art, to an intersection labeled *Denfert-Rochereau*. "*Denfert* is a muddling of *enfer*," said Clare. "Inferno. Hell." They passed through a small iron door in a stone wall, rented a flashlight from a sleepy attendant, and spent the next two hours wandering the underground maze of Paris's catacombs, a storage point for skeletons disinterred from overflowing surface cemeteries since the days of the French revolution. Clare gave him pause when she explained that the bones and skulls neatly stacked two meters high on every side of their tunnel and extending off in niches and side tunnels everywhere were thought to number about six million. "We're seeing the Holocaust in this mile or so of walking," she whispered, flicking the flashlight across the walls of thigh bones and empty eye sockets.

That night they dined with Dale's editor, Jean-Pierre . . . or, as Clare invariably called him since he had shared his thoughts about the little man's appearance, Jean-Pee-wee. The restaurant was the Bofinger near the Bastille. The food was fantastic and the atmosphere was pure upscale Alsatian brasserie—black and white tile floors, wood, brass, tall glass looking out on the rain-swept streets, and people who knew how to dine and drink in style. There were several dogs in attendance late that evening, but no children. The French knew that dining was serious business and not improved by the presence of children.

The food that night was as no-nonsense excellent as Jean-Pee-wee's monologues were nonsense *merde*. Dale had the chef's special—a stew called cassoulet that included white beans cooked with preserved goose, carrots, pig's trotters, and God knows what else, while Clare enjoyed *choucroute*—which looked suspiciously like sauerkraut to Dale—complete with wonderfully prepared versions of pork chops, bacon, sausage, and boiled potatoes. Jean-Pee-wee ordered *canard à la pressé*, which, he explained with much pleasure, literally meant duck killed by suffocation, and everyone enjoyed side dishes of heaped *pommes frites*. The Alsatian wine was wonderful.

Jean-Pierre was explaining Dale's novel *Massacre Moon* to him. "What you explained and which the American-Anglo bourgeois will never understand in their capitalist self-satisfaction of suburbs, is the— how shall we say it? The spiritual *completeness* of Native Americans as to opposite of which the *devoid* of your average United States personage . . ."

Dale concentrated on sipping the wine and enjoying his cassoulet. Clare looked up from her choucroute and smiled ever so slightly at the young male editor. Dale had seen that smile before and knew what was coming.

"The ghosts in your tale, for instance," continued Jean-Pierre. "The average American would dement himself if such should be seen, no? Of course. Whereas, for the oppressed indigenous soul, for the enlightenment Native American who is to nature as tree is to wind, ghosts are much to be understood, commonplace, beloved and welcomed, no?"

"No," said Clare with her smile deepening.

Jean-Pierre, a born monologist, blinked at this interruption. "Pardon, mademoiselle?"

"No," repeated Clare. She ate a ribbon of *pommes frites* with her fingers and turned her attention and smile back to the editor. "Indians neither love nor understand ghosts nor find them commonplace," she said softly. "They're scared to death of ghosts. Ghosts are almost always considered the pure evil part of a living person and are to be avoided at all costs. A Navajo family will burn down their hogan if a person dies inside, sure that the person's *chindi*—the evil spirit—will contaminate the place like a cancer if they remain."

Jean-Pierre frowned deeply at her, his too-crimson mouth looking rather clownlike against his white skin. "But we are not speaking of the Navajo, with whom I spent a wonderful three weeks in your state of Arizona this two years past, but of the Blackfeet of Professor Stewart's novel!"

Clare shrugged. "The Blackfeet are as terrified by ghosts as the Navajo. At least the ghosts in European tradition—say, the ghost of Hamlet's father or Scrooge's partner Marley—have personalities. They can reason, talk, defend their actions, warn the living of the folly of their ways. To the Plains Indians—to almost all Indians—the spirit of a dead person has no more personality than a fart."

"*Pardon?*" said Jean-Pierre, blinking. "A . . . faret?"

"*Un pet,*" said Clare. "Just a noxious gas left behind. Ghosts in Indian traditions are always evil, always unpleasant, absolutely one-dimensional—less interesting in their way than the powerless shades in Hades that Orpheus and Eurydice visited."

She was obviously speaking too quickly for Jean-Pierre. Dale guessed that his editor had understood no words after "*un pet.*" "If mademoiselle refers to the indigenous people of the United States as 'Indians,' " said Jean-Pierre, his voice dripping Gallic sarcasm, "then mademoiselle has no understanding of indigenous people."

Dale started to speak then, but Clare encircled his wrist with her thumb and forefinger and squeezed. She smiled sweetly at Jean-Pierre. "Monsieur Pee-wee must certainly be correct."

The editor had frowned again, paused, started to speak, and then changed the subject, moving his monologue along to the current political folly in the United States, explaining the vast conspiracy of moneyed interests—probably Jews, Dale interpreted—who controlled all reins of power in that benighted country.

Later, at Gestapo headquarters, in their bed, with the moonlight flowing over the rooftops of Paris and falling on their naked bodies, Dale had whispered, "Is this real? Are we real? Is this going to last, Clare?"

She had smiled at him from inches away. Dale was not sure, but he did not think that it was the same smile that she had showed Jean-Pee-wee in the Alsatian brasserie. "I can only think of Napoleon's mother's favorite quote," she whispered back.

"Which was?"

"*Ça va bien pourvu que ça dure—*"

"Which means?"

"It goes well as long as it lasts."

Dale awoke in the basement of The Jolly Corner. It was late morning. His restarted and reset watch said 10:45, and a weak, sluggish light filtered through the slits of the grimy basement windows. Padding in his slippers, still in the old sweatsuit he wore for pajamas, he went up to the kitchen. The farmhouse was cold and drafty, and the sunlight outside looked as weak and hung over as he felt. The rain from the night before had frozen into long icicles that hung outside the windows and door like prison bars. The refrigerator and cupboards were almost empty. He was starved and hungry for something other than the cereal and milk he always ate for breakfast, hungry for something like rich, black coffee and warmed croissants with melted butter dripping on them. He wondered if he had dreamt about food.

He walked into the study and stopped. The computer was on. The stupid quote from Milton was still on the screen, as was his ultimatum from the previous night:

>**Tell me who you are or I'll shut this fucking computer down forever.**

Beneath that, this:

>**I could isolate, consciously, little. Everything seemed blurred, yellow, grafted onto daylight. Maudlin evasions, theopathies—every recollection formed ripples of mysterious meaning. Everything dies, unwanted and neglected—everything.**

Irritated by the double-talk on the screen and by a half memory of disturbing dreams and by the real memory of his conversation with Mab and his failure to wait for Anne's call, Dale hurriedly blocked the passage and reached for the DELETE key.

He paused.

Rereading the paragraph of nonsense brought words, almost a phrase, to mind. *Icicles. Sisters. Sybil.*

He shook his head. He had a headache and he was out of food. Even the fucking bread was moldy. He'd go shopping and worry about this later.

An hour later, Dale came out of the KWIK'N'EZ carrying his three plastic bags of groceries and froze in place. Derek and his four skinhead friends were standing at the pumps between Dale and his Land Cruiser. Their two old Ford and Chevy pickups were the only other vehicles on the rainy tarmac.

Dale paused just outside the gas station/convenience store's doors. He felt a surge of adrenaline and panic and instantly hated himself for being afraid.

Go inside and call the cops . . . the state police, if not the sheriff's office. He glanced over his shoulder at the fat and acned teenage girl behind the counter. She met his stare with a bovine gaze and then deliberately looked away. Dale guessed that she was probably a girl-friend of Derek's or one of the other skinheads . . . or perhaps she served all of them.

Hefting the plastic bags and wishing they were heavier—filled with heavy cans of vegetables, perhaps—Dale stepped off the curb and began walking toward the clustered skinheads.

The leader—the man in his mid-twenties with a swastika tattooed on the back of his right hand—showed small, irregular teeth in a wide grin as Dale approached. He was holding something in his hand, hiding it.

Dale felt his legs go weak, and again he was furious at himself. In an instant he played out the fantasy of the boys parting for him just long enough for him to get his loaded Savage over-and-under out of the backseat, of blasting away into the asphalt to frighten them, of knock-ing the lead skinhead down, of kneeling on his chest and banging his fucking skull into the wet pavement until blood ran out of the mother-fucker's ears . . .

The Savage was not in the backseat. In any fight, Dale knew, the skinhead would have all the advantages—experience, meanness, will-ingness to hurt another person. His heart pounding uselessly, Dale abandoned his fantasies and tried to focus on the unpleasant reality of now.

"Hey, Professor Jewboy motherfucker," said the skinhead leader, reminding Dale that this crew had heard of him through the series of anti-militia articles he'd stupidly written. The anti-Semitism of these so-called patriotic groups had been one of his major themes.

Now losing your teeth and getting cut up will be your major themes, he thought as he stopped in front of the five young men. He wanted to tell them to get the fuck out of his way, but he didn't trust his voice to be steady. *Wonderful. I'm fifty-two years old and I just discovered that I'm a coward.*

A blue Buick drove into the gas station lot and pulled up to the closest pumps, right where Dale and the five losers were standing. The old couple in the front seat stared bleary-eyed and uncomprehending at the boys as the sullen gathering moved aside.

The interruption gave Dale the chance to hurry to his SUV and clamber inside. The leader leaned close to the driver's-side window just as Dale clicked the locks shut. The boy standing closest to Derek dragged a key along the left rear quarter panel of the Land Cruiser.

If I were a real man, thought Dale, *I'd get out and beat the shit out of that kid.*

Dale drove off, hoping that would be the end of it. No such luck. The five skinheads scrambled to their pickup trucks—Derek and the next-youngest hopping into the white Chevy, the leader and two of his older friends crawling into the scabrous green Ford with the oversized tires. Both trucks roared to follow Dale out of the KWIK'N'EZ lot.

Dale paused at the entrance to the county road. Should he head south a couple of hundred yards to the entrance to I-74? Once on the interstate, he could drive straight to Peoria. If the punks followed him he would flag down a police car or go to the police center he dimly remembered on War Memorial Drive. Or should he turn north toward the Hard Road and Highway 150A, then back west to Oak Hill Road and north to the sheriff's station in Oak Hill? That wouldn't make much sense. Not with Sheriff C. J. Congden there. One of these punks was probably C. J.'s kid. They probably all attended skinhead gatherings together and lent each other white robes for their cross burnings.

Dale turned north toward the Hard Road. He'd be damned if he'd flee to Peoria whenever some assholes made threatening noises.

Why not? he thought. *Why not just drive straight to Montana?*

The two pickups followed him to the Hard Road, the green Ford leading Derek's white Chevy.

Dale paused again at the Hard Road. The trees and water tower of Elm Haven were visible just a mile or so to the west. Straight ahead stretched the narrow, asphalted lane—too narrow and roughly paved to be called a road—that cut between fields for two miles before connecting to County 6. Dale had come that way on his drive to the KWIK'N'EZ, staring out at the muddy fields and remembering again how the lane used to be two tractor tracks across the field, heavily used by locals but absolutely impassable in the mud season. Uncle Henry and Aunt Lena had told stories of the local farmers waiting with their teams of draft horses to pull out the unlucky Model Ts and fancy new Ford coupes—a lucrative business during a muddy spring.

Dale drove straight ahead down the lane, the truck's tires hissing on the soft asphalt and melting slush.

If the skinheads had any idea of pulling alongside him and causing trouble, there was no opportunity for them to do so on this skinny stretch of potholes. The road was wide enough for just one vehicle, and there were deep drainage ditches on each side.

Dale glanced in his rearview mirror. The two pickups were following closely. Dale could make out the pale oval face and black eyes of their leader behind the wheel of the Ford.

Dale tried to estimate the age of the pickups and whether they had four-wheel drive. He thought possibly no on the Chevy, but the Ford probably did. At least, the expensive, oversized off-road tires suggested four-wheel capability.

What the fuck do I think I'm doing here?

The lane ended at County 6 just south of the Black Tree Tavern. A mile or so north and he'd be at The Jolly Corner. The Elm Haven water tower was just visible to the west.

Dale turned east onto Jubilee College Road.

You're nuts. This county road ran east about seven miles to Jubilee College State Park, but there was nothing this way—hills, narrow bridges over creeks, a few farmhouses. *But the road's wide enough for them to pull alongside—force me off the road.*

Dale floored it. The big straight-six Toyota engine growled and got the two and a half tons of vehicle moving smartly.

The two pickups behind him were honking—either in exultation at Dale's stupidity or in anticipation of what came next.

Dale drove seventy-five miles per hour down the poorly maintained county road, the Land Cruiser lifting high on its springs at the tops of hills, hunkering in the steep little valleys. The skinhead leader pulled his green Ford alongside as they roared up the next hill.

A car coming the other way and someone dies, thought Dale.

They crested the hill together. There was no car coming the other way. The white Chevy pickup loomed in Dale's mirror—actually contacting his rear bumper. The pickups honked their horns; the skinheads waved from the open windows.

The punk in the passenger seat next to the lead skinhead lifted a hunting knife and gestured with it, only two feet away from Dale. The punk's window was down and he was shouting and cursing above the roar of the wind and engines and tire hiss on wet asphalt.

Dale ignored him and accelerated down the hill. Jubilee College Road was wide enough for two vehicles here, but the bridge over the creek at the bottom of the hill was wide enough for just one.

The green Ford lurched ahead, but Dale had vehicle mass, engine displacement, and desperation on his side. He reached the bottom first and swung in ahead of the Ford. The three vehicles roared across the narrow bridge and accelerated up the next hill.

That was the bridge where Duane's uncle Art was killed in that same summer of 1960, thought Dale. *Someone forced Uncle Art's old Cadillac off the road and into the bridge railing there.*

Then Dale had no more time to think as the green Ford pulled alongside again and the white Chevy surged close behind him.

Dale tapped the brakes. The white truck behind him slammed on its brakes and fell back rather than rear-end the Land Cruiser. The

Ford swerved in front of Dale's vehicle and pulled ahead. Dale braked again, braked harder, the Chevy pickup actually skidding behind him now, and then Dale locked the steering wheel hard left. The Land Cruiser turned, almost tipped, skipped across asphalt, and literally slid into a gravel side road running north toward a line of trees. The shotgun-pelleted yellow sign in the frozen weeds at the side of the road read DEAD END.

Why did I turn there? Dale thought wildly. The two pickups had already backed up on Jubilee College Road and pulled onto the gravel road a hundred yards behind him. *What the hell was I thinking of?*

The answer came to him in a mental voice not quite his own: *Gypsy Lane.*

NINETEEN

I KNEW what Dale had been thinking the instant he turned east on Jubilee College Road. I knew why he had done this seemingly sense-less thing even before he did.

Gypsy Lane had been one of the magical places for us boys in the late 1950s and the first year of the decade of the 1960s—my last year of life. Of all our places to play, Gypsy Lane had been the most mysteri-ous. Kid legend had it that the old wagon road had been used more than a century earlier by caravans of Gypsies who plied their trade across the Midwest, keeping to little-used back roads rather than the main thoroughfares. Kid legend also had it that the Gypsies had been driven out of Elm Haven, Oak Hill, and other nearby towns after chil-dren had gone missing—kidnapped for their blood, was the opinion of the townspeople—and the Gypsies, still needed by farm folk for their elixir cures and fortunetelling and knife-sharpening tools, had discov-ered this old lane through the thickest forest, a path broadened to wagon width by the Quakers and other builders of the Underground Railroad running slaves north a day's walk at a time in the years before the Civil War, and then the Gypsies had taken the lane as their own, moving from Oak Hill to Princeville, Princeville to Peoria, Peoria north toward Chicago on this secret highway in the moonlight, their horse carts and caravans creaking through the darkness and leaf shadow.

To get to Gypsy Lane, Dale and the other town kids hiked up Jubilee College Road to County 6 past the Black Tree Tavern, where I would meet them outside the Calvary Cemetery. We'd all cross through the cemetery—brave in the daylight, more than a little nervous if we returned at dusk or after dark—climbing the back fence, crossing the pastures and meadows there, crossing a wooded valley, then reaching Billy Goat Mountains—an abandoned strip mine and gravel quarry—and finally entering the old woods, the original and uncut forest, where Gypsy Lane remained only as a sunken roadway, carpeted by moss and deep grass, overhung by brambled branches. The expedition usually included Dale and his kid brother, Lawrence, Mike O'Rourke, Kevin Grumbacher, weird Jim Harlen, and sometimes some of the other town boys—only very rarely a girl, although Donna Lou Perry, the pitcher in their all-day baseball games, occasionally came along.

I always brought up the rear. I was fat. Even on the hottest summer days, I wore heavy flannel shirts and thick corduroy pants. I set my own pace. The guys didn't mind. They'd take a break every once in a while and let me catch up. We rarely followed the sunken path more than two or three miles, usually ending our hike on this very county gravel road on which Dale had just turned, then retracing our steps to the cemetery, then heading back to town, me waddling north alone to The Jolly Corner. On those spring, summer, fall, and occasional winter days, I walked along Gypsy Lane with the guys, not believing in any of the legends or myths about it, assuming that it was an old unpaved farm road that had been bypassed by the county and state roads fifty or sixty years earlier, but enjoying the walk and the dappled shadow and thinking my own thoughts.

The reason that Dale's subconscious had come up with Gypsy Lane as a possible way to throw off his pursuers is that he remembered that the sunken lane ran most of the two and a half miles between this dead-end road and County 6 at the cemetery. It had been a rough and sunken path then, but passable. Billy Goat Mountains, where we boys had often played, was an obstacle course of ponds and slag heaps and huge hills of dirt and gravel. Dale's subconscious, if not his frightened conscious mind this day, had realized that the odds were good that his Toyota Land Cruiser, with its high clearance, exceptional four-wheel low gear, and locking front and center differentials, had a better chance of making it up Gypsy Lane and across Billy Goat Mountains than did the rusted and clapped-out pickups chasing him.

But he had forgotten something. We had hiked Gypsy Lane more than forty years ago. Things change.

Before he saw the gray wreck of the abandoned farmhouse ahead on his left, Dale had remembered Gypsy Lane and smiled to himself. He'd wanted some difficult terrain in which to lose these skinhead punks. This should be perfect.

The green Ford was roaring closer now, throwing gravel and ice thirty feet in the air. Dale could see the pale faces behind the reflective windshield, even make out the black tattooed swastika on the back of the leader's hand as he drove. For a second, Dale's burst of confidence abandoned him. *What if these kids wanted to hurt him seriously . . . to kill him?* He'd led them to a perfect place: abandoned, isolated, empty. It could be spring before someone found his body.

Too late to worry about that now, thought Dale, and swung the Toyota off the dead-end road into the snowy and brambled yard of the abandoned farmhouse. It was just as he remembered it from the end of their long hikes down Gypsy Lane. Behind the farmhouse and to the left began the . . .

"Shit," whispered Dale.

Where Gypsy Lane had come out into open pasture when he and his brother Lawrence and Duane and their friends had hiked it four decades ago, a mature forest now grew.

"Shit," Dale said again and concentrated on weaving between the trees. He was doing only thirty miles an hour now, but even that was too fast. Mud and snow flew from the rear wheels. He dodged a bare oak, but slammed over a sapling. Suddenly the Land Cruiser was sliding on a steep hill made ski-slope slick by a thick carpet of leaves. Dale had no idea where he was. There was no sign of Gypsy Lane.

The two pickups had also been required to slow behind him. The leader of the skinheads was a lot braver than Derek driving the white Chevy truck—the green Ford plowed through small fir trees and knocked over thick bushes and more saplings in its eagerness to get at Dale. The green Ford was gaining.

Dale stood on the brake, managed to miss by inches a black-trunked maple tree that would have totaled the Land Cruiser, and slid the heavy truck the last hundred feet to the leaf-filled bottom of the gully.

Where the hell am I? He clearly remembered that their Gypsy Lane hikes had always ended with a triumphant exit from the forest, across that pasture, past the empty farmhouse . . .

No, there had been a final hill to climb to get up out of the lane. They'd always had to wait at the top for Duane to catch up.

This had to be it. This shrub-filled, leaf-filled, forested gully had to be the old Gypsy Lane. *Which way?* Gypsy Lane in his memory ran east and west, but this gully ran mostly north and south. Straight ahead—east—was not an option now, since the hillside ahead was far too steep even for the Land Cruiser in four-wheel-low, and the trees on the hillside grew only a foot or two apart. Dale glanced up the hill he'd just descended.

The green Ford was thirty feet away, sliding, the skinheads inside screaming. They were going to ram him.

Dale slapped the Toyota into four-wheel drive and accelerated madly, tires whining as they dug through half a foot of dead leaves. The big vehicle sloughed, almost went into the small creek to his right, and then pulled ponderously ahead just as the green pickup slid through the space where Dale had been two seconds earlier.

I should just get out and fight them. Dale ignored the mental suggestion. If this was Gypsy Lane, it had become nothing more than a muddy, snow-and-ice-filled gully filled with trees almost as old as Dale. He quit worrying about that and concentrated on keeping the big SUV moving, sliding and sloughing up inclines, bouncing over stones and fallen trees, sometimes driving into the shallow creek to avoid trees and deadfall. The green Ford roared and spit its way along behind. Farther back, Derek's white Chevy gamely came on.

The gully was bending toward the east. It seemed very dark down here now. Dale expected an unclimbable hill or deadfall to stop him at any turn. The straight-six Toyota engine growled as it pulled the SUV over another rise between narrowing gully walls.

This was Gypsy Lane. Thirty feet wide here—it had widened out near its terminus at the county road—but still recognizable as the hidden lane the kids had enjoyed. Even the overhanging trees appeared the same. There were fewer trees growing in the lane itself now, although Dale had to dodge and swerve to avoid those that were there.

Before the skinhead in the Ford could catch up, Gypsy Lane narrowed further. Old stone walls were visible on either side, a black fence of mature trees growing from the stone. Dale drove on eastward, hearing and feeling rocks and low stumps scraping the metal guarding the Land Cruiser's underside. The Ford bounced and slewed its way along, fifty feet behind. Much further back, the Chevy kept pace.

This is nuts, thought Dale ten minutes into this madman's slow-motion chase. *I should have driven to a police station.*

And have C. J. Congden help you? came a voice.

The air seemed to brighten, the trees back away, the ditch that was

Gypsy Lane widen and release its claustrophobic grip. Dale accelerated up a steep rise and came out into an open pasture.

Billy Goat Mountains. Less than a mile from the cemetery and County 6.

The quarry ponds had long since been filled in, but the gravel heaps and dirt hills that they had called Billy Goat Mountains were still there—lower and more rounded and weathered than Dale remembered, none of the rises more than twenty feet high, and all with tenth-generation grass and weeds growing out of the mud, but still there. The former ponds were wide sloughs of mud from the snow and sleet and freeze and thaw. For Illinois kids who had never seen a real mountain, or even a serious natural hill, the slag heaps and gravel piles of the old quarry had been mountains enough. And now they had to be mountains enough again for Dale.

But the old quarry went on farther than Dale remembered. The mud flats and muddy hills stretched ahead for a quarter of a mile or more. Beyond that he could see a hint of the lane leading east to the rutted service road that ran south of Calvary Cemetery to County 6. But could even the Land Cruiser cross this expanse of mud?

Dale actually stopped. There were tree lines half a mile on either side, but he remembered the woods there being thick and deep. Certainly impassable by vehicle. *Probably a whole different forest now anyway,* he chided himself.

He looked behind him. The Ford 250 pickup came up over the rise. The skinhead hanging out the right window still brandished his knife.

Dale drove into the slough.

The Land Cruiser bogged down almost immediately. Even in four-wheel drive, all the heavy vehicle could do was slip and slide and throw mud and ice crystals high into the air. The green Ford pickup slammed into the mud and came sliding on, its skinhead occupants looking as reckless and demented as the average SUV driver in SUV commercials on TV.

Before he lost all momentum, Dale pushed the button that locked the center differential. A lighted diagram appeared on the instrument panel, showing the locked rear axle. Dale pushed a second switch, locking the front differential. His nimble SUV suddenly turned into a tank. Locked wheels dug into the mud and moved the mass of metal ahead slowly. The green Ford plowed after him, obviously in four-wheel-low. Derek had hesitated before accelerating out onto the mud flats and the loss of momentum decided the issue: the white Chevy pickup bogged down after sixty or seventy feet, the spinning wheels only dug it deeper into the icy quagmire, and the pickup stopped, sank another six inches to its running board, and stayed where it was.

Dale glanced in his mirror long enough to see Derek leap out of the driver's side of the Chevy and sink halfway to his knees in the mud. Not being a fast learner, the other young skinhead had seen Derek jump and *still* jumped out the passenger side of the pickup, where he flailed around and dropped his knife in his attempt to keep from falling face-first into the mire. But the green pickup with the three older gang members in it continued slewing steadily after Dale's Land Cruiser.

It was, thought Dale a minute or so later, one sad excuse for a car chase. The two heavy vehicles—Dale's huge Toyota fifty feet or so ahead of the scabrous green pickup—were slipping and sliding and slopping across the mud flats at a top speed of about one half of one mile per hour. Dale's Land Cruiser had the advantage of expensive differential locks and Japanese engineering. The skinheads' truck had the advantage of larger tires, greater horsepower, and a felon—perhaps a killer—at the wheel: someone who probably didn't recognize how crazy his actions were. All Dale knew for certain at this point was that if the skinheads in the Ford did catch up to him, they'd be more furious and violent than they would have been at the KWIK'N'EZ.

Two-thirds of the way across the bog, Dale realized that he had a serious choice to make. Ahead of him were the sad remnants of Billy Goat Mountains—a line of gradual hills, perhaps twenty feet high, that ended east of the final hundred feet or so of slough before solid ground again, all within sight of Calvary Cemetery. To try to climb those hills might be fatal for Dale—if the Cruiser bogged down or slid backward he'd be at the mercy of the skinheads. To head north or south to bypass the hills would just prolong the slow-motion chase another fifteen or twenty minutes and almost certainly result in the Land Cruiser and the Ford pickup slogging out onto solid ground just fifty feet apart. This whole absurd Gypsy Lane detour would have been for nothing.

Dale floored the gas pedal and accelerated onto the first hill of slag and mud. Halfway up the incline, Dale knew that he wouldn't make it. At first the Land Cruiser had dug in and climbed, but he hit a patch that was especially steep and especially muddy. The big SUV slid sideways. Dale fought the wheel, tapped the brake to arrest the slide, and floored the gas pedal to keep the momentum going sideways on the muddy slope, but then had to swing the steering wheel lock to lock the opposite direction just to keep the heavy truck from swapping ends. The Land Cruiser dug in again with all four locked wheels and hauled itself crablike up the slope to the summit.

At the top of the hill, barely as wide as his SUV was long, Dale stopped, panted, and stared. The north slope of the slag heap was twice as steep as the side he had just climbed. At the base of it, the mud and snow had melted into a virtual bog. Dale glanced over his shoulder.

The Ford pickup had built up enough speed to take a healthy run at the slope and now was climbing it at twice the speed Dale had managed. He could see the skinheads and the leader screaming, their mouths wide and black, the leader's knuckles white on the steering wheel as the pickup's oversized tires threw mud fifty feet into the air behind it.

Dale kept the gear-select in four-wheel-low and actually accelerated down the nearly vertical slope. Gears ground in protest, but the gearing, the locked differentials, and the Land Cruiser's massive compression slowed him and kept him aimed straight all the way down. The heavy SUV hit the mud and water like a giant boulder, digging the wheels in above the hubs, but Dale fought the wheel and kept it pointed north, mud, water, and ice spewing wide on either side and kicking up a rooster tail behind him. Fifty feet and he slapped off the locking differentials, kept it in full-time four-wheel drive, and shifted to second gear, gaining the solid ground in a final lunge. The windshield wipers pounded away, scraping the smallest gap in the mud there so that Dale could see to drive.

He stopped the truck where the lane to the cemetery began and looked back again.

The skinhead had paused a long minute at the summit and then followed Dale's lead by gunning the Ford straight down the hill. But the pickup's torque and gearing failed it. Halfway down, the green truck swapped ends, then slewed and yawed again. It hit the mud at the bottom of the hill, sliding completely sideways. The useless oversized tires immediately sank three feet into the bog and the pickup flipped on its left side, half burying its cab and hood in mud and water.

For a long minute there was no movement, and then all three of the skinheads crawled out the open passenger-side window and balanced precariously on the tilted side of the truck. One of the henchmen tried walking out onto the tipped and tilted side of the pickup's carrying bed, the young man's arms pinwheeling as he lost balance. He hit the mud and went up to his waist.

Dale realized that he had the urge to lock the Land Cruiser's differentials again and drive back to the pickup—not to help the three skinheads, he realized a second later, but to run over the miserable bastards, driving them so deep in the mud that they'd only be found five hundred years later, like those peat mummies in England. Dale tried to laugh, but his hands were shaking now as he gripped the wheel and his heart pounded as he came off the adrenaline rush that had been driving him. He realized that he had never been so angry—or at least not since he had been a kid in Elm Haven. Some of the wild energy and anger of that mostly forgotten year came back to him now with fragments of memory itself—*We killed that goddamned rendering truck that was chasing us.* He didn't understand the thought, but he recognized the echo of it in his current fury.

Driving slowly now, Dale headed west on the rutted lane that ran along the south boundary of Calvary Cemetery. At County 6, he got out, opened the gate, drove through, and closed it behind him. He knew that the skinheads would be walking this way soon—although not that soon, given the mud they had to wade through—but he doubted if they'd be pulling their vehicles out of the mud all that soon.

They don't have to, came the unbidden thought. *All they have to do is turn north here and walk to The Jolly Corner.*

Dale mentally shrugged. The anger was stronger than the post-adrenaline shaking now, and he felt the fury crystallizing in his chest like a clenched fist. He had his shotgun at the farm. And new shells. Let them come.

The Jolly Corner was dark when he arrived. Icicles from the day's thaw and freeze hung like cold teeth in front of the side door. Dale went from room to room, turning on lights as he went. No one was waiting for him. The Savage over-and-under was in the basement where he had left it, unloaded, propped against the wall. Dale took the box of .410 shells, loaded one, and carried the weapon back up to the kitchen. He made sure the door was bolted with the chain lock on. *Let them come.*

He walked into the small study. A message glowed on the dark screen. It was not the bit of poem he had last seen there, or his challenge for the unknown e-mailer to identify himself or else, but a verbatim repeat of the earlier message:

> **>I could isolate, consciously, little. Everything seemed blurred, yellowed, grafted onto daylight. Maudlin evasions, theopathies—every recollection formed ripple of mysterious meaning. Everything dies, unwanted and neglected—everything.**

When Dale had first seen it, it had made no sense, but now it stirred a dim recollection of something written by Vladimir Nabokov. Now he remembered the story in question—"The Vane Sisters"—and immediately recognized this text as a riff on a playful acrostic in the last paragraph of that story. Treating the computer message now as an acrostic, Dale could read it easily, jumping from first letter to first letter of each word—

>Icicles by God. Meter from me, Duane.

TWENTY

DURING the last months that Clare Hart was a student at the University of Montana—before she left for Princeton and her real doctoral program—she and Dale spent most weekends at his ranch and found themselves snowed in for five days and nights that final April.

He had left Anne and the girls. Everyone on campus seemed to know what was going on. The head of Dale's English department seemed amused by it all, his colleagues were obviously either interested or repelled or both, and the dean let it be known that she was mildly annoyed. Affairs with students happened and affairs between faculty and graduate students were common enough, but Missoula was still a small enough and rural enough town that no one liked to advertise the fact of such liaisons on campus.

Dale and Clare had gone up to the ranch on a Friday—he from the small apartment he had rented in town after leaving home, Clare from the apartment she still leased—and by late morning Saturday the county highway was impassable, the half mile of driveway was under four feet of blowing snow, the phone wires were down, and the electricity was out in the ranch house. It was perfect.

They chopped wood and sat close to the wide fireplace in order to stay warm. They crawled under the down coverlet on the bed and made love to stay warm. The kitchen stove worked off the large propane tank, so there was no problem cooking. Dale had stocked months' worth of canned goods and the large freezer was out in the utility shed between the ranch house and the barn, so they just opened the freezer doors—the temperatures plummeted below zero every night—to keep the frozen food from spoiling. Dale actually used a snow shovel to clear the propane grill on the ranch house deck to barbecue steaks their second evening there.

During the day they cross-country skiied or snowshoed along the ridges and valleys. The sunlight was brilliant between sudden snow squalls, the sky cerulean when glimpsed between shifting clouds. The wind blew almost constantly, whipping snow off the branches of Douglas firs and Ponderosa pines, drifting snow higher along the west wall of the ranch house, and burying the access road under undulating white dunes. On the third day Dale and Clare snowshoed down to the county highway, but it was immediately obvious that although plows had come along the day before, the wind and fresh snow the night before had closed the road again. They went back to the ranch house and built a fire—it took Dale ten matches to get it going—and took off their clothes and made love on a Hudson's Bay blanket in front of the hearth. Dale said later that he had calculated that they had only enough firewood to last until the following December.

It was on the last night before the roads were cleared that Clare told Dale that he seemed haunted. That day the county highway had been opened, the phones were working again, and a neighbor with a snowplow had promised to clear Dale's access road as soon as he finished a dozen other jobs nearby, probably early the next morning. Dale had told him that there was no hurry.

It was long after dark and Dale and Clare were lying in front of the dying fire, a thick quilt beneath them, the red Hudson's Bay blanket above them. The rest of the ranch house was dark and cold. Clare was closest to the fire and had turned away, toward the failing fire, propping herself up on her right elbow, so that her buttocks and hips were all that touched him. Her left arm, shoulder, and rib cage were outlined in red from the embers beyond and seemed to pulse from some internal heat of their own. Dale had been half dozing, too lazy to stoke the fire and get the room warm enough for them to retreat to the bedroom, when he heard her speaking softly to him.

"Do you know why I chose to be with you?"

He blinked at the coolness of her tone, but quickly realized that it must be the prelude to either a joke or a compliment. "No," he said, rubbing his palm down the red-limned curve of her shoulder and arm. "Why did you choose to be with me?"

"Because you're haunted," whispered Clare Two Hearts.

Dale waited for the punch line. After a long moment of silence broken only by the settling of embered logs, he said, "What do you mean? Haunted?"

It was dark enough now that he did not see her shrug, but felt the slight motion under the curve of his palm. "Haunted," she said. "Touched by something dark. Something from your childhood, I think. Something not completely of this world."

The wind rattled the high window ten feet from them. In daylight, the view looked through the trees into the long meadow going down past the barn toward the lake. Now it was just darkness pressing against glass with the wind as its fingers. "You're joking," said Dale. He had to fight the urge to remove his hand from her cool skin.

"No."

"Is this the Blackfoot mystic talking?" said Dale. He kept his tone light. But he remembered their camping trip that first weekend on the ridge near the reservation. "Or the descendant of some Italian witch?"

"Both," said Clare. She did not turn toward him.

"I thought that houses were haunted, not people," said Dale. He tried to banter, but his tone was straining around the edges.

Clare said nothing. She no longer propped herself on her elbow but lay on her side, her arm crooked over her head as if in sleep. The embers had dimmed so thoroughly that all he could see of her was the pale glow of her skin in the starlight reflected from the snow piled outside the window.

He removed his hand. The cold air in the ranch house settled heavier on them where they lay on the floor. "Why would you choose to be with someone because he's . . . haunted?" Dale asked into the darkness.

"Because it's growing stronger," whispered Clare. She seemed half asleep, or perhaps completely asleep, talking in her sleep, a medium in her trance. "It's reached a quickening. Something dead is struggling to be born."

Dale felt the cold air under the blanket then, as tangible as a third body between them. Clare was, indeed, sleeping. She began snoring softly.

Someone was banging on the door.

Dale struggled up out of sleep. For a minute he was confused, but then he noticed the brass headboard of the old bed, the oak bulk of the floor console radio at the foot of the bed, and the weak winter light coming through the high basement windows. *Duane's bed in the basement.*

The banging came again.

Dale pulled off the quilt and sat on the edge of the bed. The .410-gauge shotgun was where he had left it, propped against a bookcase. Dale remembered that he had loaded it after coming home from the truck chase the evening before. He did not remember falling asleep in the bed with his clothes on, but he had.

Someone was pounding on the kitchen door.

Dale slipped into his shoes, tied them, tucked in his shirttails, picked up the shotgun, checked to make sure it was loaded, closed the breech and clicked on the safety, and walked upstairs.

The clock in the kitchen said ten-thirty in the morning. Dale peered through the curtains on the little window in the door before opening it.

Michelle Staffney was on the stoop holding three large grocery bags. Dale could see a plastic-wrapped ham protruding from the largest of the plastic bags, the pink meat looking vaguely fleshlike and obscene.

"Open up!" shouted Michelle. "It's cold out here!" She smiled at him. She was wearing bright red lipstick and her cheeks were pink.

Dale propped the shotgun out of sight but within easy reach between the kitchen counter and the stove, and unlocked the door.

Michelle bustled in, bringing in a blast of cold air with her. Dale had time to notice her truck parked in the frozen mud turnaround, notice that the snow was mostly gone and that the day was sunny in its weak, winterish way, and then he closed and locked the door behind Michelle. He turned his attention her way as she tossed her long down coat over the back of a chair and got busy removing cans and bottles and jars and the ham itself from the three bags.

"Well, I would have called you, but of course I couldn't since you don't have a phone here and refuse to keep your cell phone turned on or whatever, so I just made the decisions myself." She removed two bottles of red wine from a skinny brown bag that had been concealed in the grocery plastic. "I hope you like Merlot. I do. So I just bought two yesterday before the stores closed. And I decided to keep it simple . . . you know, just ham and baked potatoes and green beans. But I got a wonderful Sara Lee pie for dessert." As if submitting it as evidence, she removed an apple pie from the plastic and held it up.

"Great," said Dale, totally confused. "But what's the . . . I mean, why are we celebrating?"

Mica Stouffer née Michelle Staffney paused in the act of reaching for a water glass from one of the high cabinet shelves, and Dale noticed how tightly her white blouse was pulled over her large breasts. He glanced away as if inspecting the bottles and cans and ham on the counter.

Michelle took time to run some water from the tap and drink before answering. "I hope you're joking, *Professor* Dale Stewart. Today is Christmas Eve."

They had dinner in mid-afternoon, before the thin daylight faded completely. Dale had showered and shaved and dressed in chinos, a clean shirt, and a dark brown leather sport coat while Michelle made coffee and began to fill the old house with rich smells of cooking. They had glasses of wine while the ham was cooking and opened the second bottle of Merlot during dinner. They ate at the kitchen table. Michelle had brought two stubby candles in her purse. Dale had tried not to think of Clare when he lit the candles with his gold lighter, and now the dimming daylight was augmented by candlelight on the table rather than from the brash overhead bulb. Dale had felt disoriented and light-headed when he awoke, and now he felt absolutely drunk. He amazed himself by telling Michelle all about the slow-motion truck chase the day before, emphasizing the farcical rather than frightening elements, and they both laughed. Dale poured more wine for both of them.

"I read that story you were talking about," said Michelle after they had cleared the table. Coffee was brewing in the coffeemaker and the apple pie had been warmed in the oven, but for now each of them was enjoying a final glass of wine. "You know," she said, " 'The Jolly Corner.' "

Dale only vaguely remembered talking about the Henry James story, but he nodded. "Did you like it?"

Michelle sipped her wine. Her red hair gleamed in the candlelight.

The light was all but gone from the square of window over the sink behind her. "I don't know if I like it," she said at last. "Actually, I thought it was pretty weird."

Dale smiled. When he spoke, he worked to keep his voice from sounding condescending. "Yeah, I have to confess that I find a lot of James's stuff heavy going. You know what Dorothy Parker said about Henry James?"

Michelle Staffney shook her head.

"She said that he chewed more than he bit off," Dale said and laughed. The air smelled of coffee and pie. The last of the wine tasted rich. He had left five skinhead punks wallowing in the mud of Billy Goat Mountains. All in all, he felt pretty good.

Michelle shook her head as if dismissing Dorothy Parker's clever comment and getting back to the subject. "I read the thing three times, but I still don't think I understood it. I mean, Spencer Brydon sees this ghost in his old house—this alter ego—this horrible version of himself. Who he might have been."

Dale nodded and waited. The wine was almost gone.

"But was it real? The ghost, I mean?" Michelle's voice was low, throaty.

Dale shrugged. "That's the interesting thing about Henry James's fiction," he said, hearing the echo of Professor Stewart's lecturing tone in his voice despite his best efforts. "The ghost—his old New York home, haunted as it was—they're all external manifestations of the mind itself, aren't they? The merging of the external and internal? Reality for James—at least in his fiction—was always metaphorical and psychological."

"Alice Staverton saw it too," Michelle said softly.

"Pardon me?"

"The girlfriend," said Michelle. "Miss Staverton. The one who's cradling Brydon's head in her lap at the end. She saw the ghost—the bad Brydon—at the same time that he did. She tells him that. And she liked the bad one . . . was attracted to him."

"She was?" Dale said stupidly. He had taught the story a score of times—almost always to first-year students—but he had never really focused on the footnote fact that Miss Staverton had seen the same ghostly image, much less that she said that she *liked* the monster.

"Yes," said Michelle. "And she liked the other Brydon—missing fingers, rough appearance and all—because it was *him*, the ghost Brydon, not the real, wimpy Brydon, who said that he wanted her."

"Wanted her to come find him," said Dale. "To help him."

It was Michelle's turn to shrug. "That's not the way I read it. I heard her say that the other Brydon, the Mr. Hyde one, *wanted her*. Like in wanted to take her to bed. As if it took this other Brydon, the monster Mr. Hyde one, the crass American merchant version of Brydon, to tell her that he wants to fuck her. And that's why she shocks the wimpy Brydon—who's still lying on the floor with his head in her lap at this point, I think—when she says, 'He *seemed to tell me of that . . . So why shouldn't I like him?*' "

Dale set his empty wine glass on the table and stared at her, dumbfounded. All the years of teaching this story . . . how could he have missed this possible interpretation? How could the various James scholars have missed it? Did James himself—that master of self-sublimation—miss it as well? For a moment Dale could not speak.

"All I know for sure," continued Michelle, "is that it would make a shitty movie. No action. No sex. And the ghost isn't all that scary. So, Professor Stewart. Shall we?"

Dale shook himself out of his reverie. "Have coffee and pie?"

"Go upstairs and fuck," said Michelle.

Dale follows her upstairs in candlelight, feeling thick and removed, watching things unspool in slow motion, as if in a dream.

This is no dream, Dale.

He suggested the basement bed instead, saying it was warmer there, with more light and . . .

"No," said Michelle, carrying the candles to the base of the stairs. "That's a boy's bed."

A *boy's bed?* thought Dale, realizing at once that it was indeed a boy's bed, and a dead boy's bed, but what difference did that make? All the beds in the house belonged to dead people.

"Why don't you get the quilt and the blanket from the daybed in the study?" said Michelle.

"The study is warmer, too. . ." began Dale.

Michelle had shaken her head. "The computer is in there. Just get the quilt and a blanket."

Dale fetches the quilt and the blanket and returns to the stairs, not understanding the comment about the computer, not focusing on it, not focusing on anything. Their shadows climb the stairs with them. Standing on the landing at the top of the stairs for a moment before entering what had been the master bedroom, Dale wonders idly why there is no electricity to the second floor.

The Old Man rewired it. Cut the wiring to the fuse box.

Michelle encircles his wrist with her fingers at the entrance to the bedroom. The candle flame is reflected in her strangely glassy eyes. *Contact lenses*, thinks Dale. *And too much wine.*

Dale starts to speak, can think of nothing to say. The candle she had handed to him below drips hot wax on his wrist. He ignores it. It is strangely warm up here.

"Come," says Michelle Staffney. She leads him into the room.

The excitement hits him the instant he crosses the threshold, but this time it may be as much because of Michelle's slim fingers on his wrist, or the sight of candlelight on her pink cheeks and red hair and open blouse, or the mingled scent of perfume and woman rising from her flesh as if activated by the small flame in her left hand.

"I know how this room affected you before," she whispers and sets her candle on the bedside table. She takes his candle from him and sets it beside hers, removes the quilt and blanket from under his arm, and smooths them onto the old bed—first the blanket, smoothing it down, then the red quilt. Their shadows move across the faded wall-paper and ripple on the closed drapes.

Dale continues to stand there stupidly, watching, as she turns back the edge of the quilt and steps closer. He smells the shampoo scent of her hair. Michelle kisses the side of his neck, presses her right hand against the small of his back through his sport coat, and slides the pale fingers of her left hand down his chest and across his belly until they find and hold his erect penis through his cotton trousers. She looks up at him.

"Aren't you going to kiss me?"

He kisses her. Her lips are full and very cool, almost cold.

Michelle smiles and uses both hands to remove his sport coat. There is no place to put it. She drops it on the floor and begins unbuttoning his shirt. When her fingers drop away and move to her own blouse, Dale finishes unbuttoning his own shirt, pulling the tails out of his trousers.

Michell drops her blouse on the floor next to his jacket and unbuttons her skirt. Her bra is white, lacy, strangely virginal-looking. Her full breasts rise palely above white lace. Freckles on her throat give way to the whiteness.

She unhooks Dale's belt and slides down the zipper of his fly. Then she goes to one knee, pushing his chinos and boxer shorts lower, and takes his stiff penis in her mouth.

Dale gasps not just because of the sudden assault of intimacy but because her mouth is as cold as if she had been chewing an ice cube a second before.

What are Anne and the children doing right now? On Christmas Eve?

Dale angrily shakes away the alien thought.

Michelle stands again, smiling, her red lips moist. Both hands replace her mouth now, sliding up and down the moist shaft of his penis. She whispers, "Aren't you going to help me undress?"

Awkwardly, literally throbbing with excitement as her cool hands stay on him, Dale slides her skirt down and off. She temporarily releases her hold on him and steps out of her shoes as he pulls her white underpants lower. Dale notices that her red pubic hair is cut in a narrow vertical strip; he has seen this form of trimming in magazines and in movies but never in real life. Suddenly he is aware that Michelle Staffney will know all sorts of Hollywood secret pleasures, sex tricks that women in Missoula, Montana, have never heard of. The thought would normally make him smile, but the sight of her standing there, naked except for her white bra, legs slightly apart, thighs curving inward and the pale pink lips of her vulva glowing moistly in the candlelight, does not allow him to smile.

Her arms curve behind her and she drops the brassiere. Her breasts are huge, pale, round, with pink areolae. They are as high and firm as the breasts of any seventeen-year-old girl.

False. No longer real.

Dale blinks away the thought and watches as she squeezes his penis a final time, turns back the down comforter again, and slides onto the blanket. The bed squeaks. There is no pillow. She raises her left leg slightly and props herself on her right arm. Dale can never remember being so sexually excited, not even with Clare.

"Are you coming in?" Michelle asks, lifting the comforter higher in invitation.

Dale suddenly feels a slap of cold air, almost as if another presence has entered the room through an invisible door in the wall. He turns, startled, but sees only his absurd shadow—stiff penis rising—imprinted on the faded wallpaper.

"Dale?" Her whisper is soft but urgent.

He turns back to her, seeing the candlelight dancing in her eyes. Her nipples are hard.

This is not right, Dale.

"This is wrong," says Dale.

"What are you talking about?" She reaches for his hand, but he pulls it back. Her cool fingers close around the head of his penis. "It doesn't feel wrong," she says softly, smiling at him in the candlelight. The flames stir as if to a slight draft.

Dale steps back, not understanding his reaction, feeling a stab of infinite regret as her fingers slip off the hot head of his cock.

This cannot happen, Dale.

"This isn't going to happen," Dale says dully. He feels as if the floor of the room is rising and dropping, pitching like the deck of a ship during a stormy night crossing.

Michelle pulls her hand back, sits up, lifts her other pale hand, cups her full breasts, and raises them. Her lacquered nails shine as she plays with her nipples. "Come here," she whispers.

Dale makes himself look away. His shadow is that of a hunchback, a circus freak, unstable and dancing in the wildly flickering candlelight. Suddenly the air is freezing. He sees his breath fog in the cold air and smells the tang of frozen mold. He does not look back at the bed.

Fato profugus.

"Fate's fugitive," gasps Dale, having no idea why he is saying it.

"Dale . . ." It is a throaty entreaty, little more than an exhalation behind him as Dale scoops up his clothes, dropping his left shoe and retrieving it again, leaving his socks behind as he stumbles down the stairs.

Michelle stood clothed and stiff by the kitchen door. She would not look at him.

"I'm sorry . . . I don't understand why . . ." Dale stopped. "I'm sorry," he said again.

The woman shook her head and pulled on her coat.

"The extra food . . ." said Dale, turning back to the counter.

"Leave it," said Michelle. "Enjoy the pie." She unlocked and opened the door, her back still turned toward him. She had not met his gaze since coming downstairs fully clothed, face pale.

He reached for her, touching her shoulder through the coat, but she shrugged off his hand.

"I'm sorry," he said again, hearing how stupid it sounded even in his own ears. "Perhaps another time . . . another day . . ."

Michelle laughed. It was an oddly strange sound—hollow, deep in her throat, not feminine at all. She stepped out into the darkness.

"Wait, I'll get the flashlight," said Dale. He grabbed the flashlight from the counter and hurried out the door to help her cross the frozen ground to her truck.

The black dogs came invisible out of darkness, three leaping on Michelle and two jumping at Dale where he stood on the concrete stoop. The hounds were huge, larger than dogs could be. Their eyes were bright yellow, their teeth white in the glow from the kitchen. Dale had time to swing the flashlight like a club, lighting the jackal eyes of the closest black dog, and then their paws and the mass of both hounds knocked him backward, his head hitting the kitchen door hard, the flashlight flying away beyond the stoop and illuminating nothing.

Michelle screamed once. Between black bodies, Dale caught a glimpse of her red hair rolling. The three dogs roiling above her seemed larger, more ferocious. Their growling and snarling filled the night.

Only half conscious, bleeding from his torn scalp, Dale rolled out from under one of the black dogs and tried to get to his feet. The second hound hit him from behind and Dale pitched forward onto the frozen ground, feeling the wind go out of him. The black hounds were ripping and tearing at Michelle not twenty steps away.

Dale kicked back, felt his boot connect solidly with dog ribs, heard the howl almost in his ear, and struggled to get to his knees, crawling toward where the larger three dogs seemed to be ripping Michelle apart.

The two hounds whirled around him, their jaws higher than his head, their eyes burning yellowly. One snapped at his shoulder, seizing his leather sport coat and ripping it, pulling him off his knees and tumbling him onto his face in the frozen mud. Dale covered his face as both hounds ripped his sport coat from his back, tossing it back and forth between them. Their slaver fell on his hair and cheek. He rolled on his back, balling his hands into fists.

"Michelle!" he screamed. There was no answer except for the snarling and growling.

The larger of the two hounds that had hit him leaped across him now, the other black dog growling out of sight above and behind him. Dale hammered at the black wall of the largest hound's chest as the animal straddled him, setting a huge paw on his chest like a lead weight. The animal's breath was sulfurous, rank with carrion rot.

"Get . . . the fuck . . . off," gasped Dale, grabbing the giant hound by the loose skin at its neck as if it had a dog collar and thrashing to throw it off him. The black dog snarled and snapped, its teeth missing Dale's face by less than an inch. The fourth hound had run back to join the others in their assault on the now silent woman. Dale could hear the dogs moving away in the darkness, toward the sheds and barns, but dragging something . . . dragging something.

Dale screamed again and slammed his fists into the jackal ears of the hound above him. The dog leaped back.

Rolling onto his knees again and struggling to stand, Dale got a last glimpse of Michelle—just her pale legs and one hand, no longer flailing but dragging limply—as the four black dogs dragged her out of the last light from the open kitchen door, toward the black fields and the unseen barn. The dogs were snarling and snapping, tugging first one part of her and then another.

"You fucking goddamned fucking . . ." screamed Dale, blood running into his eyes and the earth seeming to pitch and roll as he staggered toward the pack of hounds. He could not see them or their victim now. Dale remembered the shotgun, hesitating only a second before turning back to get it. Even if it cost him a few seconds, he would be useless out there in the dark with the beasts unless he had a weapon.

Dale swung back to the concrete stoop and had just stumbled up onto it when the fifth dog hit him again—leaping through the air, its

black coat gleaming silver-black in the yellow light from the kitchen—
and then both he and the hound were flying off the stoop, striking the
wall of the farmhouse once before bouncing away. Dale fell facedown
in the black dirt, felt the earth rise like a wall below him, and felt himself sliding backward down it, toward the snarling hound behind him,
into darkness.

TWENTY-ONE

AND then what happened?"

"I already told you what happened next."

"Tell us again," said the deputy sheriff.

Dale sighed. He was very tired and his head hurt. The local anesthetic was wearing off where he had received nine stitches for the cut on his head, and a tetanus shot made his arm ache even through the throb of various bruises. But the headache was the worst part. The nurses had let him get dressed again, and now he and the sheriff's deputies were talking in an empty lounge just off the emergency room at the Oak Hill Hospital. It was a little after three in the morning, but there were no windows in the lounge and the fluorescent lights were very bright. The air smelled of burned coffee.

"After you left the farmhouse," prompted Deputy Presser. He was the older of the two men in uniform but still in his twenties, with a florid face and short-cropped blond hair. "How long was that after you say you lost consciousness?"

Dale shrugged and then regretted the movement. His arms and

shoulders and ribs ached as if someone had been kicking him with hobnailed boots. The headache stabbed behind his eyes like so many steel darts. "After I left the farmhouse," Dale said slowly, "I walked to the KWIK'N'EZ at the I-74 exit."

"But you say you had a cell phone. You could've used it before you got to the KWIK'N'EZ."

"I said that I couldn't find the cell phone," Dale said softly, so as not to aggravate the headache. He tried to place words between waves of pain. "I looked in my truck, but I couldn't find it. Maybe it slipped down between the seats. The Land Cruiser's interior lights weren't working. I could have looked in the house, but I thought it was important to get out of there and call for help."

"Your sports utility vehicle would not start," said the deputy in a monotone. He was glancing at the cheap spiral notepad in his hand. Dale could see the price sticker with its bar code still on the back of the notepad.

"My sports utility would not start," confirmed Dale. "The battery . . . it wouldn't even turn over."

"But Deputy Reiss got it started on the first try using the keys you lent us," said the sheriff's deputy. He glanced at the younger deputy sitting on the other side of the table. The younger man nodded seriously in confirmation.

Dale started to shrug again but then nodded. "I don't know why it didn't start earlier."

"And you have no phone at your residence. At the residence you currently lease?"

Dale took a breath. Nodded again. They had been going over this in one form or another since midnight. "You're sure there's no sign of Michelle?" he asked the younger deputy.

"Nope," said Deputy Dick Reiss. His name badge was pinned over his left shirt pocket.

"It's dark out there," said Dale. "Did you check the big barn?"

"Taylor and me checked all the barns and sheds," said Deputy Reiss.

Dale saw for the first time that the young man had a small wad of tobacco tucked between his cheek and gum.

The older deputy held up the notepad as a gesture for Deputy Reiss to shut up. "Mr. Stewart—do you prefer 'Mister' or 'Professor'?"

"I don't care," Dale said tiredly.

"Mr. Stewart," continued the deputy, "why did you walk the three miles to the KWIK'N'EZ? Why not to a neighbor's house? The Fallons live just a mile and a half north of you. The Bachmanns are just three quarters of a mile back toward the Hard Road—right before the cemetery."

"Bachmanns?" said Dale. "Oh, that's who live in Uncle Henry and Aunt Lena's house now."

Deputy Brian Presser returned a blank gaze.

Dale shook his head again. "If we're talking about Uncle Henry and Aunt Lena's old house just north of the cemetery, it was dark. There were no vehicles in the driveway. A big dog was barking in the side yard. I kept walking."

"But why the KWIK'N'EZ rather than into town, Mr. Stewart?"

"I couldn't remember where there was a pay phone in town," said Dale. "I thought there might be one at the post office or in front of the bank, but I couldn't remember. And it seemed darker in that direction. When I got to Jubilee College Road . . . well, I could see the lights of the KWIK'N'EZ just a mile or so ahead along the cutoff past the Hard Road." He touched his throbbing temple. "It seemed . . . safer. A straight line."

Deputy Presser wrote something in his tiny notepad. Dale noticed that the deputy's fingers went white with the tension of holding the pen and that the fingers bent almost concave in the same too-tight way that some of his students at the university had held their pens while taking notes.

Dale cleared his throat. "I didn't actually make the call," he said. "I was . . . well, I sort of lost consciousness again when I got to the gas station. I just asked the night man there to call the police and then I sat down on the floor next to the frozen foods until your deputy arrived. Not Deputy Reiss. The other one."

"Deputy Taylor," said Deputy Presser.

"The sheriff's not involved?" asked Dale. He had been relieved to the marrow of his bones when C. J. Congden had not responded to the call.

"No, sir," said Presser. "The sheriff's taken his family up to Chicago for the holidays. He'll be back day after tomorrow. Did you say you knew the sheriff, Mr. Stewart?"

"A long time ago," said Dale. "We went to school together. A long, long time ago."

Deputy Presser looked up at this, then made a note in his notepad.

"Jesus Christ," said Dale, shaking with fatigue and the aftereffects of shock, "aren't you going to get some people to look for Michelle? Those . . . animals . . . might have dragged her anywhere. She could still be alive!"

"Yes, sir. Come daylight, we'll have some folks out there. But tonight we've still got to get some things straight. You say she drove a white Toyota pickup truck?"

"A Tundra, I think," said Dale. He looked up at the two deputies. "It must still be parked there at The Jolly . . . at the farm."

"No," said Presser. "When Deputy Taylor and Deputy Reiss here drove out to the old McBride place, there was no white pickup. No vehicle whatsoever . . . except for your Toyota Land Cruiser, of course. Which started right up when Deputy Reiss tried it with the keys you gave him."

Dale could only frown at the two men for a moment. "No pickup?" he said at last. "No other car?"

"No, sir," said Deputy Presser, jotting notes again. "Are you sure you saw the vehicle you say Miz Staffney arrived in?"

"Yes," said Dale. "Wait . . . no. I don't remember seeing her truck yesterday. But . . . I mean . . . she had to have driven there, right? It's too far to walk from town . . ." For a wild moment, Dale felt his heart hammering with hope. Michelle must have not been hurt too badly if she could have driven her truck away. Then he remembered the snarling and snapping of the hounds and his heart rate slowed, the surge of hope fading. "I don't understand," he said. "Did you check her house in town?"

"Yes, sir," said Presser. "We checked the house you told us about. There's no one there. No vehicle in the drive there, either."

Dale breathed out and looked down at his hands where they lay as heavy and clumsy as poorly executed clay sculptures on his thighs. His chinos were filthy and spattered with his own blood.

"You say she arrived at the farmhouse in the daylight, though?" asked Deputy Presser.

"Late morning," said Dale. "Or very early afternoon. I was sleeping late. She woke me. We started cooking the dinner shortly after she arrived."

"And you never noticed what vehicle Miz Staffney arrived in?"

"No," said Dale. He looked the young deputy in the eye. Then he turned his gaze on the younger deputy, who stared back while chewing his tobacco. "Look, I asked earlier, but neither of you answered. Did you find blood there? Torn clothing? Signs of a struggle?"

"We found blood where you hit the door," said Deputy Reiss, moving the chaw aside with his tongue. "We found that sports jacket you talked about. It was all tore up, just like you said."

"And Michelle? Was there any sign of . . . of the dog attack?"

Before the younger deputy could answer, Deputy Presser raised the notepad to silence him again. "Mr. Stewart, we're going back out to the McBride place now, to look around again. We'd like your permission to search the house itself. Deputy Reiss there stood in the kitchen and shouted in to see if the lady was inside, peeked in a couple of rooms, but we'd like your permission to really search in the house. Could be, if she was hurt, she might be in there out of sight somewhere."

"I'll go with you," said Dale, struggling to get up.

"No, sir, that's probably not a good idea," said Deputy Presser. "The doctor here says that it might be better, because of the knock on your head, if you stayed in the hospital until tomorrow noon or so for observation."

"I'm going," said Dale. He held on to the back of his chair, blinking away the dizziness that came with the waves of headache.

"Your call, Mr. Stewart," said Deputy Presser. He and the other deputy led Dale through the empty ER, past the curious nurses and interns, and outside to where a Sheriff's Department car idled in the driveway, its exhaust roiling up and surrounding them like fog.

Dale rode in the back of the cruiser and felt like a prisoner—wire mesh grille between him and the two silent deputies up front, no window or door handles in the back, and the stink of urine and desperation rising out of the ripped upholstery. Evidently even small counties like Oak Hill's and Elm Haven's had their problems. Dale felt his heart begin to pound heavily as they drove up the lane to The Jolly Corner, the dead trees gaunt at the edge of the headlights.

Deputy Taylor was waiting in his idling vehicle. For a minute the four men stood in the dark side yard, the three deputies talking softly among themselves while Dale's gaze flicked repeatedly to the night-dark fields beyond the dim glow of the lights. "Could I have the keys?" he asked.

"Pardon?" said the deputy who had shown up at the KWIK'N'EZ hours earlier. Taylor was short and fat.

"Car keys," said Dale. He took them from the deputy and crawled up into his Toyota SUV. The truck started immediately. Dale turned on the overhead light and found his cell phone where it had slipped down between the center console and the passenger seat. He thumbed its on switch, but the display showed the charge depleted. Dale slid the phone into his shirt pocket and joined the three deputies on the stoop. He was cold and shivering without a jacket.

The kitchen was just as he and Michelle had left it after dinner—dishes rinsed but piled on the counter, the apple pie cold next to the empty coffee cups. Dale remembered that Michelle had turned off the coffeemaker before they had gone upstairs.

Deputy Presser stepped over to the stove and pulled the Savage over-and-under shotgun from where it had been propped against the wall. He broke it open, removed the unfired .410 cartridge, and raised his eyebrows while looking at Dale.

"I kept the gun loaded because of the dogs," said Dale.

"So you'd seen them dogs before," said Deputy Reiss from where he stood looking into the empty dining room.

"I told you both that I'd seen the dogs before. Just never so . . . big."

Deputies Presser and Reiss exchanged glances. Dale noticed that Presser had slipped the shotgun cartridge in his jacket pocket. He handed the weapon to Deputy Taylor, who remained standing by the outside door.

"I'm freezing," said Dale. "I'm going to go downstairs to get a sweater."

"We'll come with you," said Deputy Presser. To Taylor, he said, "Larry, you look in the rooms up here."

The basement was, as always, warmer than the upstairs. Dale pulled a heavy wool sweater from his stack of clothes near the bed and slipped it over his head while the two deputies looked around the room, shining their flashlights behind the furnace and peering into the empty coal bin. Michelle was not hiding anywhere.

Upstairs again, Deputy Taylor reported that there was nothing on the first floor. Presser nodded and stepped into Dale's study. "What's that mean?" asked the deputy, pointing his heavy flashlight at the IBM ThinkPad's screen.

The message on the otherwise dark screen read, **>Hrot-garmr. Si-ik-wa UR.BAR.RA ki-sa-at. Wargus sit.**

"Is that German?" asked Deputy Presser.

"I'm a writer," said Dale. He was stalling for time and trying to translate the message himself. He had never seen it before.

"I asked you if it was German or something."

Dale shook his head. "Just double-talk. I'm writing a science fiction novel, and I'm trying to get the sound of some alien's speech."

"Like Klingon, you mean," offered Deputy Reiss from the hall.

"Right," said Dale.

"Shut up, Dick," said Deputy Presser. The deputy walked out into the hall, leaving Dale to continue staring at the screen. If any of the deputies read Old English—a long shot, Dale knew—he might be in trouble. But as far as he could tell, only the first and last parts of the message were in Old English. "Hrot-garmr" translated as fire, but literally meant "howling dog," as in the howling funeral pyre they built for Beowulf's or Brynhild's funeral in the old epics. "Wargus sit" translated into "he shall be a *warg*"—that word again. "Warg" meant an outlaw who had literally become a wolf in the eyes of his comrades, a worrier of corpses, someone who, like Indo-European werewolves, deserved to be strangled.

"Mr. Stewart? What's upstairs?"

Dale came out into the crowded hall and looked up to where Deputy Presser stood five steps up the staircase. "Nothing's up there," said Dale. "It's been sealed off for years. I just took the weather plastic down a few weeks ago. It's empty." He shut up, realizing that he was babbling. His heart pounded in syncopation with his throbbing headache.

"Mind if I take a look?" asked Deputy Presser. Without waiting for an answer, the deputy switched on his flashlight and loudly climbed the stairs. Deputy Reiss followed. Taylor went back into the kitchen, still carrying Dale's empty over-and-under. Dale hesitated a few seconds and then went up the stairs.

Both men were in the front bedroom. One of the candles on the bedside table had burned out in its own pool of wax, but the other one was still burning. The blanket and the quilt on the bed were still mussed from when Michelle tossed them back as she got up to leave just . . . *My God*, thought Dale . . . just hours earlier. It seemed like days.

Deputy Presser lifted the quilt with his long flashlight and looked at Dale for an explanation. Dale met his gaze and stayed silent.

The three looked in the other room—dark and empty except for the child-sized rocking chair still in the middle of the room—and then clumped downstairs to the kitchen again.

"Are you going to search for her outside?" asked Dale. His throat felt raw and his head pounded worse than ever.

"Yeah," said Deputy Presser. "In the morning. Deputy Taylor here'll stay with you until we get back."

"To hell with waiting until morning," said Dale. Someone had brought his flashlight inside from where it had fallen during the dog attack and set it on the counter. Dale tried it. It worked. "I'm going to search the fields and outbuildings now."

Deputy Presser shrugged. "Larry," he said, talking to Taylor, "you stay with him here at the farm until we get back. If Mr. Stewart goes looking, you stay near your car radio in case we need to get in touch. If he don't come back in an hour, you radio dispatch. You got that?"

"But Brian, it's cold and dark out there as a . . ."

"You do what I say." Presser looked at Dale. "We'll be back some-time in the morning. Mr. Stewart, I suggest you get some sleep rather than wander around the farm in the dark, but Larry'll be here in case you need help."

"I don't need for Deputy Taylor to stay," said Dale. "But I'll need my shotgun."

Presser took the weapon from Taylor. He shook his head. "Sorry," he said with absolutely no tone of regret. "We're going to have to keep this at the sheriff's office for a while. Just in case."

"Just in case of what?" said Dale, truly mystified.

The deputy looked Dale hard in the eye. "You say there's a woman missing here. You say dogs got her. Well, if a woman's really missing, maybe something other than dogs got at her. We may need this shot-gun for tests."

"Oh, for Christ's sake," said Dale.

Presser gestured for Deputy Reiss to follow him, motioned for Deputy Taylor to stay where he was, and he and Reiss went out to their car and drove off. Dale glanced at the clock. It was a few minutes after 4:00 A.M.—still three hours until the first pale hint of sunrise.

Dale pulled on his winter peacoat, which was hanging on a hook by the door, switched on the flashlight, and went outside.

You shouldn't ought to go off alone," shouted Deputy Taylor from the circle of light on the stoop.

"Come with me, then," called Dale, not turning, walking toward the first outbuilding.

"I gotta stay near the car radio!"

Dale paid no further attention to the deputy. At the edge of the muddy turnaround, he whisked his flashlight beam through the frozen weeds, stabbed it behind the fences, swept it around the outside of the chicken coop. Nothing. Dale slammed the frozen door to the coop open and peered inside, moving the light from walls to nests to floor. For a second it looked as if someone had piled a dozen small, dark-metal coffins in the coop, but then Dale remembered moving Mr. McBride's punch-card learning machines out here. Dark stains were everywhere, but they were the old, dried, faded stains. A fox had gotten into the coop when there had been chickens here, he had told Michelle. *Or a dog.*

The next several outbuildings were also empty. Dale's flashlight beam moved across hanging sickles, scythes, grass cutters, plow disks, extra cornrollers, harrow disks, unnamed blades—all rusted red-brown. His flashlight beam was fading, the batteries dying.

Dale walked farther from the farmhouse, its few visible lights seeming very far away. Out by the rusting gas tank, which hung like some great spider's egg from the iron girders, one pair of wheel ruts led to the barn, another south along the fence at the edge of the empty field. Dale walked out into the field, slapped the flashlight hard against his palm to brighten the beam, and repeatedly called Michelle's name into the night, pausing each time to listen for any response from the dark fields. Nothing. Not even an echo or distant dog bark. Dale walked up and down the rutted lanes, shining the flashlight beam on bare patches of mud, hoping for dog prints, a human bootprint, a shred of cloth . . . anything as a sign. The ground was frozen and unrevealing.

Panting slightly now, his breath fogging into the freezing predawn air, flashlight glow as dim as a dying candle, Dale walked to the giant barn and leaned his weight into sliding back the huge door. The warped wood and rusted steel screeched in protest, but finally opened enough for him to slip in.

The harvesting combine still filled the space, the cornrollers reaching for him like faded red teeth.

"Michelle!!"

Something rustled in one of the high lofts, but it was too small a sound to be a woman. *The hounds couldn't have hauled her up there.* He shined the light up toward the impossibly high rafters and hidden lofts, but the cone of light was too dim now to reach that far. *But if she escaped the dogs, she could be up there, hiding, injured.*

Dale tucked the flashlight in his jacket and climbed the nearest ladder, feeling the rot in the wood and smelling the rot in the boards and straw of the barn itself. The structure was old and the ladder soft. He made sure that he never had both hands holding a single rung at one time—if one rung let go, he wanted to be connected to something solid.

Thirty feet up and he was high enough to peer over the edge of the wall and into the dark void of the first loft. The roof of the combine— the same combine that had killed his friend Duane forty years ago, chewing him up like so much offal?—was below him now, looking scabrous in the dying light. Dale shook the flashlight again, but this time the beam only dimmed further.

This loft was empty except for matted straw, some rotted tack, and a skull.

Dale crawled into the loft area, feeling the thin, rotted wood creak beneath his weight, groping ahead for the skull. It barely filled his palm, the long yellow teeth pressing toward the blue vein in his wrist.

What the hell had it been? A rat? It seemed too large for a rat. A raccoon or fox? How did it get up here?

He set the skull back, swept the flashlight uselessly back and forth toward the other black rectangles of the loft, and called Michelle's name again. The only response was a fluttering of a barn owl or sparrows in their nest.

The flashlight died completely before he started down the ladder. Dale tucked it into his jacket and checked the luminous dial of his watch, noting that his arm was shaking from either the terrible cold or the strain of climbing, or both. It was just 4:45.

Dale left the barn door open when he walked back to the house, half hoping that the hounds would jump him in the dark along the way, wanting to know that they were real. He gripped the long barrel of the useless flashlight so hard that his fingers cramped.

The deputy's car was idling and the deputy was snoring in the front seat, his police radio cackling static audible even through the raised window glass. Dale left him sleeping and went into the house. It was still cold inside. He turned up the thermostat, heard the old furnace click in, and walked into the study. He had forgotten the computer.

>**Hrot-garmr. Si-ik-wa UR.BAR.RA ki-sa-at. Wargus sit.**

Dale rubbed his cheek, feeling the beard there. He was very tired, and his headache had grown worse rather than better. He found it difficult to focus his eyes on the screen. "Howling dog"—as if for fire. "He shall be a *warg*." But what the hell was the middle part? After another moment of thought, during which he half dozed, Dale typed—

>**What the hell is the middle part?**

A moment later he snapped awake, realizing that he had dozed off in his chair while waiting for an answer. *The screen never answers when I'm here.* Aching everywhere, his head and lacerated scalp throbbing, Dale pulled himself out of the chair and walked out to the kitchen. He peered through the glass—the deputy was still there—and then locked the door and went back into the study.

>**It is Hittite.**

Dale sighed and rubbed his cheek again. He had to try twice before he could type out his next question without misspellings.

>**What does it *mean*?**

This time he walked to the bathroom, holding himself upright with one palm against the wall as he urinated into the bowl. Flushing the toilet, washing his hands, staring at his pale and red-eyed image in the mirror, he felt as if he were observing and feeling everything through a waterfall of red pain. He walked back into the study.

>**zi-ik-wa UR.BAR.RA ki-sa-at means "thou art become a wolf."**

Dale felt a surge of rage through the pain and fatigue. He was so fucking tired of games, he could throw up.

>**Why the hell do you send me these messages in code if you're just going to translate them for me?**

Even before he had walked back from the kitchen, he knew he had wasted a question. This was absurd. The computer screen seemed to agree with him, since there was no reply. He hurriedly typed—

>**Who has turned into a wolf? Me?**

This time Dale walked to the head of the basement stairs and paused. Big band music was coming from the console radio down there. Hadn't it been off when he and the deputies had been down there? Wishing that he still had his loaded shotgun but almost too tired to care about what was waiting for him, Dale went down the stairs.

The soft lamps near Duane's old brass bed spilled soft yellow light onto the pillows. The wine crates and wooden shelves of paperbacks were reassuring in their familiar clutter. The furnace rattled and breathed with its usual sound. The radio dial glowed, and the old music played softly. Perhaps he had turned the radio on without thinking about it when he was down here. Or perhaps the station had been off the air for a while when the deputies were here with him. Who cared?

His legs felt leaden as he climbed the stairs and went back into the study.

>LU.MES hurkilas—the demon entities who are set to capture wolves and to strangle serpents.

"Well," said Dale to the empty room, "thanks for nothing." He switched off the ThinkPad and fell onto the daybed, still fully clothed, his muddy boots hanging over the edge. He was asleep before he thought to pull a blanket up over himself.

TWENTY-TWO

URING their last months together, before and after the late-spring blizzard that had snowed them in at the ranch, Clare and Dale had spoken—at first via banter but then more seriously—about being together. Clare had been accepted into an elite medieval studies graduate program at Princeton and would be leaving in July to meet some of the other anointed scholars there and prepare for the coming years. In June, Dale heard himself offer to join her there so that they could be together.

"I'll finish the fall semester, take that sabbatical I've been putting off, and head your way."

"What would you do there?" asked Clare. "Around Princeton?"

"Maybe they need a lit teacher. Some nontenure-track guy to teach freshman comp."

Clare said nothing, but her silence showed her skepticism.

"Seriously," said Dale, "what am I going to do here in Missoula without you? I'd be like Marley's ghost hanging around someplace that's dead to me."

"Isn't it the ghost who's supposed to be dead?" said Clare. "Not the place?"

"Whatever," said Dale. "Actually, I've always thought that it was the ghost who was vital and the place that died. That's why ghosts can be seen—they're more real than the thin, faded version of the place. You know, like Lincoln's ghost in the White House."

"Interesting," said Clare. They were cleaning out the stables at the ranch, and now she paused to rest on a pitchfork. "You're serious? About coming east?"

"Absolutely," said Dale. He realized even as he said it that he had not been serious, not up to that moment, but that now the plan meant more to him than anything else in the world. At the same instant, he felt the relationship between them swing as if on the hinge of his intentions; up to that moment he had been the locus, his hometown, his university, his classes that she was auditing, his family here in Missoula to be dealt with—but now he would be the guest, she the focus of action and attention. As if acknowledging this further, Dale said, "What I'll really do is write my serious novel and learn how to be a good house husband while you're at the library studying *The Song of Roland* or whatever the hell it is. When you come home in the wee hours, I'll have a hot meal waiting and give you a back rub when we go to bed."

Clare had looked up at him then, almost startled, with something like alarm visible in her eyes in the instant before she looked back toward the horses. Perhaps, Dale thought, it had been the use of the word *husband*. Whatever the reason, her glance had given him the first solid foreboding of their final breakup just three months in the future.

As if denying the possibility of that, he had stepped forward then, pushed her pitchfork away, and hugged her tightly, feeling her soft breasts through the denim workshirt. If there was a second or two of awkwardness on her part, it fled as soon as she returned the hug and raised her face for a kiss. One of the horses—Mab's roan, probably—showed jealousy by kicking the stall gate.

* * *

Someone was knocking on the door.

Dale struggled awake, registered that he was lying on the daybed in Mr. McBride's study still fully clothed and that his head still hurt like a sonofabitch, and then the pounding resumed. He looked at his watch. 9:15 A.M.—they had promised to have people here for the search at first light. "Goddamnit to hell," muttered Dale.

Groaning, rubbing his whiskered cheeks, he went out to let Deputy Taylor in.

"Where are they?" asked Dale as the heavyset deputy stepped into the kitchen, swinging his arms to get warm and eyeing the empty coffeemaker. Taylor had obviously also just been awakened.

"You're supposed to come with me," said the deputy, nodding toward his idling car outside.

"What are you talking about? Deputy Presser said he'd bring some people at first light for the search and . . ."

"I got a radio call. You're supposed to come with me right now."

"To the sheriff's office?" asked Dale. "Have they found Michelle?" Dale's skin went cold then with the absolute certainty that they had found her body.

Deputy Taylor shook his head, although Dale couldn't guess which part of the question he was answering. Hopefully both parts. "You gotta come now," the deputy said, pulling Dale's peacoat from the hook.

"Do I have time to grab a quick shower and change my clothes?"

"I don't think so," said the chubby deputy, holding out the peacoat.

"Am I under arrest? Do I have to ride in the back of your car?"

The question seemed to surprise the deputy. For a few seconds he could only blink. Then he said, "Uh-uh," but without conviction.

"In that case," said Dale, "I'm going to go brush my teeth. That's non-negotiable."

*　*　*

Dale rode up front, in silence. The clouds were low and leaden this Christmas morning, and it was beginning to snow with that slow steadiness that often meant a real accumulation. Dale was surprised when Taylor turned into Elm Haven rather than taking the road to Oak Hill, but he knew where they were headed as soon as the car turned north on Broad Avenue.

The old Staffney house and barn looked in bad shape in the dim light, paint missing, the barn leaning, all the windows dark. The only vehicle in the driveway was another Sheriff's Department car. Deputy Presser came out from around the back of the house as Taylor led Dale down the driveway.

"Michelle?" said Dale. The cold hand closed around his heart again. If she had driven here, injured, it was possible she could have died here in the house that she and that Diane woman had been renovating. *But the deputies said yesterday that the house was empty. And her truck's not here.*

Deputy Presser shook his head and led them up onto the back porch. He used a key to let them in the back door.

"Don't you need a warrant for this?" asked Dale, following Presser into the cold kitchen. The place smelled of mildew and rat droppings.

"The Staffneys don't own it any more," said Presser, sliding his hands back in his jacket pockets. It was colder in the kitchen than outside. "The bank over in Princeville has had the paper on this place since Dr. Staffney's wife died in the home a few years ago."

"But Michelle said . . ." began Dale and stopped. He realized that the kitchen was not just empty, it was *abandoned*. Plaster had fallen from the ceiling, exposing the bare ribs of lathing, and cabinet doors had long since been ripped off. Dust and droppings and chunks of plaster lay everywhere on the counters. Sections of the tile floor had been torn up and other sections destroyed by a leak from the ceiling. The ancient stove had been pulled out of place, with parts of it missing. There was no refrigerator. Pipes and gas valves and plumbing had been disconnected. The sink itself was filled with broken glass and mold, as if someone had broken bottles in there and left it many years before.

"I don't understand," said Dale. "Michelle said that she and her friend had been working on the place, bringing it up to snuff so that she could sell it."

"Yes," said Deputy Presser. "That's what you told us last night." He gestured for Deputy Taylor to hand him the long flashlight, flicked it on, and nodded for Dale to follow him down the hall into the other rooms.

Dale stopped in shock at the end of the stale-smelling, plaster-cluttered hallway. What had been a downstairs bathroom to the right showed a toilet ripped out of the floor, broken ceramic in the shattered sink, and an empty spot where an old claw-footed bathtub might once have crouched. The dining room and living room were worse.

The broad wooden boards in both rooms had been torn out, leaving only the upright edges of obviously rotted two-by-fours with a black drop to the unlighted basement visible between them. Even if the three men could have tiptoed successfully across the old support beams, there was nowhere to go; the once-grand staircase to the second floor was completely gone. Someone had long since torn out and scavenged all of the stairs, banisters, newel posts, and fixtures. Above the huge hole to the basement where the stairway once rose, the ceiling had collapsed. Dale could see all the way through the hole to the broken second-floor ceilings and even through the water-damaged roof to the low clouds. It looked to Dale like photos from London during the Blitz, some buzz-bombed tenement in Soho. Snow blew down the ruined shaft and disappeared into the basement, white flecks being absorbed by absolute black.

"She said that she and the Diane woman were fixing it up . . ." he began again and then stopped. *I dropped Michelle off here after I saved her from the black dogs at the schoolyard that night. She went inside. I told the deputies this.*

Dale fell silent and just watched the two men watching him. "You

knew this in the middle of the night at the hospital when you were taking my statement over and over," he said.

Deputy Presser nodded. "We knew that no one has lived here or
stayed here in the past ten years. We know more now. Go with Deputy
Taylor in his car." Presser turned on his heel and clomped out of the
dead building.

Dale had imagined the sheriff's office to be in the tall old courthouse
on Oak Hill's central square, but it turned out to be in a low, 1960s-
modern brick building a block from the courthouse. There were a few
offices with venetian blinds closed, an artificial Christmas tree with
one string of colored lights blinking on the dispatcher/receptionist's
counter, and enough cubicles for four or five deputies. Presser had
Dale walk back to the furthest cubicle, where two glass walls met. The
view was across the street to Gold's Deluxe Bowling Center. The
building was boarded and closed.

Well, thought Dale as the deputy waved him to an empty chair, *at
least they haven't booked and fingerprinted me yet.*

"Deputy," he began, "I swear I don't understand. Michelle told me
that she and the other woman were living in that house when I met
her . . . saw her here in Oak Hill for the first time a few weeks ago.
That's where she had me drop her off the night she called me about
the dogs by the school. The sheriff can verify that . . ."

Presser held up one hand in the same motion he had used to silence
Deputy Reiss. Dale shut up.

"Mr. Stewart," said Deputy Presser, "I need to tell you about your
rights. The sheriff has called me—he's going to be back late tomorrow
or early the next day—and he wants to talk to you, but he's authorized
me to carry out this interview. You have the right to remain silent . . ."

"Oh, Jesus," said Dale. "Am I a suspect?"

"Let's say that you need to know your rights right now," said the
deputy. "You've probably heard this a million times on TV, but I've got

to do it. You have a right to an attorney. If you cannot afford an attorney, one will be appointed for you . . ."

"Christ," repeated Dale. He felt as if someone had knocked the wind out of him again. His headache throbbed. "So I'm a suspect in Michelle's disappearance."

"No, you're not," said Presser. "Anything you do say can be held against you in a court of law. Now, would you like to call an attorney, Mr. Stewart?"

"No," Dale said dully, knowing that he was being a fool and not caring.

"I'm going to turn on this tape recorder, Mr. Stewart. Are you aware of it and do you agree to me taping this interview?"

"Yes." It was an old-fashioned reel-to-reel recorder, and Dale could see the reels turning, the brown tape sliding through its gate as Presser spoke into the microphone, giving the date and time of the interview, giving Dale's full name and his own, and positioning the microphone on the desk. Both the deputy's voice and his own sounded very distant to Dale. "If I'm not a suspect in Michelle's disappearance, what am I being read my rights for? What other crime has been committed?"

"I'll ask the questions during this interview," Deputy Presser said flatly. "But I will tell you that it's against the law to file a false report alleging that a crime or kidnapping or violent incident has occurred when it has not."

Dale felt like laughing. "Oh, a violent incident has happened all right, Deputy. And Michelle Staffney is out there somewhere, possibly dying, because we're wasting time here with you interviewing me. *That's* the crime."

"Mr. Stewart," Presser said, obviously ignoring everything Dale had just said, "would you please read this?" He opened a thin file folder and slid a printout across the desk to Dale.

Dale first noticed the black-and-white photo of Michelle Staffney in the left column. The AP article was dated a little less than two years earlier.

HOLLYWOOD PRODUCER CHARGED WITH DOUBLE MURDER

Hollywood producer Ken Curtis was arraigned today in Los Angeles Superior Court for the January 23rd shooting murder of his wife, actress Mica Stouffer, and her alleged lover, Diane Villanova. Ms. Stouffer, the screen name for Michelle Staffney Curtis, had been separated from her husband for three months but was still involved in what friends called "a stormy relationship" with the producer. Curtis pleaded not guilty today and it is expected that his attorney, Martin Shapiro, will invoke the insanity defense. "Ken was obviously not in control of his faculties at the time," Shapiro told reporters.

Curtis is known primarily as the producer of the successful *Die Free* films starring Val Kilmer. Mica Stouffer, a member of SAG for thirty-one years, had done bit parts for most of that time. Diane Villanova, with whom Ms. Stouffer was living for two months prior to the fatal shooting, was a screenwriter with such credits as *Fourth Dimension* and *All the Pretty Birds Come Home to Roost.*

Both Stouffer and Villanova were pronounced dead on the scene at Ms. Villanova's Bel Air apartment last January 23 after neighbors called the police about—

Dale quit reading and set the piece of paper on the desk. "This has got to be a mistake," he said thickly. "A joke of some kind . . ."

Deputy Presser removed two more pages from the file, slick old-fashioned thermal fax pages this time, and slid them across to Dale. "Can you identify either of these women, Mr. Stewart?"

They were morgue photographs. The first photograph was of Michelle—mouth open, eyes almost closed, but with a slit of white showing from beneath the heavy eyelids. She was on her back and top-less to the waist, her perfect, pale augmented breasts flattened by gravity and the photographer's flash. There were two perfectly rounded bullet holes at the top of her left breast and another—with a wider entrance wound—just below her throat. Another bullet hole was centered in a bruised discoloration in the center of her forehead.

"Michelle Staffney," said Dale. His throat was so thick that he could hardly speak. He looked at the second photograph. "Christ," he said.

"Curtis used a knife on her after he shot her," said Deputy Presser.

"The hair and shape of the face looks like Diane . . . like the woman I met with Michelle . . . but . . . I don't know." He handed the photos back to Presser. "Look, your sheriff saw me with Michelle—with this woman."

Presser just stared. "And when did you say that you first saw these two women in Oak Hill, Mr. Stewart?"

"I thought . . . I mean I saw them about six or seven weeks ago. A few weeks before Thanksgiving, I think . . ." Dale stopped and shook his head. "Could I have a drink of water, Deputy Presser?"

"Larry!" shouted Presser. When the other deputy appeared, Presser sent him to the water cooler.

Dale's hand was shaking fiercely as he lifted the little paper cup to drink. He was stalling for time, and he knew that Presser knew it. The deputy had paused the tape recorder, but now he started it again.

"Is this woman from the news reports—Mica Stouffer, aka Michelle Staffney—the same woman that you say was attacked by dogs and carried off at the McBride farm last night, Mr. Stewart?"

"Yes," said Dale.

There was a long silence broken only by the tape hiss.

"Mr. Stewart, are you on any sort of medication?"

"Medication?" Dale had to stop and think a minute. "Yes, I am."

"What kind is it, sir?"

"Ah . . . Prozac and flurazepam and doxepin. One's an antidepressant . . ." *As if the entire world doesn't know that,* thought Dale. ". . . and the others are to help me sleep."

"Are these medications prescribed by a psychiatrist?" asked Deputy Presser.

Is it any of your goddamned business? thought Dale. He said, "Yes. They're prescribed by a psychiatrist in Montana where I live."

"And have you been taking them regularly?"

No, thought Dale. When was the last time he took his meds? Sometime before Thanksgiving? He could not remember. "I've missed some," said Dale. "But I only take the doxepin and flurazepam to sleep and it was about time to wean myself from the Prozac anyway."

"Did your psychiatrist say to do that?"

Dale hesitated.

"Are you on any psychoactive or psychotropic drugs, Mr. Stewart? Any medications for schizophrenia or similar disturbances?"

"*No*," Dale said, more stridently than he should have. "No." At this point in a movie, Dale would be screaming, *Look, I'm not crazy!*, but the truth was that this had hit him like a sledgehammer and he suspected that perhaps he was coming unhinged. Unless he was dreaming this encounter with the deputy, then some other memory was false. The photograph of Michelle, dead, cold on a Los Angeles morgue slab, had been real enough. *Perhaps Michelle has a twin sister . . .*

Right, Dale mentally answers himself. Has a twin sister who comes back to Elm Haven with this Diane Villanova person's twin sister, and then passes herself off as Michelle Staffney for no reason . . . Dale shook his aching head. He remembered the Staffney family from when he had lived in Elm Haven forty years ago. Michelle had no sisters.

"Mr. Stewart?"

Dale looked up. He realized that he had been cradling his head, perhaps muttering to himself. "My head hurts," he said.

Deputy Presser nodded. The tape recorder was still running. "Do you want to change the statement you made to us about the dogs attacking you and Miz Michelle Staffney?"

Still rubbing his head, Dale asked, "What's the penalty for false reporting, Deputy?"

Presser shrugged, but punched the PAUSE button on the recorder. "Depends on the circumstances, Mr. Stewart. Tell you the truth, this situation's mostly been inconvenience, it being Christmas Eve when you called for help, what with only four people on duty last night and you tying up three of them and all. But as far as I can see, no real harm's been done yet. And you obviously *did* injure your head last night, Mr. Stewart. That can cause some funny reactions sometimes. Do you remember how you hurt your head?"

The hellhounds knocked me against the door while they were ripping Michelle apart and dragging her into the dark, thought Dale. Aloud, he said, "I'm not sure now. I know how crazy this sounds, Deputy."

Presser started the recorder again. "Do you wish to change any of your statement, Mr. Stewart?"

Dale rubbed his scalp again, feeling the stitches there and also feeling the pain and throbbing just under the bone of the skull. He wondered if he had suffered a concussion. "I've been depressed, Deputy Presser. My doctor—Dr. Charles Hall in Missoula—prescribed Prozac and some sleeping medication, but I've been busy and—upset—in recent weeks and forgot to take it. I admit that I haven't been sleeping much. I'm not sure how I hurt my head last night and Michelle . . . well, I can't explain that, except to say that things have been a bit confused for me the last few months." Suddenly he looked up at the deputy. "She brought a ham."

"Pardon me?" said Presser.

"Michelle brought a ham. We ate it yesterday. And some wine. Two bottles. Red. That's something physical. We can check that. Maybe some other woman who . . . anyway, we can check the ham and the wine."

"Yes," said Presser. "I have Deputy Reiss out doing that today. We found a receipt in the Corner Pantry bag in your kitchen. Deputy Reiss is going to talk to Ruthie over at the Corner Pantry and then visit the few liquor stores in the county."

"You searched my kitchen?" Dale said stupidly.

"You gave us permission last night to search the house," Deputy Presser said stiffly.

"Yeah." Dale lifted the small cup to drink some more water, found it empty, crumpled the cup, and tossed it into a wastebasket. "Am I under arrest, Deputy?"

Presser shut off the recorder and shook his head. "I mentioned that the sheriff wants to talk to you tomorrow or the next day. We could keep you here until then . . ." Presser made a vague gesture toward the far wall, behind which Dale guessed there were jail cells. "But you might as well wait at your farm."

Dale nodded and winced at the pain. "I don't suppose you're going to give me my shotgun back. The black dogs might be real, you know."

"Deputy Taylor'll drive you back to the farm," said Presser, ignoring Dale's question about the over-and-under. "Don't go anywhere without letting us know. Don't even think about leaving the county. But there's one thing I think you should do, Mr. Stewart."

Dale waited.

"Call this Dr. Hall," said Presser.

TWENTY-THREE

IT snowed all the rest of Christmas Day. Exhausted and confused, Dale stood at the study window and watched the deputy's car disappear into the snow, and then just stood there watching the snow continue to fall. After a long period of this during which his thoughts were as vague and opaque as the low gray clouds, Dale went over to his ThinkPad and powered it up. Switching from Windows to the DOS shell, he typed after the blinking C prompt—

>**Am I cracking up?**

Dale did not expect an answer—certainly not while he sat there waiting—and he did not receive one. After a while he wandered out to the kitchen, washed the plates, and tidied up. Someone—Michelle last night?—had put Saran wrap around some of the ham and placed it on the second shelf of the refrigerator. Dale knew that he should be hungry, since he hadn't eaten since dinner the night before—*Did I really* have *dinner last night, or did I imagine it as well?*—but he had no appetite now. Dale pulled on an extra sweater and his peacoat and went out into the snow.

Several inches of wet, heavy snow had accumulated in the turn-around. Dale headed west, past the white-shrouded sheds and the barn—its large door still slightly open—out toward the low, flat hill above the creek. There were no dog tracks on the rutted lane, no human footprints in the corn-stubbled field, no sign of an injured woman dragging herself.

Am I nuts? It seemed probable. Dale realized that the deputy's advice had been sound—he should call his therapist. Dale might have called from Oak Hill if not for the presence of the deputy during the ride back.

It was snowing harder when Dale reached the small rise where Duane had buried his faithful collie, Wittgenstein, that same summer of 1960. The trees along the creek running north and south were indistinct in the snowfall, and Dale could not see even the barn, much less the farmhouse. Sound seemed muted. Dale remembered days like this from his childhood in Elm Haven and elsewhere: a day so still that the slight thrumming of one's own heartbeat or pulse sounded like the settling of snowflakes.

1960. Dale tried hard to remember the details of that summer. Nightmares—he remembered nightmares. White hands pulling his younger brother under his bed in their shared bedroom in the tall white house across from Old Central in Elm Haven. The ancient school itself, boarded up and awaiting demolition, but burning mysteriously at the end of that summer before the wrecking balls could bring it down. A green glow from the shuttered cupola atop the monstrous old building. The kids had created legends and spooky tales around that school. And some of those legends seemed real after Duane died in these very fields that summer.

Dale turned slowly around. Below the slight rise, a few shattered cornstalks were the only hint of even faded color against the featureless white, rows upon rows of slight mounds that had been high stalks even this summer past.

What the hell happened to our generation? Dale tried to remember his college energy and idealism. *We promised so much to so many—especially to ourselves.* He and other professors his age had often commented on it—the easy cynicism and self-absorption of today's college-age students, so different from the commitment and high ideals of the mid and late 1960s. *Bullshit,* thought Dale. It had all been bullshit. They had bullshitted themselves about a revolution while really going after exactly what every previous generation had sought—sex, comfort, money, power.

Who am I to talk? Dale tasted bile as he thought of his Jim Bridger books. It was work-for-hire these days: a set fee for a series of formulaic frontiersmen-and-Indian-maiden tales. They might as well have been bodice rippers for all the serious intent that Dale had brought to the writing the past few years.

Sex, comfort, money, power. He had obtained everything on the list but the last—and had schemed and connived in faculty politics to obtain even his pathetic version of that over the years—and what had it brought him? *Thanksgiving and Christmas dinner with a ghost.*

Dale left the low hill and began walking south along the creek, using the wooden cross-braces to climb over fences. A dog was barking far away to the west, but Dale could tell from the sound that it was just a run-of-the-mill farm dog, a real dog, a mortal dog. *As opposed to what? My hellhounds?*

Dale wished that he believed in ghosts. He could not. He realized that everything—life, love, loss, even fear—would be so much easier if he did. For decades of adulthood now he had tried to understand the psychology of people who prided themselves in believing in ghosts, spirits, feng shui, horoscopes, positive energy, demons, angels . . . God. Dale did not. It was a form of easy stupidity to which he preferred not to subscribe.

Have I gone crazy? Probably. It made the most sense. He knew that he had not been sane when he had loaded the Savage over-and-under a little more than a year earlier and set the muzzle to the side of his head and reached to pull the trigger. He could recall with perfect tactile memory what that circle of cold steel had felt like pressing into the flesh of his forehead. If he was crazy enough to do that, why not all this?

All what? Dining with ghosts? Imagining being seduced by the sexiest girl in sixth grade? Writing questions and answers and acrostics to himself on the computer?

If Michelle had been a ghost—if ghosts existed, which Dale did not believe for a second—why would *she* be here? She barely knew his dear friend Duane McBride. Twelve-year-old Michelle Staffney, the doctor's daughter, simply did not play with raggedy-ass boys like Duane or Harlen or Mike or Kevin . . . or Dale. Besides, Michelle Staffney aka Mica Stouffer had hated Elm Haven. She had lived in California for more than thirty years and—it seemed absolutely certain—had died there. If she were going to haunt someplace, why not haunt the Bel Air home of her lover, Diane Villanova, where both of them had been murdered? Or better yet, haunt her husband's place—the esteemed producer of the Val Kilmer *Die Free* series.

Jesus. Dale shook his head at the banality of the world. The movement shook free snow that had been clinging to his hair. He realized that he'd not brought so much as a baseball cap and his hair was soaked, his face sheened with melted snow. It was cold.

Dale looked around and realized that he had walked to the little woods not far from the Johnson farm. The black dogs had followed him this far a few weeks ago. *Had they?* There was almost certainly a real black dog somewhere in all this hallucination—a visual trigger for these fantastic illusions—just as there was probably a real, living red-haired woman that he'd glimpsed at the Oak Hall City Market some weeks ago that had made him obsess on the memories of the sixth-grade sex grenade, little Michelle Staffney.

Anne's hair is an auburn red—in the right light.

Dale rubbed his face, realizing that he had forgotten his gloves as well as his hat. His hands were chapped and red with cold.

The hellhounds could be behind you right now, moving silently through the snow, stalking you. He turned slowly, not feeling real alarm.

Empty fields and falling snow. The already dim light was fading farther. Dale checked his watch—four-thirty. Could it be so late? It would be hard dark in half an hour. The snow had accumulated to seven or eight inches now, wet, soaking through his chinos . . . the same bloody chinos he had been wearing the night before. It was his blood, of course, from where he struck his head on the door during his fall. *What made me fall? Who made me fall?*

He walked back toward the unseen farmhouse, cutting diagonally across the frozen fields and climbing two more fences where they came together at a post. He was approaching the barn from the south along the fenceline there when the house came into view, a dark gray shape against the dark gray evening.

A Sheriff's Department car was in the drive, but it was the bigger vehicle, years older than the ones the deputies drove. The sheriff's car.

C. J. Congden stood near the chicken coop, gray Stetson covered by one of those clear plastic hat covers that state troopers and county mounties wore when it rained or snowed. Congden had his hand on his holstered pistol and was tapping the white grip of the gun. He was grinning.

"Thought you had orders to stay in the house, *Professor,*" the big man said.

"They told me to stay at the farm," said Dale. "I'm at the farm." His head began hurting in earnest again. His voice sounded dull even to himself. "Did you have a good Christmas vacation trip, Sheriff?"

Congden grinned more broadly. His teeth were yellowed from nicotine. Dale could smell the cigarette and cigar smoke on the fat man's jacket. "So, you all through telling ghost stories, *Professor?*"

Suddenly Dale felt as if someone had put snow down the back of his neck. "Wait a minute," he said, reaching out as if to grab Congden's jacket. The sheriff stepped backward so as not to be touched. "You were *there.*"

"Where?" C. J. Congden's grin had gone away. His eyes were cold.

"At the schoolyard that night. You *saw* her. Presser had so convinced me that I was nuts that I almost forgot . . . you *saw* her. You spoke to her."

"To who?" asked Congden. He was smiling slightly again. It was dark enough now that Dale had to lean closer just to see the expression on the former bully's face under the brim of the cowboy hat. With no lights on in the house, the big structure seemed to be disappearing with the last of the winter daylight.

"You know goddamned well who I'm talking about," snapped Dale. "Michelle Staffney. You offered to drive her home, for Christ's sake."

"Did I?"

"Fuck this," said Dale. He brushed past Congden and started walking up toward the house. "Arrest me if you're going to. I've had enough of this shit."

"*Stewart!*" The noise was at once a bark and a command. Dale froze and turned slowly.

"Come here a minute, Stewart. I want to show you something." Congden took a step back, half turned, and took two more steps. Toward the barn.

"What?" said Dale. Suddenly he was afraid. It was dark out now, really dark. He had no flashlight. Once, in that same summer of 1960, C. J. Congden and his pal—Archie?—had stopped Dale along the railroad tracks outside of Elm Haven and Congden had aimed a .22 rifle at Dale's face. It was the first time that Dale Stewart had felt absolute, knee-weakening, bladder-loosening fear.

He felt it again now.

"Come here, goddamnit," growled Congden. "*Now!* I don't have all day."

No.

"No," said Dale.

Go to the house. Hurry.

Dale turned and began walking quickly, expecting and fearing the fast strides behind him or the gleam of hounds' eyes ahead of him.

"Stewart, goddamn you to hell, come *here*! I want to show you something in the barn!"

Dale broke into a clumsy run, ignoring the pounding in his head that throbbed every time his boots struck the frozen earth through the snow. He couldn't see the house. It was too dark.

Dale almost ran into a barbed-wire fence, realized that he was behind the chicken coop, and ran to his left and then to his right again. The house became visible as a shape in the darkness. Dale threw a glance over his shoulder, but he could not see Congden in the gloom. Snow stuck to his eyelashes and threatened to blind him.

"Stewart, you pussy!" came the sheriff's voice, but from Dale's right somewhere in the dark, closer. "Don't you want to know what happened?"

Dale thudded up the cement steps, threw open the door, slammed it behind him, locked the main lock, and threw the heavy bolt. His head throbbing, he turned slowly in the dark kitchen, listening for movement or breathing in the house. If there was any, he could not hear it over his own panting and the pounding of his heart.

He peered out the window, but even the sheriff's car was lost to the gloom and the heavy snow. *Jesus, that son of a bitch has a gun. And I don't. And he's crazier than I am.*

Not turning on a light, Dale went down into the basement and felt along the wall near the crates of books. The big console radio was playing 1950s hits softly, its glowing dial the only light in the room. *There it is.* Dale hefted the Louisville Slugger and carried it back up to the kitchen. It was no match for the huge .45 Colt pistol Congden carried in his holster, but perhaps in the dark—

In the dark. Dale peered through the window, standing to one side so that he could not be seen himself. Suddenly he had the image of C. J. Congden's face pressed against the glass less than an inch from his own, teeth yellow, skin yellow, tongue lolling.

Holy fuck, thought Dale, instinctively raising the bat. There was no face at the window. Congden wasn't anywhere to be seen in the few feet he could see in the dark. *Maybe he drove off when I was getting the bat and I didn't hear the car.*

And maybe he didn't.

Maybe he's already in the house with you.

Dale realized that he was shaking, his hands clutching the Louisville Slugger so tightly that his fingers were cramping. *Jesus, God, I am losing it. I'm coming apart at the fucking seams.*

Dale slid down the wall against the stove, still holding the bat as he sat on the old tile and pressed the side of his face against the cool metal of the stove itself. He felt the melted snow in his hair running down his temple and cheeks. *The cold circle of the muzzle.* Dale was glad that Presser hadn't returned the Savage to him—he felt so low and frightened at the moment that pulling the trigger seemed almost a welcome escape. *Would it fire this time?* Dale thought, *Yes.*

There was a movement outside on the stoop just a foot away through the door. Snow dropping from the eaves? A stealthy footstep, those scuffed cowboy boots? Someone shifting an ax from his left hand to his right?

Sitting on the linoleum floor, face against the stove, Dale Stewart closed his eyes and slept.

The thing was banging the door inches from Dale, clawing to get in. Dale jerked awake, crawled on the linoleum still half asleep, found the baseball bat, and lifted it as he got to his feet.

Daylight streamed in through the curtains across the kitchen door. He had slept through the night. Someone knocked again, and Dale peered out at a sheriff's green jacket, a badge, a Stetson. It wasn't C. J. Congden. A newer Sheriff's Department car idled in the turnaround. The snow was more than a foot deep, and the only break in it was from the parallel tracks of the sheriff's tires.

This sheriff, a man in his thirties with a lean face, saw Dale and motioned for the door to be opened.

Dale blinked and set the baseball bat between the wall and the stove. It took him a few seconds to fumble the locks open. Cold air curled in when he opened the door and the man on the stoop—a smaller man than Congden, leaner and shorter than Dale—took a step back like a properly trained encyclopedia salesman, showing his deference to the homeowner.

"Professor Stewart?"

Dale rubbed his chin and nodded. He realized that his hair must be wild, and that he was still wearing the same soiled and wrinkled chinos, shirt, and sweater that he had put on for Christmas Eve dinner two days earlier.

"I'm Sheriff Bill McKown," said the man in the sheriff's jacket. "You mind if I come in?"

Dale shook his head and stepped aside. The man's voice was deep and slow, his manner assured. Dale himself felt as if he was made of torn paper and broken glass and might cry at any second. He took a deep breath and tried to force calm into himself.

Sheriff McKown removed his Stetson, smiled, and seemed to glance around casually, but Dale saw that the man was taking everything in. "Everything all right here this morning, Professor Stewart?"

"Sure," said Dale.

McKown smiled again. "Well, I just noticed that you answered the door with a baseball bat in your hands. And you seemed to be on the floor before that."

Dale had no explanation, so he offered none. "You want some coffee, Sheriff?"

"If you're making some for yourself."

"I am. I haven't had my morning coffee yet." *That was an understatement*, thought Dale. "Have a seat while I make some," he said aloud.

McKown watched silently while Dale fumbled out the Folgers can, filled the coffee pot with water, poured it into the coffeemaker, cleaned the filter under the tap, spooned out six servings, and got the thing percolated. Dale's fingers felt swollen and clumsy, useless sausage balloons.

"That's an interesting report you filed on Christmas," said McKown, accepting his mug of coffee.

"Cream or sugar?" asked Dale.

McKown shook his head and sipped. "Good." Dale tasted his and thought it tasted like cloudy bilge water.

"You feeling any better now?" asked the man with the sheriff's badge.

"What do you mean?"

McKown nodded. "Your head. I hear you got nine stitches and maybe a light concussion. Any better?"

Dale touched his scalp and felt the crusted blood under the old bandage. "Yes," he said. "The headache's better this morning." It was.

"You want to talk about the report? The woman you said went missing? The dogs? Anything?"

Dale sipped his coffee to gain time. Should he tell McKown about C. J. Congden's visit?

No. Tell him nothing.

"I know how crazy the whole thing sounded," Dale said at last. "It sounds crazy to me. I guess your deputy told you that I've been on some medication for depression . . ."

McKown nodded. "Did you get a chance to call the psychiatrist in Montana? What's his name?"

Tell the truth.

"His name is Charles Hall. And no, I haven't had time to call yet."

McKown drank some coffee and set the mug down. "We called him, Professor Stewart. Just to check that you were a patient of his."

Dale tried a smile, knowing how ghastly it must look. "Am I?"

"Not anymore," said the sheriff. "I've got some bad news for you."

Dale could only wait. He had no idea what the man was talking about.

"Dr. Charles Hall died on December nineteenth," said McKown. "We talked to his answering service and then the doctor on call, Dr. Williams. That's a woman, Dr. Williams."

Dale stared. When he could speak, he said, "Was he murdered?"

McKown lifted his coffee mug but did not drink from it. "Why do you ask that, Professor Stewart?"

"I don't know. The way things have been going . . . wait, you're serious about this? Charles Hall is dead?"

"An auto accident on December nineteenth," said Sheriff McKown. "Evidently he was on his way back from a long weekend skiing in Telluride, Colorado, when a drunk came across a center line." McKown took a pink while-you-were-out slip from his stiffly ironed breast pocket and set the paper on the kitchen table. "This is Dr. Williams's number. She wants you to call her as soon as you can so she can talk to you and make sure your prescription's refillable — that sort of stuff."

Dale lifted the slip and stared at the phone number. "Did you tell her . . . about Christmas? About me?"

"We confirmed that you'd been a patient of Dr. Hall's and did ask her what you were being treated for. She didn't want to talk about anything — it's all confidential — but we told her that there was a possible missing person situation and that we just had to clarify that you weren't delusional. She looked at Hall's file on you — she's taking half his patients, another doctor took another half — and she confirmed that you were just being treated for depression and anxiety."

" 'Just,' " said Dale.

"Yes," said Sheriff McKown. "Well, she wants you to call her as soon as you can. I guess you can't from this place, though."

"No," agreed Dale. *Charles Hall dead. That prissy little office with the windows looking out on the tops of the trees. Who would use that office now?*

"My deputy tells me that you seem to remember that you and I went to school together, Professor Stewart."

"What?" Dale looked up from the pink piece of paper in his hand. "Sorry?"

McKown repeated the statement.

"Oh . . ." said Dale and stopped. He knew that he was coming across as a mental deficient as well as a lunatic, but his head was too full of conflicting information to process things right now.

"Might have been my uncle, Bobby McKown," said the sheriff. "He graduated high school in '66, so he would've been about your age."

"I remember Bob McKown," Dale said truthfully. "He used to play ball with us. Go hiking out at Gypsy Lane with us."

The sheriff sipped coffee and then smiled thinly. "Uncle Bobby always told us little ones about that Bike Patrol you guys had going then. Bobby always wanted to be in it, but I guess you had enough members."

"I don't remember," said Dale.

"Do you remember anything more about the other night, Professor Stewart? Anything about the dogs?"

Dale took a breath. "I'm pretty sure I've been seeing real dogs around here, Sheriff. There were paw prints the last few weeks . . ."

McKown's expression was pleasant enough, but Dale saw that the man was watching and listening very carefully.

"I've never had hallucinations or delusions before, Sheriff," Dale went on, "but I'm prepared to be convinced that I'm having them now. I'm still . . . depressed, I guess. I haven't been sleeping too well. I've been trying to work on a novel, and that's not going very well . . ."

"What kind of novel?"

"I'm not sure what kind it is," said Dale with a self-deprecating chuckle. "A failed one, I guess. It was about kids—about growing up."

"And about that summer of 1960?" asked McKown.

Dale's heart rate accelerated. "I guess it was. Why do you say that, Sheriff?"

"Our uncle Bobby used to talk about that summer occasionally— very occasionally—but more often than not, he *didn't* talk about it. It was like being a kid in Elm Haven back then was one long sunny day, except for that summer."

Dale nodded, but as the silence stretched he realized that McKown wanted something more. "Bob McKown knew Duane McBride . . ." Dale gestured toward the old house around them. "Duane's death that summer came as a real shock to a lot of us kids. We handled it in weird ways, if we handled it at all."

"I've read the case files," said McKown. "Mind if I have some more of this good coffee?"

Dale started to get to his feet, but McKown waved him back down, went to the counter, refilled his own mug, brought the pot over to top off Dale's cup, and set the pot back in the coffeemaker burner. "Who do you think killed your friend Duane, Professor Stewart?"

"The sheriff then and the Justice of the Peace . . . J. P. Congden, C. J.'s father . . . determined that it was an accident," said Dale, his voice unsteady.

"Yeah, I read that. Their report and the coroner's report said that your friend Duane just started driving this combine in the middle of a July night—the combine didn't even have its corn picker covers on—and they say that somehow this Duane, who everybody says was a genius, managed to fall out of the cab of that combine and then have the machine run over him, tearing him apart. You buy that, Professor Stewart? Did you buy that then?"

"No," said Dale.

"I don't either. A combine would have to drive in a full circle to run over someone who had been driving it. The corn pickers are in the *front*. A paraplegic would have time to get out of the way of a combine doing a full turn. I presume the coroner knew that about combines, don't you?"

Dale said nothing.

"That particular coroner," continued McKown, "was a good friend of Justice of the Peace J. P. Congden. Do you remember that Duane McBride's uncle, Art, died that same summer? A car accident out on Jubilee College Road?"

"I remember that," said Dale. His heart was pounding so hard that he had to set the cup of coffee down or spill it.

"The sheriff's office then, all one of him, found some paint on this uncle Art's Cadillac," continued McKown. "Blue paint. Guess who drove a big old car those days that was blue?"

"J. P. Congden," said Dale. His lips were dry.

"The Justice of the Peace," agreed Sheriff McKown. "My uncle Bobby tells me that ol' J. P. used to have the habit of racing people's cars toward bridges like that one where Duane's uncle got killed, and when folks hurried to cross the one-lane bridge ahead of him just to stay on the road, old man Congden used to pull them over and fine them a twenty-five-dollar ticket. Twenty-five dollars was real money back in 1960. You ever hear those stories, Professor Stewart?"

"Yes," said Dale.

"You all right, Professor?"

"Sure. Why?"

"You look sort of pale." McKown got up, found a clean glass, filled it with tap water, and brought it back to the table. "Here." Dale drank.

"My uncle Bobby knew J. P. Congden and his kid, C. J., real well," continued McKown when Dale had finished with the water. "He said they were both bullies and bastards. C. J., too."

"You think that J. P. or C. J. ran Duane McBride's uncle into that bridge abutment?" asked Dale, working to hold his voice steady.

"I think it would've been right up old J. P.'s alley, his sort of bull-shit," said McKown. "I doubt if he tried to *kill* Arthur McBride. Just shake him down, probably. Only the bridge ruined that plan."

"Did anyone accuse him of it?"

"Your friend Duane did," said the sheriff.

Dale shook his head. He did not understand.

"The report says that Duane McBride, age eleven, called the state police—you remember that the sheriff then, Barnaby Stiles, was a good ol' boy friend of J. P. Congden—but the report says that one Duane McBride reported the paint match between his uncle Art's Cadillac and the Justice of the Peace's car."

"And did they investigate?"

"Congden had a great alibi," said McKown. "Over in Kickapoo drinking with about five of his pals."

"So they dropped it."

"Right."

"*After* Sheriff Barney told J. P. Congden that Duane was on to him."

McKown sipped his coffee, showing no sign of how bitter the brew was.

"And did J. P. Congden have an alibi for the night *Duane* was killed?" asked Dale. His voice was shaking now, but he did not care.

"Actually, he did," said McKown.

"Same five cronies at the bar, I bet," Dale said.

McKown shook his head. "Not this time. Congden—J. P. Congden—was in Peoria at a traffic court seminar thing. At least half a dozen officers of the law were with him that night. But how old was C. J. Congden that year, Professor Stewart?"

"Sixteen," said Dale. He had to force the words out through still-dry lips. "Whatever happened to C. J. Congden, Sheriff McKown?"

McKown flashed a grin. "Oh, he ended up where most small-town bullies do . . . he was elected county sheriff here four times."

"But he's dead now?" said Dale.

"Oh, sure. C. J. stuck the barrel of his pearl-handled .45 Colt in his own mouth in '97, no, the summer of '96, and blew his brains all over the inside of his double-wide." McKown stood. "Professor Stewart, you're not under arrest or anything, and I'd sure love to talk to you some more, but I think it's important that you call this Dr. Williams in Missoula. You look tired, sir. How about if you get showered and shaved, and I'll drive you into Oak Hill? You can call from the station house. Then I'll drive you back here myself. How does that sound?"

"Fine," said Dale. He got to his feet like an old man.

"Would you mind if I just looked around this house for a minute, Professor Stewart?"

"Search it?" said Dale. "I don't mind. Your deputies already went through it."

McKown laughed. For a small man, he had a big man's easy laugh. "No, not search it, Professor. Just look around. I've never been in here and . . . well, you know. We lived on a farm about four miles from here when I was growing up and between local legends and Uncle Bobby's stories and with the crazy old lady who lived here after Mr. McBride died, this was our local haunted house."

McKown walked into the dining room. "This looks empty, but not especially haunted."

Dale went into the study to get some clean clothes to take down to the basement for after his shower. The computer screen had his question from the day before and another line under it.

>**Am I cracking up?**
>**Absolutely.**

The sheriff walked through the front parlor and into the hall just outside the study. Dale killed the power on the ThinkPad and closed the lid.

"I'll just be a minute," said Dale, heading down the stairs. "Help yourself to the last of the coffee."

TWENTY-FOUR

For two weeks after Clare had left him, Dale would call her apartment number and hang up as soon as she answered. He had blocked his number so that she could not use *69 to know who had called. After a week of almost nightly calls like this, her phone suddenly refused to accept calls from any blocked phone. Dale removed the block from his phone and called the next evening. An answering machine picked up. He called again at half-hour intervals all that night. Only the answering machine responded. Dale listened intently to the silence behind the machine's robotic tones, beeps, and hisses, but there was no hint of Clare there. The next evening, the same thing. Dale began calling every fifteen minutes all through the third night. The phone rang. The machine picked up. Dale became certain that she was not home any of those nights.

The next day, Friday, Dale had no classes. He made a point of telling several fellow faculty members that he was going on his annual autumn camping trip to Glacier National Park. He even called his old house when he knew that Anne would be away and left a message on that machine—Anne had recorded a new message to take the place of the old one with his voice on it—telling her where, roughly, he would be camping in Glacier in case he did not return for classes on Tuesday. Leaving this information had been his practice for years—the only year he had skipped it had been the first time he had driven Clare to the park and Blackfeet Reservation—and Anne would know that it was only old habit.

Dale flew to Philadelphia and drove across the river into New Jersey and on to Princeton, arriving just before dark. He had never been there before, and he found Clare's apartment—she had given him the address way back in July when she first found it—with some difficulty. Her apartment was in a small duplex several miles from the university campus. Dale sat in the rented car for fifteen minutes before working up the nerve to cross the street and ring her bell. She was not home. She did not come home that night. Dale knew this because he sat in the car until 4:00 A.M. watching, slumping down out of sight when a police car drove by twice, urinating out the passenger side door into a lawn gone to weeds rather than drive away to find a rest room.

About ten-thirty the next morning—a beautiful, crisp, red-leafed autumn Saturday—Clare arrived in a Chevy Suburban that Dale knew was not hers. A young man in his late twenties, a blond young man with very long hair and a Nordic face, was driving the Suburban. He and Clare went into her apartment. They did not hold hands or hug, nor did they touch in any way while Dale watched them, his car hidden only by leaf shadow, but Dale could sense the intimacy between them. They had obviously spent the night together.

He sat in his car and fiddled with his beautiful Dunhill cigarette lighter and tried to decide how to confront her, confront them, what he could say without appearing like the biggest loser and asshole in existence. He could think of nothing.

Five minutes later, Clare and the blond man came out of the duplex. She was carrying the same green nylon duffel she had brought to the ranch so often and the battered rucksack she had brought with her on their first trip to Glacier and the reservation. She and the man were laughing, deep in conversation as they threw her bags in the back of the Suburban, and neither looked across the street to where Dale sat as they clambered into the big vehicle and drove off.

Dale followed them, making no effort to avoid detection. Tailing someone was easier than it looked in the movies. They drove back the way he had come from Philadelphia, took the I-295 bypass around Trenton, then drove about twenty miles south on Highway 206, eventually turning east on Highway 70. By the time the big Suburban turned southeast onto Route 72, the traffic had thinned out considerably. Dale was vaguely aware that they had entered—or were about to enter—the relatively empty part of New Jersey known as the Pine Barrens.

Clare and her lover turned south again on Route 563 and drove eleven miles—Dale clocked it on his rental car's odometer—before pulling left into a parking lot amidst a cluster of ramshackle buildings. The sign out front said PINE BARRENS CANOE RENTAL.

Dale drove on another mile before finding a good turnaround spot in the tiny crossroads town of Chatsworth and then drove back slowly. A river ran along the west side of the highway for this stretch, and he caught a glimpse of Clare and her lover in a canoe heading south, downriver, before they disappeared around a bend in the river. He turned into the canoe rental place and parked next to the empty Suburban. Dale walked past the main building, noted the high stack of firewood there and the chopping stump and the ax embedded in it and the pile of wood chips and unstacked wood, looking as if the owners were preparing for a hard winter, and then he was waiting for the teenaged boy in khaki pants and a green Pine Barrens Canoe Rental shirt to finish helping two women shove off into the easy current.

"Howdy," said the boy, looking at Dale long enough to register the dress pants and street shoes and to dismiss him as a canoe rental client. "Can I help you?"

Dale studied the canoes and kayaks lined up on trailers and at the river's edge. "How much to rent a canoe?"

"Thirty bucks," said the teenager. "That includes life jackets and paddles. Cushions are fifty cents extra. Three bucks each for a third or fourth person. More than four people, you need a second canoe."

"I'm alone," said Dale, feeling for the first time how true those words were.

The boy shrugged. "Thirty bucks."

"How far do the canoes go?"

The kid looked up from counting cash and smiled. "Well, they'd go to the ocean, but we like to retrieve them before that."

"Well, how far is a normal trip, then? The two women who just left? How far are they going?"

"Evans Bridge takeout," said the boy as if Dale should know where that was. "They'll be lucky to get there before dark."

"How about the couple before them?" said Dale. "They going to Evans Bridge?"

"Uh-uh. Those folks were camping. They'll be at Godfrey Bridge Campsite in four and a half or five hours. Then they plan to go on down to Bodine Field tomorrow where we'll take them out."

"How do you know they'll be camping at Godfrey Bridge?"

"You have to have a camping permit before you can do a two-day rental. They showed me the permit." The boy looked at Dale. "You a cop?"

Dale tried to laugh casually. "Hardly. Just curious about canoe trips. My girlfriend and I have been thinking about taking one."

"Well, you'd better make up your mind by next weekend if you're planning to rent from us," said the boy, sounding bored and disinterested again. He was lifting kayaks onto a trailer. "We close for the winter after then."

"Do you have a map I could have of the distance to campsites and such?"

The boy took a wrinkled photocopy out of his back pocket and handed it to Dale without looking at him again.

Dale thanked him and walked back to the car.

The gravel turnoff from Route 563 to Godfrey Bridge Campsite was only about ten miles south of the put-in point. Dale had expected a developed campground, but at the end of the gravel road there was only the river, some metal fire pits set back under the trees, and two portable toilets. Thick forest pressed in on all sides. The camping area was empty. Dale glanced at his watch. It was a little after two. Clare and her boyfriend should be along between 6:00 and 7:00 P.M. The afternoon was clear and silent—no insect sounds and little animal or bird noise. A few squirrels scampered in the trees, but even their autumn play seemed hushed. Occasionally a cluster of canoes or a lone kayak would float by, the people either brazenly loud or as silent as the absent insects. None of the canoes carried Clare.

Dale walked back to his rental car, drove it a few hundred yards up the gravel road to an overgrown logging road he'd noticed, pulled it back out of sight, and popped the trunk open. For a while he stood staring into the trunk at the ax he had taken from the canoe rental place.

Professor Stewart? You get ahold of the psychiatrist in Montana?"

Dale looked up from the table where he was sitting drinking bad coffee out of a Styrofoam cup. The sheriff had shown him to a tiny room with a bare table and telephone and left him to make his call. There was no two-way mirror in the wall, but there was a tiny slit in the door and Dale guessed that this—sans telephone—was what passed for an interrogation room in the Oak Hill sheriff's office.

"Yeah," he said.

"No problems?"

"No problems," said Dale. "Dr. Williams told me what you did about Dr. Hall's accident and agreed to phone my prescription into the Oak Hill pharmacy. Actually, I'm pretty sure that I still have some medication left back at the farmhouse."

"Good," said McKown. The sheriff slipped into the only other chair and laid a manila folder on the table. There was a paperback book under the folder, but Dale could not see the title. "Are you willing to talk to me for a minute?" asked the sheriff.

"Do I have a choice?" Dale was very tired.

"Sure you do. You can even call a lawyer if you want."

"Am I under arrest or suspicion for something other than being crazy?"

McKown smiled tightly. "Professor Stewart, I just wanted to ask your help on a little problem we have."

"Go ahead."

The sheriff removed five snapshot-sized glossy photos from the folder and set them out in front of Dale as if inviting him to play solitaire. "You know these boys, Professor?"

Dale sighed. "I don't know them, but I've seen them. I recognize this kid as Sandy Whittaker's nephew, Derek." He tapped the photograph of the youngest boy.

"You want to know the names of the others?"

"Not especially," said Dale.

"This one you should know about," said McKown, sliding the photograph of the oldest skinhead out by itself on the tabletop. "His name is Lester Bonheur. Born in Peoria. He's twenty-six. Dishonorable discharge from the army, six priors including felonious menacing, assault with a deadly weapon, and arson. Only convicted once for auto theft, served just eleven months. He discovered Hitler about four years ago the way most folks discover Jesus. These other punks are just . . . punks. Bonheur is dangerous."

Dale said nothing.

"Where was the last place you saw these five men?" McKown's pale blue eyes were too intense for a poker player.

"I don't . . ." began Dale.

Tell him the truth. Tell him the whole truth.

The sheriff's stare grew even more intense as Dale's silence stretched.

"I don't know what the place is called," continued Dale, completely changing what he was going to say, "but it's that muddy old quarry area a mile or so east of Calvary Cemetery. When we were kids, we called the little hills there Billy Goat Mountains."

McKown grinned. "That's what my uncle Bobby always called the old Seaton Quarry." The grin disappeared. "What were you doing there with these troublemakers, Professor?"

"I wasn't doing anything *with* them. The five of them were in two pickup trucks, chasing me. I was in my Land Cruiser."

"Why were they chasing you?"

"Ask them," said Dale.

The sheriff's stare did not grow any friendlier.

Dale opened his hands above the tabletop. "Look, I don't even know who these skinheads are except for him . . ." He tapped the photo of the youngest boy again. "Sandy Whittaker told me that her nephew was a member of this local neo-Nazi group. They threatened me when I first got here in October. Then the other day—"

The day before Michelle Staffney showed up on Christmas Eve.

"The day before Christmas Eve they jumped me at the KWIK'N'EZ. You can ask the fat girl who works there. I got in my Land Cruiser and drove away. They chased me in their pickup trucks. I took the back way from Jubilee College Road and lost them at the muddy old quarry area."

" 'Back way' is right," said the sheriff. "That's all private land. Why would you drive across country like that with these bad boys after you?"

Dale shrugged. "I remembered Gypsy Lane. It's an old overgrown road that we used to . . ."

"I know," interrupted McKown. "My uncle Bobby talked about it. What happened out there?"

"Nothing," said Dale. "My truck got through the mud. Theirs didn't. I drove on back to the McBride farm."

"Were the boys all alive when you left them?" McKown asked softly.

Dale's jaw almost dropped. "*Of course* they were alive. Just muddy. Aren't they alive now? I mean . . ."

McKown swept the photos back into the folder. "We don't know where they are, Professor Stewart. A farmer found their pickup trucks out there in the mud yesterday afternoon. One of the pickups got turned on its side . . ."

"Yes," said Dale. "I saw that. The green Ford followed me up and over a muddy hill there and tipped over at the bottom. But both boys— both *men*—got out of it. No one was hurt."

"You sure of that, Professor?"

"Yes, I'm sure. I saw them hopping around and cursing at me. Besides, the chase—even the truck tipping over—all happened in extreme slow motion. No one was going fast enough to get hurt."

"Why do you think they were chasing you?"

Dale held back his anger at being interrogated. "Sandy Whittaker said that Derek and his pals had read on the Internet some essays I wrote about right-wing groups in Montana," he said slowly. "The skinheads called me names both times they encountered me—'Jew lover,' that sort of thing—so I presume that's why they wanted to hurt me."

"Do you think they would have hurt you that day, Professor?"

"I think they would have killed me that day, Sheriff McKown. If they'd caught me."

"Did you want to hurt them?"

Dale returned the sheriff's hard gaze with a hard look of his own. "I would have happily killed them that day, Sheriff McKown. But I didn't. If you've been out there you must know that. They must have walked out of that muddy mess and left tracks."

"They did," said McKown. "But we lost their tracks up at the cemetery."

Dale almost laughed. "You think I jumped them up at the cemetery? Killed all of them? Hid their bodies somewhere? Just me against five skinheads less than half my age?"

McKown smiled again. "You had a weapon."

"The Savage over-and-under?" said Dale, literally not believing this conversation. "I didn't have it with me."

McKown nodded, but not reassuringly.

"And it's a single-shot," Dale said with some heat. "You think I went home and got the over-and-under, went back to the cemetery, and shot them all? You think they'd just stand around there and wait to be shot while I reloaded?"

McKown said nothing.

"And then why would I call you about the dogs and Michelle . . . about this delusion of mine the next day?" Dale went on, losing the heat of anger and almost faltering. "To throw you off the trail of the skinhead murders?"

"Doesn't sound very likely, does it?" McKown said agreeably.

"Not something a sane person would do." Dale's voice sounded bleak even to himself.

"No," said McKown.

"Are you going to arrest me now, Sheriff?"

"No, Professor Stewart, I'm going to drive you back to the McBride place and let you get on with your day. We can stop over at the pharmacy on the way so you can get your prescription. And I will ask you to stay around the area here until we get some of this confusion cleared up."

Dale could only nod.

"Oh, there is one other thing."

Dale waited. He remembered that Peter Falk as Columbo always said that right before trapping the suspect into confession.

"Would you be so kind as to sign this for me?" McKown moved the folder and slid a copy of *Massacre Moon: A Jim Bridger Mountain Man Novel* across the scuffed tabletop. The sheriff unbuttoned his shirt pocket to retrieve a ballpoint pen. "It'd be a real treat if you could sign it 'To Bill, Bobby's Nephew.' We're both real big fans."

*   *   *

It was only early afternoon when Dale got home. The sheriff touched the brim of his Stetson and drove off down the lane without coming in. The house was cold. In the study, the ThinkPad was open and turned on.

>**Did you really kill Clare, Dale?**

TWENTY-FIVE

THE five black dogs returned shortly after midnight. Dale watched from the darkened house, through the kitchen window and then from the dark dining room and then from through the parlor drapes and then from the study as the hounds circled the house, their pelts and eyes picking up the starlight, their forms visible only as negative space against the softly glowing snow.

Dale softly slapped the bat against his palm and sighed. He was very tired. He had not slept all day or evening, and the sleep the night before had been while sitting on the kitchen floor. Now, as then, he knew that if the dogs wanted to come in, they would. They were larger than ever. Larger than barrel-chested huskies, taller than wolfhounds. If they wanted to come in, the kitchen door would not hold them out.

Feeling an urge not dissimilar from an acrophobic's desire to leap from high places, Dale found it pleasing to consider opening the door and going out into the night, allowing them to drag him down and off. *At least the waiting would be over.*

He went into the darkened study. The only light here was from the glow from the words he had not disturbed in almost twelve hours.

>**Did you really kill Clare, Dale?**

He decided to do this thing. To have a conversation. He leaned over to type.

>**Are you really Duane?**

No new words appeared while he watched, of course, so he took the bat and walked the short circuit down the hallway to the kitchen and back, checking to make sure that no hounds had forced their way in through any of the unprotected windows. The question went unanswered. He had not really expected an answer.

He tried again, typing, walking, finding a response this time, tapping in more words, walking, reading, thinking, and then typing again. In this way a sort of asylum conversation ensued.

>**I didn't kill Clare. I didn't kill anyone.**
>**Then why did you remember doing so?**
>**It wasn't a memory. Perhaps a fantasy. And how do you know what I'm remembering or fantasizing?**
>**Have you reached the point, Dale, where you can't tell your fantasies from your memories?**
>**I don't know, Mr. Phantom Interlocutor. Perhaps I have. Are you a phantom or a memory?**

No response on the screen when Dale returned. He tried again.

>**Look, if I'd killed Clare Two Hearts, I'd be in jail right now. The memory—the fantasy—had me follow her to New Jersey and kill her and her boyfriend at a public campsite. If it had**

happened that way, I would have left clues everywhere—
plane tickets, talking to the kid at the canoe rental place, car
rental bills, credit card signatures, probably footprints and
fingerprints. I would have flown back to Montana a gory
mess. Ax murders aren't antiseptic acts, you know. The cops
would have arrested me within twenty-four hours. Old
boyfriends are the first suspects.

>If the police know there is an old boyfriend. Why would
Clare tell anyone in her new life at Princeton about you,
Dale? What did she call you that time you thought she was
joking—"My first foray into the gray-haired set"? Why
would she reveal that to anyone in her new life?

>My hair's not that gray.

Dale made his loop, found no new words on the screen, read the
exchange that was there, and laughed out loud in the dark house.
"Jesus Christ, I'm certifiable." He turned off the computer.

A soft voice said something indecipherable upstairs.

Dale got the flashlight and went up, leaning into the cold draft flowing down the staircase. There was a light. He hefted the bat, feeling his
heart pound faster in his chest but also feeling no real fear. Whatever
was there was there.

The remaining candle in the front bedroom had been re-lighted. It
flickered as he entered, and his shadow danced on the mildewed wallpaper.

"Michelle?" There was no answer. He smashed the candle with the
baseball bat, the flame skittering across floorboards before dying, and
then went downstairs using only his flashlight.

Outside a dog howled.

Dale turned on the kitchen light, found the yellow legal pad he kept
on the counter, and started a shopping list for the morning:

- plastic sheeting
- nails

After a moment of thought, he added:

- new shotgun and shells

A different dog howled somewhere in the dark farther to the west, out toward the barn. Dale checked the flimsy door locks, turned out the light, and went downstairs to the basement.

It was warmer there. He turned on the soft lamp near the bed, got into his pajamas, and crawled under the thick comforter. The sheets felt clean, the pillows soft. He tried to read from an open paperback— *Swann's Way*, open to the "Swann in Love" section—but he was too sleepy to make sense of the words. The big console radio was whispering dance music, but Dale was too tired to get up and shut it off. Besides, the glow of the wide dial was reassuring in the dark.

The starlight was visible through the small, high windows near the ceiling. Occasionally a dark shape would occlude the stars, then another would glide by, but Dale did not notice. He snored while he slept.

This night is where my friend Dale passed the point of no return. What was going to happen here was going to happen. He knew that even as he slept. There was no going back.

Dale did not feel like an unintelligent character in a sloppily told tale. This was his *life*. Everything in the past year or two had seemed to lead him here—to this house, to these events, to this pending conclusion to all doubts. In an age when his generation sought to hide all reality behind simulation and feigned experience, Dale had to know what was *real*. What was memory and what was fantasy? And there remained the simple fact that despite everything, Dale did not believe in haunted houses or ghosts. This disbelief ran deep as marrow, and his belief in this disbelief was as stubborn as bone. Dale believed in mental illness and in schizophrenia and in the uncharted confusions of the mind, but not in ghosts.

More important to his decision to stay these last few days of his life at The Jolly Corner was his perception—was his *understanding*—that whatever was happening to him had to be resolved *here*. This cascade of insane events had come to him in the form of a coming to life of something vital, a stirring of energies, a preparation for birth. Or perhaps a preparation for death. Either way, Dale believed, labor had been induced in this cold farmhouse out in the ass end of Illinois, and some rough beast was slouching toward The Jolly Corner either to be born or to die.

And there was the final fact that Dale knew that he could not go home now—could not show up at Anne's and Mab's and Katie's door in this shape—could not return to the shreds and tatters of his former life in Missoula without this thing being resolved, these questions answered.

Once, when talking with Clare during a long hike in Glacier Park, he had asked her what she thought the topography of a human life might look like. She suggested that it was an inverted cone measured out in units of potential—infinite at the top, zero at the bottom—and that the decreasing radials around the diminishing outer shell of the cone could be measured in accelerating time as one grew closer to old age, death, dissolution. Dale had thought this a tad pessimistic. He had suggested that perhaps a human life was a simple parabola in which one never knew when the apogee—the highest, most sublime point—had been achieved.

"Maybe this is your apogee," Clare had said, gesturing to the pine forest and the lake and the distant peaks and to herself. Somewhere nearby in the trees a Clark's nutcracker had scolded them.

"Not yours?" he said, pausing to hitch up the chafing backpack straps.

"Definitely not mine," Clare said in that offhand tone of casual cruelty that somehow seemed strangely attractive to him then—cosmopolitan, perhaps.

But Dale had wondered about that topography of a lifetime later, both before and after Clare and the sure grasp of his sanity had left him. Recently, it had amused him to think that the ribbon of his life might be twisted in a mad Möbius loop, curling back on and through itself, inside becoming outside, losing entire dimensions even while acquiring some impossible continuity.

Christmas had been on a Tuesday this year. Dale half expected to be arrested or dragged off to the loony bin by the weekend, but although Deputy Presser showed up to check on him—to make sure that he hadn't left—on Saturday and Sheriff McKown came by late on Sunday, no one grabbed him and clasped him in handcuffs or strapped him into a straitjacket.

Both times Dale saw a sheriff's car coming up the snowy drive, he was sure it was C. J. Congden. What would he do if it was? He had no idea. Each time the car drew close enough to be identified, Dale felt something like a sense of disappointment that it wasn't Congden.

"How are you doing out here, Professor?" asked Sheriff McKown on Sunday afternoon. Dale had just been leaving for a walk, and the sheriff walked down to where Dale had paused near the large gasoline tank behind the generator shed. "Everything all right?" asked the sheriff.

Dale nodded.

"This amount of snow is something after all these warm, dry winters, huh?"

Dale asked, "Have you found the five skinheads?"

The sheriff had removed his Stetson and rubbed his fingers around the brim in a motion that reminded Dale of one of C. J. Congden's habits. Perhaps all cops with cowboy hats did that. "Nope," he said. "Their families haven't heard from them, either. But there is one piece of interesting news."

Dale waited.

"We have an old bachelor farmer who lives north of you who's gone missing," said McKown. "Bebe Larson. Him and his old Chevy Suburban disappeared on the day before Christmas Eve."

"Do you think I killed him as well as the skinheads?" asked Dale.

McKown put his Stetson on slowly. "Actually, I was thinking that maybe Mr. Larson ran into your friends on County Six and they might have borrowed his truck and maybe him as well."

"You think those boys are capable of kidnapping?" said Dale.

"I think Lester Bonheur is capable of anything," McKown said flatly. "And the others are just along for the ride."

Dale shrugged. "I'd like to go into Oak Hill sometime this week to get some provisions," he said, amusing himself at the use of the word "provisions." Pretty soon he'd be talking like one of his mountain man characters.

"That'd be fine," said Sheriff McKown. "I trust that you'll be coming back here until we get all of this other stuff cleared up."

"Does all this other stuff include the return of my property, Sheriff? The over-and-under, I mean."

McKown rubbed his chin. "I think we'd better hang on to that weapon until we find those boys, Professor Stewart." The small man hesitated a moment. "Have you been taking the Prozac?"

"Yes," lied Dale.

"The other prescription stuff too?"

"I haven't had to," Dale said. "I've been sleeping like a baby." *Like the dead.*

"Have you talked to this Dr. Williams in Missoula again?"

"I haven't been away from The . . . from the farm," said Dale. "No phone."

"Well, maybe you can talk to her when you come into Oak Hill."

"Maybe," agreed Dale.

When the sheriff got back in his vehicle, Dale leaned over and tapped on the driver's-side window. The glass whined down. "Sheriff," said Dale, "are you and your deputies going to be checking on me every day?"

"Well, we're concerned about you, sir. And there's this outstanding issue of the false report."

Dale said nothing. Snow was falling gently on his bare head and eyelashes.

"But why don't you give me a call when you're in Oak Hill this week, just tell us when you're heading back here. Then we'll drop by sometime later in the week and make sure everything's all right here." When Dale just nodded, McKown said, "Well, if I don't see you before Tuesday, you have a Happy New Year, Professor Stewart."

Dale stood back and watched as the sheriff's car turned around in the quickly falling snow and headed down the snowy lane. He noticed that the car's wheels rolled over the fresh paw prints in the snow as the sheriff drove away.

That afternoon Dale changed his mind about buying plastic sheeting for the second floor and nailed up two sheets to cover the opening. The thin cotton did almost nothing to keep the cold air from flowing down the staircase, but the barrier offered some psychological relief.

Dale worked on his novel all the rest of that afternoon and evening, forgetting to eat, forgetting to pause even to go to the bathroom. The house grew quite cold as night approached, but Dale was lost in the hot summer days of his childhood and did not notice. He was almost three hundred pages into the novel by then, and although no distinct plot had emerged, a tapestry had been woven of leafy summer days, of the Bike Patrol kids wandering free around Elm Haven and the surrounding fields and woods during the long summer days and evenings, of endless hardball games on the dusty high school ball field and wild games of hide-and-seek in the deep woods near the Calvary Cemetery. Dale wrote about the Bootleggers' Cave—not deciding whether his band of friends would find it or not—and he wrote about friendship itself, about the friendship of eleven-year-old boys in those distant, intense days of dying innocence.

When he looked up from the ThinkPad, it was after midnight. His computer and desk lamp were the only lights on in the house. A cold draft curled through the Old Man's study. Dale saved his book to hard disk and floppy disk, checked DOS for any phantom messages—there were none—and walked through the dark house to the kitchen to make some soup before turning in.

"Dale." The whisper was so soft as to be almost indistinguishable from the hiss of the hot water heater or the rough purr of the furnace waiting to light again. "Dale." It was coming from the top of the darkened staircase.

No, not darkened. There was a light on the second floor, up there behind the taut, white wall of sheet. Seeking out no weapon, not even thinking about finding the baseball bat or crowbar, Dale climbed the cold stairs.

The light was only a dim glow from the front bedroom. *The candle again.* A shadow moved between the bedroom door and the wall of translucent white sheet. Dale watched as the center of the sheet seemed to ripple in a stronger breeze, then bulged ever so slightly outward. He moved to the top step and leaned closer. Six inches from his face, the sheet took on the definite impression of a nose, a brow, eye sockets, full lips.

Michelle or Clare?

Before he could find a resemblance, the bulge receded, but another disturbance moved the thin cotton toward him lower down. Three ripples, then five. Fingers. Dale looked down and could see the perfect shape of a woman's hand, palm toward him, fingers straining against the sheet. He waited for the sheet to rip free of the nails. When it did not, he moved his own left hand to within an inch of that slowly moving white hand in the cloth. Less than an inch. His fingertips were millimeters away from touching the pressing fingertips through the sheet.

"No," whispered Dale. He turned and went slowly downstairs. When he looked up the staircase again, the glow was gone and the sheet was as flat and vertical as the edge of some ageless glacier. He went into the kitchen and made some tomato soup, using the last of his milk to mix half-and-half with water in the can just as his mother had shown him when he was ten years old.

* * *

He had just dozed off in the basement, listening to the big band music as usual, when a sudden silence made him snap awake.

Dale sat up on the edge of Duane's old bed. The radio console had gone dark. Had he shut it off? He didn't remember doing so. But the reading lamp was still on, so the fuse hadn't blown. Suddenly he felt a slight chill. "Aw, no," he whispered to the empty basement.

Sliding out from under the quilt, setting the book of Proust he'd been reading safely on a wine-crate bookcase, Dale stepped over to the large console radio and wrestled it away from the wall.

The inside was empty. No wires, no tubes, no lights for the dial, no works at all. Dale looked at the interiors of the other radios he'd listened to over the past two months. All empty.

He went back and sat on the edge of the bed. "This," he said to no one in particular, "is just plain *stupid*."

Suspecting on some deep level that this would be the last night he would ever sleep in Duane McBride's home, Dale slid back under the quilt and listened to the wind rise outside in the dark.

TWENTY-SIX

THE sunrise of the last day of the old year, the old century, and the old millennium did not dawn; it seeped in like an absentminded spill of sick light, its stain of lighter gray blotting slowly beneath a shroud of darker gray. Dale watched it from the kitchen where he had been since 5:00 A.M., drinking coffee and looking out the small windows, watching the snow fall just beyond the frosted panes and sensing the movement of black hounds circling farther out.

The snow was already ten inches deep, and it continued to fall. The stunted trees along the long lane had become as fanciful as twisted bonsai inked into some Japanese watercolor, snow-laden, abstracted. The outbuildings no sooner appeared in the weak morning light than they tried to disappear behind accumulating drifts and blowing snow. Even the white Land Cruiser was up to its black running boards in snow and wore rounded cornices and caps on its hood and windshield.

Dale checked his provisions—smiling again at the word—and decided that he had enough canned goods and bread to last for a few days. A part of him knew that he would not need a few days' worth of food, but he worked at ignoring that voice.

It was a good day to write and Dale wrote, conjuring up summer days while winter pressed cold and flat against the study's single-paned glass. When he took a break for a late lunch sometime before 3:00 P.M., the daylight was already ebbing, draining out of the day like gray water out of a sink. Dale returned to the computer but could not concentrate on the passage in the scene in the chapter that had seemed so alive only moments earlier. He shut down Windows and stared at the DOS screen.

>**ponon yo-geblond up astigeo**
won to wolcnum, ponne wind styrep
lao gewidru, oopaet lyft orysmap,
roderas reotao. Nu is se raed gelang
eft aet pe anum. Eard git ne const,
frecne stowe, oaer pu findan miht
fela-sinnigne secg; sec gif pu dyrre.

Dale had to smile at this. His ghostly interlocutor was becoming less imaginative—this message was Old English, of course, but it was hampered by the ghost's (or Dale's computer's) apparent lack of diacritics and proper Old English letter forms. For instance, Dale knew immediately that what his ThinkPad script—set up to work with his HP Laserjet 4M printer—had shown as "āstīgeð" should have been rendered "astigeo," and what looked like "oopaet" on his screen should be "oðpæt." More importantly, even without translating it all, Dale knew at once that this was a passage from *Beowulf*.

Dale had brought Seamus Heaney's brilliant 2000 translation to Illinois with him and now he went to the basement to retrieve it. He found the cited passage in lines 1373 to 1379 in the description of the haunted mere:

When wind blows up and stormy weather
makes clouds scud and the skies weep,

**out of its depths a dirty surge
is pitched toward the heavens. Now help depends
again on you and on you alone.
The gap of danger where the demon waits
is still unknown to you. Seek it if you dare.**

Dale contemplated a response to this, decided that none was needed, and reached to shut off his computer. He paused then and opened Windows instead, clicking on the Word icon. Rather than calling up the file for the novel he'd worked on every day for the past two months, he opened a clean document page and began typing.

To Whom It May Concern:

Everything that I've lost, I've lost because I fucked it up. It's no one's fault but my own. I think that I've spent my life either trying to be someone else or waiting to become me and not knowing how. I've come too far out to this place and I don't know the way back.

At least a few things make more sense. After all these years, I finally managed to read part of Proust's À *la Recherche du temps perdu* — the title is translated on this edition as *Remembrance of Things Past*, but I remember Clare telling me that a better translation would be *In Search of Lost Time*. It's shameful for an old English major, much less a writer and professor of English, to confess to never having read this classic, but I'd picked it up a hundred times over the decades and never gotten past the boring first section. This time I found it lying here in Duane's basement, opened it randomly to the section called "Swann in Love," and read that straight through. It's brilliant, and so funny. The last paragraph made me laugh so hard that I started crying—

"To think that I've wasted years of my life, that I've longed to die, that I've experienced my greatest love, for a woman who didn't appeal to me, who wasn't even my type!"

When one reduces one's life to a series of meaningless obsessions, the last stage is to turn other people into obsessions.

I wish I'd been a better husband and father. I wish I'd been a better teacher and writer. I wish I'd been a better man.

Who knows? Perhaps the universe, or life, or *something* important that we can't see, is a Möbius loop after all—that by sliding down one side of things we can come out on the other. Or maybe not. I'm very tired.

Finished, Dale reread the letter and saved it to hard disk. He glanced at his watch and then had to look again. It was twelve minutes before midnight. The evening and night and year and century had almost slipped away while he was writing. Dale considered printing the thing, but there was no paper in the printer and he was too exhausted to replenish it.

"It doesn't matter," he said aloud. If anyone was interested in finding the note, they would look in the computer. He left the machine on and went down to the basement, searching around the worktable for the bundle of clothesline he had seen there on the day he'd moved in. It was only clothesline, perhaps thirty or forty feet, but it was thick and expertly coiled. Dale wondered if it had been Duane or his Old Man who had coiled the rope with the easy expertise of someone who had worked with his hands all of his life. It didn't matter.

Dale took the rope up to the kitchen, untied one end, and used a butcher knife to cut a three-foot length of line from the bundle. He furled this in a loop, left the main bundle of rope on the counter, and carried the knife, a flashlight, and the short loop of rope up the stairs to the second floor.

He paused as he reached the white barrier of sheets at the top of the steps, then plunged the knife into the taut fabric, ripping down and sideways as if disemboweling an enemy. The closest sheet separated with a long slash down the center, but the sheet behind that one showed only a ragged cut. Dropping the knife, and slipping the rope and flashlight into his pocket, Dale used his hands and fingernails to open the cut wider, tugging, clawing, and finally biting his way through the thin cotton like some predator chewing its way out of its own amniotic sac.

The second floor was dark and cold. Nothing stirred. Ignoring the front bedroom, Dale flicked on the flashlight and walked to the rear bedroom.

It was just as he had last seen it—the children's rocker in the center of the room, the ungainly chandelier above it, the complicated water stain spread across the ceiling ten feet above the floor.

Trying not to think and mostly succeeding, Dale entered the room, set the flat-bottomed flashlight on the floor so that it threw a circle of light on the ceiling, and concentrated on knotting the end of the rope into a noose that would not give way. When he was done, he stared up at the chandelier. It looked sturdy enough to hold five men his weight. The spreading water stain all around it kept shifting in the yellow light, one minute looking like a fresco of warring men and horses, then curling into storm clouds, then resembling nothing so much as a spreading pool of blood. Dale blinked and looked away, sliding the rope and knot through his hands.

I've been wandering between worlds since the night the shotgun shell misfired. Time to choose one world or the other.

The child's rocker held his weight as he stood on tiptoe, tossed the loose end of the rope around the central axis of the metal chandelier, made a triple knot that would not give way, tugged on it, lifted his feet and hung there a minute from his hands, then found the child's rocker under his soles again. Even with some stretching, his feet should stay two feet and more off the floor.

Dale slipped the noose around his neck, tugged it tight, and kicked the chair out from under him. *This isn't right. I shouldn't . . .*

The clothesline cut deep into his neck at once, cutting off all air. Flashbulbs exploded behind his eyes. Instinctively, Dale kicked and flailed, reaching above him to grab the clothesline, but the slip knot pulled even tighter and his fingers skittered and slipped on the rope, unable to give him enough leverage to lift his own weight for more than a second or two before the choking began again.

The room seemed to come alive around him—shadows leaping from the water-stained ceiling into the corners, dark forms dancing around and below him like Indians whirling around a campfire. The room filled with voices, a multitude of sibilant, urgent whispers hissing at him.

Dale felt unconsciousness flapping around him like a raven's wings, batting against his face, trying to enfold him. Then the flapping of ravens' wings became the triumphant howling of hellhounds. He tried to grab the rope and lift himself again, but his hands had lost all strength and his swelling fingers slipped off the rope even as the clothesline cut deeper into his neck. Dale's vision grew red and then slid into black even as he kicked and coughed.

His last sensory impressions were of great movement, of noise exploding around him, of sharp sticks or skeletal hands striking him and clawing at him, and then of flying into the night, falling into blackness.

TWENTY-SEVEN

DALE coughed, blinked, and tried to breathe. He was lying on the floor, there was something heavy lying on him, and the flashlight had been knocked over, its beam stabbing out through the bedroom door. He was getting some air, but the rope was still choking him, cutting into his throat.

Dale reached up and pried the noose looser, his own nails cutting into the already torn skin of his neck. Finally he had the constriction loose and he pulled the rope free, tugging the line through the slip knot and throwing it away from him into the cold darkness. He got to his knees, bits of lathing and plaster falling from his shoulders and hair, dust settling around him. Dale struggled to his feet, retrieved the flashlight, and shined it around the room and then upward.

The entire heavy chandelier had come down on top of him. No, most of the damned *ceiling* had come down around him. The chandelier's metal cable still snaked upward into the attic and its bolts were still firmly embedded in parts of the ruined ceiling that had fallen, but the cable had played out enough slack during the ceiling's collapse to keep Dale from strangling. Shifting the flashlight beam, Dale could see all the way to the torn and dripping interior of the rooftop twenty feet above him. The water had dripped through the ruined shingles and roof for years, decades, one drip at a time, soaking the plaster, rotting the lathing, weakening the ceiling. What had seemed like an hour of kicking and slow dying to Dale had been only a few seconds before the whole mess gave way.

He started to laugh, but the attempt hurt his throat. He ran his fingers along his neck—bruised, torn skin, but seemingly nothing worse.

"Jesus," he said hoarsely into the darkness. "What a fuckup." The phrase seemed so funny to him now that he had to laugh, sore throat or no sore throat. Then he began to weep. Dale dropped to his knees and sobbed like a child. He knew only one thing at that moment—*he wanted to live.* Death was an obscenity, and it had been obscene to court it the way he had. Death was the theft of every choice and every breath and every option the future had offered him, pain and promise alike, and Dale Stewart had always hated thieves. Death was the cold silence of King Lear; it was the *never, never, never, never, never* that had chilled him from childhood on. From the day Duane had died.

Dale had no idea what he was going to do next, but he was finished not only with hurrying death, but with embracing the cold and solitude in this sad simulation of death. He wanted to go home—wherever home was—but not this way, not here, not so far from any real home he might have left behind.

Dale got to his feet, wiped the tears and snot from his face, lifted the flashlight, and went out of the room and down the stairs without a look back. It was time to sleep. He would decide what to do in the morning. He went into the study just long enough to turn off his computer and flick off the lights.

Suddenly headlights illuminated him through the frosted study window, the white light sliced into thin shafts by the blinds. Dale went to the window but could see only the headlights, high and bright, far down the driveway, as if a vehicle had just pulled in from County 6. Snow was falling heavily between the headlights and the farmhouse.

Dale muttered, "The snow's too deep. They'll never get down the drive." What he thought, though, was, *This was what Duane saw that night, alone, the night he was killed.*

He walked down the hall and through the kitchen, turning on lights as he went, and then stepped out on the side stoop. Perhaps it was the sheriff, coming with news. *After midnight on New Year's Eve. Not likely.*

The lights came closer, showed how deep the drifts really were, how insistent the snowfall, and then swerved to illuminate the mounded Land Cruiser before swinging back into the turnaround. Somehow the big vehicle had made it down the lane.

Not C. J. Congden. Dale could see that it was a Chevy sport utility, huge, dark, all four wheels churning.

Clare's boyfriend's Suburban.

He shook that thought out of his head. This Suburban was older, more battered. Hadn't McKown said something about . . .

The left rear truck window rolled down even as there came a brilliant flash of light and an explosion. Sharp stones seemed to pelt Dale's right side, tearing his shirt to shreds, swinging him around, dropping him to one knee even as the porch light exploded and went dark. Something had cut his forehead and ripped at his right ear, but before he could register the wounds, the Suburban's doors swung open and dark figures emerged, silhouetted against the vehicle's interior lights. The skinheads. They were carrying rifles or shotguns.

Bleeding, hurting, Dale flung open the kitchen door and threw himself inside, into the light, clawing across the linoleum even as a second shotgun blast blew the window out of the door, scattering broken glass everywhere.

Dale kicked the door shut and slammed the locks, throwing himself back against the wall and out of the line of fire. With the window broken, it would take the skinheads five seconds to rush the door, reach through, and throw the locks back. Or they could just kick in the damaged door.

He risked a look. They were not rushing the door. The Suburban's headlights still burned and all four of its doors were open, interior lights still on. The vehicle was empty. The five men had scattered out of sight, leaving a riot of trails in the deep snow.

Two more shots roared. The kitchen window on the south side blew in and more glass rattled over the counter, into the sink, onto the kitchen table. Dale crouched and covered his face.

Another shot from the east side—a rifle shot this time—and simultaneous with the sound of the shot came the crash of glass breaking in the front parlor.

Where's the baseball bat? The crowbar? He could not remember. Along with a powerful surge of adrenaline came the absolute knowledge that he wanted to live. He bobbed up just long enough to slap off the overhead light and then he was crawling down the hall, turning that light off. There were no windows in the hallway. If he could wait out the attack there or . . .

Glass broke in the dining room, and this time there was a loud *whu-ump* followed by a blast of heat and light. Crawling on his belly, right arm bleeding from shotgun pellets and his left elbow sliced by broken glass, Dale peered into the room and saw the drapes aflame, the wallpaper beginning to ignite.

Molotov cocktail. These bastards meant business.

A shotgun blast took out the front window. Someone tried the locked and sealed front door, then fired a rifle bullet through the wood. Voices shouted back and forth behind the farmhouse. Laughter. Another gasoline bomb exploded—in the kitchen this time—throwing flame across the hallway and into the dining room ten feet from where Dale crouched.

He had a choice now—upstairs or the basement.

Dale was crawling toward the basement steps when he remembered the computer. *The letter. The novel.* Jumping to his feet, he ran into the study, realized he was visible in the lighted room, and grabbed the ThinkPad, ripping it free of its power cord and throwing himself back toward the hallway just as a shotgun blast exploded the window, scattered the blinds, and ripped the wallpaper above him.

Shouts. Wild laughter. The dining room and kitchen were both ablaze now, cutting off his retreat out the side door unless he was willing to run through flames.

All in all, he had time to think, *I prefer the dogs and ghosts.*

Clutching the laptop computer to his chest, Dale pounded down the steps to the basement as more shots and explosions ripped into the rooms above him.

He'd left the basement light on, and the space seemed safe and inviting after the insanity upstairs. Plan A had been to squeeze through one of the slim, high windows—he had done it once when he was eleven—but one glance told him that he would never fit now. A second glance showed him a thick boot kicking in the window on the south wall, above the empty console radio, and a wine bottle filled with gasoline came flying in, bounced once on Duane's bed, and shattered on the concrete floor. The burning wick had been knocked out somewhere on the trajectory and this Molotov cocktail did nothing but spread gasoline over the quilt, bed, books, and floor, but Dale knew that there would be another bomb in a second or two. The fact of that made him both furious and sad. This basement space and its forty-year-old contents were the last real remnants of his friend Duane's life.

Another window exploded inward, from a shotgun blast this time. The light must be attracting their attention. Dale had to shut off the light, but first he had to find the hammer and crowbar—not to use as weapons, but as tools.

The hammer was on the worktable against the east wall. He could not find the crowbar or flashlight. No matter. Dale stuck the hammer in his belt, wrestled a brick loose from a brick-and-board shelf on the worktable, and flung it across the room, breaking the lamp and throwing the room into darkness just as another Molotov cocktail came through the south window. This one exploded, throwing flaming gasoline all over the worktable even as Dale ran full tilt for the opposite end of the basement room, sliding around the furnace and clambering through the opening to the coal bin. He almost dropped the computer but clutched it to his chest with his left hand as he used the hammer in his right hand to rip the nails and screws out of the plywood barricade on the south wall of the coal bin. Already the basement was filling with smoke and he could hear heavy thuds upstairs, although whether this was footsteps from the skinheads in the burning building hunting for him or collapsing masonry, he had no idea.

The board ripped away, and Dale jammed the hammer in his belt again and fumbled for his Dunhill lighter. His right jeans pocket, where he always kept it, was empty, and for an instant Dale felt pure panic, but a quick patting located the lighter in his left pocket. It flicked to light on the first try, as it always did.

Dale was already scuttling down the dank tunnel, taking no notice of the remnants of old bottles already in the tunnel or of his own torn and bleeding right arm and scalp. Odds were that this was no bootleggers' escape tunnel—more likely an unfinished basement project from the 1940s or '50s—but the breeze he had felt and heard weeks ago suggested that it must open *somewhere*.

But not in an opening big enough for you to fit through.

It didn't matter. Even twenty feet away from the burning basement and house was better than nothing.

No it isn't. The fucking tunnel is already filling with smoke. There was no way that Dale could just hunker down here and let the skinheads burn the house down, hoping that they would not wait around to comb the ruins. The fire—he could feel its heat against his back as he shuffled along on his knees—was sucking the air right out of this tunnel. He'd be dead from asphyxiation long before he died of burns. This tunnel had to go somewhere or he was finished.

The flickering lighter showed that the wall he'd seen the first time he had peered down the tunnel was not the end; the shaft angled six or eight feet to the northwest, then continued on an indefinite distance straight ahead to the west. But the old passage had caved in much more here away from the foundation of the house. The roof of the passage dropped from four feet in height to a ragged three to a hole not much more than fifteen inches high. Dale did not hesitate, but wriggled onto his back, held the ThinkPad tight to his chest, extended the lighter back and over his head, and kicked forward through the narrow slit, his sneakers sliding in the mud. Everything smelled of sewage, and for a second he was sure that just the flame of his lighter was going to ignite methane gas and set off an explosion that would lift the burning house right off its foundations and surprise the hell out of the skinheads.

It did not explode, but rats scurried over Dale's groin, chest, and face, evidently fleeing the fire in the basement. He ignored them and kept kicking and writhing, moving west an inch at a time.

The tunnel opened out again to something like the original passage, and Dale flopped back on his knees and kept pressing ahead. The lighter illuminated rotted boards in the mud and stone overhead, and Dale realized that this was indeed a tunnel, a sort of crude mine, and that Duane's bootlegger tale was probably correct.

Another two or three minutes of scrabbling and the tunnel ended in a rock and mud wall. No doglegs or side passages here. Dale was panting, swinging the flickering lighter in an arc behind him. Despite the cold hair striking Dale's lacerated scalp, smoke was billowing into the tunnel behind him, curling toward him.

Cold air on my scalp. Dale lifted the lighter and looked up. A narrower shaft, no less than three feet wide, ran straight up. There seemed to be three very faint stripes of light perhaps eight feet above Dale.

There was no way for him to get up there. No ladder, no rungs, no footholds—just mud and rock and darkness.

Dale had not lived in the mountain West for almost twenty years for nothing. Flicking the lighter off and pocketing it, he removed the hammer from his belt, flipped it around to present the claw side, slammed it into the hard clay as high as he could reach, wedged his knee against the far wall, and began to climb. It would have been infinitely easier if he'd had both hands to use, but he continued cradling the computer to his chest while using his injured arm and hand to pound in the claw, lift himself with upper-body strength while bracing himself with one extended knee, then repeat the process.

He banged his head against something solid. Using what seemed the last of his strength to hold himself in the narrow chimney, he shifted the hammer to his left hand and felt above him. Boards. Very solid boards. It was as if he had reached up and found the roof of his coffin.

No.

Pressing against both walls of the shaft with his knee and back, he grabbed the hammer again and began pounding and slashing madly at the solid ceiling, not caring how much noise he was making. Let the skinheads find him. Anything was better than being buried in this stinking shaft as it filled with thicker and thicker smoke.

The hammer was not working. He dropped it into darkness and took the risk of shifting his weight, putting his right sneaker sole on the slippery wall behind him and extending his right arm across the gap to brace himself while he wedged up as high as he possibly could, almost horizontal to what must be wooden floorboards above him, his back and shoulder against the wood. In a final wild surge of adrenaline, Dale flexed in both directions, feeling lacerated muscles in his right arm tear, not caring, almost dropping the ThinkPad but clutching it in time, pressing upward in the darkness until his neck muscles audibly popped and the veins stood out on his forehead.

The rotted boards overhead splintered, gave, splintered again. With his balance failing, Dale made a fist and punched his way up through the rotten wood, punched again, then reached up and wedged his elbow over the edge just before he fell. He widened the hole, using his laptop as a battering ram, and pulled his head and shoulders up through the splintered opening.

He was in the chicken coop. Dale could see gaps in the east wall and around the door illuminated by brilliant red and yellow, flames from the burning house a hundred feet away. He slid the laptop across the rough floor, pulled himself out of the hole, and set his eye to the crack between the door and its hinge.

The Jolly Corner was fully engulfed in flame. Parts of the roof had already caved in, and even as he watched, flames exploded out both the first-floor kitchen window and the corner second-floor window. Silhouettes moved in front of the flames, cavorting, carrying weapons. The five skinheads ran back and forth, high-fiving one another and leaping into the air. They seemed to have no concern that the Elm Haven fire department would show up, and this late on New Year's Eve, this early on New Year's morning, they were almost certainly correct in their confidence. Dale could see the gleaming skull of the chief Nazi skinhead, Lester Bonheur, as he directed two of the others to get back around the front of the burning building, obviously hoping that the Jewboy nigger-loving professor would run, burning, from the building so that they could shoot him.

But the skinheads had eyes only for their conflagration. Dale stayed on his belly, trying to slow his panting and pounding heart. All he had to do was hide here until the bastards left or until the flames died enough for him to slip out and make his way across the snowy fields to the Johnson farm to call for help. He wasn't going to freeze to death yet. The heat from the burning building was strong here even a hundred feet away. The skinheads could not wait all night with impunity—the farmhouse would be collapsing in fifteen or twenty minutes anyway, convincing them that Dale was dead—and there should be no reason for them to search the chicken coop or other outbuildings.

All Dale had to do was stay put and wait.

"Don't bet on it, Stewart, you cowardly fuck." The voice was infinitely cold and totally dead, and it came from directly behind him.

TWENTY-EIGHT

C. J. Congden was sitting against the back wall of the chicken coop not ten feet from Dale. He did not look good. Even in the flickering red light filtering through the chinks in the east wall, the skin of Congden's face glowed mold-white and green. His eyes were sunken and opaque with white, as if covered with fly eggs. The ex-sheriff was not wearing a hat tonight, and as Congden turned his head slightly, Dale could see the exit hole the suicide .45 slug had left in the back of his skull and the fragment of bloody hair and scalp hanging over that hole as if in an obscene attempt at concealment.

Congden grinned, showing a black gap where the recoil of the pistol he had fired into his soft palate had knocked out his front teeth. That pistol was still in his hand, and now the thing aimed the weapon at Dale, its white fingers looking like bloated worms on the trigger guard and pearl handle. Congden's mouth did not move when the voice spoke, and the sound seemed to come from the thing's bloated belly. "Time to go out and join the party, Stewart."

Dale reached for the hammer in his belt and then remembered that he had dropped it down the hole. "Fuck you, Congden," he whispered. He had no intention of going anywhere, not knowing whether this apparition from hell could harm him but having no doubts as to what the skinheads would do. "Fuck you," he said again.

Congden seemed amused by this. His mouth opened wide for a grin and continued widening, stretching impossibly and terribly wide, fat cheeks and jowls rippling as if in a high wind. The thing's mouth became nothing more than a widening hole, as ragged as the hole Dale had just burst through, broken teeth substituting for splinters. In a literally heart-stopping moment, Dale realized that he could see *through* Congden's skull within that rippling maw, through the hole in the palate and out the back of the thing's head.

A noise issued from Congden then: at first a hissing, a tea kettle beginning to announce itself, but then the hissing rose until it became the rush and roar of a fire hose, then a boiler pipe exploding steam, and then a siren.

Dale crouched on his knees and clapped both hands over his ears. It did not block the noise. Nothing could block that noise. Congden had raised his ruined face toward the ceiling of the bloodied chicken coop and seemed to be hauling in air through the wound in the back of his skull as the screaming whistle roared from the funneled mouth. The skinheads *had* to hear this.

Dale surrendered, swung around, flung the door of the chicken coop open, and staggered out into the snow and naked light of the burning farmhouse.

One of the skinheads saw him and set up a hue and cry before Dale had run thirty steps toward the darkness of the fields. Injured as he was, Dale would have preferred taking his chances reaching the Land Cruiser and driving away for help, trusting his four wheel drive once again to keep him ahead of the other vehicle. But the keys to the Land Cruiser were in his peacoat pocket, and the peacoat was hanging on the hook in the kitchen.

That entire kitchen side of The Jolly Corner's first floor was a wall of flame throwing red light like a spotlight toward Dale as he followed the lane toward the barn, jogging from side to side in the deep snow, trying to put the chicken coop and other outbuildings between himself and the screaming skinheads. Twice he fell, each time leaving bloody streaks in the snow. Both times he clawed his way to his feet and staggered on through drifts up to his knees. Even the falling snow seemed blood red in the light of the burning house.

How bad was I hurt? How much blood have I lost? The pain was no worse than it had been, but his entire right side from shirt collar to pant cuffs was soaked with his own blood now. Dale felt light-headed and fought vertigo with each running, staggering step.

Out away from the fire now, running left past the fueling station and into the fields. It was darker out here, if he could just keep low, head for the creek and the woods a mile southwest.

They can follow my trail in the snow. Dale looked behind him and saw not only the path he was leaving through the drifts but the bloody smears like painted arrows.

The skinheads were whooping like cowboys, throwing open doors to the outbuildings and throwing the last of their Molotov cocktails inside. The old shed holding Mr. McBride's antiquated punch card learning machines went up in a ball of flame.

The skinheads were firing their shotguns and rifles into the shadows behind the outbuildings now, the muzzle flashes bright against the dark structures. One of the silhouetted figures found Dale's track in the snow and began screaming above the din.

I'll never get across that field. Dale knew that he did not have the strength left to run that far even if there were no snow slowing him down. The punks would be on him in minutes.

He slid to a halt in the snowy field. The barn was to his right. Perhaps he could climb to the lofts, hide in the maze of rafters up there in the dark.

One of the skinheads flicked on a handheld spotlight, throwing thousands of candlepowers in a single, blinding beam stabbing across the field. Dale ran toward the barn anyway. It was the only thing he could think of.

Using a flashlight to freeze sparrows in the barn, then shooting them with BB guns. The black eyes staring. He slipped and fell, crushing frozen cornstalks under the snow, then staggered ahead on his knees, fighting his way to his feet again.

Something in the farmhouse, perhaps a gas main, suddenly exploded upward in a curling mushroom of flame and noise. The silhouettes of the skinheads paused a moment by the sheds, looking back at their handiwork. Dale glanced that way, praying to see flashing red lights, emergency vehicles, Sheriff McKown's car rushing to the rescue. Everything to the east was dark and lost to sight in the falling snow.

He was still a hundred feet from the barn when he lost his footing in the dark and fell again. Dale hit hard on his right side, and this time the pain was very bad. He got to his knees and looked back at the burning farmhouse, noting but not really thinking about all of his books and other possessions burning in there.

What was the word in the Eddic poem for the hero's funeral pyre?

Hrot-garmr. *"Howling dog." Flames like a howling dog.*
zi-ik-wa UR.BAR.RA ki-sa-at. *"Thou art become a wolf."*

Kneeling there, hearing the punks shout and howl off to his right, knowing that he was no hero but just an injured and terrified middle-aged man unused to violence and afraid to die, Dale still wished that he could become a wolf. If he became a wolf, he would rip the throat out of the nearest skinhead before the others killed him. If he became a wolf, he would taste their warm blood even as they killed him.

He did not become a wolf.

Dale had just struggled to his feet again when the huge door to the barn exploded outward, ripped away its steel slide suspension, and seemed to plow through the snow toward him in slow motion. Then the door fell away and Dale saw that it was the huge combine lumbering toward him, the thirty-foot-wide harvesting extension shifting snow aside like a plow from hell, its corn head covers missing so that its open maw revealed picker units with their exposed snapping rolls and lugged gathering chains grinding.

This is the last thing Duane McBride ever saw.

The glassed-in driver's cab, twelve feet above the whirling blades and flying snow, was illuminated by weak interior lights, and Dale stared at the face of the driver, shifting like a poorly done digital effect in a movie—first Bonheur's, the oldest skinhead's, leering face, then the Congden corpse face, then Bonheur's, then Congden's. The interior light went out. Dale turned and ran.

Forty-one years earlier, Duane had run deeper into this field and died. Dale swung left, back toward the burning farmhouse and its outbuildings, desperate to put something—anything—between himself and the machine lurching and chewing behind him.

Halfway to the nearest shed, Dale knew that he was not going to make it to the chicken coop and other outbuildings. And the shouting in the darkness there told him where the other skinheads waited. Running only thirty feet in front of the rusted gatherer points and whirling chains and snapper rolls, Dale cut right and lurched through the drifts toward the fueling station. There was a chance, just a chance, that he could climb the support girders around the two hundred–gallon fuel tank, jump from there to the roof of the old generator shed, and leap down to the safety of the other outbuildings from there.

Dale leaped for the metal support trusses, slashed his palms on the rusted metal of the girders, pulled himself up with his feet scrabbling against the big cylindrical fuel tank for leverage, and managed to get ten feet above ground level when the giant combine smashed into the tank, ripped the support girders out of the ground, and drove the whole complex into and through the rear of the generator shed. Dale was thrown fifteen feet into the air, and it was only luck and the mysteries of ballistics that brought him down twenty feet north of the combine rather than headfirst into the churning snapper rolls. As it was, the giant machine lurched several yards further, corn pickers boring into and chewing up the rusted fuel tank while spewing gasoline over the combine and everything around it. Just the inertia of the ancient combine smashed the rear wall of the generator shed to kindling while the corn head's gathering points spewed back splinters and rusted steel within the geyser of gasoline.

Stunned, the wind knocked completely out of him despite the cushioning effect of the foot of snow he had landed in, Dale lay on his back and watched Bonheur's face melt into C. J. Congden's face, both visages leering at him from the high driver's cab. Dale heard the old transmission grind and the combine backed away from the wreckage, the fuel tank still stuck on the corn picker points like a rust-colored rat in a terrier's teeth. The combine ground another thirty feet back, shaking and scraping the skewered tank off its snapper rolls, and then turned back in Dale's direction.

Dale had crawled a few feet north, away from the huge circle of fuel-reddened snow, but he knew that he did not have the strength to rise and run again. He barely made it to his knees to face the giant machine.

The combine's harvesting lights snapped on, pinning Dale in their merciless beams.

"Not this time," gasped Dale. He pulled Clare's gift of the Dunhill lighter from his pocket and flicked it. It lighted at once. Almost wearily, Dale tossed the lighter six feet into the circle of soaked snow.

The flames leaped ten feet high at once, roaring in a circle around the combine, leaping up the soaked snapper rolls and climbing like blazing ivy to the high grain bin and soaked driver's cab. The glass there blackened and buckled. Then the fire ignited the remaining fuel in the lacerated storage tank, and the explosion lifted the front of the combine five feet in the air while blowing Dale twenty feet in the opposite direction.

Dale rolled in the drifts, using his hands to rub snow on his flash-burned eyebrows and hairline.

For a minute the combine just burned steadily, the flames having not yet reached its own interior fuel tank, melting snow, curling paint, and superheating old steel and iron with a hiss that filled the night.

Hrot-garmr, Dale thought dully. *Funeral flames like a howling dog.* The heat from the flames was intense, but almost pleasant after all the wet cold.

Then, slowly, amazingly, the door to the flaming cab opened and a human figure engulfed in fire stepped out on the burning grain bin deck and jumped out to lie facedown and burning in the snow.

Dale was vaguely aware of the other skinheads fifty feet or so behind him, silhouettes against the other fire—The Jolly Corner—but none of these forms moved. "Shit," said Dale and staggered to his feet. He rushed as well as he could to the burning man's side, dragged him out of the circle of burning fuel, and threw snow on the back of the man's burning jacket and flesh until the flames were smothered. He rolled the man over. Skinhead Lester Bonheur's features were burned red down to the muscle layer, and his eyes were flickering as if from an epileptic fit.

On his knees next to him, Dale sagged backward and shouted to the unmoving skinheads back by the sheds, "For God's sake, go for an ambulance." None of them answered or moved.

The burned shape in front of him seemed to gain mass, rolled over, and got to its knees. "It looks like I have to do this myself," hissed the corpse of C. J. Congden and lunged at Dale, knocking him onto his back and grabbing him by the throat.

Dale's gasping breath was visible in the air as he clawed at Congden's tightening fingers. No breath came from Congden's broken, open maw. The thing was terribly strong, its rotted mass heavy on him, and Dale felt what was left of his own strength slipping away with the last of his breath.

"Fuck you," Dale gasped up into Congden's contorted death mask, and then Dale surrendered—not to Congden, not to those fuckers behind him, but to forty years of resistance, letting the wall in his mind crumble like chalk. With the last of his breath, Dale shouted into the night, "*Gifr! Geri! Hurkilas! Osiris sews healf hundisces mancynnes, he haefde hundes haefod!*"

Congden's rotted fingers tightened on Dale's windpipe, cutting into the flesh of his neck, and the mouth lowered as if ready to suck the last breath from Dale if necessary. Instead, Dale used his last breath, to howl defiance.

"*Anubis! Kesta! Hapi! Tuamutef! Qebhesenuf!*"

Then there was no more breath with which to shout or breathe, and the Congden thing laid its full weight upon Dale, who sensed but could not see the five hounds knocking aside four skinheads, not leaping on them but past them, and then the first and largest of the impossibly huge jackal dogs hit Congden with a noise like a sledgehammer striking a rotten watermelon and ripped Congden's head off with one swipe of its massive jaws.

Congden's arms and fingers continued to choke Dale.

The hounds were all on Congden now, ripping the animated, headless corpse literally limb from limb and then limb from torso, black dogs running through flames from the burning combine and then circling back as if the flames did not exist, growling, snarling, and fighting each other in their hound-frenzy over the lacerated torso and scattered parts.

"Jesus fuck," cried one of the distant skinheads, and Dale dimly heard them running back toward the burning farmhouse and their Chevy Suburban.

Dale staggered to all fours, shaking the last of Congden off his chest and legs. Blazing-eyed hounds knocked Dale to one side and snatched up the rotted bits—a cowboy-booted foot, a fleshy ribcage trailing intestines, a half-fleshed jawbone—and then ran with them into and through the flames, disappearing into the darkness beyond. Dale rolled onto his side and looked over to where Bonheur still lay in the trampled snow. Smoke rose from the man's dark form. Dale could not tell if he was breathing.

Dale tried to get to his feet, aware that the burning combine's fuel tank could ignite any second, but found that he could no longer stand or even kneel. He rolled on his belly and started crawling back through the mottled snow toward the sheds and blazing farmhouse.

Flashing red lights and flashing blue lights. A half dozen vehicles, all with lights flashing, in the turnaround near the farmhouse, and more emergency vehicles just visible on the driveway. Dale caught a glimpse of the skinheads raising their arms, dropping weapons, of a fire truck, of men rushing with hoses and other men running and stumbling through the drifts toward the burning combine and him, and then Dale decided it might be a good idea to rest a minute. Belly down in the snow, he put his burned forehead on his bloody forearm and closed his eyes.

TWENTY-NINE

ON the third day, I rise again and leave this place—the hospital, the farm, the county, the state.

But on the first day I almost do not wake at all. Later that evening, the doctor confides in me that they were concerned, that my vital signs showed someone slipping more toward coma than wakefulness or recovery, and that they do not understand, since my injuries had proved essentially superficial and had been dealt with during the night. I could have explained the near-coma state to him, but would probably have found myself in a straitjacket. On that first day and evening in the hospital, Deputy Brian Presser and Deputy Taylor were there, and together they irritated the doctor by insisting on taking a videotaped statement from me, as if I were on the verge of death after all. I told them the truth, mostly, although I said that I could remember nothing after the first explosion of the combine.

When it is my turn to quiz them, I ask, "Did anyone die?"

"Only Old Man Larsen," says Taylor.

For a second I must look blank, for Deputy Presser says, "Bebe

Larsen, the guy they commandeered the Chevy Suburban from on the day before Christmas Eve. Derek and one of the other kids confirmed that the five of them were pretty pissed when they hiked out from the quarry that night. They roughed the old man up a bit before tying him up and sticking him in the back of the truck. He was dead when they got to one of the other kid's sister's house in Galesburg."

"Heart attack," says Deputy Taylor. "But the skinheads didn't know that."

"Lester Bonheur?" I ask. My hands are bandaged for burns. My right side and right arm hurt from where they removed bits of buckshot, and I have stitches holding my scalp in place on that side. My eyelashes and eyebrows have been burned away, my hairline has receded three inches because of the flames, and I have goopy salve over much of my face. It all feels wonderful.

"Bonheur's still alive," grunts Deputy Presser, "but he's burned all to hell and gone. They're transferring him to the St. Francis burn unit in Peoria tomorrow morning. The docs think he'll live, but he's going to have a shitload of skin grafts ahead of him."

"Hey, Professor," says Deputy Taylor, referring to something he had asked earlier during the taped interview, "who *was* that other guy there at the fire . . . the one the kids say they saw? The one who looked like he was dead?"

I close my eyes and pretend to sleep.

On the second day, Sheriff McKown shows up with some magazines for me to read, a Dairy Queen milkshake for me to drink, and the ThinkPad computer. "Found this in the chicken coop," he said. "I assume it's yours."

I nod.

"We didn't turn it on or anything, so I don't know if it still works," says McKown, pulling a chair and settling into rather gracefully. "I presume there's no evidence on it . . . at least none relating to this weird series of events."

"No," I say truthfully. "Just one bad novel and some personal stuff." Including a suicide note, but I do not say that.

McKown does not pursue it. He ascertains that I am healthy enough to answer a few more questions, takes out an audiotape recorder and his notebook, and spends the next hour asking me very precise and logical questions. I answer as truthfully as I can, providing often imprecise and rarely logical answers. Sometimes, though, I have to lie.

"And those rope burns on your neck," he asks. "Do you remember how you received those?"

I automatically touch the torn tissue on my throat. "I don't remember," I say.

"Possibly something when you were crawling through that tunnel," says McKown, although I know that he knows that this is not the case. "Yes."

When he is finished and the notebook is put away and the recorder is off, he says, "Dr. Foster tells me that you can leave here tomorrow. I brought a present for you." He sets a single key on the moveable tray hanging over the bed.

I lift it. It is darkened with carbon and the plastic base of it has melted slightly, but it looks intact.

"It still works on your Cruiser," says Sheriff McKown. "I had Brian drive it over. It's in the lot outside."

"Amazing the key survived the fire and that you found it," I say.

McKown shrugs slightly. "Metal's like bones and some memories . . . it abides."

I look at the sheriff through my puffy, swollen eyelids. Not for the first time am I reminded that keen intelligence can be found in unlikely places. I say, "I imagine that I will have to stay around here for quite a while."

"Why?" says Sheriff McKown.

I start to shrug and then choose not to. The bandages are very tight around my right side and ribs, and it already hurts a bit to breathe deeply. "Arraignment?" I say. "More depositions? Investigation? Trial?"

McKown reaches over to where he has set his Stetson on my bed, lifts it, and unnecessarily re-creases its crown. "One more interview this evening with Deputy Presser," he says, "and I think we've got all the information we need. You won't be needed for the kids' arraignment and I doubt if there'll be a trial . . . about the burning of the farmhouse and their attack on you, I mean."

I sit in my hospital bed and wait for more explanation.

McKown shrugs and taps the brim of his hat against his knee. The crease in his gray-green trouser material is very sharp. "Derek's and Toby's and Buzz's confessions pretty well agree that they came to burn you out and hurt you on New Year's Eve. And you didn't use any sort of deadly force . . . all you did is try to run. It's not your fault that Bonheur was such a moron that he drove Mr. Johnson's combine into the fuel tank."

I nod and say nothing.

"Besides," continues the sheriff, "the real crime here is the death of Bebe Larsen. But I don't think that will come to trial either. Three of the boys are juveniles, they'll get plea bargains and spend some time at a juvenile center and then waste my time on probation around here. And the other two will cop to lesser charges rather than face murder. If Bonheur lives, and I guess he's going to, he'll be going away again for a while. Can I ask you a question, Professor Stewart?"

I nod again, sure that he is going to ask about the extra figure the skinheads say they saw struggling with me in the light of the fires, even though I've stated in all the interviews that it was Bonheur who tried to choke me before collapsing again.

"The dogs," he says, surprising me. No one has mentioned the dogs in all the formal interviews during the past twenty-four hours.

"A lot of people and vehicles stomped that snow down before daylight, but there were still a few paw prints," he says and settles his Stetson on his knee and looks at me.

I suffer a shrug. I think, *Homage to thee, Oh Governor of the Divine House. Sepulchral meals are bestowed upon thee, and he overthroweth*

for thee thine enemies, setting them under thy feet in the presence of thy
scribe and of the Utchat and of Ptah-Seker, who hast bound thee up.

Why had a lonely nine-year-old boy on an isolated Illinois farm in the late 1950s chosen Anubis to worship, going so far as to learn the ancient deity's language and ceremonies? Perhaps it was because the boy's only friend had been Wittgenstein, his old collie, and the boy liked the jackal god's head and ears. Who knows? Perhaps gods choose their worshipers rather than the other way around.

The question had been whether to tell Dale that he was never at risk from the Hounds. The Guardians of the Corpse Ways, like jackals cleansing the tombs of undeserving carrion, are protectors of the liminal zone at the boundaries of the two worlds. Like phagocytes in the bloodstream of the living, they are not just psychopomps, protectors of souls during the transition voyage, but scavengers, seeking out and returning souls who have crossed that boundary in the wrong direction and who do not belong on the east bank of the living, no matter how terrible the imperative of the torment that has brought them back there. But who is to say that Dale had not been at risk? He had, after all, volunteered to travel to the west bank necropolis in attempting to kill himself, and in that sense at least, summoned Osiris to weigh his heart in the Hall of the Two Truths.

"Professor, you all right? You seem to have gone away for a minute there."

"I'm all right," I say huskily. "Tired. Side hurts."

McKown nods, lifts his Stetson, and stands. He turns to go and then turns back. *Columbo*, I think, remembering Dale's earlier thought. Instead of asking some final, insightful, damning question, McKown gives me information. "Oh, I looked through Constable Stiles's files for 1960–1965 and found something interesting from 1961."

I wait again.

"It seems that Dr. Staffney, Michelle's father, the surgeon, called Barney Stiles in late March of that year and demanded that C. J. Congden, his old henchman Archie Kreck, and a couple of other local thugs be arrested . . . for rape. According to Barney's sloppy report, Dr. Staffney said that these boys—well, Congden was seventeen then, so not quite boys—these punks had taken his daughter for a ride, driven her out to the empty McBride house—Mr. McBride had moved to Chicago and the place was empty then before his sister moved in— driven her out to the empty McBride place, and raped her several times. Did you know anything about this, Professor?"

"No," I say truthfully.

McKown shakes his head. "Dr. Staffney dropped the charges the next day, and as far as I know neither he nor Barney ever mentioned it again. Michelle was only in seventh grade then. My guess is that J. P. Congden, C. J.'s father, threatened the good Dr. Staffney."

Neither of us speaks for a moment. Then Sheriff McKown says, "Well, I just thought I'd let you know." He walks to the door, his hat still in his hand, but pauses a moment. "If you're not needed around here, I imagine you'll want to get going when you're released from the hospital tomorrow."

"Yes."

"Heading back to Montana, Professor?"

"Yes."

McKown puts his hat on and tugs the brim down slightly. His light eyes look intelligent but colder with the official hat on. "And if there's no trial or anything, you're not planning to come back this way, are you?"

"No."

"Good," says McKown, adjusting his hat again before leaving. "Good."

On the third day, they wheel me to the door of the hospital—hospital policy, it seems—and let me walk to the Land Cruiser. The day is cold but absolutely cloudless. The sunlight and blue sky suggest the possibility of spring even though it is the first week of January. Deputy Taylor has brought by a red wool mackinaw for me to wear, since my coats had burned in the farmhouse with my other possessions, and I appreciate it as I walk the chilly hundred yards to where the SUV is parked. I wonder for a minute if the taxpayers had paid for this largesse, but the coat hangs on me, two sizes too large, and I guess that it's a castaway from one of the bigger deputies.

Unable to resist, I drive the Land Cruiser back to The Jolly Corner by way of Old Catton Road, bypassing Elm Haven. There is no crime scene yellow tape at the entrance to the drive, so I turn into the lane.

It is shocking to come down this familiar long driveway with no farmhouse at the end. All that remains of The Jolly Corner is the brick and stone foundation, a four-foot-high remnant of one charred wall of the kitchen, and the tumbled, burned mass of debris falling into the open and black basement. The fire was quite thorough, and I am amazed that they found the key to the Land Cruiser.

Snow in the area all around the ruins of the house has been trampled down by emergency vehicles and footsteps. Far out behind the chicken coop and other sheds, I can see the black, skeletal-steel remains of the old combine. Numerous vehicles have plowed channels through the snow coming and going from there as well. The big barn looks vulnerable with its giant door missing.

I do not even consider getting out of my truck.

Driving back down the lane, I am slightly startled by the sight of a sheriff's car turning in from County 6. I pull to the right to let it pass and roll down my window when the car stops and Deputy Presser gets out. He peers into the front of my vehicle with the professional curiosity of any cop during a traffic stop.

"On your way out, Professor?"

"Yes."

"I see your laptop's working." He nods toward the ThinkPad, open and activated on the passenger seat, its screen saver cycling.

"I was never any good at folding road maps," I say and touch the computer's Pointing Stick. The screen saver disappears, and the Rand McNally road map of the United States is on the screen. My route from the Midwest to Missoula is highlighted in bright green.

Presser chuckles and then lifts a long, canvas-covered object. "Sheriff McKown said that I might catch up to you here. He said that you might want this."

It is the Savage over-and-under, of course. Probably freshly cleaned and oiled, if I know McKown at all.

"No," I say. "I won't be needing it. Give the sheriff my thanks and tell him to donate it to a department yard sale or something."

Presser looks doubtful for an instant but then salutes me with a tap to the brim of his Stetson, sets the weapon in the backseat of his vehicle, and drives on to The Jolly Corner to turn around.

I drive south along County 6, past Uncle Henry's and Aunt Lena's old place, up the first hill, and past Calvary Cemetery. A single figure stands far back there in the snow amidst the headstones, and there is no car parked outside the black iron gate. The figure seems to be wearing olive or khaki and a campaign hat. I give him only one glance. If there are other ghosts here, they are not mine.

At the intersection with Jubilee College Road, I consider driving into Elm Haven a final time but then dismiss the thought. Elm Haven itself is a sort of ghost in this new century, and I will spare no time for it.

I drive ahead down the cutoff road toward the interstate. Less than a mile later, where I must cross 150A, I have to wait a minute for several trucks heading toward Peoria to rumble past.

The black screen on the computer blinks.

>A long time, do you think?

The road is clear now, but I wait to reach over and type—

>No, not long. I'm sure of it.

I have no specific plan for the coming weeks or months. However long Dale needs to recuperate and recover, to become one again, is however long I will . . . not possess, never possess . . . but do my best to maintain life's forward movement for him.

I suspect I will see Anne and Mab and Katie some time after I return, and I hope that I do something to help and nothing to hinder Dale's intentions in that regard. I do not know his precise plans.

Sometime in the coming week or so, I will call Princeton, talk to some people, and then wait until I hear Clare Hart's voice on the line before I hang up. He has no urge to speak with her, but it may allow Dale to sleep better when he returns if he knows she is alive and well.

If the gift of these weeks—and it is a gift, deliberately given to me, just as I have twice given Dale the gift of another chance—if this gift stretches to a month or two, I think that I will resume work on Dale's novel. The truths of sunlight and summer and childhood friendships in it are real enough, but it is all too earnest and serious of purpose and artsy, I think. Perhaps I'll add playful elements as well as the darker secrets and silences that Dale had been too fearful or hesitant to face. Perhaps I'll have fun with it—turn it into a horror novel. Dale can always change it later if he insists on committing lit'ra-chur. Or together he and I can twist reality like the Möbius loop it is.

I cross 150A and turn right down the interstate access ramp at the KWIK'N'EZ without looking back. Sheriff McKown has topped off the tank and even with this gas-guzzling monster, I can be to Des Moines or beyond before I have to think about stopping.

Once on I-74 the way goes on ahead open and free to the west, and so do I.